A FLIGHT IN THE HEAVENS

Book One of The Theurgy of The Gods Series

Gabrielle Gagne-Cyr

The characters and events portrayed in this book are fictitious. Any similarity to real persons, living or dead, is coincidental and not intended by the author.

E-BOOK ISBN-13: 978-1-7776520-1-2
PAPERBACK ISBN-13: 978-1-7776520-2-9
HARDCOVER ISBN-13: 978-1-7776520-0-5

Cover design by Elita Maalouf
Font design by GemFonts & Paul Lloyd
Library and Archives of Canada Cataloguing in Publication
First Edition 2021
Manufactured in Canada

1 2 3 4 5 6 7 8 9 0

Notes

This novel was written in Canadian English. You will notice the cultural impact from both its UK heritage and US influence. For those readers out there who may not be familiar with the style, I hope you will appreciate our unique Canadian hybrid flavo(u)r!

Science Fantasy

A subgenre that draws upon elements derived from both fantasy and science fiction; a universe where technology gains increasing significance as opposed to more traditional medieval settings.

Steampunk Fantasy

A retrofuturistic subgenre that incorporates elements from the insdustrial era, juxtaposing ancient mechanics with modern technologies.

Though not steampunk in its essence, this book incorporates some of its tropes. Think of it this way, friends; this is a world where the future clashes with the past. It has swords and machine guns, flying airships and tricorns.
Basically, it has the best of everything.

Cheers, friends.

Chapter I

Slay tumbled down against the floor of the damp cell. The door creaked behind him as the beeping sound of the security system called it into motion. He drew himself halfway up and sat back against the cold stone, legs sprawled open before him.

What an idiot.

He'd just set foot in the capital of Letholdus and already found himself in this predicament. At least they'd brought him to a control post. No sane person wanted to find themselves in the doomed Prison of the Anemas where, once in, no one got out. Regardless, many awaiting judgment in the posts ended up there not long after.

He hoped his sentence wouldn't be so absolute.

He drew a hand behind his neck and began massaging it. As he twisted his head from side to side, he felt a jolt.

Horrible receded eyes stared at him from the corner of the room.

The dark circles under the man's eyes had nothing to do with a lack of sleep nor the veins that sagged the skin around them as though his sockets were sucking it in.

Slay's chest accelerated. His breathing grew laboured.

The daemon.

Relax, it's only a picture.

He looked away. Every cell in the control posts had a similar image imprinted on its walls.

It was a reminder.

He glanced over his shoulder at the obscured face of the placater who had locked him in. The guard's armour went from head to foot, adjusted red steel, the daemon's crest anchored in the middle of his chest. He was holding a standard submachine gun, and a sword was on his hip. A knight of the peace.

Fucking pricks.

The placaters, he damn well knew them. They had invaded nearly every last piece of territory in the lands of Iscar, their presence a relentless knife hanging over their heads.

Since Daromas the daemon had snatched control of the government, he had cemented his undisputed influence from one end of Iscar to the other, his placaters an ever-growing anthill of soldiers reminding them of the threat under which they lived.

Slay had spent his life on the remote islands of Benetos, long spared by the placaters. When the army had disembarked, the soldiers' arrival had been cause for much tribulation. For, *to create a unified Iscar, everyone had to comply with the daemon's decrees.*

Yeah right, he thought. *Rather, to entertain this fucking dictatorship.*

He peeked again over his shoulder, wincing. There was that cold, deadened gaze, still glaring at him.

He scrubbed his burning eyes, fingers wiping the stubborn dust that had clung to his lashes. He stood up, his pants now whiter than black where they had touched the ground. He stepped near the gate and leaned over the bars.

A place for rats.

Control posts were common. This was where troublemakers were brought in. If their offence was judged serious, they were taken to the Anemas prison. If not, they would languish in the checkpoint for a few days, even months, at the leisure of the placaters.

His gaze fell on the cell in front of his. One person was lying on the floor, legs crossed and feet facing him. Another stood against the wall of the backroom and was staring up at the ceiling, the picture of the daemon imprinted next to him. The man looked bored.

"When do we eat around here?" he asked his neighbour.

The man's eyes blinked his way. "You were expecting to eat?"

Slay put his head down and shook it. "Here I was, hoping to get a free meal. If I'd known, I would have been more careful." He gestured at the nearest guard. "I guess these guys don't like to be messed with. Who would have thought that throwing scraps at one of them would get you thrown in a control post?"

"Yeah, who would've thought?" replied the man, his smile growing.

"What brought you here, friend?"

The stranger drew closer to the door of his cage. He was a lanky sort of chap, with brown hair trimmed below his shoulder. He wore a lean face and a nose that was a bit too large for his thin features. "We went looking for trouble as well, it would seem," he answered. "What's your name, mate?"

Most people who found themselves in prison or the posts these days were guilty of *disrupting the placaters' peace.* Whatever that meant. "Slay," he replied. "You?"

"Darvis." The man bowed and gestured his hand in the Letholdian salute, open palm arcing up.

Slay pointed to the guard. "Any chance we're going to the Anemas?" His pulse started beating faster at this though he kept his expression light.

Darvis glanced at the figure lying beside him while caressing the short spot of hair that had begun to grow on his chin. "Say, Farrah. How many times have we been sentenced to the Anemas as of now?"

The woman nudged her chin to him. "I'm not counting anymore."

The man's hands gestured up. "See, not everything's doomed if you know how to work the system."

He looked at them. Where he came from, you couldn't run away from a charge of offence. Yet again, there weren't many places to hide on an island. The number of beatings he had gotten when he was younger? *That* was what *he* couldn't count. "I guess when you live in a big city, the rules are different."

Thank the gods.

The woman moved into a sitting position and brushed the dust on her hands against her green cargo pants. His eyes went round at the sight of the person standing up. He had somehow been imagining a portrait far removed from the one he had in front of him.

She was stunning.

He could not recall seeing a more beautiful woman. Her brown hair fell over her white t-shirt in cascades of lustrous wavy locks. Her olive-toned features defined each of her angles. Her eyes, almond-shaped, were painted a dark green and chestnut colour and seemed both watchful and self-assured.

She smiled and Slay bet she had no idea how every man probably melted in front of those lips.

This prison trip was worth it after all.

She came closer to the bars, head facing Darvis. "Making friends?" she asked while placing a palm on her slim waist. The cropped shirt she wore revealed a hint of a tanned stomach underneath.

The man lifted his shoulders. "The enemy of my enemy is my friend?"

She grinned and Slay thought that he would much rather be in Darvis's place right now.

The woman turned to him. "I'm Farrah," she said in a soft and yet confident voice. "You must be a newcomer in Letholdus?"

"I'm just passing through," he replied, his back becoming straighter. "I'm from the Islands of Benetos but I'm going to Racketeer Bay." His tone was playful, afraid it might sound silly to say this out loud.

Racketeer Bay was home to the pirates of Iscar and was under the authority of the daemon though he had dismissed its residents as unsavoury. No one had any doubt under whose control it was, but even the daemon knew that some people were better kept at a distance.

In the case of pirates, it was better to ignore their lot and leave them to their dealings than make outright enemies out of them.

It also happened to be better for the government making use of their services.

Darvis's expression narrowed. "You're a pirate?"

"Not exactly. At least, not yet." He glanced once more at the guards and lowered his voice. "They say Racketeer Bay isn't under the grip of those freaks."

Farrah tilted her head to the side. "Just a different kind of control though." She looked straight at him. "If you wish for freedom, you won't have it as long as power is in the wrong hands."

Slay dropped his fingers from the bars. "We all want that, but it's not about to happen."

She looked at the placater, brow furrowed. "Only as long as our people continue to do nothing, watching from afar in muffled agony."

He gaped at her. Most didn't talk so freely of rebellion. It was much safer to keep their mouths shut and pretend that the daemon was the best thing that had ever happened to them.

Most were very good at pretending.

"Well, nothing much we can do," he answered and felt that his riposte was not up to par with Farrah's eloquence.

She looked his way and curved her warm smile. "That's why nothing changes," she replied before peering at Darvis. "Better get ready."

The lean man stared in the same direction she was facing. Slay heard noises coming from outside, noises that sounded a whole lot like gunfire and shouts. It was now his turn to look around at the entrance of their block.

A blast propelled the gate inside, hitting a placater around the waist. Both of the guards collapsed on the floor as several dark shapes entered the post.

The placaters ran their ammunitions towards the entrance, their fire welcomed by the newcomers. Through the cloud of particles, projectiles flew in and in no time the soldiers were lying on the ground, their metal overalls protecting them little against the impact of bullets.

One of the assailants, a huge man wearing black garments and an armoured mask went towards Darvis and Farrah's cell. He was holding the keycard of the locking system he had retrieved from one of the bodies.

The gate creaked open the moment the card slid past the screen.

Farrah took the newcomer's arm in hers. "Thank you, Thorick."

The man nodded in silence while Darvis emerged from the room. "Give me the key, I'll go around," he said, holding out his palm. Thorick gave the device away, and Darvis shoved it in front of the screen to Slay's cell, promptly opening his door.

He stood there, gawking at the others. "I'm guessing this is not the first time you guys have done this?"

"And I guess it's your lucky day," Darvis answered.

The lean man was already rushing past to the other cells, freeing their residents. "Who are you people?" Slay asked Farrah.

The woman was rearranging the weapons the big man named Thorick had brought along with him: two handguns on the side of her cargo pants and a holster with shoulder straps holding twin kukri swords on her back.

She barely offered him a glance. Her expression had become both serious and watchful. Two other newcomers were waiting at the entrance, also wearing dark clothing and masks. "We're rebelling against the daemon," she answered. "I guess that makes us insurgents."

The instant Darvis returned, Farrah and her cloaked friends left.

"Where are you going?" Slay asked the lean man, trotting after him.

"Away from here."

They came to a halt next to the exit. Farrah crouched beside it, both guns in hand, and Thorick took position on its other side. Outdoors, armoured placaters were gathering.

Reinforcements were on their way.

Slay hovered behind Darvis. He was usually the first to row into battle, but these guys seemed to know what they were doing. He somehow felt that he would get in their way if he were to act on impulse. "Can I come?" he asked, eyes peering over the man's shoulder.

"I don't make the calls around here, mate." Darvis pointed to Farrah. "She does."

He glanced at the woman and felt more intimidated than before. Without the faintest interest in them, she bolted out the door, Thorick on her heels. Slay rushed after them while they engaged the placaters that had greeted their escape.

He sprinted towards the closest body and retrieved the MP5K submachine gun from the dead hands of its previous owner. He shot its nozzle up, his bullet firing into the head of the nearest placater.

He veered around and saw that his new *friends* were fleeing down the street.

Damn it.

He accelerated after them and it wasn't long before they halted around a corner. He noticed people's gazes flitting right and left to peer at their group as they went about their business.

"Oh, you're still here," Darvis said. "Better keep up if you wanna stick around."

They were off again.

They proceeded down street after street, past shops and came to another stop inside a narrow alleyway.

"We've lost them." It was one of the hooded figures that had spoken, a woman. She pointed to Slay, head tilting to the side. "What do we do about him?" She had a small, pleasant voice, young and vibrant.

"He's good, love," answered Darvis. "We broke him out of the post."

"Could be a spy," said a gruff voice. Another of the dark figures.

Darvis chuckled. "A spy, Warwick? In a lowly post? This ain't the Anemas, mate."

The man answered nothing.

Farrah awarded him a look. "You'd better make up your mind. Go your way or come with us."

All of their eyes were on him. He pressed his tongue over his lips. "You broke me out of a control post and fought off those placaters in the middle of the daemon's capital. I'm intrigued."

Farrah fully glared at him, one hand rising to her waist. "I don't care about your *intrigue*. I'm asking if you're ready to die. If not, you can leave now. I don't need an observer blocking our way."

Slay's lips parted like a child whose mother had given him a slap to the head. He closed his mouth and grinned. "I'm a fighter. Fuck Daromas, I'm in!"

Not that he would have ever said that to the daemon's face.

And not that he had any clue what the hell he was getting into.

Farrah twisted back to her hooded companions. "Let's get a move on."

They began removing their cloaks, Slay watching as the people underneath revealed themselves.

The man named Thorick was wearing a charcoal silvered armour that protected him from his forearms to his shins. His broad, middle-aged face and dark eyes made him appear fierce and yet, also serene-looking. He sported a thick, tidy beard around his jawline and his-salt-and pepper hair was tied up in a bun. His skin was the same olive colour as Farrah's. Both were Letholdians without a doubt.

He wasn't the sort of guy you'd want to pick a fight with; he was *huge*!

The other newcomer, the woman who had spoken, revealed herself as a petite, blue-eyed blonde, whose hair fell a few inches below her shoulders. She looked younger than the rest, dynamic and friendly, though she was also giving off that *down to business* vibe these people seemed to have. Unlike the others, she only removed the mask part of her attire. The black shozoku garments she wore nevertheless suited her.

Cute, he thought. *I didn't know rebellion was so attractive...*

The last member, Warwick, was a mature-looking man. His face bore more than a few aging lines and marks, and his close-cut, greying hair gave him the appearance of a man of action with a military past.

As soon as they had removed their garments, Farrah ordered them to get going. They took different routes, the beautiful leader leaving to one side with Thorick and the soldier while Darvis guided them down another path.

Slay craned his neck back to witness the woman's departure and felt a hand gripping his shoulder. "Come on," said the lean man with a hint of impatience.

"Aren't we leaving together?" he asked as he caught up to them.

It was the younger woman who answered him. "We're going to the same place, just not using the same route."

"What's your name?" he asked her, coming to terms with Farrah's form fading into the distance.

"I'm Essan," she replied, eyes passing over him.

"And… you're all a part of a team or something?"

"Yeah, or something," she answered, a grin growing on her lips.

They began walking amongst the townspeople. "You guys make me feel as though you're gonna eat me when we get to whatever place we're heading for," he told her, a corner of his mouth twitching as he did.

Essan burst out laughing. She had a nice giggle like bells chiming in the wind. She gave him a once-over. "Well…" She tugged at the brown leather jacket he wore over his white tank top. She then took a gander at his short, sandy-blond hair and ragged beard. "Maybe after a bath," she finished.

Slay pursed his lips and narrowed his eyes. "Now I can tell my mom that avoiding baths *does* save lives."

She chuckled. "We're not telling you much because we don't know much about you," she explained, her tone becoming more serious.

He winced. "Fair enough."

Their walk down the streets of Letholdus resembled more of a zigzagging marathon of lefts and rights, Darvis steering them on the opposite side of the road each time they went past a hovercar carrying a patrol. A lot of soldiers were out and about for the preparations of Daemon's Day.

Daromas, the *daemon*, or he who would think of himself as half-human and half-god.

Fifteen years before, one week from now, Daromas had usurped the throne of King Redamastys Athlos. This was an event that required festivities even though only a handful of people would celebrate. Most would bow their heads in front of the procession as they hid their tears of anger.

On that day, the royal family had been assassinated at the hands of Daromas and his seven commandants. The news had jolted the whole of Iscar and resentment had poured in the face of this absolute distortion of justice though not many had lifted a finger to do something about it.

The king had warranted his own defeat when he had made the most powerful person in all the lands his general. For Daromas was no normal soldier.

Long before, he had acquired the theurgy of the gods, which was the capacity to conjure an almighty deity to fight by his side. And he who partook in a union with a god had no rivals to challenge him.

Israthel was his name, the Bearer of the Night, the ultimate patron of dusk.

No one knew how Daromas had acquired such an ancient and destructive force. Overpowering and absolute, night fell upon any who bathed in the shadow of the obscured god.

Through time, the daemon had gathered seven soldiers, dark commanders who had also wielded the power of theurgy, all bowing to their treacherous master. After twenty years of loyal service, the general and his defenders of the realm took over an entire kingdom from the inside as easily as if they had been playing a game of chess.

The general had assassinated King Redamastys and any who'd stood up against him using a magic greater than any living man could face.

On that day, Iscar had bowed down to intimidation.

In his thirst, Daromas had expanded his army of placaters, the keepers of his new domain. Over time, he had broadened his reach, creating a network of fear where Daromas removed any who did not fit his vision. Control posts were built all over the kingdom, and the four great prisons were revamped, the Anemas prison towering as the greatest, and vilest, one of them.

As the years went by, their lives became infused with the looming shadow of constant terror. Though a few had risen against the dictator, none had come close to bringing down this tyranny.

For what human could defeat a god?

The cost for trying was more than anyone was willing to pay.

As time passed, fewer people had revolted against the new regime and most now lived a passive existence of torment.

Looking now at Darvis and Essan, Slay thought that maybe insurrection wasn't so dead after all.

"This way," said Essan. She crossed over a bridge suspended above a canal before heading down the stairs on its other end. She then went to the back of the walkway and jumped into the shallow waters underneath. Slay widened his eyes at this, but nonetheless followed after Darvis.

They trudged inside the tunnel for a short while before coming to a halt in front of a gate. The younger woman knocked on it a few times and waited. She then knocked on it a different number of times and waited some more.

The hinges sprung into motion, and the rusty door drew ajar. A man stood behind it, big-bearded and narrow-eyed.

Essan tapped a hand on his shoulder as she walked him by. The joints groaned behind them as they proceeded into the passage and came up in front of a round cavity going down a ladder.

Down the rabbit hole, Slay thought.

They made their way to the bottom and entered the gigantic underworld maze. It was a gloomy abyssal tunnel illuminated by sparse electric torches, a perfect hideaway really. Even if the military ever got inside this place, they would probably lose themselves in these passages.

Essan guided them onwards for a while, down the left corridor, and so on and so forth, before she came to a stop and pushed open a door Slay had completely missed. It stood where light did not meet the entrance, its colours blending with those of the background wall.

Inside, Slay found a whole new world of rooms in this beneath the earth place where people lived.

Blankets were lying on the floor, maps and trinkets were amassed on massive wooden tables and a few dilapidated bookcases adorned the walls. At the back, a weapon stool, clothing and even some food had been stacked on broken shelves.

He looked at the different connecting areas, each similar to the others. It was an immense chamber built inside intersecting walls, creating an illusion of smaller, more intimate rooms.

The rebels gave him quizzical stares as he went in. At least a dozen people were going about the chambers, but he guessed that many more lived inside this apparent renegade hideaway.

When he noticed her near the back of the communal room, Slay ogled Farrah. The beautiful woman was looming over a work table, conversing with a dark-skinned man wearing short, curly, white hair and an ill-kept beard of the same colour.

When Essan and Darvis made their way towards her, he felt more than happy to move in the same direction.

"The daemon's float will be coming down Queen Street after twelve," Farrah was telling the man. "We need everyone in position by that time. We can start sending teams earlier during the day to avoid suspicion."

The older man pointed his finger at the map. "Arcanum's going to be posted in the public square, right where the chariot takes a turn."

Darvis joined Farrah's side. "Let's just hope all goes according to plan."

"The float follows the same route every year," she replied. "Thousands of people will attend; it shouldn't be too hard to camouflage ourselves."

"You guys wanna assassinate Daromas, the daemon?"

Farrah stared him down, eyes narrowing.

The lean man put a hand on Slay's shoulder. "You know mate, we don't know much about you...."

He glanced at Essan. "Is this the moment you eat me?"

She giggled and looked apologetically at Farrah who had arched an eyebrow. "No, we're not gonna eat you," answered the renegade leader. "Although we would like to know what you're doing here."

Slay stared at the different foreign faces of the people who surrounded him. What *was* he doing here? In truth, he didn't know. He had left the islands seeking a better life. Maybe he was looking to take out his anger. Maybe he was searching for a life of his own.

Maybe he was trying to find a reason to become something.

And these guys... they were something.

He stared at Farrah because he felt that she was the one he had to convince. "Where I come from, things are different. It's a village, so the placaters know you on a first name basis. The more they hate you, the more they make an example out of you." He lifted his shirt and revealed a dozen marks all over his torso.

"They make a fool out of you, and your family pays for it. You don't own anything. No money, no self-respect. We're all a bunch of machines trying to hang on to nothing. I didn't want that life anymore, so I left. I thought that I could find myself if I got away from the placaters and somehow Racketeer Bay seemed like the only option.

"Then, I met this guy." He pointed to Darvis. "And suddenly I'm standing next to a group of people fighting placaters in broad daylight as though it's usual business!" He locked his eyes onto Farrah's, her expression revealing nothing. "Now that I'm here, it seems like a nice place to be. I'm good with taking out the daemon if that's what you're asking. Fuck, who doesn't want to kill that asshole?"

He tried on a grin and lifted his hands in midair though cold sweat had drenched his palms at the thought of the words he had dared utter out loud.

He felt a slap against his back and heard Darvis chuckling. "Yup, I think he's good."

Farrah's eyes warmed and she offered the tiniest smile. "We don't have a choice anyway. If we don't have trust, we don't stand a chance." She put up a hand in front of him. "So, I hope we can trust you… hmm?" She was staring at him and Slay realized that she wanted to know his name.

He felt disheartened that she had not been listening when he and Darvis had introduced one another. "Slay." He took her fingers and shook them. "And you're Farrah." She rewarded him with no more than a curt nod. "Right." He believed that a change of subject was required. "What's the mission?"

Darvis said, "We're gonna try to kill Daromas on Daemon's Day."

"Okay." He put his hands on his hips, nodding to himself. "Okay," he repeated and wiped his chin with his palm a few times. "You guys sure have guts. What are you going to do about the commandants?"

Farrah resumed her exploration of the map. "You have to understand that our plan is not to survive." She peered up at him, eyes gauging his reaction. "We're going to take position around the area and initiate our firing when Daromas's float passes by. Most bullets won't reach him and believe me, the commandants *will* come for us before we've even begun doing any of this."

Slay's breath caught. "This is a suicide mission."

A quiet sort of pause followed this. Like when a crowd grows silent after a person said something they shouldn't have.

Darvis took a steadying intake of air. His eyes looked set, but Slay thought that they revealed certain sadness. "Yeah, mate. So we can offer the rest of Iscar a chance. I think it's worth it."

He gripped his lower lip between his front teeth, taking this in.

"Losing nerve?" Essan said, bumping his arm with her fist.

Slay dropped his shoulders. "That's… something."

Farrah sloped against her desk and crossed her arms. "Don't worry. If you want out, we won't force you to come. No one is. We'll only ask you to remain here for the rest of the operation with those of us who'll be staying behind. If things go amiss, they'll be the ones running the resistance. They'll decide what to do with you."

She looked at the older man standing beside her and he gave her a nod.

He wanted to answer, but she had resumed her work, apparently done with them. Darvis grabbed him by the shoulder and gave him a quick nudge. They left Farrah and the older man to their talking.

"Listen Darvis, about the plan… " Slay began. "It seems like one hell of a long shot."

"Having second thoughts?" the man replied.

"I mean… it's just…"

Gods, Darvis. These guys have gods!

Darvis was nodding and one corner of his lips was pulling up. "We're not completely stupid. We've got an ace up our sleeve."

Slay blinked a few times. "An ace?"

The lean man grinned crookedly, but did not grace him with an explanation.

"Darvis, I don't know if…"

He stopped him short. "You don't have to answer now. Think about it for a while. We've got a few days to spare. Why don't you talk to other people, eh? Get to know us a bit."

"Yeah, I guess I'll do that," Slay agreed. "I'm free to leave, right?"

Darvis laughed as he retreated. "Don't be silly. Of course you can't leave. We barely know you."

And he was gone.

Chapter 2

As it turned out, Slay wasn't allowed to leave. Though he had felt uneasy about this, he understood the reasoning behind it. In fact, he got to learn a lot about these people.

After the first two days, he had counted around two dozen of these renegades roaming the hideaway, men and women of different ages and backgrounds unified in a cause they thought paramount.

Their group had been around for more than eight years. When most had stopped resisting the daemon, Farrah's gang had kept the candle of their own revolt burning. She was both the initiator and leader of the insurgence.

She had been eighteen when she and Thorick had assembled their band of renegades and since had been a cause of constant nuisance for the placaters. "Although," said Darvis, "the daemon probably isn't aware of our existence. We're insignificant to him."

However unimportant they were to Daromas and his commandants, they had made a difference in the lives of many. The renegades had built a network of communication that enabled them to rush to the rescue of those persecuted by the placaters and bring a semblance of justice in the streets of Letholdus.

They had increased their numbers with time, and Slay came to both admire and feel inspired by the warriors who partook in their group.

They wanted to make a difference and did something about it.

That was important. Really important.

Their contagious ambitions were reeling him in. His family was dead and he had nothing left but a shadow of a previous life taken from him. Perhaps his good fortune had had him stumble upon the very people whom he could identify with—men and women who had lost something and were grasping at what remained.

Heck, he'd spent the few last years provoking placaters with no regard for his personal safety. This wasn't any different. Why cower now when this mandate was far more crucial?

Because of the daemon.

Yeah, that's the difference. At the mere thought of the man, he felt the jitters.

Essan visited him, too. Orphaned at the age of five, this youngest group member had since roamed the alleys of the capital, referred to as a *street rat.* She had learned to fend for herself, how to hide and steal. She had become an apprentice of the twilight and knew how to get info, disappear without a trace and fight in silence. Slay had been right; her outfit *did* fit her well. She was a warrior of the dusk.

Essan had a sweet disposition. She was easily ten years younger than him, not much older than eighteen. Everyone in the group liked her, akin to a child they all took care of even though she wasn't a little girl anymore. Perhaps they wanted to make amends for the emptiness she had endured as an orphan for so long.

He also tried talking to Thorick, but the big man had answered him with a neutral look of poised scrutiny when he had.

When he inquired about him to Essan, she giggled. "Of course he didn't reply, silly. He doesn't have a tongue."

Needless to say, this took him aback.

Thorick had been a guard at the late king's court. When the daemon had usurped the throne, the knight had declined to join in the new regime and Daromas's commandants had sent him to the Anemas. That was before the prison had had its makeover and been revamped into the pit of despair it now was.

They had tortured him and asked him to comply, but nothing

they had done had broken the man. He had kept mute. So they had taken his tongue, for *one who does not speak does not need one in the first place.*

He had lingered in there for weeks whilst Iscar had been shredded to bits. The armour he now wore most of the time hid the wreckage of his body, torn apart at the hands of torture.

At the beginning of Daromas's chaotic reign, people had resisted the new ruler. Back in those early days, friends could still be found, and Thorick had escaped prison with the help of a guard who had known him. The name of that guard had been Darvis.

The knight had fled the city, but Darvis had stayed behind. Years later, unable to continue the farce of his life as a placater, the lean man had deserted his post. Years more had passed before he had reunited with Thorick and signed up with the rest of the gang.

"Must suck not to be able to talk," Slay said.

"I don't think he minds it," answered Essan. "His presence is sometimes better than any words spoken."

Slay tried talking to Farrah a few times but felt more like a nuisance to her than anything. Far from discouraging him, he had turned to the others to get to know her more. Essan wasn't much help on the subject. It seemed to him that both women were close and the youngest would not speak out of respect for her elder.

She just said, "She doesn't fear him."

"Everyone fears the daemon," Slay replied matter-of-factly.

Essan bobbed her head. "She fears what he can do. She fears the repercussions of his acts. She fears his regime. But she doesn't fear *him*. That's why we follow her."

That was all she told him, but these words said a lot.

Darvis had chortled openly when Slay had approached him on the matter of Farrah. After a minute or so, he had fled the man's side, his cackle following his retreat. Definitely no help there.

Thus, he had resolved to gaze at her from afar.

He was not the only one compelled by this leader. The renegades' respect for this woman was a mixture of inspiration and devotion. Her charisma was unchallenged, but it was her presence that captivated him most. She was a person of impressive demeanour, both secure and determined, and he had found himself hoping that she would survive the following days.

He also conversed with the other man who had broken him out of the control post, Warwick, and, as he had presumed, he had been a lieutenant in King Redamastys's army. Most of the scars adorning his face had been the result of confrontations with the placaters since.

After Redamastys's death, Warwick had vanished amidst the dirtiest parts of the city. But when whispers of revolution had reached his ears, he had sought the opportunity to reclaim his honour and joined Farrah.

The man had briefed Slay on their procedures, explained their training regimen and styles of combat. He also took him to the armoury, and he was free to choose whichever weapon of his liking. Soon, two axes rested on each side of his tarnished leather belt.

They had then trained together for a few hours. In no time, Slay had removed his vest, his forehead glistening with sweat, his shirt drenched.

"Your style is somewhat brutal but effective," Warwick told him. "I guess those muscles of yours aren't just for show. You know how to fight, son."

Slay grinned. He had been the best fighter on the islands. Maybe this didn't look like much compared to the rest of Iscar but where he'd come from, people were brawlers. Being the best amongst them, that wasn't saying nothing. Yes, he knew how to fight, and he was damn good at it.

On the eve of the daemon's celebrations, Darvis approached him.

"How are ya doing?" the man said as a greeting.

How indeed.

"You guys are my new favourite people," Slay answered. "But I can't shake the feeling that I'll never see you again after tomorrow."

The man chuckled. "Come with me, I'll tell ya something."

They went and sat right on the floor of an adjacent rooms, apart from the other renegades. "Arcanum's our safeguard," began Darvis, leaning both forearms on top of his knees.

"Arcanum?"

He nodded. "You heard that I used to be a placater, eh? Arcanum was my partner. We never stopped being in touch since my desertion, and now he's fed up with this bullshit," Darvis continued. "He doesn't want out, he wants *out*."

Slay drew his arms around his chin, blinking at the man. "Out?"

"If all else fails, he's the one that's gonna kill the daemon. We'll have provided him with the distraction."

Slay's eyes widened. "How is he gonna do *that*?"

"He's going to be posted at the parade near the central square. When we open fire, both commandants and placaters will be called in to defend the daemon. They've never stationed Arcanum close to him before, but on that day, they'll expect him to cover Daromas when we make our move. If our bullets miss their mark, he's gonna go in and slit that asshole's throat."

"The commandants will kill him for this," Slay replied darkly. "You'd have to be crazy to put yourself in that position."

At the mere thought of being in proximity to the daemon, his pulse had begun beating faster and a rotten stench had fluttered his nostrils. Slay had no idea how Daromas smelled, but this felt like an appropriate scent.

Darvis gave him a look and Slay remembered. "Oh."

Out.

"Why didn't you tell me this from the start?" he asked, frowning at the floor.

Darvis slanted his head back. "You already know why."

"Does that mean you trust me now?" He smirked and so did the lean man.

"I guess it does. You'll be keeping with me throughout the operation though. You know, just in case."

"Uh, as in, if I try to betray you—"

"I'll put a bullet through your head. Yup." He patted Slay's leg and got up. "Arcanum's doing this for all of us. His sacrifice might give us a chance to live. To truly live."

"Many things could go wrong, Darvis."

The other man grinned good-naturedly. "Whatever you decide, it's your choice, mate."

Slay swallowed.

Everyone was solemn on that next morning when Farrah addressed the group and took them through their plan.

"I know we've never done anything of this sort," the renegade leader said. "I also know that I'm asking a lot." She lowered her gaze, her features hardening. "I wish I didn't have to ask any of you something like this. I wish we could live in a world where no one had to die to make things right. I wish we didn't have to sacrifice a man's life to achieve our goals."

She glanced back up, looking more forceful than ever. "But here I am, asking if you are willing to put your lives down with me for Iscar and all of its citizens! Whatever happens, know that I am humbled that I fought alongside you. It brings me peace to do what I must. And remember," she finished, eyes hardening, "*he* is just a man. Nothing more."

A collective sort of shiver ran through the room and for a moment, it felt like they were about to throw their plans out the window.

"I'm ready, boss," declared Darvis, fist lifting up though his lips were quivering and he looked as though he hadn't slept all night.

Nor had Slay.

Every time he had tried to, Daromas's godsforsaken orbs had been staring at him, stealing what little hopes he'd had of sleeping.

No more words were said, no more sounds. Like Darvis, the group had brought their fists up as Farrah had gazed over them.

After a minute or so, one of them had lowered his hand and the others had followed. In absolute silence, they had taken position around the communal hall and had hung their heads. Slay could hear some of their whimpers, the sounds of their fear taxing his resolve.

The first group had left not long after.

The wait was the worst part of it. Slay had done circles around the room so many times that he could no longer count them. More than once, he had drawn his axes and tested their blades against his fingertip, cutting himself in the process. After a few times, he'd figured the weapons were in good condition and had left them alone. He'd paced on, his index finger stuck in his mouth as he'd sucked on its bloody tip. All the while, the words *what the fuck* were the only thing that he could think about.

When it came to his and Darvis's turn to take their leave, they'd made their way to Farrah.

"Are you sure you want to do this?" she asked, eyeing him.

He attempted a smile. "Yeah. I mean, maybe we'll become heroes today."

There was no way he was turning his back on these people now. He was no coward.

That hothead part of him also had a way of screwing him over.

She grinned. Though its sincerity wasn't questioned, he found something controlled in its appearance, a depth hidden right underneath the facade she seemed to wear.

"I bid you good luck," she said.

He left, remembering the warmth in her eyes, the only thing that kept his stone-laden feet going.

Farrah looked on as Darvis and the new enrollee, Slay, exited the room. She knew their attempt on the daemon came at a high price, but she was tired. Year after year, she had wasted away in pointless battles and nothing had changed.

How many more years like this?

Iscar could not keep at it for much longer. The daemon was crushing their souls, and they were delving further into the pit of this desolation. She was not willing to spend another minute in this inferno.

This wasn't a question. It was an answer.

She gestured at Thorick and Essan. "We're next; are you guys ready?"

Essan smirked and plastered her armoured mask over her mouth, embodying the role of the martial arts assassin that she was. She had lined up sharp knives on her back, and concealed countless other arsenals inside her shozoku garment. "Of course I am!"

Thorick pulled a hand around his back, patting the enormous hammer that served as his weapon of choice. He had also retrieved two hunting rifles from the armoury and hung them on the leather harness he wore over the left shoulder of his metal chest piece.

He gave her a smile, and she knew he would be with her till the end as he had always been. He was a bit of the father she had lost long ago and she counted on him like no other.

She adjusted the straps of her kukri swords on her back and checked that she had properly loaded both of her one-arm hand guns. She then pulled her fingerless leather gauntlets on and tugged on the necklace she wore inside her shirt. She finished by pushing back the hair that had flowed across her face and nodded to the others.

"Let's go."

The alleys surrounding Main Street and Queen's Street were flooded with citizens. Thousands of people had swamped the central square and the adjacent lanes leading up to the palace, crowding both sides of the daemon's procession route for the celebration.

Farrah, Essan and Thorick made their way through the sullen mass whose smiles echoed the presence of nearby placaters. She did not fake one as she disappeared inside the sea of Letholdians, her features contorted with the lines of her upcoming task. She went through the crowd, ignoring the leering gazes falling appreciatively on her as she pushed amongst them.

She was used to their stares. Ever since she had become a woman, people had looked at her this way. Countless times, their belittling ganders had made her feel akin to a piece of meat commanding an audience. She did not care for such behaviour.

She was not an object of pleasure for their base needs.

She sometimes wondered whether she had gained part of the internal strength she possessed due to their failure to see her for the person that she was.

They elbowed people aside as they made their way inside the central square tavern, which was packed to boot for the occasion, and they walked up to the innkeeper. Huddled between a few other clients, Farrah requested the room she had booked weeks before.

The clerk scrolled a hefty finger down his registry, hummed and waved them up the stairs. Her stomach tightened with every step she took, while she actively worked on keeping her fingers from balling into fists. Though she felt submerged by thoughts of what they were about to do, her vision had never been so clear.

The innkeeper led them inside the plain room, and just as soon rushed back to his business. With the door creaking shut behind them, Farrah walked over to the window and opened the pivoting glass.

The noise was deafening outside. She moved a chair closer to the windowsill, Thorick and Essan doing the same beside another. The parade was set to begin. According to her calculations, Daromas would arrive in less than an hour.

Essan dropped her head against her forearms, which she had folded along the edge of the sill. "Now we wait," she muttered.

Farrah nodded, gaze fixed ahead. *Now we wait.*

Darvis and Slay were caught in the midst of the flock, a short way from the procession's route so that if something went amiss, they could attempt to flee.

Or rather, *when* something went amiss.

There was no doubt in Darvis's mind that even *if* Arcanum killed the daemon, the commandants would make them atone abundantly for their sin.

He watched their surroundings and spotted a few of their own people on the other side of the street. Alongside a couple of brave volunteers, Warwick was standing right beside the float's trajectory. Though their location offered the best vantage point, it came at increased risks for his and his comrades' lives.

These poor souls had almost no chance at survival. In the event that Arcanum failed, it was on them to finish the job, which pretty much translated to a death warrant.

Warwick had known this and when Farrah had objected, claiming that it should be *her* in his stead, he had argued with her: "What are you thinking? You're our leader, we need you!"

She had replied with as much courage, "Then it makes that much more sense that I be on the front!"

Darvis and the others had intervened.

Their vehement refusal had displeased her, and their squabble had lasted some time. After a while, Essan and Warwick had taken her aside and had muttered things they could not hear. When Farrah had returned, she had nodded her approval with no other word spoken.

Warwick wanted to do this. He was old, tired, and like Arcanum, he wanted to redeem himself for failing their late king all those years ago. Though it seemed improbable, Darvis still hoped that the rugged man would survive the day.

Just perhaps.

Slay was standing next to him. The islander had cleaned his short beard and shaved the sides of his hair the day before and he looked now far more presentable for a man who might be about to die.

He appeared nervous though his stance was steady. He had settled his pale green stare ahead of him, looking unfocused.

Darvis lowered his gaze and noticed that the islander was flexing his arms in and out. *Poor fella*, he thought, regretting getting him out of jail. He then blinked around upon hearing the noise of restrained applause.

The congregation was heading their way.

"Get ready," he said while glimpsing into the distance.

No placaters were in the vicinity. Most of them had formed a guard of honour on each side of the street, creating a human barrier between the crowd and the daemon's float. Others yet stood behind the mass of people, tasked with keeping order and monitoring the horde by encouraging shouts of acclamations.

Rows of banners were lined up between the placaters, depicting each of the commandants' faces, their hollowed stares akin to the embrace of death lurking over them.

Darvis tried searching for Arcanum amidst the soldiers, but they all looked the same, and he was feeling far too restless to play "spot the differences."

Just around the corner to Queen's Street, Arcanum had told him a few days before. *If anything comes up, I'll send word.*

Darvis had gone out every day at their meeting place since and no messages had appeared, save on the last day.

I'm going out. Cheers, friend, the scribbled note had said.

His breath becoming rattled, he looked up at the incoming float.

The hovering platform was a display of opulence. Its silver, sculpted frame was enriched with patterns of encrusted jewels. Columns of marble supported a ceiling of cascading, mulberry silk curtains embroidered with branches of laurels. A gigantic regime screen stood at the end of the vehicle, facing the rear crowd. It depicted the ever-seeing stare of the daemon, glowering at his subjects as he sat on the float with his back to them, a camera planted in front of him.

There he was. In the middle of the transport, sitting on an argent throne.

Daromas the daemon.

Darvis's core shrunk and his leg shook. He jostled his head a few times, seeking composure, but when his gaze fell to the man's eyes, his index finger began tapping the side of the leg that was already trembling.

The stare was inhuman, leeching. It was like rot decaying on a skull or the eyes of a vulture, *waiting.*

Waiting for a feast.

Dressed in a stylish black suit, the man was posing with a straight back. The metal leather of his shoes matched the sharp crown that sat on top of his head. A short, powdered, black-and-white beard covered his face and his dark hair was slick and ordered under his headdress.

What a charade. This was not a celebration. It was a demonstration. It was fear being instilled. It was a *reminder.*

Two commandants were standing by his side, clad in their red-and-black uniforms. At the front stood another two, while the remaining three were posted at the back. Every one of them had those same eyes, the same wicked, rotting orbs.

It was a result of the toll, the paid price for wielding the theurgy of the gods.

Ever since these commandants had formed a connection with their deities, they had been cursed. Year after year, their greed siphoned their vitality.

They were changing into something less than human, turning into creatures of the underworld—Daromas most of all. Perhaps that was because he had attained his god before the commandants. Perhaps that was because he had given it more of himself than the others had.

In any case, the man was slowly morphing into a human version of a harpy.

Slay had darted for his rifle, and Darvis rushed ahead before he could put his fingers on it. "Relax, mate, it ain't time yet," he said, his nerves jumping at this.

The islander lowered his hands and surveilled his surroundings.

The newcomer's eyes were as round as saucers and sweat was drenching his face. He wore the expression of a mad person.

Maybe that's what they all were.

Warwick and him weren't exactly near each other, but Darvis was taller than most and though he had cursed his height many times in the past, it had served him well. When his eyes crossed the older man's, they gave each other the slightest nod, and the gesture felt like goodbye.

Darvis took a shaking breath. His insides were bloated, his mind caught in a cloud. Glimpsing sideways, he knew at once that Slay felt the same way.

The daemon was almost on them.

Darvis had stopped looking at the *man.* If he had, he wasn't certain he'd had the courage anymore to be a part of this.

He gazed back towards the central square tavern, counted the windows and looked on.

And on.

A black tissue was blown out the window.

"Five seconds, mate."

Slay's eyes went wide and he hoisted his rifle, hands shaking.

"Four seconds."

Warwick was also getting into position, his two acolytes imitating his movements. The placaters nearby took no notice of them. They had turned their heads towards the chariot in submission. Arcanum was somewhere in their midst, readying himself for his fate.

"Three seconds."

The commandant on the corner of the float glided his gaze in Warwick's direction. The stern lines of his ghostly face became a frown.

"Two, one…"

"Daemon!"

"Now!"

As a darkened purple blob expanded in front of Daromas, sounds of rifles fired from all directions while countless bullets made their way towards the vehicle.

Everything stopped.

The gunpowder from their weapons caught in a suspended cloud of potassium nitrate. Their munitions were rendered useless and remained devoutly perched in place as though time and space no longer mattered, each of them at a different distance and angle from the daemon.

Their hearts pounded to the drums of their quietened limbs. They were trapped inside their bodies, unable to move or make a sound.

The arch of purple mist had revealed a skeletal creature. Beams of violet were shining from the eyes of the skull-like features of the thing that had appeared.

A drape of scarcely visible strands had covered the entire float and encompassed its surroundings, its strings catching everything inside their almost-invisible web. The light that had illuminated the creature's orbs reverted on itself and disappeared, exposing empty cavities where pupils should have been. His bone-fingered hands were hovering above his head, holding the hood he had lifted to unleash his mysterious power.

The skeleton lowered his white-knuckled fists and dropped the cloak over his face. At once, the projectiles fell in a blaring clatter that echoed throughout the silent audience.

Movement was allowed again and their limbs regained the freedom to act of their own accord.

They stared in disbelief at the tall figure that had appeared. He had opened his bony palms in front of his chest, making a cross out of his forearms, face hidden under his imposing cap. Particles of smoke poured through the shredded fabric of his gown, forever kept in motion in the stillness of the frozen universe he could create.

Their gaze had fallen upon the God of Darkness, Shalowhith.

Darvis had never seen a deity with his own eyes. Their presence was from beyond this plane, and no man could match their strength.

Come on, Arcanum! he thought, pulse yammering inside his head. *Now!*

The placaters were rushing around the float, protecting their master from the intruders. He saw a few of them climbing on the chariot, pointing their rifles up. At this, Darvis's heart beat faster than it ought to have been capable of.

Daromas was yet seated. His expression had not changed though the knuckles holding the armrests of his throne were white.

And he couldn't have looked further from fright.

He drew a long finger up and beckoned to Shalowhith's wielder by curving it once. Commandant Ykbara glided towards her god, her stride resembling that of a puppet pulled by strings. A purple glow enshrouded the general's fist, the sign that she had conjured a deity.

She whispered something and Shalowhith opened his palms again. The whole populace was holding its breath, waiting to see what doom would befall on them.

Crisp strands of white and silver darted out of the tip of the skeleton's fingers. They flew above the god's head and drifted in midair until one of them quaked and dove down. It sprinted towards Warwick at a speed that no one could have matched. Before the man could open his mouth, it charged against his neck and anchored itself at the base of his skull.

His weapon tumbled from his hands, his eyes widened in fear, his fingers still as though he were yet clutching his rifle. Rendered immobile, the man could do nothing but shift his pupils.

He was the first victim of the spell.

The filaments had begun to drop one at a time as though they had been searching for a target all this time, and promptly, other renegades became their prey. Ten bone fingers, ten strands. Ten of his companions stunned as they awaited the placaters' arrival.

"Lower your gun, *fool*, and don't make a move!" he whispered to Slay, who was gaping at the scene.

Cursing, he witnessed a commandant making his way to Warwick.

By the gods!

Everything was happening too fast.

His mouth fell when a gigantic sword struck Warwick in half, his face now a distortion of what it had been, his two acolytes soon receiving similar fate.

What is Arcanum doing?!

Both commandants and placaters had formed a barricade around the daemon.

Do it!

Mayhem had erupted and yells of panic exploded in his eardrums as people began trampling over each other in their hurry to flee from the scene. The strands that had ensnared the dead renegades had withdrawn from their necks and were seeking new targets.

"We need to go!" he shouted to the islander.

The blood in his veins had turned cold; the fear that had clenched his intestines was wrestling them as though wanting to wrench them out of his abdomen.

Slay's eyes were watching on in terror, and realization finally hit Darvis. "Oh, shit!" He darted around the other man and found a silver string hanging from his skull. "Fucking hell!" he cursed as people ran past them.

He clutched the strand with his fist and pulled on it. Blood gushed down his fingers as it cut through them. He retrieved his pocketknife, sweat trickling down his temples as he began hacking the filament with it.

The string yielded and as it did, it fell from Slay's neck. The islander took a deep breath as though he had just emerged from the depth of the sea.

The hair on Darvis's forearms stood up. Shivers ran down the length of his back. A tremor took ahold of his fingers. He looked over his shoulder. Though he could not see Shalowhith's face, it was as though the horror was driving his purple glower into his soul.

"Let's go!"

They started to run as if the underworld was on their tail.

And it was.

The moment the violet beams flared up, Farrah grasped the edge of the windowsill as she witnessed the unfolding events. They had awakened the beast, and he was about ready to devour them.

She knew of Shalowhith, knew of the creature's terrible powers arising from darkness.

Gods had different skill sets, unique to each and every one of them. Shalowhith's magic was the faculty of control. It allowed the god to stop anything from moving, enabling its master to dispose of any adversary that required swift defeat.

Shalowhith almost never stirred, but for the cloak surrounding him, which moved as though it was caught under the spell of its own ability.

Farrah witnessed Warwick's splintered halves topple like a fragile piece of paper ripped in two. Gritting her teeth, she withdrew her gaze from the gruesome display and focused it on the silver strands now plunging into the frightened crowd.

Amidst the cacophony of the fleeing denizens, she could hear the shrieks of the panicked renegades, the sound of their cries dying the moment a string caught their necks.

They were apparently chasing every man and woman who had raised a gun on Daromas, as if the god had put their faces to memory when they had all stood frozen with their weapons lifted.

She drew her eyes shut, her breath accelerating. When she opened them again, she focused on the placaters rushing to the daemon's side, surrounding him.

She would have to put her trust in Arcanum.

Shalowhith was about to find them, and it was only a matter of time before a commandant followed through on the spell.

"Close the windows!" she bellowed at the sight of a string diving their way.

Thorick and Essan sprung into motion just as Shalowhith's strand came crashing into the glass surface they had drawn shut, not a second too late. The string recoiled on impact, but just as soon, it attempted to pierce through the glass again. They startled a few steps back, eyes round as the tip nudged its head repeatedly against the window in an unnerving clatter of ceaseless pecking.

As though it had a mind of its own, the wire stopped moving altogether, its tip pointed at them. The silence that followed felt just as foreboding as the rummaging it had been making only seconds before.

"It's waiting for us to come out," quaked Essan.

"Not if it can't see us." Farrah bolted towards the entrance. "We'll go through the back, Shalowhith can't put his gaze on us there!"

They hurried through the building and ignored the clerk's shouts as they sped towards the kitchen and made their way to the back and out in the alleyway. They drew to a sudden halt, tottering on tiptoes, their shoulders slanting back.

They were face to face with half a dozen placaters.

"Halt!" one of them said, pointing his gun to her.

Her kukri sword was already at his throat, slashing it open. Thorick's enormous hammer crashed against the soldier next to him while Essan flashed a finger knife into the eye of a third one. The battle was soon over, the placaters bathing in their blood at their feet.

"Right on cue."

They heard a restrained clapping coming from the other end of the street where the voice had emerged from the shadows. Farrah glowered at the man walking down the alley, disquiet gripping her.

Commandant Husar. A general known for his love of torture and tormenting habits. A man as repulsive on the inside as he was on the outside.

In his late thirties, he was the youngest of the commandants. He wore a ragged mane of red hair and a clean-shaven face. His bottomless, darkened eyes revealed no warmth, and his mouth painted a haughty smirk of annoyance.

Farrah positioned herself for a fight, but her gaze drew to Husar's hand. It was the colour of a mud-encrusted path after a heavy rain.

He was not alone.

They sprung away from the lethal assault. Several swords had flung their tips down on them from above and split the soil where they had stood a second before.

The Warlord, Illmeth, a seven-sword-wielding celestial being twice the size of Thorick, rose in their wake.

His face was draped in the mask of barrenness where flawless skin devoid of features stood instead of his visage. Though he held both of his weapon arms before him, five other hovering ones were angled at their necks. They had before them the most accomplished sword expert and stood no chance at defeating him. With the power of a thought, any one of those soaring weapons could end their lives in a single thrust.

"Oh my, you guys are in trouble."

Farrah could not answer. The blade of the sword rested heavily against her throat. She glared at the man, her eyes filled with loathing as he glided towards them.

Both the daemon and the commandants shared a similar walk, which resembled that of a slithering snake or an undead wraith. Their feet were light against the ground and their limbs hardly moved as they ghosted about.

"How are you going to pay for this, I wonder?" Husar asked. His voice was like the sound a person makes when caught in between radio channels, that distant frequency you aren't supposed to hear. It was the voice of a god wielder, the echo of a human shell being feasted upon.

Handcuffs were fastened around their wrists and they were brought back to the now-empty central square where the daemon awaited their arrival.

Farrah staggered on the floor of the float as, next to her, Thorick and Essan received the same treatment. She swayed to her knees with some difficulty and peered to her side.

Darvis and a few other renegades were there as well. Her heart skipped a beat when she witnessed the lean man's bloodied face and dazed expression. He offered her a wink, but his eyes did not fool her. He looked petrified.

Her sight next sought Daromas, yet very much alive.

She grew still. Where was Arcanum?

Something was wrong. He should have acted by now. Many

soldiers surrounded the daemon, but there was no way of knowing which one of them he was.

Daromas was watching them through the emptiness of his indented cavities. His head quivered from time to time as though the discourse in his mind caused him mute disbelief.

Shalowhith was nowhere to be seen. The power of theurgy was intricate in its nature and terribly energy consuming in its application. The deity's presence lasted for as long as their wielder could control them before they returned to the void whence the projection came from.

Daromas rose from his seat.

His movements were slow and deliberate as he approached them. Like Commandant Ykbara and Husar, he had a strange sort of spastic stroll, akin to a lifeless doll carried by an invisible source.

He took a rasping breath, nostrils flaring and lungs heaving like a man suffering from pneumonia, and then whispered something under it. The incoherent mumble flew inside the wind like petals ripped from a rose.

He wobbled all the way to the end of the row, hand lifting as he twisted back around. His chest had turned first, feet following as though both halves of his body weren't connected. His long fingertips prowled like the feet of a spider on the scalps of their heads as he paced along the line they made.

Mumble mumble, the voice went.

When the arachnids touched the fringe of her hair, Farrah's stomach lurched. Her eyes were downcast, staring at the silver-clad feet as they glided past her.

Her brain wanted to shut down.

When he reached the other end of the row, he faced the empty central square, chest heaving somewhat, breath wheezing. As though the doll was cranked back to life, he returned to his seat and squatted before it like a man about to put his hands through dirt as he began his gardening.

He grabbed the bottom of the throne and lifted it. The chair drew back like a jewelry box revealing its contents. He removed his jacket and rolled up the sleeves of his white shirt before he rummaged inside the treasure chest.

When he brought them back up, his hands were covered with blood.

He flipped something behind his back, and it went lumping on the floor of the float in front of them like a gelatin dessert.

A red and wet gelatin dessert.

He began flinging different things out of the hidden compartment, slowly amounting to an ensemble of human meat.

The long-awaited feast for the jackals.

Mumble, mumble went the raspy radio voice. "Ah, there it is." Those were the only words she caught.

He lifted the biggest piece out, the *piece de resistance.*

A human head.

Daromas drew himself up, one hand holding the head by its hair, the other by its flesh, right underneath the neck. The daemon's mouth was opening and closing, taking in short, audible breaths, eyes staring at the head the same way they looked at everything else.

He peered around at them and pointed with his finger at the face he was carrying.

It was Arcanum. A very dead Arcanum.

Farrah felt like vomiting. The stench of the rotting corpse was forcing its putrefaction into her nose.

The head was dropped on the floor like a ball left forgotten and the daemon dragged himself towards them again, body jerking all the while. Chains bound their hands in forged metal and a commandant stood behind each one of them.

They were trapped.

He stood on tiptoes in front of them, lowered his cheeks between his palms and stared at the renegades. His gaze was scrutinizing like that of a curious animal, head tilting from side to side every few seconds.

"I *know* everything, my little moppets," rasped the frequency. "I *see* everything." The eyes flashed and Farrah felt nauseated.

He wheeled around, and clicked his tongue a few times before darting his head back. The gesture seemed wrong in the midst of all his previously long ones. He drew an excruciating pneumonic breath and beckoned at the nearest placater.

"Bring back the cameras."

Slay was shaking. As soon as Shalowhith's enchantment had released him, he and Darvis had fled. They had wasted no time looking over their shoulders as they had.

When he had cornered into the first alley, he had waited for Darvis to catch up to him. But the lean man hadn't shown up.

He had searched around for signs of him. They had been separated in the aftermath of the frantic crowd. But even as the mob had begun to disperse, there had been no traces of Darvis.

Slay approached the side of the building and peered over at the square.

There he was! Right in the middle of the site, unmoving.

Fuck.

Shalowhith had not allowed him to escape as he had done Slay. Worse, a group of placaters had assembled around him. There was no saving him, nothing that he could do without getting the both of them killed.

What am I supposed to do? He was not one of the renegades. Was he supposed to run off and pretend that he hadn't known any of them? Or should he forfeit his life by trying a stupid and desperate heroic act?

As he stood rooted in place, it felt as though Shalowhith yet had his string upon him.

Before long, the deity released Darvis from his power and the placaters shackled him. The soldiers took him on the daemon's float alongside other insurgents.

At least some of the renegades were yet alive, captured perhaps but still breathing. What about the rest of them? Surely others had escaped. Had they gone back at the hideout? Should he be heading back there as well?

Another group was now being escorted towards Daromas's chariot.

Bloody hell!

He had hoped that Farrah would have fled at the first sight of danger, but he was looking now at her proud figure being taken in with the others. Worse, Thorick and Essan were by her side, the placaters forcing them to their knees in front of the daemon.

What else had they expected? We never stood a chance....

Darvis's friend hadn't showed up and it was so darn sad to see that their efforts had been for naught. All these years of fighting and they were to die like dogs, never to be remembered. *So fucking sad.*

He heard footsteps behind him and looked around. Fearing the arrival of a placater, he found instead someone he had not expected.

It was the man with the white beard, the one that Farrah had been conversing with back at the hideout. He was advancing as if on a straight line, his frail body covered with coatings of fabric, and was making his way towards the central square.

Slay ran up to the man and grabbed him by the shoulders. "Hey! You need to get out of here, real bad stuff is happening!"

The man focused his weary, bloodshot stare on him. Layers of sweat dripped his face, lower lip quivering. "Oh, I know you. You're the newcomer," he replied dreamily. He looked like a twig just about ready to snap.

"Yeah, Slay. Listen, old man, we need to get out of here!"

The man took his hand inside his own and waved it away, not ungently, and resumed his walk. Slay peered down and noticed blood tainting the side of the man's leg.

He did not stop him this time but contemplated the hunched form as it followed the road. Did they have a backup plan he hadn't been told about?

He didn't even know the man's name.

The daemon was standing in front of the cameras. He had removed the crown from his hair, and a repetitive twitch in his left eye had him blink too many times for a normal person.

"My people," he began, voice distant. "You are nothing without me." He pointed at the renegades, lashes batting as the twitch in his eye gained momentum. "These people are *nothing*."

There was an odd quality to this voice. It was as though the man's emotions had all but disappeared. Had it come from anyone else, it would have sounded dull, a weapon to lull a child to sleep.

"Look at their faces. *Remember* them."

He patted the hairs on his head as though placing them, and it had the effect of a man tapping his brain mechanically. "Remember today," he rasped on in his monotone voice. "Etch into your minds every detail of this event."

Farrah's muscles tensed as he walked up to his commandants and requested a knife be given to him before making his way towards the row of renegades.

Her eyes were filled with sting though she would have wanted them to be made of stone. She had known for some time now that they would be executed but hadn't known when nor how. It would seem that Daromas had decided to end their revolt right here, in the bud, by making an example out of them.

This was the better alternative. Torture at the hands of the Anemas would have proven worse fate.

As the daemon turned his stare on the first man, Farrah realized that she would have to watch as her allies were killed, one after another, before her turn would come.

She searched Essan and Thorick's gaze. The knight looked as though he had made peace with his fate and had lowered his head in prayer. Essan, though, was trembling so much that Farrah could almost feel her shivers reaching her.

When the younger woman locked eyes with hers, Farrah attempted a smile and it was the hardest she had ever tried. Essan quivered one of her own and though it was ambivalent and as coerced as hers had been, it comforted Farrah nevertheless.

She's so young, she thought. *I should have never let them follow me in this nonsense....*

She faced her other side. Darvis's head was angled to the ground.

Blood was running down his cheeks in heavy streaks, and she wasn't even certain whether he was conscious or not. Not long before, he had stopped moving altogether.

Mumble mumble, the daemon was saying.

Her eyes focused away.

Daromas was angling the cameraman's lens towards the rebel's face. He had dropped on his knees, his red-buttered fingers tugging on the camera's sunshade bellows.

Mumble. "A bit to the left, maybe."

The poor cameraman was doing all he could to keep up with the daemon's abrupt tilts. "This looks perfect, Daemon. Thank you."

Also satisfied with his work, the daemon was now facing the objective, knife upright like a surgeon about to operate. The commandant standing behind the renegade had clasped his palms on the sides of the man's head, holding it in place.

"We resume in three, two…" the cameraman was saying.

Daromas cleared his throat resoundingly and Farrah could almost taste the daemon's phlegm inside her mouth as he scraped it.

"See now," Daromas's deadened voice declared as though he was reciting some medical textbook, "how I treat insurgence." He snatched the renegade by the hair and brought the knife closer, tip inching towards his closed eyelids.

"Look away!" Farrah cried out to Essan who drew her eyes shut at once.

The man's scream as the knife burrowed inside his cornea turned her body numb.

What happened afterwards, Farrah did not know. She had averted her own gaze. After a few minutes, the yells had all but stopped, and all she could hear now were scarce moans.

And then nothing.

The woman beside the rebel with a knife up his eye was sobbing and whispering prayers to the gods.

No gods were going to help her today. They had already joined the people who towered above them.

Daromas had wiped the sweat from his forehead and smeared it with the blood of his victim. He let out a short huff and coughed a few more times before he got back on his feet.

He waved at the camera idly so it would follow.

This time, the knife hovered above the woman's head as it began scalping the back of her hair. Her shrieks sent a flock of birds flying away from the nearest building.

The man to her right had been left abandoned on the floor, and wasn't moving anymore. Nor would he again.

Shortly, the woman's body came to meet his.

Mumble, mumble. "You got it all?"

"Yes, Daemon."

"I want those close-ups right."

"Naturally, Daemon. Anything you want."

Mumble mumble. "Maybe a little tilt?"

"We'd be losing the top of the head but if that's what Your Excel—"

"Oh." Mumble. "No, that wouldn't be good."

The daemon inched a few steps to the side and halted in front of the following insurrectionist. Only he and another now stood between Daromas and Darvis.

In one fell stroke, Daromas charged the knife inside the man's mouth. The blade pierced through the back of his head, his blond hair now painted red where it had.

He crumpled beside the other victims.

Before the daemon could resume his execution, however, a commandant drew closer to him and whispered something in his ears. Daromas's eyes flew over the general's shoulder. A man was making his way towards the float accompanied by a group of placaters.

"I'll take care of him after," Daromas muttered.

The commandant insisted. "He said he's one of them."

Mumble. "… surrendered?"

"He says he has information that might be of interest."

Daromas stared hard at the older man the placaters were dragging on the vehicle. "… see what he has to say when I'm done with the others."

Not a second later, his knife had begun hacking through the nerves and muscles holding the neck of the man standing next to Darvis.

Darvis looked up with some difficulty when two silver-clad feet appeared in front of him. They slipped somewhat when they did, and the daemon had to grip the cameraman's arm to prevent a fall. So much blood surrounded Darvis that it formed a pool threatening to spill on his navy trousers.

"… new shoes. Dammit." More mumbles.

Darvis's vision felt shrouded as he darted it up into the daemon's expression. All he could see was those darkened holes, sucking him in.

Though yet untouched by flowing blood, his navy trousers became wet with fear.

He swivelled his head to the left and noticed that Farrah was by his side. Her eyes looked haunted. She seemed sad.

Now, *why* was she sad? This wasn't right. He tried on a grin, and the skin around it hurt a whole lot.

She answered with a smile of her own.

That's good. She looks much better this way.

A hand grabbed his face, shielding her from his sight, and something sharp entered his ear.

The moment his eardrum split, his ordeal began.

Farrah clenched her jaw. Blood had spattered over her face and it felt warm as her heart grew cold.

Darvis's body fell backwards. She could sense something welling up in her eyes, but there was no sadness to be found in the look of disdain she gave the man now moving in front of her.

Daromas did not seem to mind it. His expression was displaying that same emptied appearance it had worn for the past hour.

He put the knife to her forehead.

Farrah steadied her glower on him. "Daromas," she hissed through her teeth, "you..."

"Daemon!"

Farrah stared at the older man in disbelief. What was *he* doing here? He wasn't supposed to be a part of the operations, she had made certain of it!

He had gone up the float and was standing some ways behind Daromas, a horde of placaters guarding him on each side.

Daromas wheeled around, and again, the lower torso followed through as if it was detached from the rest of his body.

"He's not one of us," she uttered at once.

Daromas did not so much as pretend to hear her.

Droplets of red stains were dripping at the base of the older man's robes. He was staring at Farrah, smiling as he bowed to her. The daemon's eyes widened, and it gave the impression of a man on drugs trying to understand the picture he had in front of him.

His feet began gliding towards the older man.

Tick.

He froze and his head cocked to the side.

"Daemon! Please, step back!" said one of the commandants while another carried Daromas away. "This man might be dangerous!"

"We've searched him, Commandant Grieves," answered the soldier next to the older man. "There's nothing on him."

"Search him again," demanded the so-called Grieves.

The placater began to shuffle through the man's clothes. After a while, the soldier looked back to his superiors, shrugging.

"Take off his clothes, you idiot," ordered Commandant Husar.

The placater started removing the layers of clothing over the man's head, and it soon became apparent that he was wounded. Blood had soaked the fabric the soldier had uncovered under the first one.

When the placater removed the last shirt, it revealed the older man's frail, naked chest. "What the...?" He took a step back.

Farrah's eyes also widened at the sight.

The man's stomach was barely holding itself together. Layers of surgical glue were doing a poor job of retaining his abdomen, cut open in two. Protruding from it was a scarcely visible metal canister compacted inside his belly.

A body cavity bomb.

And from the appearance of the timer on it, it was about to go off.

As a look of horrified comprehension dawned on Farrah's face, the older man gazed up to her.

His eyes were truly warm.

Tock.

His body broke apart the moment the ignition sparked off. The commandants rushed in front of the daemon, shielding him from the explosion.

The last thing she saw was Daromas's face, mouth opening and closing as he rasped a few rattled breaths.

A flash of light took fire on one of the commandant's palms. A god was on its way and it would arrive in time to protect the daemon but too late for what was about to come next.

All went blank.

Smoke expanded out of the man's body and exploded all around as though a volcano had breathed life.

It was not any bomb; it was a military-grade chemical device. These canisters packed such a punch that their discharge spanned a cloud of shrouds that encompassed everything up to a hundred-mile radius.

He hadn't been trying to kill Daromas; the old man had given them a chance at freedom and she was not about to let his sacrifice be in vain.

"Let's go!" she shouted.

She pushed up onto shaking legs and threw herself down from the float. Unable to calculate the distance of her dive, she hit the ground hard, her shackled hands unable to cushion her fall.

She made it back to her feet as other bodies collided near her. "With me!" she called out in her companions' approximate location.

Confused shouts followed their flight as the all-encompassing, expanding mist blurred their vision. They ran through it, not knowing which direction they were taking.

CHAPTER 3

Slay had witnessed everything from his place of hiding. While his brain had been trying to make sense of what was happening, three people had escaped the cloud of smoke.

Holy fuck! It's Farrah and the others!

He gesticulated with his hands as he ran up on their flanks. Farrah looked over and veered his way. "Here!" he shouted at them and they followed him as he took them around the corner where he had just been.

Shots were fired and placaters began emerging from the mist. "Kill them!" one of them yelled.

The chase was on and they had nothing else to defend themselves but their feet to flee and their resolve to survive. They swerved around the nearest street and went down the alleyway. As they did, a huge weight was heaved off of their shoulders, for the commandants' spectral stares were no longer on them.

"This way!" Essan shouted. She bypassed Slay and led them down another avenue.

He followed the younger woman who obviously knew her way around better than he did. They flew past a placater cohort who looked twice their way before charging after them.

Slay spun on his heels and retrieved the hatchets he was carrying on his hips. "Come on!" he bellowed at them. He had been aching for a fight and was the only one who could protect the others. It was *his* turn to do something.

He drove his axe inside the chest of the first soldier before thrusting his second weapon into another man's skull. He veered towards the last one and took him out as efficiently as he had done the other two.

He retrieved his hatchet from the first cadaver and came face to face with the renegade leader.

"Cut our manacles!" she asked, showing him her back.

"Get on the ground," he told them, and all three stooped in front of him.

He hurried to Farrah and lowered his axe against her shackles. The metal clanked as she pulled her hands apart. At once, she reached towards the MP5K gun of the closest placater and grabbed it as her own as Slay freed the other two from their manacles.

A commotion resounded ahead. Farrah jerked her head around as she shoved the guns she had picked up into Thorick and Essan's arms. "They're on to us. Let's go!" the renegade leader said, her voice commanding.

They hurried off once more, Farrah taking the lead this time.

"Where to?" asked Essan. "Back to the hideout?"

"Everyone has seen our faces on the screens. We cannot stay here, we have to go!"

"We're leaving Letholdus?" exclaimed the other woman.

Farrah pulled her lips tight. "Until things calm down and we figure something out."

They proceeded down the streets. Everyone they met along their route stared at them with their mouths agape and far too knowingly for their taste. The citizens' expressions didn't look as intrigued nor as uncaring as they had been the last time they had fled through the capital.

Terror had imbued their glares.

The regime's screens were screaming at them, Daromas's larger-than-life features scowling on the monitors.

"*There is nowhere to hide,*" the voice was saying. "*I am already here.*"

Their faces had been plastered all over the screens, Daromas's own appearing in and out in conjunction with theirs. All in Letholdus would know who they were by now.

"*I see you.*"

"How are we supposed to get out of here without the placaters noticing?" asked Slay breathlessly, eyes opening up at the sight of the daemon's staring at them through the monitor. It almost felt as though the daemon could see them. "They will be on the lookout for us at every exit point!"

"*I am everywhere.*"

Farrah didn't answer. She continued on, seemingly knowing where she was going.

"*Where are you going, my little moppets?*"

After more than an hour of scurrying around, they came to a halt. Farrah had brought them to a crouch behind a few barrels barricading the entrance of a deserted alleyway. The sun had initiated its descent and soon darkness would be their ally, granting them cover under the night sky.

Slay didn't know where they were, but from the appearance of the area, they had entered the better part of the city. The people strolling about were wearing much wealthier-looking attire and the houses were far grander and more elaborately designed than they had been in midtown.

Farrah motioned with her hand, and they made their way down the lane after her until she had set foot in front of an elegant cyan antiquated mansion.

A single lantern on the clean-cut yard illuminated their way as she led them by the fence and up the path. She knocked on its door a few times. They heard bustling noises on the inside, soon revealing its resident as he came up to its entrance. His curious expression turned to shock when he noticed the people standing on his porch.

The man looked to be somewhere in his forties. His sharp reddish-brown beard was carved in a diamond shape. He wore an elegant gentleman's suit: dark pants, white shirt, and a burgundy vest. Over the attire, he sported a black overcoat and a top hat of the same colour. Metal pieces and straps accentuated his whole garb, and round reading glasses sat on the end of his fine nose. Even his boots were made of prime leather, and the cane in his right hand seemed more for the sake of appearance than anything.

The man was unquestioningly an aristocrat. "Farrah!"

"Aslor, can we come in?"

"Of course." He hurried them inside, eyes glimpsing outside before closing the door behind them.

The so-called Aslor guided them to his living room, a prosperously decorated red and brown parlour. From the looks of the extravagant pieces that garnished the room, he was a collector of some sort.

The gentleman gestured towards the sofas before taking a seat himself, looking restless. "I saw it all," he began in a polished accent that spoke of his rank. "It's all over the screens!"

Farrah sighed, her voice grim. "We don't have time. We need to get out of here, and you're the only one I could trust with this task."

Aslor nodded, his lips pursing. "I know. The daemon's placed a wide-scale warrant for your arrest." He got up, palms pressing against his lap as he did. "There's no time to talk; you're quite right." He beckoned with his hands. "Come along."

They followed him down the staircase that led to the basement. When they reached its bottom, the man strode inside the spacious room and inputted a few numbers on the board of the rear end wall. Hinges sprung into motion and a door slid to the side, revealing a hidden chamber.

Dozens of different gun types, weapons and armour positioned on metal stools were scattered around the room.

"Better stock up before you take your leave."

"Thank you, Aslor," Farrah said and gave him a tired but earnest-looking smile.

The gentleman bowed a little. "But of course..."

They equipped themselves with similar items as those that had been confiscated earlier. Then, using a pair of pliers, Aslor removed the shackles they were still wearing on their wrists.

"All set?" he asked after he had finished taking Thorick's manacles off.

Essan drew closer. "You have a plan?"

They went up the stairs again. "I am always at the ready, young Essan, whenever my leader calls upon me." He glanced back and gave Farrah a nod. "This is what I do, after all."

She returned the gesture.

They entered a room near the front of the house and when Aslor lit it up, it revealed a medium-sized, red hovercar sleeping inside a hangar.

"We don't even have these models where I come from, they're so damn expensive!" Slay said as he circled around the vehicle, eyes lingering over each of its details.

Aslor waved a hand, looking abashed. "Please come along," he mumbled as he opened the front door.

They followed him inside, Farrah sitting by the man's side and the others at the back. The car promptly slid above ground level and hovered about three or four feet off the floor.

They began their way down the path at cruising speed, the engine purring smoothly as they did. By now, the sun had set and the streets were almost deserted. Most Letholdians had headed inside to the confinement of their homes, wary of the day's events.

Sandwiched in between Thorick and Essan, his shoulders hunched, Slay was trying hard to calm his nerves. This stillness had him replaying visions of Daromas and these were threatening to accelerate his breathing again even though they weren't running anymore.

Essan had been shivering the entire time, her left leg bouncing against his. The huge guy, Thorick, had been contemplating the passing streets outside, body erect and unmoving.

Unable to tolerate the flow of his thoughts any longer, Slay stretched inside the space between Farrah and Aslor. "So, uh, mister, what is it that you do exactly?" he asked, elbows angling against their headrests.

The gentleman kept his eyes on the road, his left arm resting on the windowsill. "I am a merchant," he replied. "I mostly excel in trades."

"You're a member of the group?"

It was Farrah who answered. "Aslor doesn't take part in our operations. He is our main supplier and funds our activities. You can say he is our patron of sorts."

"Oh. You're the bank."

The trader chortled. "I am a supporter of the cause and I do what I can to help."

Farrah said, "A lot of what we have done is thanks to the finances you have brought us. You are a key member of the organization."

"You are too kind…."

Slay stared ahead and noticed that they were heading towards the capital's port. "How are you gonna take us out of here?"

Aslor's fingers flittered against the wheel. The man appeared nervous by nature but genuine in his intentions. "Oh yes. I have a plan. Although, I cannot guarantee its success, mind you."

It was Essan's turn to draw closer to the driver's seat, and Slay made space for her. "Is it dangerous?" she asked.

The gentleman shook his head though his tone didn't seem too confident. "I don't think so… although we'll have to do quite a lot of convincing."

Farrah turned to him, frowning. "You're asking one of your clients to smuggle us out of town, aren't you?"

Aslor glanced her way, seemingly appraising her reaction.

"One of his clients?" Slay asked.

Essan bumped Slay on the shoulder. "Yeah, Aslor's a trader from the merchant lands of Keshui. He deals with all kinds of people. They carry stuff to him and they take his things out of the city."

"Oh, I see." He smirked. "I bet that all your deals are totally legal, eh?"

Aslor made a slight pout. "I do believe there is nothing wrong in earning a profit when it does not hurt anyone else."

Slay patted him on the shoulder. "Of course, I get ya."

"Anyway," the trader went on, fingers prodding his glasses, "my client won't be easy to persuade, but if there's someone who can smuggle you out, it's her." He peered at Farrah. "In fact, I think it is imperative it be *her*."

"Why is that?" she asked.

"My dear, if things go wrong, she is perhaps the only person in Iscar who could defy a commandant and yet survive the encounter. I doubt she ever would, mind you, but what you need right now are strong allies by your side."

"You're asking a pirate." Farrah's tone felt disapproving; so was the shape of her brows.

"I know what you're thinking," Aslor added, hearing the rebuff in her voice. "But it's not as bad as you believe. We've had countless dealings in the past. She never disappoints and always keeps to the agreement."

"Pirates keep their promises as long as the first party remains the highest bidder," she replied.

Aslor put a hand up and glanced at her over his spectacles. "Also, she has just about as many reasons as you do to hate the daemon. He had her father murdered and she bears no love for his killer, Commandant Trent."

Slay could hardly control himself any longer. "How about you tell us who it is?"

Aslor focused his stare ahead, finger tapping on the wheel a few times. His gaze then flitted to Farrah, looking like a child seeking approval. "Captain Feras Sadahl."

Her eyes grew large. "The daughter of Corsak Sadahl?"

Slay's mouth fell open. "Holy shit, her father was *the* sovereign of the pirates! How are you gonna convince one of the most powerful sky corsairs to help us?"

The gentleman's tone turned skittish again. "I can't say that we are well acquainted, and I do not know whether she will agree to help us. But I have a decent amount of gold to offer and she is not shy of risks."

Farrah's pointed gaze had not wavered from his face. "Feras Sadahl is just as dangerous as any of the seven commandants. By escaping a lion, we might be giving ourselves over to a wolf."

"No, no," Aslor replied. "She won't betray us. It is imperative we come to her carrying the best arguments we can give; this I can agree on. She is no ordinary pirate and may not be receptive to our cause unless we can make her understand it."

Though Farrah did not appear swayed by the gentleman's words, Slay was ecstatic. He was about to meet the infamous Captain Feras Sadahl.

Corsak Sadahl had been the greatest pirate to roam the skies for over two decades. He had been a giant of the heavens, feared and beloved throughout Iscar.

When Daromas had attempted to cast them out, Captain Corsak had resisted the daemon's rise to power and made it his cross to keep the pirates' freedom to do their business. Some said that it was through his efforts that the daemon had agreed to this pact with them; that they could resume their way of life as long as they admitted to being under his governance.

In a historic turn of events, shortly after they had struck the deal, Commandant Trent had ambushed Captain Corsak in the middle of Racketeer Bay and executed the pirate sovereign.

Perhaps Daromas had had a change of heart. Perhaps he had wanted everyone to know that any who defied him could not expect to live.

Ironically, the daemon had upheld his end of the bargain and the pirates had retained some laws of their own. Not to say that they were free. Rather, he had offered a semblance of freedom to be used to his advantage.

Feras Sadahl, Corsak's daughter, had acquired her standing in part due to her famous lineage and in part due to her willpower. Ever since her father's assassination, she had made a name of her own, independent of his. A warrior of reputation foremost, she had been born and bred to take over the footsteps of her father and was now possibly the richest captain around, known for her charisma and talent for business.

Hers was a name that inspired admiration from all those who bore the title *pirate.* Feared by the common folk, tolerated by the daemon and his commandants, and idolized by the ruffians.

"They say her father fought against a dragon and lived to tell the tale," Essan told them.

Farrah was gazing ahead at the approaching marina and Slay couldn't decipher whether she was angry or simply anxious. Aslor kept on stealing glances her way, seemingly wondering the same.

"Farrah," the trader said after stopping the vehicle. "If you don't want to do this, I can find you another way out."

She shook her head. "No… I trust you. We'll go with your plan."

The gentleman inclined his chin, her amnesty all he required. He opened the car's door and exited, looking pale. "Let me do the talking. She knows me and I'm used to dealing with pirates."

Aslor began fiddling with the cuffs of his jacket and Slay wondered whether the man was trying to sound more confident than he was.

The trader led them along the docks. They strolled past three ships before he drew them to a halt next to the most majestic of them.

The *Celestial Dragon* had been the property of Corsak Sadahl before his daughter had inherited it through his demise. She had made a few changes over the years, and the galleon was now more grandiose than ever.

Flying airships were similar to their sea counterparts in most ways. Though sea vessels only dipped in waters, their soaring cousins were provisioned with colossal side wings that hoisted them up into the sky and folded on themselves upon landing.

Gigantic rocket propellers situated at the rear end drove the ships upwards at liftoff, whilst smaller ones dispersed along the keel kept the vessel well balanced and fluid throughout its flight. As per their original shapes, airships could also be piloted in waters and were commonly landed in them and anchored at the same quays.

Captain Feras Sadahl's galleon was enormous. The *Celestial Dragon* had a reinforced hull and keel of thick, black titanium. The material used for the rest of the ship was rich grenadil wood, embellished with layers of detailed carvings sculpted inside fine slats of white-painted sandalwood. The bow and bowsprit wore a grout finish made of pure gold and covered the galleon's surface with a canvas of opulent marquetry.

The sails bore the ominous, dark-coloured symbol of all pirate transportation and high upon its main mast drifted the unmistakable black flag carrying the dragon skull and twin cutlasses emerging from its orbs—the Sadahl crest.

The galleon's figurehead featured a crisp, ivory sandstone dragon, its mouth agape. Slay thought that if ever he was aboard a vessel and saw this nightmare coming his way, he would believe his days numbered.

The *Celestial Dragon* was a testimony to the Sadahl family lineage and power, and its captains were just as impressive.

Aslor headed towards the gangway that linked the pier to the galleon's main deck. A man, sitting on a barrel next to the bridge, rose to his feet and blocked the passage before the trader could step on it.

He was well built, tall, and dark-skinned. His coarse beard ran down his naked chest and his spotless shaved skull gave focus to the single gold loop that adorned his right ear. He wore bulky ash-coloured pants, long boots, and a scimitar hung from his belt.

Aslor gave him a gesture of greeting. "Good evening, quartermaster Kerok. Could I, mayhap, have a word with the captain?"

The man's eyes were surveilling their dishevelled group, his expression betraying no emotion. "I thought our dealings were over, Mister Aslor?" he replied in a deep baritone.

The gentleman attempted a smile that ended up looking queasy. "I have a new deal which may be of interest to Captain Sadahl."

Kerok did not reply nor budge as they waited for an answer, the renegades growing increasingly nervous under his glare. After a conspicuous amount of time, he beckoned them up the gangway.

They followed behind and made foot onto the main deck of the airship. Other members of the crew took notice of them and were soon stopping whatever it was they were doing to stare at the newcomers instead.

The quartermaster gestured to a woman standing near, her hands holding a pad and pencil. "Capt'n," he said, "Mister Aslor wants to see you."

Feras Sadahl turned around, her posture angled into confidence.

Her tailored leather pants ended just over her pointed-toe ankle boots, her shoes revealing subtle designs carved into their sleek hide. Her ample white shirt had been rolled up on her left elbow, displaying an arm covered in tattoos that travelled the length of her jewelry-adorned fingers up to the side of her throat. She kept all three buttons of her shirt opened, disclosing a strong collarbone and a few golden medallions that dangled around her neck.

A dusky leather sash circled her waist and bound itself to her leg where hung a blunderbuss holster. A shotgun and a cutlass sword were fastened between her shoulder blades by a bandolier strap racing across her chest, a pistol nestled in its middle.

Farrah stared for a moment at the pirate's other arm, or rather, what had replaced it.

The right side of her shirt had been removed and bound to her shoulder was an intricate golden, mechanical limb, a fantastic piece of function and hardiness. It had taken the place of the missing arm and also made her look all the more intimidating.

The corsair gave the pad she was holding to a crew member standing next to her. Farrah noticed how her piercing gaze went from one of them to the other, and how every new face increased the frown on her own.

"Mister Aslor, I see you have brought a dangerous cargo." Her voice was firm, yet annoyed. This was not auguring well for them.

Other pirates had gathered topside, eager to get a look at the newcomers.

"Captain," the trader answered, "we are good business partners, and I think that you may be interested in my offer."

The corsair's brow rose, her face depicting cynicism.

Feras Sadahl had a fierce beauty to her chiselled face, penetrating and charismatic at once. Her wavy, dark brown hair fell under her tricorn hat. Her golden-coloured eyes stood under acute brows, and a scar ran under her right eye all the way to the other side of her sharp nose.

Something magnetic emanated from her presence, commanding respect and bearing. It was no wonder she had become famous at such a young age.

She waved her palm at the renegades. "Perhaps you are not aware, Mister Aslor, that these people's names have made the Red List. Anyone caught having dealings with them is to suffer similar fate as the one they'll receive when the daemon gets his hands on them."

There was a low sort of rumble at the back of the captain's voice when she talked. The one you would expect a feline to have if it had the means to speak.

Though Aslor looked discomfited, he did not let her comment discourage him. "Yes, I am aware," he replied. "I believe, however, that it may be possible for you to take these fugitives away from Letholdus so that no one needs suffer said fate. I will, without a doubt, give you more than a fair deal in exchange." The gentleman bowed a little.

The captain made a scowl and nodded curtly. "You want me to take aboard my ship four red-listed criminals?" She scoffed, her tone turning leery. "Mister Aslor, you must believe me mad or utterly stupid to think I would agree to this. Being on the Red List is analogous to a death sentence at the hands of the Anemas. I may be a dealer of good fortune, but I am no idiot."

The trader's smile was fading by the seconds. "Of course you are no imbecile, Captain," he answered. "We came to you because you are the only person with the means to help my colleagues." He tried on a grin. "Don't we all want to make the daemon lose once in a while?"

The corsair smirked, and this particular smile felt more contemptuous than anything. "Please do not insult my intelligence with empty talk. You may take your offer to someone else more willing to die meaninglessly."

She turned around, apparently done with them.

Farrah came to the trader's help. "Captain," she interrupted her. "You are right, this is not your fight. You have every reason to deny the risks of having us on your ship, but won't you reconsider? We have the means to repay our debt and promise to make it worth your while."

She turned to Aslor, eyes seeking his. "Oh yes," he added without blinking. "Five thousand gold pieces."

The captain's face had grown mocking. "Forgive me, but unless you are hiding quite a bit of those gold pieces under your shirt, Mister Aslor, payment does not seem to be as available as you are making it appear."

The gentleman began to fidget. "Well, no, we do not have it on us… but as soon as you have brought us elsewhere, we can settle our affairs at the nearest bank."

The pirate laughed. It was a cold one, devoid of pleasure. "Of course you will, and perhaps we'll still be alive to receive due payment. Forgive me, but I would rather not take the risk." She crossed her arms over her chest. "You may leave now. Rest assured I will be graceful enough not to alert the authorities that you were here."

"Please, Captain," Farrah urged, taking a step forward. "I know our cause isn't yours, but I beg of you. We had to look on as our people were butchered in front of our eyes." Her stare sought the renegades' faces. "I cannot stand having more of them hurt."

The corsair dangerously bridged the distance between them and levelled her head with hers. "Their lives were lost because of your own foolishness." She drew back. "I will not let my men die so you can save yours."

"No one needs to die!" she argued. "If we leave now, Daromas won't know we were aboard your ship, nor that we had dealings together. You can take us to the nearest city and we will be on our way at once, I *promise.*"

"Miss, I saw you on the screens earlier. You are presently the most famous faces in all of Iscar. What valiant efforts you have shown us." The captain's eyes became a scowl, her mouth looped upside down and her voice grew harsh. "And what idiocy."

The pirate lifted her chin towards the renegades. "What did you expect? Your masquerade in the central square today was an irresponsible act reflective of the ones who planned it. You may be willing to throw away your lives, or other people's lives for that matter, but you are just wasting them."

The words cut through Farrah, but she kept her voice controlled and collected herself as she faced the pirate's glower. "These people were killed because they believed in a better Iscar," she replied, lips pressing together. "Do not call it meaningless when you know nothing of the strength these men and women needed to rise against persecution. Their lives mattered and their deaths matter as much."

The captain came even nearer, the corner of her mouth distorting as she did. "You are quite something." She exhaled through her teeth. "You prance around heroically, all the while asking others to sacrifice themselves for you. Then you wonder why so many had to die? Why don't you get your head out of the daemon's ass and take a hard look at your own face." Her upper lip drew up in distaste. "I will not let my men be killed for you."

Farrah's chest tightened at this. "I've never asked anyone to die for me!" she retorted. "And I am not to blame for the sins of the daemon.... I loved these people and they believed, as I do, that a better Iscar *can* exist if we strive for it. They *chose* to lay down their lives, the same as I did." Her breasts heaved once. "Do not belittle me as though I am an ignorant child, Captain Sadahl. We knew the dangers and faced them because change can't happen unless we stop running from our fears."

The pirate gave a short laugh. "That's very noble. Did you, however, think about the consequences that your absurd act would cause others? Hmm?" She lifted both brows, head hovering over hers. "Thanks to you, the daemon will now double his efforts to oppress the people. He will make routes more difficult to travel, arrest anyone he will imagine of being of assistance to you and make our lives more of a misery than they were before." She gave Farrah a snarl. "Today you helped no one. You made things worse."

Farrah stared pointedly at the captain of the *Celestial Dragon*. She had been trying hard to keep her guilt at bay, yet knew that the corsair had spoken some words of truth.

Admitting this did not make her feel weak.

Perhaps their actions *had* made things worse, and it was a tragedy that some had died today, yesterday and all the years before. Yet, people would continue to suffer as long as the daemon was in charge, whether they challenged him or not. She would much rather die fighting the regime than waste it in the melancholia of their despondent lives.

The pirate was right, but she was also wrong.

She lifted her glare into the corsair's austere expression, arms still held over her chest. "Your father was killed at the hands of the daemon," she began in a low voice. "He died because Daromas wanted to make an example out of him. We cannot let this go on. You of all people should understand that!"

The lines on the captain's face had somewhat softened at this. "Listen, I do want the son of a bitch to die," she replied, looking sideways. "But losing my father only goes to show that fucking around with the daemon only brings tragedies. I am not running away from it. I am keeping the people I care for alive. *This* is what matters to me." The pirate dropped her hands to her side, fingers dangling near her blunderbuss. "I will kill Trent one day for what he has done to my father, but the time for his atonement has not come yet."

Farrah kept her gaze on the corsair though she somehow felt like fleeing her sight. "I also want the people who matter to me to live," she replied in a clear voice. "We're on the same side, Captain, we can help each other...."

The pirate's features tightened, annoyance creeping back. "You are wrong. We are not on the same side. I cannot help you and you may go, *now*." Her tone left no opening for arguments.

Farrah stared at the captain, her expression now imbued with scorn. The corsair did not appear to mind the challenge.

"Capt'n!" a person called. It was one of the crew members. "The soldiers be comin'! Them hovercars juss' got docked not far from the *Dragon*!"

"Lift the gangway at once, Dahara. No placater is setting foot on my ship," growled the pirate, looking bothered by this interruption.

The woman who had warned them hurtled towards the galleon's entrance, a few crew members following suit.

The captain leaped towards Farrah. "You better hope they're not coming for you," she said with bite. "Master Kerok," she went on while taking large strides towards the dock side of the vessel, "please have our *guests* clear out from view."

Kerok wound around them, but Farrah flew past him and planted herself in front of the corsair. "What are you going to do?"

The captain's brows were knitted. "Do not be troubled. I will be courteous enough to get rid of this nuisance for you though I cannot imagine why I would be so cordial. As soon as they have gone, you will leave my ship and I hope I can count on your honour to keep me out of your future dealings."

Her voice was sharp and did not invite an answer. She shoved Farrah aside and leaned over the bulwarks.

Kerok took Farrah by the arm and guided her back to the others, beside the stairs that led up to the bridge. Farrah stooped next to Thorick, her face draped in the wrinkles of worry.

The captain did not appear as anxious as Farrah felt. Her shoulders held back, she was leaning against the bannister, relaxing into a powerful stance that inspired strength.

The corsair had every right to refuse their offer and be unwilling to put her crew in harm's way for red-listed strangers she knew nothing about. But Farrah hated that she had treated them as if their life's work was stupid and meaningless.

What did a pirate know of rights and wrongs?

"What happens now?" whispered Slay.

She did not look his way. "We'll have to find another solution. Let's just hope the placaters won't come aboard the ship and Captain Sadahl keeps to her word."

They heard footsteps arising from below and silenced their voices.

Feras was watching the soldiers, her face depicting nothing as their stares lifted up to hers. "Under orders of the daemon, we are to inspect every ship. Lower the bridge at once."

She drew up a nonchalant palm. "Have you not noticed my colours, friends? This ship is exempt from searches."

Though the officer's voice remained firm, the placaters around him had shuffled on their feet. "I know who you are, Captain Sadahl. No ship, no matter whom it belongs to, is exempt from the present search. As long as the fugitives are yet on the loose, the daemon has put down a state of no quarters. You hold no rights in this matter and *will* comply."

Feras grinned a side smirk. "I'm glad you know who I am," she answered in a low, snarling sort of voice. "Are you certain that you wish to make me comply?"

The placater's chin had nudged back at her words, and anger had risen in his tone. "You assuredly will, Captain, or we will have to use force against you, and the daemon will hear of your behaviour!"

She tilted her head, her face aloof. "You will use force against *me*?"

The pirates around her sniggered. At that, the officer in charge seemed shocked. The others, however, had shuffled in place with renewed fervour.

She lowered her forearms on the handrail. Most of her crew had assembled on the side of the vessel or hung on ropes, their expressions mocking.

The placaters glanced at each other and one of them murmured something at their officer who hushed him up with the palm of his hand.

"Is this your final answer, Captain?" he asked. Feras shrugged and the placater swore. "This is a direct affront!"

He whirled on himself, the others following as he darted towards their hovercars.

Her mischievous expression faded away, her eyes growing serious as they tracked their movements.

Kerok came by her side. "Capt'n?"

She stared off for a few seconds more, then wheeled around and strode towards the renegades.

The corsair glared at each of them. "I will regret this," she declared with contempt. "It will be ten thousand gold pieces. You may take it or leave it, but know that my patience is running thin."

Aslor's mouth fell, gaze distraught. "Oh well, yes… that should be… agreeable…."

She then looked at Farrah and said, "Thanks to you, my galleon and crew will never have dealings again in Letholdus, not to say the difficulties we will face elsewhere. You'd better be worth my while." Her voice was like acid.

Farrah answered nothing. They would be safe, and that was probably more important than a hurt ego.

The captain spun around. "Master Kerok, ready the ship for liftoff. From the looks of it, reinforcements are on the way and I'd prefer not to provoke a fight. We may yet remain on the daemon's good side when this is over."

Kerok left at once, shouting orders to the rest of the crew in preparation for their departure. The corsair headed up to the bridge where the main controls and monitors of the galleon resided.

The group stood rooted in place, at a loss for words. Aslor moved nearer to Farrah whose gaze had surrendered to a world of thoughts. "Hmm, Farrah, I am not certain I will be able to settle our debt in a single payment…."

She lifted her hand to her chest, fondling the necklace under her shirt. "Don't worry, Aslor. Give what you can and I'll take care of the rest."

Regardless of her words, the trader still appeared anxious.

She looked up at the captain of the *Celestial Dragon*, standing at the helm of her vessel. The corsair's expression depicted more or less nothing as she contemplated the ship's monitors.

"Capt'n!" shouted the woman named Dahara, running up the stairs leading to the bridge. "They've noticed our movement, the placaters be boardin' their hovercars! I fear they're gonna waylay us!"

"Let them try," replied the pirate.

Kerok imputed a few coordinates in their sky charts. "Ready for lift off, Capt'n."

The corsair grabbed the wheel between her fingers, her quartermaster taking position in front of the controls, pressing keyboards and moving levers with expertise. The ship began to glide through the water and drifted away from the ledge.

They heard some commotion on the pier. Hovercar engines were turning on, placaters shouting as they sped towards them. Their bullets ricocheted against the titanium forepeak, the dragon figurehead scowling at the intruders as it drew away.

"Return at once, Captain!" yelled the officer, his car coming to an abrupt halt near the dock's edge.

The pirate ignored the soldier. She turned the sizeable black wooden helm around, and the vessel followed her movements. It wheeled back and darted towards the open waters. As it began gliding further down, a booming sound arose from under the galleon as its propellers breathed to life.

"Release the wings, Master Kerok, and the wind sensors," ordered the captain.

The giant, batlike wings unfolded and expanded on both sides of the ship as compact boxes flew up and surrounded the vessel. A blueish glow ignited the tip of the metal cages and Farrah could have sworn she had seen a film erupting from them, draping the galleon's figure before becoming invisible.

Those boxes, called wind sensors, were assigned to the preservation of the ship, preventing the outside weather from affecting its temperature. Linked to one another, these invisible shields engulfed the whole structure and regulated the galleon. Tasked with keeping the harsh winds at bay, these tools ensured that no crew member took a plunge in the abyss as a result of a flurry.

The ship started to rise over the surface of the water, its propellers creating a gushing tempest underneath as they heaved upwards.

Promptly, the *Celestial Dragon* darted towards the horizon and out of reach of the gunfire, the capital quickly shrinking from sight.

Farrah took a breath as she looked over the bannister. Letholdus seemed so different from her new viewpoint… not as threatening anymore.

And yet, something had broken inside of them.

The illusion of safety. They had grown too confident and had forgotten to be afraid.

Daromas had reminded them.

Essan grabbed her by the shoulders. "We made it out…." she said. Her voice sounded sweet and Farrah felt grateful that she was yet by her side.

She searched for Thorick's gaze, and he smiled. Her breath siphoned out of her lungs and she realized that she had been keeping it in all this time.

"What a fucked-up day," Slay huffed.

"Forgive me," she began, eyes cast downwards. "I wish things had gone differently. I almost got us all killed." Her sternum clenched. "Many were…."

Darvis, Warwick, Arcanum and all the others. Those violent deaths would never be forgotten. It would haunt them for the rest of their days and many of their nights.

Thorick was shaking his head from side to side, his expression warm.

"Don't you start this," Essan whispered, her eyes closing. "We knew the risks involved. We trained for this, trained for all the possible scenarios. Although this was not the one we wanted, we were ready for it." She opened her eyes and the tears held in them shimmered in the night. "I guess that's what makes it a bit easier; some part of me had already begun the grieving process."

Essan let out a long, shaky breath through her nose, her hands lifting to her heart. "We've lost many people over the years. This time is no different. Though I wish I could forget this day ever happened, I can't regret that we've tried." She grinned, and her lips trembled as she did. "Anyway, we already have enough of that pirate making us feel like idiots. Let us not add to this ordeal with our own guilt."

Farrah inclined her head. No matter the amount of planning, nothing could come close to the weight of failure. The weight of losing friends.

"Thank you, Essan," she told the other woman and both shared a look of understanding. It was a painful look, imbued with hurt, but it also conveyed their resolve. Essan grinned and though she seemed about ready to crumble, her stare was set.

Eyes also glistening, Thorick put his hands together, backs facing forward, and bowed down.

He was offering a prayer to the gods.

Slay stared at his feet. He had gotten to know Darvis in the last few days and thinking back on how he had died gave him a pit in the stomach.

He owed the guy his life and wouldn't forget it.

"What went wrong?" he asked in a low voice.

Farrah had hung her head at his words. "Either we were betrayed or Arcanum was," she replied with a frown. "Whichever it was, he did not deserve the death he received."

Essan had clasped her hands around her waist at these words, gaze running blank. Farrah drew closer and draped her fingers on her shoulder.

"What do we do now?" he asked, glad that he couldn't replay in his mind the memory of what had transpired on the float. Unlike the others.

Farrah stared up at the corsair and the members of her crew. "What we must."

CHAPTER 4

The captain retreated on deck while Kerok steered the ship inside the gloomy abyss of the night.

She paused in front of Aslor, wearing a disparaging expression. "It seems we were able to leave without too much of a fuss. We may yet encounter trouble if they've figured you lot are aboard my galleon."

"We are well aware of the risks you are taking, Captain, and are indebted to you and your crew." His tone was as apologetic as his words had been. "Rest assured you will get your payment without fail."

The pirate shrugged and gave Farrah a look. "You certainly appear grateful." She lifted an eyebrow before turning back to the gentleman. "The sooner I'm rid of you, the better."

Aslor bowed a little. "Of course...."

"Well?"

"Uh, yes, Captain?"

"Where to?" Her tone was growing impatient, and she had crossed her arms again.

"Yes, of course..." Aslor stole a glance Farrah's way, expression begging for her help.

She said, "Can we have some time to figure out our next move?"

The corsair did not bother to look at her. Her face was cut from stone as she focused it elsewhere. "I will not let my ship wander about while you people figure your problems out. I need a destination." Her glare finally went to her. "*Now.*"

"Give us until tomorrow," she replied, and then added, "please."

She noticed how the pirate's eyes had widened at that and felt that the corsair had just about had it with her extra cargo.

"Captain," Aslor said, "nothing would make us happier than to comply. You have rescued us and we are thankful for your help. We only wish to be prudent. Our situation is precarious; we must choose our destination wisely, for our sake but also for your people's safety, not to forget the successful delivery of the required payment. If it would please you, this wee bit of extra time would bring about a more secure outcome for us all."

The pirate gave a smile and like the last one, it had the power to cool melting ice. "You are very intelligent with words, Mister Aslor," she answered before giving them her back.

"Are we in accord?" wheedled the gentleman after her.

The corsair gestured with her hand as she drew away. "Time is of the essence, my friend. If you want more, you may pay more."

Aslor retrieved a handkerchief from the pocket of his burgundy vest and wiped his forehead with it. "I guess we have a deal," he mumbled.

Essan shook her head. "Pirates," she whispered, her tone sounding more impressed than admonishing.

Slay, for one, was irrevocably enthralled by these changing tides. In the span of a day, he had made an attempt on the daemon's life, had escaped death at the hands of the commandants and, not to forget, a god. He now stood aboard Captain Feras Sadahl's *Celestial Dragon*, flying the skies in the company of the renegades' gorgeous leader and three other members of their group.

He scrutinized Farrah's expression. She didn't look nearly as excited as he felt. "You okay?" he asked her.

She glanced his way, her beautiful face a mask of turmoil. "Yes," she answered simply.

She was a tough one to get close to. Although, considering what the renegades had witnessed today, he could understand their bland expressions and reluctance to recall any of its events. They all looked like people who hadn't slept for days. He probably did too.

They were interrupted by the pirate they had met earlier, Dahara. She was smaller than most and though her gestures were somewhat rugged, there was also a softness about her. Her short, unruly hair looked cut by a lion's claws and her clothes seemed a bit too large on her, perhaps in an attempt to hide her curves.

"Hi y'all, I'm Dahara. The Capt'n asked me to take y'all to yer cabins. Ye wanna have a little run first 'round the *Dragon*?"

"That would be lovely," answered Aslor, head inclining.

She beckoned at them and they fell in step alongside her. "Here we be on the main deck. All the way up there, t'wards the stern, be the quarterdeck, whar the wheelhouse be."

The galleon was enormous and Slay figured that walking from one end to the other would not be a short stroll. Dahara next motioned towards the doors beside the staircase they had been hiding under before, right below the quarterdeck. "These would lead y'all to the capt'n's sittin' room. Now, come on o'er this way."

She gesticulated some more and they followed her along the side of the promenade deck. She walked them to the other portion of the galleon, chatting the entire time. "There be the stem, and near the figurehead," she pointed ahead, up another set of stairs, "be the fo'c'sle deck."

Instead of bringing them to said stairs, she guided them near an entrance. "Here," she continued, leading the renegades to a doorway, "will take ye inside the ship."

She opened the magnificently carved wooden doors and they entered a richly decorated saloon hall. On its left side lay a large table surrounded by smaller ones. It was where the pirates ate though they usually carried the tables out at night to dine under the stars. On its other side stood a lavish living room where the crew could talk, play games and relax.

Dahara gestured further to the back and said, "There be the galley kitchen." She motioned towards a grand staircase in the middle of the room. They followed the pirate down and entered another hall with a smaller parlour at the right end corner, and on its other side, a long passageway. "These be the crew's quarters. I'll be showin' y'all to yer cabins."

She led them down the corridor, somewhere past amidships. She then opened a few doors, peeking inside to make sure they held no occupants. "That'll do," she said, gesturing to a few of them.

Slay pointed at the double glass entrance down the passageway. "What's on the other side?"

Dahara glanced over. "That'd be the capt'n's corner. There be her stateroom and her office, right below the capt'n's sittin' room I showed y'all before. The entire aft o' the ship be made o' windows. The view be amazin' there."

Slay beamed. That sounded like something he'd want to see.

"Thank you, Dahara," Farrah said before motioning to the others. "We need to get some rest. Tomorrow, we'll have to figure out our next move."

Exhausted, they entered their respective rooms.

Farrah closed the door behind her and looked around the cabin, taking in its appearance. It was a cozy room, larger than she had expected and as clean as the rest of the galleon.

Her berth easily held two people and she even had a sofa and table. It appeared that Captain Sadahl liked to keep her crew and guests in the same glamorous décor as the remainder of her magnificent ship.

She strode across the cabin and sat back against her bed, feeling drained and wishing for nothing more than for this day to end.

She was trying hard to keep her daunting thoughts at bay at the sight of her massacred allies flashing before her eyes. She felt too empty and exhausted to even cry about it.

Not that she ever did. She had run all out of tears a long time ago. It was all she could afford, lest she surrendered to grief.

Her stomach still lurched every time she thought of Darvis, and the things that had come out of his…

She closed her eyes, and the visions became worse. Her hands flew to her ears as if forcing silence would somehow help mute her mind.

What were they going to do? They had no plan, no home, no anything, and it was on *her* to lead the others out of the hole she had driven them into.

As she lay back against the soft pillow of her berth, she reflected on the words the corsair had spoken.

Today, you helped no one; you made things worse.

She felt a knot in her throat. It was easy for Captain Sadahl to judge them; she knew nothing of their endeavours and pains, nor how their resistance had made a difference in the lives of many.

It was peculiar that she had smuggled them out of Letholdus after she had been so categorical on not doing so. Would she have done the same if the placaters hadn't shown up?

Not that it came cheap.

They would have nothing left after this expensive deal and she would do everything she could to repay Aslor in time.

Too worn out to reflect on her thoughts longer, she fell asleep with her clothes on, dreaming of darkness and worries. The last thing she saw before she dozed off were those two bottomless holes, the veins surrounding them reeling her in like boulders sinking her down.

When the group had gotten out of bed the next morning, they had reconvened. The five of them were all that was left of their insurrection and they had become the most sought-after fugitives in Iscar.

The Red List was a unique inventory made up of few names, those who had caused the daemon such slight that he would have an entire army after them if it meant catching them. No costs or manpower were spared for the capture of red-listed criminals and this had given them pause.

"I'd like to know everyone's position," Farrah said.

Essan had sat next to her on the bench of the flashy dining room table. "You mean, what do we want to do from now on?"

"I won't force any of you to continue this rebellion," she explained. "Retiring far from this would be more than a valid alternative."

"What are *you* going to do?" asked Slay.

She took a steadying breath. "I've made a promise a long time ago and I intend on keeping it. I will kill Daromas, and won't stop until I have."

It was Thorick who answered first. He lifted his oversized hand and placed it to his forehead before arching it in Farrah's direction.

He would follow her.

"Farrah," came Essan's voice. "What we faced yesterday brought me nightmares that I'll never forget. And I won't lie, at the thought of…" Her words trailed off and her eyes became glassy. Aslor put a hand on her shoulder and though she had jumped at his touch, she nonetheless returned to them.

"Our mission is still the same," she went on, voice feebler than before. "I will follow you even if I'm scared shitless." She clutched her lower lip between her upper one as her body hunched on itself. "To be honest, I've never been so afraid in my entire life." Her mouth twitched as she attempted a smile. "It hurts how scared I am."

Farrah lifted from her seat but Essan put both hands up to tell her that she was alright. She sat back down, her eyes crinkled with concern. "But you know what?" added the younger woman. "It just makes me want to kill him even more."

Farrah's stare remained hard. "Essan, maybe—"

"No." She shook her head from side to side. "I'm doing this! I'm not leaving you. Not now, not ever. I need you, and sometimes I like to think that you need me too."

"Essan…"

The silence that followed was heavy with the weightiness of their emotions.

"She's right," said Slay, his shoulders lifting. "We're already fucked. Better to go down fighting."

She released Essan from her worried gaze and turned it on him. The islander gave her a quivering grin, and it brought one to her lips though her features were yet woven in turmoil.

He was scared.

Courage, she thought, doesn't mean that a person isn't afraid. It means having the strength to rise above the fear so it does not consume you.

"Hem, hem."

Their heads moved towards Aslor. The gentleman readjusted his glasses and pulled on the sleeves of his jacket. "I can't say I'm the best warrior, but I can get around pistols," he began. "I can't very well return home and would not abandon all of you when I may yet be of use."

Farrah opened her mouth. She had not expected this from him. He had never joined them in the field before. "Aslor, are you quite certain?"

The man raised a glinting expression. "I would follow you everywhere, Farrah. Now, more than ever."

Her voice stuck, rendered mute by her friends' decisions. "We must all be crazy," she muttered, head shaking a few times though a grin had formed on her lips.

"I'm still processing," replied Slay and Aslor nodded his support.

"Thank you, everyone," she answered, her gaze gliding over to them all. "To have you by my side means the world to me."

The islander bumped his palm against the table. "We're set! So how do we piss off the daemon now? Uh, without actually seeing him again. I've had enough of these commandants for a lifetime."

After a few shivers had run down their spines, they had started a lengthy conversation. What *could* they even do considering they were fugitives?

"To be honest," Essan said, sitting up on her knees, palms stretched on the table. "I am not aware of anything happening outside the capital. This is already further than I've ever been before. I wouldn't know where to start."

"I learned certain things when I was younger, but Iscar has changed immeasurably ever since," Farrah replied with a sigh.

Aslor nodded and began pulling on his beard using his index finger and thumb. "And my knowledge is restricted to the dealings I've had in the past from the comfort of my home."

Slay pursed his lips and sat his chin against his knuckles. "There's our problem. We're a bunch of foreigners who don't know much about Iscar. I left the islands a few months ago, but I still feel lost in this big world."

Essan watched the pirates as they went about their usual business. Most of the crew were still having breakfast, enjoying a leisurely morning. "*There* are people who certainly know about this big world," she muttered.

She was right. If there were people who knew a whole lot about Iscar, it was those who spent their lives travelling it. And they were not aboard *any* ship; the *Celestial Dragon* had a reputation to its name.

"How about we ask that girl, Dahara?" Slay asked as if he'd had a flash of insight.

They glanced around some more and found her still at table. Farrah got to her feet and noticed how the majority of the crew had turned their stares on her when she had. Apparently, pirates were just as obvious with their gazes as the rest of Iscar. She clenched her teeth and hovered beside Dahara.

The woman lifted her face to meet hers.

"Might we have a word with you?"

The pirate opened her mouth and continued on chewing her food. "Ye wanna talk to me?" Farrah said yes with her head. The woman glanced her up and down before answering with a shrug. "Sure thin', suga'."

She untangled herself from her seat and Farrah heard some of the crew members' whistling as she did. Dahara grinned and shoved them off. "Take no harm from them, dolly," the pirate said, noticing her expression. "They don't mean no disrespect."

"And yet," Farrah replied.

Slay was staring at the pirates leering. He supposed he wasn't the only one who had noticed how particularly stunning the renegade leader was.

He wondered if she knew herself.

Farrah was not the self-absorbed type. She was poised but never acted for the sake of appearance. She held no desire to please or to be pleasing for that matter, and though she was self-assured, she also seemed stuck inside her head more so than outside of it.

From what he had observed so far, she wasn't pursuing any personal relationships, be they friendly or romantic in nature. It was as if she maintained an invisible chasm around her, disconnecting her from the people in her life, except for a few select ones.

She sat in front of him, oblivious to the stares of the crew. He wondered what sort of men she liked, privately enjoying the prospect of being that person. Yet, some unknown part of him felt that he would be doomed to remain one of the onlookers, hopelessly vying for her attention.

"What do ye want from me?" asked Dahara, taking a seat.

Essan lifted herself up. "We were wondering if you could tell us of places known for resisting the daemon?"

Dahara's expression grew fearful as she drew back. "What are ye people thinkin', goin' after the daemon after what happened yesterday?"

"I know it seems ridiculous." answered Farrah. "But this is what we want."

The woman gaped at her as though she had just said the most absurd thing she had ever heard. She lowered her head down and shook it. "Your choice. I don't be judging."

"So, uh, do you know?" Slay asked again.

Dahara scrunched her bushy eyebrows, face hardening in thought. "I don't be knowin' much 'bout that. This ain't somethin' we care much about, us the crew. Rebellion ain't our cup o' tea, if ye be knowin' what I mean."

Farrah said, "Perhaps there is someone who might be aware of such a place?"

The woman scratched her chin. "Well, the capt'n would surely be in the loop, be me guess."

"Will she want to help us?" asked Essan.

Dahara glared. "What d'ye mean?" she replied, her tone changing somewhat.

Essan moved her hands about as though fumbling to make up for something. "Oh, I only meant that she might not be willing to assist to us considering… everything."

"I don't see why not," the pirate replied as if this was the easiest answer in the world.

Essan nodded. Slay, on the other hand, felt dubious. He had the feeling that Dahara underestimated how disapproving the captain had been of them.

"Yes, thank you, we shall do that," ended Aslor, smiling as he clasped his fingers on the table.

Dahara rose from her seat and gave Farrah a wink before leaving, the pirates nearby resuming their banter as she did.

"I think you have an admirer, or many actually," said Essan, giggling, the amusement clear in her blue eyes.

Farrah rolled her own. "Right," she answered. "Though I'd prefer not to, I guess we're talking to the captain."

Feras opened her begrudging eyes. Mornings weren't fun; she much preferred the night. She stretched and headed towards the sumptuous windows of her apartments, looking out at the sun, blinking at its darting light.

She put some clothes over her black briefs, exited her room, and went up the luxurious staircase before emerging topside.

"Mornin', Capt'n!" a member of her crew swabbing the deck said in greeting.

She waved at him, grinning idly. It was too early to talk.

She moved further down the spar deck and entered the saloon

hall. She walked up to a cart and poured herself a cup of coffee. As she took her first sip, she glanced about and noticed her guests huddled around one of the dining-room tables.

She made a face and turned on herself. It was definitely far too early to deal with these guys.

"Tell the cook to have breakfast brought outside for me, would you?" she asked a member of her crew. She drew outside the hall and sure enough…

"Captain, a word if you please?"

She stared up at the heavens, coercing a smile to her face. "Mister Aslor?" she inquired while walking on.

"Captain, we are currently at talk for a destination."

Feras widened her eyes. "How relevant of you to tell me." She glanced around and slapped another smile on. That woman was with the gentleman, her expression as uptight as it had been the night before. "You are more than welcome to talk to me when you have arrived at a conclusion, which I hope will be soon," she finished. She then widened her eyes some more to further encourage them.

"Certainly, Captain," answered the trader. He was fiddling his top hat between his fingers. "We are not well versed in the affairs of the world, however, and thought that you might offer some advice?"

Feras paused in her steps. "If you wanted me to choose a destination, you could have told me from the start."

Aslor gestured with his hands. "I have not explained myself well! What I meant to say is, perhaps you've knowledge of groups, people like us who yet resist the daemon in other parts of Iscar?"

Feras contemplated him long enough to renew the twitch in his fingers. "You wish to go on resisting Daromas after what happened yesterday?"

It was the woman who answered. "Yes," she said rather simply, but her tone wasn't asking for any sort of approval.

Feras squinted and then chuckled. "You people sure are driven, I'll give you that." She resumed her way towards a table nearby and sat on the bench.

Farrah and Aslor looked at each other before taking a seat in front of the corsair.

The pirate dropped her lashes, the sun flashing in her eyes. She put a palm up to block the light and said, "Oh, you're still here."

Farrah made a face. Aslor fretted by her side, growing increasingly nervous. "Have you knowledge of someone who could help us?" she repeated.

A crew member came by and lowered a platter of food in front of the corsair. She thanked him and took a leisurely bite out of the greasy sausage. Farrah stared, but said nothing, far too aware that the other woman held all the cards.

The pirate drank a sip from her cup. And then another. "Can't help you."

"You didn't even think about it," she puffed out. Aslor placed a hand on her shoulder.

The captain's eyes were on her, wearing the ghost of a smile. "I don't need to," she replied. "No one's stupid enough to rise against the daemon for one thing and make it known for a second. Thus, I cannot have heard of any such groups, can I?"

Farrah said nothing. She stared sideways at the clouds, wanting to look somewhere other than at the captain's face.

"Mayhap you are aware of a place where we could lie low?" Aslor went on.

The captain took a few bites more before exhaling a languorous sigh. She wiped her mouth and pushed her plate back. "I thought you wanted to fight."

Aslor rearranged his glasses. "Well, yes, but you just said…"

"I *said* that I didn't know of any such groups. What do you want to do, fight or lie low? It seems more and more to me that you people have no idea what you're doing."

Farrah frowned at the pirate. "I already told you that we want to fight the daemon."

The corsair nodded. "So you keep on repeating. So why don't you *fight* him?"

Farrah opened her mouth and shook her head. "Perhaps you haven't noticed, but our situation makes this hard."

The pirate drew her forearms on the table and intertwined her fingers. "One thing I know about life is that if you desire something, you do your homework and work to get results. You people say you want to rid us of Daromas but seek to join some far-off group to fight the placaters. Real good, you're basically emulating a child playing with ants but scurrying away from the centipede in your room."

She put up a hand. "*Then*, you decided you wanted to kill that centipede." She dropped her palm flat on the table. "But as soon as you got close to it…" She tiptoed her fingers around her plate and towards them. "It scared you off and you went running for cover. The next day, instead of learning that perhaps a broom would make it easier to fend off that freakish-legged thing, you went back to playing some more with your ants."

The corsair angled her body nonchalantly. "If I'm not being clear, I'll put it into simpler words you can understand." She looked at Farrah whose lips tightened at the insinuation. With a hint of a smirk, the pirate said, "If you didn't kill the daemon, that's because you didn't have the means. Take out the placaters if that gives you some sort of life fulfillment, but if you were not strong enough to kill Daromas yesterday, you won't be able to kill him tomorrow or a year from now."

Farrah gazed at her. She did not appreciate being chided but knew when to keep her mouth shut. This was one of those moments. Listening to her was probably more important than preserving her dignity.

She retreated her palms to her lap. "What are you suggesting we do?"

"Stop wasting your time with the small fry and do what it takes to become stronger," the captain answered, eyes lingering on them with a look of indulgence. She then drew herself up and tipped her hat before leaving.

Aslor arched an eyebrow. "I fear that she's answered with something far removed from what we were…"

"Come," she told him.

"Oh, alright."

They made their way back inside the saloon hall where the others were yet seated. "You got anything?" asked Slay, chin yanking up when he saw them approach.

They drew their heads together so the pirates would not overhear their conversation even though most of them had already resumed their usual day-to-day business.

"And *how* exactly do we become stronger?" inquired Slay after Aslor had described their meeting with the captain. "Even if we trained day and night, I don't suppose that would make much of a difference against a god."

"Yeah," added Essan. "I'm all in with the placaters, but I think it's become clear that we simply don't stand a chance against the daemon."

Farrah, who had kept quiet up till now, said, "You're right we can't expect to defeat a commandant, not unless we engage them on equal grounds."

"What do you mean?"

She felt uneasy, still debating with the idea she'd conjured, uncertain of how it would sound. "We can't vanquish a god, but we might be able to if we had similar powers on our side."

Essan opened her eyes and mouth wide. "Are you suggesting what I think you're suggesting?"

Farrah held her breath. "We acquire our own gods."

Her words had stunned everyone into silence. Essan's jaw had dropped; Slay's lips had looped upside down, body darting back on his chair, hands gripping the table. Aslor was tugging his shirt collar, and Thorick was watching her with a mysterious look on his face.

She held her breath longer than she had anticipated. She knew how ludicrous her statement had been; the gods weren't these easily acquired gifts that anyone could get their hands on.

The deities of their realm had brought Iscar into being a long time ago. Together, they had united their powers to create the lands, the sea, the animals, and the rest. Their work done, some had disappeared forevermore. Others had lingered on and aided the humans in the development of great cities, in inspiring a way of life as well as granting advancement in technologies well before their time.

Eventually, all had returned to their heavenly plane. But many had left a piece of their souls in Iscar—a piece which had the ability to summon a projection. This earthly representation was nothing more than a shadow of the actual celestial body behind the mirror in the realm beyond this one. Though this reflection was but mere ghost, however, a god's reflection was worth more than a thousand men.

These souls dwelled in ancient shrines and secluded temples scattered throughout Iscar that were so remote, and in such perilous locations, that none ever tried getting near them. The gods were not to be awakened from their slumber; to act so recklessly meant death. Yet, the commandants *had* mustered such power.

How they had done so, no one knew. Partaking in the union of an all-powerful deity through theurgy was something that most in modern Iscar hadn't thought conceivable. But the daemon and his commandants had done it.

Not that it hadn't been done before.

In ages forgotten, when the lands were yet on the brink of conquests, writings told of the partnerships between humans and gods, and stories of great battles against foreign invaders. With time, these alliances had all but faded and remained now only a memory. These remembrances had created a space for symbols and embodiments of ideas which drove their society forth.

Oleon, the Sun God, carried the star's shine on them every day.

Thyrael, the Eclipse God, took it away.

Oltier, the God of Light, brought radiance in people's hearts.

Israthel, the Bearer of the Night, sucked it out.

From the beginning of time to its end, they would be there, upholding forevermore the balance of their lands.

All, except for Thorick, were avoiding her stare as if none were willing to voice their feelings on the matter. Perhaps they were afraid of disappointing her, worried to put into words what they all thought.

That it was impossible.

It wasn't the first time Farrah had reflected on this. For as long as she'd battled Daromas, she'd dreamt of fighting his gods with her own but had never gone through with it.

To become one with a deity meant that its wielder was willing to lose part of their humanity. And to lose one's humanity was worse than death itself. No one was ready to do *that.*

It was the price of power. The peddling of one's soul.

They all knew it too well; every day they were faced with Daromas's horrible sickness as it took form in the screen's images. *This* was what was in store for them if they went down this path.

How could she ask any of her allies such a thing? As long as they could yet achieve their goals using their own means, these alternatives had had to come first.

But their assassination had failed, and that had been their ultimate attempt, their last plan. She had already gone through them all, from plan A to plan Z, and was all out of ideas.

They were simply no match for Daromas and his commandants. Perhaps it was time to look into the elusive lands of plan *et.* They no longer had any other choices. It was their last resort.

And suddenly, it was as though everything had become clear and this had been her goal all along. Though she had wanted to steer away from this road, it felt now as if someone had placed her in the middle of it. Her core had opened up, her mind was buzzing with this revelation.

Though she couldn't put it into words, something was happening.

She was listening to the calling.

It was Essan who first broke the silence. "How are we going to do that?" Though her tone had been questioning, Farrah had heard the doubt in her voice. She was glad that she had been gracious enough to question the means and not the idea.

"I'm not certain," she replied. "For all we know, the daemon and his commandants acquired their powers of theurgy by travelling in search of them for months—if not years. Nothing is known of their ordeals, nor the challenges they faced."

She scanned their expressions and found that their stares were as bleak as the notion of them conjuring gods. "I recall some of the books I read when I was younger," she went on in a soft voice. "Our deities used to lend us their hands in combat when our lands were on the brink of wars or the thrift amongst humans was too great—re-establishing order whenever it was lost."

"Uh," interrupted Slay. "When the daemon murdered King Redamastys with the help of gods, wasn't that when chaos started?" he argued, teeth gnawing on his lower lip. "Seems to me that they created the problem in the first place. Kinda makes you question whether they're all that good."

"Yes," she answered, frowning. "But there are many gods, aren't there? Even long ago, not all of them fought on the same side. Different interpretations of what our world needs have led to different incentives behind the deities' actions.

"What if Daromas's search took so long because he had to find conducive gods to aid him on his quest, beings of destruction who desired the same thing he wanted? Wouldn't that justify their motives?"

She got up and clapped her hands against the table. "Think about it. Shalowhith, God of Darkness, Illmeth, the Warlord? Not forgetting Israthel, the daemon's deity, Bearer of the Night? These are all creatures of the dusk. And yet, there are so many others: Enamus, the Chevaleresse of Protection and Oltier, God of Light. What about these deities who would have never sided with Daromas?"

She gazed at them almost feverishly and said, "Now that the ability of theurgy has been rekindled, we are part of a new era whereby we require the presence of our gods once again.

"Surely they will answer the call once we convince them that Iscar is in danger and that eight gods of darkness have given their support to a tyrant. If our deities are meant to awake in times of disequilibrium, then I doubt there's anyone who would argue that our situation isn't that."

All of their expressions looked somewhat overwhelmed, their faces strained by the whole concept.

"So... they're just waiting for someone to call on them?"

Farrah smiled. She knew Essan would be the first one on board. "Exactly."

Aslor retrieved a handkerchief from his pocket and brought it up to his forehead. "Thus, your plan is to acquire the power of theurgy so we can battle the daemon on equal ground?" The man seemed to be pondering the words the captain had spoken earlier.

Farrah inclined her head. "Yes."

Slay scratched his temple. He was wearing that same blank expression he'd had on the day she'd met him when Darvis had just broken him out of the post. "I'm not saying it doesn't make a lot of sense. Only, how are we going to acquire such powers? Sounds to me that if they were readily available, more people would have had them."

Farrah sat down, teeth biting the inside of her mouth. "I don't think you can gain their magic simply whenever. History is filled with stories of them joining our side for a short time before disappearing for centuries. Others have probably tried in the past but received no answers.

"I'm guessing you can acquire their powers in certain critical moments and have to convince them to choose *you*. The bond between a god and his wielder is special and not everyone has what is required to achieve such link."

Essan dropped her chin into her hands. "And you think we have what it takes?"

"I believe it with all my heart."

Silence had followed these words. Then, after a while, Slay said, "Does that mean our eyes are gonna get all rotten like?"

Another silence had followed.

"It is true that partnering with a god steals a person's vitality,"

Farrah answered in a low voice. "But it was years before the commandants' began to change."

"What if it takes years to defeat the daemon?"

Pause.

Essan's smile was queasy. "I guess it's worth it," she said though it sounded more like a question than an affirmation.

"In essence, not only would we be risking our lives, we'd be losing our lives' energies," replied Slay.

"Yes."

Her face was determined. It was willing. It was resolved.

"Okay," the islander answered, sitting back. "Okay."

Chapter 5

Though they now had a plan, its intricate nature and improbable success required much thinking. If anything, where would they start? They had no clues to any of the gods' resting places, and even *if* they'd known where to go, they had no idea what to expect when they got there.

Yet, what other choice did they have? What was the point of losing years to endless warfare for a situation that was not about to change?

Though the members of her group had agreed to follow her in this folly, Farrah knew they were coddling her.

She had seen the fear in their eyes, the doubts in their voices. They did not believe in this enterprise. They had agreed to it knowing that it was a goose chase, one that kept them away from the daemon.

This was alright. She didn't need to convince them.

She would *show* them.

It wasn't as though they were empty-handed. Each of them had spent the greater part of their lives fending for themselves. They were all capable warriors, and with the assistance of the gods, they would finally have the means to stand before the commandants on equal ground.

The question still remained: Where to begin?

They'd wracked their brains for hours, trying to figure out the first stride they could take. They felt uncomfortable talking to the crew of the *Celestial Dragon*; it was imperative they kept their plan a secret or else make their situation with Daromas more precarious than it already was.

"I'm going to speak to Captain Sadahl," Farrah declared.

"I thought you'd rather not have more dealings with her?" said Essan.

She pressed her lips together. "I would rather not. But she's been of great help to us, regardless of how unpleasant she's been about it."

Aslor leaned closer, whiskers twitching. "I can talk to her if you want."

Truth be told, she would have preferred to send him in her stead, but the pirate clearly intimidated the poor man and in their current situation, insecurity was not an option. He was of a gentle nature and she appreciated that about him, but she was afraid he might not have the courage to stand up to the captain.

"No, it's okay," she answered, sparing him her thoughts.

"It's only that…" the gentleman went on. She stared at him and realized that he had his own reservations about her. "I get the feeling that she might be more willing to listen to me," he finished, looking sideways.

She furrowed her brows.

"Why d'you think that?" asked Slay.

Aslor interlaced his fingers. "Well, I know Captain Sadahl, and it seems to me that she's appeared somewhat…" he tugged on his pants' fabric, "… *discontent* with Farrah since yesterday."

He eyed her. Seeing as his words hadn't offended her, he added, "You see, the captain is usually of an uplifted spirit. But when she is displeased with someone, it rarely turns around." He held his palms in front of him like he was attempting to make up for what he'd just said. "Not that you did anything wrong, Farrah! But Captain Sadahl can be truly generous with those she keeps in her good graces and somewhat rancorous with those who've provoked her." He shuffled in his seat. "Sadly, I fear the nature of your encounter last night may have slighted her."

Farrah was not impervious to his words; she had seen the disdain on the pirate's face. Her expression softened. "Then all the more reason for me to mend things with her."

Farrah went topside but saw no traces of the captain. She noticed the quartermaster walking by and headed towards him. "Master Kerok, was it?" she asked. The strong man turned her way and nodded. He had that same look of cool scrutiny he'd had in his eyes the previous evening. "Would it be possible to talk with the captain?"

Kerok let the rope he was holding fall to the ground and motioned her to follow with an air of suspiciousness.

"The Capt'n is in her quarters," he said and led her to its entrance, near the aft of the ship.

He opened the magnificent glass double doors, which resembled those they had witnessed inside the crew's quarters, and entered the captain's sitting room.

The lounge was both cozy and ostentatious. The windows at the rear covered the entire back wall, allowing in a rich sunlight that beamed through their facade, lighting the sumptuously designed boudoir. Old furniture of royal taste decorated the room, and endless rows of bookcases adorned its walls. This was evidently where Captain Sadahl received her guests.

She followed the man down the sculpted staircase and approached the doors at the end of the passageway. Kerok knocked on them.

"Enter," said a voice.

The quartermaster slipped the door ajar and allowed her inside. "Capt'n, she asked for an audience with you," explained the man, gesturing to Farrah.

The office was of a similar taste as the impeccable sitting room. A number of books and decorations were mounted on tall shelves around the bureau and a marquetry desk stood in front of the extension of the glass tainted walls from upstairs.

Captain Sadahl contemplated them and Farrah noticed how her eyes came close to rising overhead at the sight of her.

"Thank you, Master Kerok," replied the corsair and leaned back in her seat. She gestured to one of the chairs in front of her desk and Farrah went to sit while Kerok left the room.

The pirate glued her fingers in front of her chest, elbows bent on the armrests of her quasi-throne.

Perhaps Aslor was right, she thought as she eyed the corsair's look of inconvenience.

"What can I help you with…" the captain began before stopping for a second. "Tarah, was it?"

She plastered a smile on. "Farrah."

"Of course," the pirate answered, her smile looking similar to hers.

"I will make this short, Captain," she said. "We have arrived at the conclusion that we are to match Daromas's strength if we wish to defeat him. To do so requires help of a similar nature as the one acquired by him and his commandants." She took a breath, preparing herself for a comeback. "We need the theurgy of the gods and our goal is to head out in search of them."

Farrah waited for the rebuttal, which did not come. The corsair's face looked more or less indifferent. Tentatively, she added, "We were hoping that you might know the location of some deities?"

"I may have heard of some things," the pirate replied, voice purring as she poured herself a drink from the bottle of expensive liquor standing to her right. "What is your offer?"

"My offer?"

The corsair took a sip from her cup. "Where I come from, knowledge is power. You believe I would become an informant to red-listed criminals, making myself a greater target than I already am, without compensation?" She lifted her gaze. "Seeing as we're talking about treason of the highest sort, you can't expect me to help you free of charge?"

Farrah's eyes widened and said, "You are the greediest person I have ever met."

"Then surely you've never met another pirate," replied the captain. "Where *you* come from, people may be willing to lay down their lives for you at no cost. In the real world, where *I* come from, you'll find that most are not that generous."

The pirate sat taller in her seat, a corner of her mouth lifting. "Though you are evidently ungrateful for the gesture, what I did for you was more than most would have done. My benevolence, however, has its limits. I do expect some recompense for my assistance."

"I am grateful for the help, *Captain*," she replied, voice heavy with the weight of stones. "But between you and me, the payment is exorbitant, and you are walking away from this deal with far more than we are."

"I gave you an escape and a chance at survival," the pirate answered. "I do believe that is rather priceless, wouldn't you say?"

"You are gaining riches beyond measure simply for transporting us elsewhere! I think that it is more than fair."

The corsair waved her index finger in front of her. "Oh no. You have caused me great risks by having you aboard my ship, risks that are still yet to unfold. I made outright insurrection in the eyes of the daemon the minute I fled the capital with you and your friends. You believe that my crew and I won't be sanctioned for taking such actions?"

"It wouldn't have come to that if you'd left as soon as we'd arrived," Farrah snapped back. "The placaters wouldn't have intercepted us and we'd had gone unperturbed."

The corsair dropped her mouth. "You are quite something," she declared, eyes round at the audacity of her comment. "I bet you are the sort of person not used to being denied anything. How infuriating it must be to have someone treat you as you are." Her tone had become sour. "A spoiled girl."

"Spoiled?" she replied, chest lifting up. "I have been spending the better part of the last fifteen years sacrificing everything to help those in need and battle against persecution. I…"

She stopped short. Though this encounter had definitely not

turned out how she had wanted it to, it was not in her character to get carried away. Maybe it was all these emotions that she had bottled up coming out the wrong way.

"I don't have to explain myself to you," she said quietly. "You don't know me and I can't help how you see us." She rose from her seat. "I'm sorry I have appeared ungrateful. As soon as we leave your ship, we will settle payment and will be out of your way. I'll return with a destination before the evening and I hope we can trust that the secret of our venture will remain between us."

She left the room, unable to withstand the corsair's sharp stare any longer.

Farrah had headed back to the others bearing the bad news.

"More money?" said Aslor, somewhat tripping on the words.

She nodded. "I told her we would find a solution on our own. We can't afford the captain's *help* anymore."

"I'm guessing your meeting with her didn't go according to plan?" said Slay.

Farrah did not feel like explaining. "Maybe you were right, Aslor. Next time, I'll be sure to send you instead."

The trader waved it off. "To be honest, I doubt I would have yielded different results. We're lucky to have gotten this far. I reckon we shouldn't ask for too much."

Farrah agreed. "It doesn't matter what the captain thinks. We can find our information on our own."

"Did you have somewhere in mind?" asked Essan.

She took a seat next to the others. "Yes, the research citadel in Mondos. It hosts the biggest library in Iscar. It's where some of the most advanced scholars reside. Surely, we can find something there or at least some records of the past."

"Seems like a good place to start," agreed Aslor. "Nevertheless, we'll have to be careful. Our faces may have well begun to spread around."

Farrah hummed. "Then we're settled. We'll go to Mondos."

She grinned at the gentleman. "Perhaps you'd like to inform our dear captain?"

He chuckled. "Of course."

Just as they were about to conclude their session, they jumped in their seats as a sword was flung against the tabletop and its blade rattled against the hardened wood.

Farrah looked around and stared into Captain Sadahl's serious expression, incomprehension wearing her own.

"The blacksmith Oros Belaid made this sword," explained the corsair.

She cast her eyes down on the cutlass. She knew the name.

Years ago, the man had served royalty. His weapons were some of the most intricately designed in Iscar, and it was said that hidden powers resided in them. When Daromas had killed the king, Belaid had left the city alongside other artisans and craftsmen who were unwilling to sell their work to him and his commandants.

The pirate drew her hands to her hips. "This is no ordinary weapon. If you would look at the blade's finishing, you will find its shape unmatched."

Slay leaned closer and touched its steel. Fine details etched its black and gold pommel, its metal worked to perfection. He gazed up at the pirate.

"It's pretty awesome," he replied, eyes scanning her intentions.

The corsair leaned over and picked up the weapon in her left arm, her sword hand, and stared at it. "When Oros made it for me, he told me that it was forged inside a fire imbued with igneous rocks retrieved from Ekhon's volcano, thus, conjuring flames not of this realm to work on its blade.

"Now," she pointed the tip of the cutlass to the ground, "he also explained that many have forgotten that this mountain was once the property of a celestial being, the one who gave power to these lava rocks."

The pirate gazed at Farrah, brow lifting tellingly.

She sustained the stare. "A god," she muttered.

"It is believed that a deity going by the same name is responsible for the particular abilities of those rocks." She sheathed the cutlass back over her shoulder and offered Aslor a meaningful look. "You will find him in the city of Tharan. Shall I set the course?"

Aslor blinked at the others, then fumbled up his seat. He cleared his throat as though he were addressing a member of the royal family. "That would be a good place to start I believe." He glanced at her. "Farrah?"

She nodded her approval.

The captain had already begun retreating. "We will be there by the morrow."

Farrah stared down at her hands, expression tight, then got up and ran after the pirate. "Why the change of heart?" she asked, voice catching after the corsair's back.

"Master Kerok, please set a course towards Tharan," the captain ordered her quartermaster before turning to her. "I had to make a decision. Either steer you somewhere and land by the morning or wait for days on end for you lot to make one." The corner of her upper lip twisted up. "You can understand which choice seemed more appealing."

She resumed her way, leaving Farrah frowning at her back.

Aboard the *Celestial Dragon*, most evenings were an opportunity to eat, drink and celebrate the bounty of their sky-roaming lives. Most nights, tables were drawn unto the main deck and musicians fiddled rapid folk songs that lifted everyone's spirit. The alcohol and the food were displayed in abundance and the atmosphere was, for lack of a better word, rousing.

The renegades had sat at the back of the longest table. The captain was on its other end, a drink in hand and a leg hoisted on the armrest of her chair. The pirate was jeering alongside her crew mates, her mood far more jovial than the one she had been in before.

Slay took a seat beside Farrah carrying two tankards. "Here you go." He motioned to one of the glasses.

Farrah grabbed the drink and muttered a polite thank-you though she did not bring the jug to her lips. It wasn't that she had no taste for alcohol, but a clouded mind wasn't as sharp as a clear one.

Slay was showing none of her reticence. An apparent accomplished drinker, the man had finished with his glass in a few gulps. "These guys know how to have fun," he said as he did, a boyish grin illuminating his features as he contemplated the *Celestial Dragon's* crew.

It was no wonder the notion of becoming a pirate had appealed to the islander. He seemed of a similar mind and looked right at home alongside these men and women. She wondered whether he knew of the killings, thievery and their brutal coercive ways. Would he also feel right at home holding a knife to a man's throat as others ransacked said person's home?

Of course, she'd heard the term *corsair.* In Iscar, some of the most famous faces in piracy called themselves as such, claiming this banner as a means to appear more *virtuous.* Unlike their pirate brothers, corsair captains had higher privileges and notoriety.

Crude merchants, ruthless mercenaries and hired hands, corsairs stood as elected knights of the skies, enabling their laws for the protection of trade and commerce. Corsairs, such as the acclaimed Feras Sadahl, were captains of reputation, enacting fruitful dealings and affairs that richly profited the many indiscriminately and benefitted their own pockets most of all.

Furthermore, they held rights others were denied. They were able to roam the skies freely, had access to certain exclusive ports and were exempt from ship searches. Through them, any wielding the right amount of money could partake in their unsavoury business and though all could profit from these trades, it was the affluent who could usually afford it.

Daromas himself had conceded many years ago, in Corsak Sadahl's era, to such ongoing piracy as promoting his own ideals, even requiring their services from time to time.

Regular pirates, on the other hand, were seen as outlaws acting of their own accord and furthering their personal needs. Ransacking, pillaging and robbery were at the forefront of their activities and because of this they had lower standing within the public eye.

Driven by desperation, these men and women sought to survive on their own outside of Daromas's Iscar. Pushed to the extremes by their godsforsaken lives, they were the brutal counterparts of the gallivanting corsairs.

Naturally, corsairs and pirates, they were all the same. A corsair captain stood at the helm of a pirate crew. But in the public's romantic imagination, these heroes of the heavens were swashbucklers of the realm, free to roam the clouds with their bounties, far from the reach of the daemon. They served as inspiration of *what could be.*

Though brutish and unconstitutional, corsairs were just about decent enough to fulfill the people's hopeful desire for a dream—one where great captains could make them feel something in their lives of hopelessness.

Farrah watched the crew for a while more, her worries lessening. If anything, corsairs had names to uphold. They held their clients' privacy in high regard, and their sense of loyalty to their trades were bound in their own code of honour. Corsairs could be named as such as long as the people offering said title found the captain's merit in wielding it.

If Feras Sadahl had kept the banner for so long, it meant that she had deserved it.

Her eyes swept around, and she witnessed people enjoying themselves, normal men and women partaking in this style of living that she knew nothing about.

They weren't all that different from the renegades she'd frequented back in Letholdus. Their drives were opposing in nature and yet, something about them made her feel as though they weren't such strangers after all.

The crew incorporated a similar ratio of men and women, seemingly getting along and presumably members for quite a while. Though she knew these pirates were some of the deadliest warriors in Iscar, they were really just a group of people, living in the skies of their own dreamscape.

For the first time in her life, she saw citizens of Iscar who were free.

Of course, it wasn't that easy, and no one was ever free from the shackles of the daemon. Nevertheless, these pirates might be closest to what freedom felt like. It was encouraging to be in the presence of people who knew how to rejoice and live. She wanted to give that to the rest of the world.

Farrah smiled to herself as she returned her attention to the members of her own group.

Aslor was partaking in Slay's drinking whilst showing some of the pirates a magic trick. When he retrieved what had apparently been one of the men's card, the pirate clapped him on the back. Some of the gentleman's drink spilled on his lap, a light giggle emerging from his lips as he did.

Grinning, she grabbed her tankard and took a sip.

Something leaned against her thigh and her privacy was invaded by strong smells of alcohol and sweat. She yanked her jug down and lifted a glare on the smirking crew member.

From this close a range, Farrah could count the number of hairs that garnished the man's ill-kempt, unshaven chin. She moved a few inches away but soon found herself running out of space when he drew closer.

"Ye be a damn pretty one," the pirate began, showing off a set of decaying teeth.

She rotated her head, ignoring him.

Tap tap. His fingers prodded against her shoulder. She jerked back, and the man's smile grew larger when she did.

As she was about to voice her desire for privacy, Dahara came in from behind and said, "Really, Doron, will ye leave the gurl alone? She ain't gonna fuck ye anytime soon!"

She shoved the man away, palm slapping the pirate's scalp until he got up, wearing a pitiful look on his willful face.

"She ain't fuckin' ye either, Dahara!" he replied, scowling at the woman as he left.

Dahara shook her head and took the man's seat as her own. "Go on, move along, Doron ye moron!" She gave Farrah an apologetic expression. "Sorry fer that, miss." She puffed out her cheeks comically. "And don't ye worry, ye ain't me type, so I ain't gonna go actin' like them fools."

She gestured to the pirates gathered at a nearby table. Some of the men had the courtesy to lower their gaze when Farrah peered over. Others offered ogling simpers instead.

Dahara sneered at the pirates and sat with her back against the table, her legs hanging wide open.

Farrah rearranged herself in her seat and grinned. The woman was something of a character, and there was a fondness about her that was hard to ignore. "I should thank you," she replied with a tinge of playfulness in her voice.

Dahara gesticulated with her hands. "Yeah, and I don't mean no offence, but I like me women a bit more… ye know." She moved her arms up and down, flexing them. "Tough."

Farrah felt like laughing. She smiled instead. "None taken."

"These pigs, darn it. Ye just gotta ruffle 'em up and they'll leave ye alone. They be good lads. Be juss that they ain't used to havin' such a damn fine-lookin' lass aboard the *Dragon*, 'cept fer Alena, o' course." She lifted both palms in front of her. "Again, I ain't flirtin'! But dammit, I still got me eyes." She blew out a quick snort.

Farrah chuckled and said, "I'll keep your advice in mind."

Dahara nodded as though feeling that she was doing a fine job counselling her. She lowered her head to the side as if she was about to tell her some important secret. "They gots in their weeny brains that one o' 'em stands a chance. They be hopin' I can brin' back some info."

The pirate pursed her lips. "But don't ye trouble yerself, doll face. I've got yer back." She leaned even closer. "Unless ye *do* want me to find ye a fella, eh?" She winked and shoved her elbow into Farrah's stomach.

"Oh, I'll be quite fine. Thank you…"

The pirate drew away. "Yeah, figured. At least I can tell them skippers that I tried."

Farrah hoped that Dahara's words would be enough to discourage further encounters with the most febrile crew members. "How long have you been on this ship?" she asked, steering this conversation to a less embarrassing one.

The pirate pulled on her lower lip with her fingers. "I reckon it must have been 'bout three years."

"What made you join the crew?"

Dahara dropped her elbows back. "Well, fuck me! When Capt'n Sadahl requests ye be part o' her crew, ye don't say no!" She cackled somewhat, her face brightening up.

"She's a successful pirate," she agreed, her tone contained.

Dahara glimpsed around at the captain now at conversation with her quartermaster. "Yeah, there be that," she muttered.

Farrah waited for the woman to build on her words. When she didn't, she noticed how embarrassed the pirate looked, not to mention the odd glimmer in her eyes.

Dahara cackled at her curious expression and gesticulated with her hands. "Oh, ye know." The woman's cheeks were growing pinker by the second.

"You like her," Farrah pointed out, head cocking to the side.

Dahara fluttered her fingers some more. "Yeah, well, so be it, eh?" she replied. "But forget romance and all that shit. I juss think she be one hell o' a person."

The woman was now staring at her, or from the look of her expression, seeking an approval of some sort. "I couldn't say," Farrah began, searching for the right words to keep her peace with the pirate. "I really don't know her well enough."

Dahara seemed puzzled by her reply. "Blimey gal," she answered, "ye don't need to *know* her, ye juss have to know *about* her."

Farrah shrugged. "Hearsay don't mean as much to me than my own impression of a person."

Dahara glared at her with mounting incomprehension. "Whar d'ye come from?" She pointed all ten fingers at the captain. "She be the daughter o' Corsak Sadahl, the top admiral now that he be gone!" She drew her head forth, leaving her shoulders behind. "And I mean, she emanates fuckin' animal pheromones or somethin'."

Dahara fumbled on the bench, looking as though she had perhaps said too much.

Farrah stared at the captain of the *Celestial Dragon*. "I guess we see things differently," she replied with a shrug.

Dahara grinned and dropped a palm on her leg. "In no time, ye'll know her better fer who she be," she argued with yet another one of her winks.

"I don't suppose we'll be in her presence long enough for this to happen," Farrah answered thoughtfully before her expression became playful. "Is the captain aware of your feelings?"

Dahara giggled and waved her off. "Nah, I definitely ain't her type o' gal. Not that she'd be mean about it, but I'd prefer to keep some self-respect if ye be knowin' what I mean. Ye don't go bein' dim-witted enough to chase aroun' someone like *that*."

She pondered the pirate's words. Feras Sadahl's reputation was impressive to be sure, but she also radiated something else that was hard to define.

Power?

". . . and even if I be in that league, darn it, fuck that competition."

Farrah cocked her head to the side. "Competition?"

"Yeah, I ain't the only lass who wishes for the capt'n's favour." She fluttered her eyelashes a few times. "But she only fancies a few o' 'em, and fuck, I ain't got that look." She made a gesture with her hands, enlarging her breasts, making a funny outwards motion with her lips.

Farrah laughed at the imitation and so did Dahara. Her cackling giggles had an uplifting quality to them. "See what kind I mean?" the pirate finished with a grin. Farrah nodded, her expression one of whimsical understanding. Dahara's gaze meandered back to the captain, letting a few seconds pass by before she added, "Anyway, it be good enough bein' part o' her crew."

She followed the woman's gaze.

Today, you helped no one. You made things worse.

She looked away, lips pressing against one another.

"What's up?" said Essan.

Farrah turned to her. "Hmm?"

The younger woman was staring at them both. "You two were eyeing the captain for the past minute or so."

"Dahara was helping me understand her position—that she has a crew who loves and admires her, and putting them in harm's way must have been hard for her." Her face softened. "I'll try to be more aware of this next time."

Dahara scratched her jaw. "That's what ye got from our conversation?" She shook her head, snorting. "Me guess be that I did a fine job talkin' to ye then." She rose and waved them off, staggering somewhat as she went.

"I agree with you," said Essan. "I think it was a good thing to do for the captain to take us in. It couldn't have been an easy decision, seeing as we're red-listed. Even if she *is* a pirate, no one wants to be an enemy of the daemon."

Farrah's smile widened. Essan was on the side of the people and that was a nice way of being.

"Aslor?" she asked, and the gentleman turned to her, looking like a man that had his liquor coming to him. "You know the captain, don't you?"

Aslor's eyes travelled away. "I can't say I know her all that well. . . ."

"You mentioned we could count on her?"

"Yes, yes. I have been on good terms with Captain Sadahl. Though you've had your differences, but I have come to believe that she will be considerate as long as we are fair to her, and she won't side with the daemon if such a predicament arises."

She knew she could trust him.

This was a new world, different from the one she was used to.

But it wasn't because it was unknown and strange that it meant that she had to lose herself in it.

So maybe she could also learn to trust Captain Feras Sadahl.

Chapter 6

"Tharan!" shouted the vigil from up the crow's nest.

They were waiting on the forecastle deck, the morning sun opening their way to a ragged land and its city. The captain was navigating the ship, Kerok by her side maneuvering the controls.

The renegades gazed at the incoming ground, approaching the unknown. Their sleep had been irksome and infused with restlessness. Their quest was underway even if they had no idea what they would meet along the road nor what it meant to go out in search of a god.

Tharan was a small town, a harbour of seafarers and artisans, its buildings tainted and battered by impoverished maintenance. The city functioned predominantly as a respite area for merchants and traders meeting their cargoes and exchanging goods. Unlike other great cities that swelled on riches and abundances, Tharan had been home to the leftovers of the realm: men and women graceful in their artistry but shamed by the daemon and banding together in a gathering of crafting misfits.

The *Celestial Dragon* came to an abrupt halt as it doused itself in the waters surrounding the city, soon resuming its way towards the bay. When the captain called for a standstill, they cast the anchor at a certain distance from the port. The pirate had wanted the *Dragon* to remain in the cove as a security measure as well as to discourage the placaters from boarding her ship.

The corsair had met up with them near the galleon's gangway. She was wearing a mid-calf black coat and a golden sash around her waist. Like her other shirts, the sleeve of her jacket had been fashioned to display her mechanical arm. "Get aboard the tender," she told them, her tone less than warm. "Master Kerok will stay here with the rest of the crew."

"You're coming with us, Captain?" asked Slay.

"Shall I hold your hand?" she replied. The starlight in the man's eyes dimmed. "Right," continued the pirate, "this way."

They followed her down the ladder and aboard a rowboat and proceeded towards the port.

"How did you meet Mister Belaid?" asked Essan who was sitting next to the corsair, looking flustered by their nearness. She had stuck her hands between her legs as if she was trying to make her slight frame smaller than it already was.

"My father. They knew each other of long. When Oros decided to flee the capital and settle here, it was my father who carried him on this ship. He had my sword forged after his murder by Commandant Trent as a tribute." She did not look sad or even angry as she said the words.

"And how do you figure he's gonna help us now?"

"*You*," she glared at Essan, "no." She then simpered. "*Me*, yes."

Aslor interlaced his fingers on his lap. "It is very nice of you, Captain, to point us in the right direction. We are most grateful."

"Oros, like pretty much as all of Iscar, is no friend of the daemon. He'll point you in the right direction, but the rest is up to you."

"I understand," he answered.

They arrived short minutes later on the edge of the bank and docked the rowboat on the last pier. No one paid them any heed as they went about their usual bustling business and exchanges.

"At any sign of recognition," the corsair said, her leg lifting over the ledge, "we separate." She wound around Aslor and loomed closer to him. They were about the same height, yet the woman was far more intimidating than him. "And we meet up at the Bank of Commerce so I can be done with you lot."

The trader's smiled quivered. "Don't worry, Captain, we will not run off without giving you payment." He chuckled. "We already have the daemon on our backs; we wouldn't want to add the corsairs to the chase."

The pirate quirked an eyebrow and gave him a nod. She was probably not used to people double-crossing her, and Aslor's rampant fidgeting must have been proof enough that this man would not be the first.

They began walking down the streets of the city, peering around them as they did. Thankfully, there weren't nearly as many placaters in this town as there were in the capital.

Essan trotted up to the captain. "Won't people recognize you?" she asked, eyes trailing up the pirate's impeccable figure.

The corsair shrugged though Farrah noticed her lips curving, appreciating the implication.

"We rarely come here; it's too small a city for my liking," the captain answered before pointing her finger at them all. "You people though, I don't know. There's word going around, ordering your immediate arrest. By the looks of the last communications we've received, however, the daemon is yet ignorant of your location."

"You've received communications regarding our capture?" exclaimed Farrah.

The pirate returned her stare ahead. "Yes."

She approached the captain's other side. "Why didn't you tell us?"

The corsair pouted. "Because there's nothing to tell. They repeat the same sequence every hour or so: *The fugitives are to be stopped at all costs and any who has information on their whereabouts are to report immediately to the nearest control post.* It is unknown whether you are yet in the capital or have left. As such, everyone must be on the lookout." She awarded Farrah a sideways glance. "That's about the gist of it."

"That's good for you too."

The captain fully stared at her. "For now. But we are currently in the open and your identities have become recognizable enough. Anyone who takes a second look at you will remember the images they've seen on the regime's screens. If that person happens to be a sympathizer of Daromas, everything will be over in no time for all of us."

The corsair looked into the faces of the citizens out in the streets. "And you're not helping."

"What does *that* mean?"

The pirate drew an ironic expression. "Many a few are staring at you."

Farrah cast her eyes around. She had not been paying much attention to the glares of the townsfolk, perhaps because she was so used to them that she had grown accustomed to blocking them out. "They're also looking at you," she answered rather uncharacteristically on the defensive.

The corsair grinned sideways, and Farrah expected that this particular smile was the one that made most of these women Dahara had mentioned fall for her.

"No, it's you," she retorted. "And you," she went on, eyeing now Thorick's uncannily large frame.

The knight frowned. He dropped his shoulders and lowered his head somewhat—as if that could do anything to hide his enormous physique.

Farrah lowered her face as well, brow creased while the pirate walked on the same, her gaze set in front of her without a care.

They proceeded for a short while more through the different compact streets of the busy city until the captain stopped in front of a shop. "Here we are. Better make haste, it will do no good to linger," she said before casting a look around and entering the blacksmith's store.

They made their way inside the workshop and found a man toiling on the pommel of a long sword near a blazing furnace at the back of the room.

He must have been in his sixties. His black curls had turned almost grey all around and fell on his forehead, sweat gluing the thin strands to his skin. His ragged beard held the same ashen colour as his hair, and he wore a simple apron over muscular shoulders.

He looked up when he noticed them approaching. His wrinkled eyes stared for a moment at the corsair before he dropped his tools and took her by the arm. "I hear a lot about you," he declared in a raspy voice.

"And I see you are still hard at work." The pirate pointed at the collection of weapons and armour decorating the walls of the room.

Oros sat back on a dusty-looking stool and beckoned them to do the same. They found benches and chairs lying about and carried them closer to his. "What brings the daughter of Corsak?" said the man in his strong, throaty voice.

"I need a favour. Have you heard of these people?" asked the captain, gesturing at the renegades.

Oros surveilled the room, his inscrutable eyes scrutinizing them. "Should I know about them?"

The corsair arched her hand their way. "This is the merry band who tried to murder the daemon a few days ago."

The man stood up straighter in his seat, his expression turning to one of collected intrigue. "I heard about *that*," he replied, eying them some more.

Farrah couldn't help noticing that he didn't look all that excited by their presence in his shop.

"Feras, I must say that I am startled," the blacksmith went on, gaze immobilizing on the captain. "After the murder of your father, I thought it had become clear to you that rising against the daemon bears no other end but death!"

The pirate put up a hand. "Believe me, Oros, I have part in this only due to a serious misfortune which has led me to provide transportation for these people, nothing more."

The blacksmith twitched in his seat and ran calloused fingers through his sweaty hair. "You *do* understand that being seen in the company of these people holds the same sentence as theirs?"

The corsair crossed her arms over her chest. "Indeed, which is why I've been trying to get rid of them ever since they set foot on my ship and why I need your help to end this unfortunate affair." She grounded the flats of her boots against the floor. "They only require a few answers and then will be on their way."

Oros rose from his chair and strode up to the front door, sliding the lock shut before returning. "Were you seen coming here?"

"I don't believe so, yet cannot be certain of it." The pirate smirked and added, "In essence, you are harbouring the most hated criminals in the realm."

The blacksmith grimaced. Though he appeared calm on the surface, his eyes had shimmered for a second. He was afraid. "What do you want from me?"

The captain retrieved the cutlass that hung from her bandolier strap and gave it to Oros. "You once told me that you created this sword using igneous rocks taken from Ekhon's mountain, did you not?"

The blacksmith scratched his beard and nodded.

"The volcano of the *god* Ekhon, yeah?" added Slay who seemed to be having a hard time sitting still.

Oros stared at the islander. "Aye, it is."

"Tell us more about that god, would you?" asked the pirate.

The man took a slow inhalation and put an arm on his lap. "As you would have guessed, he is the master of flames, known as the Baron of Fire."

"The deity who gave us fire at the beginning of time," muttered Aslor.

"Aye," agreed the blacksmith. "He's also in charge of our land's molten rock, the magma that resides under the earth's surface."

"What about the volcano?" asked Farrah, her expression serious.

The man swept another look around. "It's about two days' walk from here due west. Though by ship it would be a matter of half an hour, maybe less," he began, eyes casting upwards as though searching for the memory. "It's difficult to miss. Them lands turn infertile miles before you get near that volcano. There ain't much that lives in them parts, except for death, so travellers go around it, avoiding its desert at all cost. I only went there twice myself to get them rocks at the bottom of the mountain.

"The higher up, the harder your breathing. The climate be boiling and smoke pours everywhere. Once in a while, the volcano erupts, so it's better to steer clear of it altogether if you don't wanna find yourself in its path."

The captain turned a questioning stare on Farrah as though asking whether she really wanted to go there.

She chose not to return the look. "What about the god, have you seen him?"

The blacksmith lowered his gaze to his hands. "Aye, I have. That's why my second trip became my last."

"What happened?" inquired Essan, sitting up on the edge of her seat.

"I saw an outline through the mist, but there is no mistaking a god," he said in a hushed tone. "He looked at me and I felt fear like never before. I struggled to breathe while that cursed mist engulfed me and then ran as fast as my murky brain allowed me. After that, I knew it was not my place to return."

Essan inched closer, tiptoeing on feet that could scarcely hold the few inches of buttocks yet sitting on the chair. "Was he good or bad?"

Oros folded his massive arms on his chest. "He let me go, didn't he?"

"That's it?" Slay blurted out.

The blacksmith bumped the table next to him with his fist, his outburst startling them in their seats. "Darn it, boy! If that ain't enough! I dunno where you come from, but you don't see a god every day, do ya?"

"Are you sure it was a god, Gramps? Seems to me that you had some sort of hallucination because of all that mist...."

"Don't ya go and make fun of these things, laddie," Oros replied in a low growl. "I know what I saw."

A chill ran down her spine and Farrah's surroundings became silent. It was as if the deity himself had quietened the room in reverence to his power.

"No one is doubting you, Sir Oros," she said. "Only, our gods reside in their dimension, don't they? Their earthly projection is bound to their spirit altars or with their human wielder. Yet, you saw him wandering on his own?"

Oros scratched his beard once more, looking up in wonder. "I can't answer that. I only know what I saw."

She gazed down, considering this new piece of information.

The gods did not linger on this plane. What appeared before their eyes was rather a blemished copy sent to aid the humans in their affairs. For this reason, even if the projection was defeated, it had no bearing on the real deity.

Perhaps this projection also dwelled in the human realm, maintaining a permanent link between the gods in their heaven and this mortal world.

"What is it then?" asked the blacksmith. "You wanna get a look at a god, that it?"

"The less you know the better for you, sir," she answered. "It is kind enough that you've provided us with this information; we wouldn't want to bring you any troubles."

Oros's eyes settled questioningly on her face. "No matter what you're trying to accomplish, I'll tell ya this: Trudging inside this cruel desert is perilous, and I reckon that Ekhon lives on top of that mountain, which is impossible to climb on foot. Going by ship is the only way you'll get up there. However, I do not recommend it. Take my word for it, you should stay away from this volcano if you know what's good for you." He looked at the corsair, tone admonishing. "And for gods' sake, away from the daemon."

The captain nodded, her expression airy.

"Thank you, sir," Farrah answered and rose from her seat.

They followed her lead. Oros was the last to stand. "Better go through the back door. 'Tis a small town and people are bound to talk coz they're scared. And people who are afraid do strange things," he finished with a grunt.

They ducked inside the alleyway behind the workshop. Oros's omen had brought them no comfort, and they felt more agitated than before as they resumed their walk through Tharan.

"We're off to the mountain?" asked Slay.

"No," answered the corsair. "We're off to the bank." She gave Aslor a look of warning.

"Captain," Farrah began.

"No," she intervened at once. "I won't hear it. I know what you're about to say, and you can keep it to yourself."

"Oros mentioned that it would be impossible to make it to the top of the volcano on foot," she went on, feeling disinclined that she had to. "We could be there in less than an hour and…"

The captain shook her head in disbelief. "Then I'll have to bring you back. Then you'll want a lift somewhere else you'll require me to go. You'll always want something more out of me."

She stared into the corsair's honey-gold pupils, her own beseeching. "It's the last thing I will ask of you. I make it a promise."

"We can go," the pirate turned to Aslor, "to the bank."

The gentleman put a hand on Farrah's back. "It's okay, we'll find another way," he muttered.

The captain stomped off, forcing them to follow in her footsteps. "Mister Aslor," she said and her tone now implied business. "You will convey the transaction to my accounts and we will part ways. I don't want to hear from you again. Our dealings are over when this exchange is concluded. Understood?"

Aslor trotted next to her. "Loud and clear, Captain."

"We're heading to the main district, so be on your guard. The placaters will be around."

She strode down the path, Farrah wondering what they were going to do without the corsair's galleon. Travelling on foot would require too much time, not to mention the dangers they would face. Seeking another vessel would be tricky now that the whole nation was on the lookout for them, not withstanding that most who owned airships were predominantly pirates or Daromas's soldiers of the peace.

Neither of these options seemed good.

They walked past a regime screen, and she had to force herself not to stop.

She had just glimpsed her own face.

All of the screens' contents in Iscar were under the control of the government and administered by its people. Each building, each house, was under strict order to possess one. Turning on and off of their own accord, these delivered their news at Daromas's pleasure anytime of the day.

She glared at the display captured by the cameras during Daemon's Day. Her kneeled position, her cheeks doused in Darvis's blood…

"*You are mine.*"

The daemon's voice had the ability of chilling one's veins. She looked beside the screen and saw Daromas's watching glare, his poster mocking her.

"*I see you, my little moppets.*"

She ducked her head, cold sweat drenching her palms as she created fists out of them.

Chin lowered, she peeked at the citizens' expressions. Most were avoiding staring at them. This was odd, considering they couldn't keep their eyes off of them before. Now all she witnessed were faces depicting apprehension.

No, it was closer to panic.

"The bank is down this road," said the corsair, guiding them along the street.

Farrah caught up to her. "Captain," she whispered, "I think we should go back."

"And why would that be?"

"We've been spotted."

The pirate followed her gaze. Some of the denizens were dodging right out of their way, expressions fearful as they peered back at them over their shoulders. "Yes, I see what you mean," she answered, features turning watchful.

"We need to move out."

The captain pressed them on at a similar pace. "The plan doesn't change."

Farrah caught the corsair's forearm. "The placaters could be on their way!"

The pirate yanked her arm away. "By the looks of things, they already are. Might as well do the best with the time we've gotten left," she replied curtly.

"Every minute we stick around is an opportunity we're giving them to come chasing after us! *All* of us."

The corsair scoffed. "Nobody's taking me today. You lot," she sneered down at her, "I can't say."

They had just entered the shopping square and were closing in on the bank. Farrah noticed people scampering out of a nearby street, heads darting back to look behind them. "Captain! *Please*, the—"

Someone seized her by the collar, and a maddened expression infringed on her vision. "You little shite!" the man barked. "What were you thinking?!"

Thorick had soon grabbed him by the scruff of the neck and yanked him out of the way. Everyone around them had frozen, their eyes glued to the scene.

"You should've let 'em kill you!" spit the man, rolling back to his feet before darting away when confronted by Thorick's menacing bulk.

She was rooted to the spot.

"Get out of here, you're bringing us trouble!" shouted a voice.

She witnessed the citizen's pursed expression, their spite, their hate.

The corsair had crossed her arms over her chest, looking annoyed. She had taken a step back as though hoping the rest of the crowd would not associate her with them.

Farrah's face turned into a mask of stone. "Can we go?" she asked the captain.

The pirate drew a look of warning but twisted back when a hurricane of metallic footsteps made their welcome heard on the adjacent road. By the sound of things, a lot of people were coming their way and Farrah had a clear notion whom they belonged to.

The captain cursed under her breath and retrieved her shotgun from her back. She had a second to adjust it before it blew away the first placater that had entered the square. The soldiers behind him tumbled backwards as the body was propelled into them.

"Get 'em!" shouted a voice in the crowd. "It's the daemon's killers!"

"Yeah, get them!" repeated another and this soon became the chanting chorus of an angry mob.

The pirate offered Farrah an irate look while shooting down a placater. She had no doubt that she wanted to give her a few choice words, but these would have to wait.

"*Get 'em!*"

Farrah retrieved both of her handguns and shelled down the next soldiers storming the area, ignoring the crowd's outcry.

They ran back the way they came, shouts and gunshots rising in their wake. The captain had grasped her blunderbusses and taken the rear, her every bullet forcing a soldier's retreat with violent coercion.

The placaters flowed into the street, their numbers magnifying into a swelling wave. Farrah lowered herself on one knee and blasted a volley of shots into their ranks. Placaters went crawling under her assault. She bolted up again and sped after the others.

"Where to?" shouted Slay, wielding his axes in both hands.

"The ship!" Farrah yelled while stealing a glance over her shoulder at the corsair who looked about ready to swear at her. "You still haven't got your money and we can't stay here! There's no other way!"

The pirate opted for that curse as she ran after her. "I'm starting to think you're the one who called them!" she snarked and Farrah was relieved to hear a note of humour through the anger that pierced her words.

Down the streets they went until the docks were in view. They sprinted towards their tender and hopped inside while Thorick sundered the rope that held it in place.

The captain shoved a paddle into Slay's arms and both drove the rowboat through the water. The placaters had begun flooding the port and rushing the bank, wading in as deep as their red armour allowed them.

The group ducked inside the tender when the enemy's guns broached their escape, blasting pieces of wood from their improvised shield as their bullets bounced on its walls.

Their boat drifted away, the placaters pouring across the beach now making their way towards their own vessels.

The corsair drew her head up, hand grabbing on to her hat. "Better make haste, we're being pursued!"

Thorick heaved himself up, took hold of both paddles, and began swinging his muscular arms in cycles. Their tender gained life as he drove it along with mighty strokes.

As soon as they hit the side of the *Dragon*, they hurried up the ladder.

"Capt'n!" exclaimed Kerok, surprised to see the rest of the rebels in her wake. "Shall I start the engines?"

"Oh yes, Master Kerok, we must be off *immediately*."

The quartermaster left while the corsair rounded on the renegades. "If it wasn't clear before whether I had taken you aboard my ship or not, I doubt the daemon will be guessing still."

"I'm sorry that things didn't go according to plan," Farrah replied. "I didn't want—"

"You can keep your false sorries to yourself," cut in the pirate, "for I am far too certain that these changing circumstances are convenient to you though they mean a death sentence for us."

"I don't invite battles if they can be avoided," she answered. "I tried to warn you, but you chose otherwise, Captain. Had you listened, we would have averted this mess! We're stuck on this ship regardless of whether it's convenient or not."

The corsair bridged the gap between them, her nose almost touching hers as she dominated her. "I could have you thrown off my galleon!"

In a fraction of a second, Slay had drawn himself up in front of Farrah, pushing her behind him. "Calm down, Captain!" he bellowed, holding his other hand between them.

"Who the fuck are you?" the pirate snarled, angling up as she stared him down.

"Slay!" Farrah snapped. At this rate, she was beginning to think that the corsair *would* have them thrown off her ship. She brought the islander's arm away. "Please, stand down."

Slay looked dejected and she felt pity for the man. He probably had no clue what was going on and had been at a loss ever since she had first met him.

He stood back a little, eyes travelling to and fro between her and the captain. But the corsair wasn't taking her glare off him and Farrah remembered what Aslor had told her earlier. Something that had to do with her unforgiving nature.

Seeing the pirate's glower instilled with the promise of imminent threat, she felt the warning signs of escalating violence.

She moved past Slay and approached the corsair, whose murderous expression was still intent on the islander. "Captain, I know that you are angry," she began. "You're angry because we've burst into your life and have brought you only troubles. You've sheltered us, transported us and fought at our side. We know this means that you are risking everything you hold dear: your crew, your reputation and your survival, for us strangers.

"You've made yourself an insurgent now that we've been seen together. That's unfair, and I get how infuriating this situation is for you and your crew. It does not bring me warmth that we were unable to fulfill our part of the bargain today, and I hope we can remain on good terms until we've settled our debt."

The pirate had not budged the entire time, and only balanced her glare on her after she was done talking. "We are now enemies of the daemon, and we can't come back from that. You're right; this situation *is* unfair." She folded her arms and looked away.

The following silence burdened the tension she already felt.

"I will take you to your mountain, and you'll get your god," finally concluded the pirate. "Then, you better kill that swine of a daemon so that this hassle will have been worth something." She unfolded her arms and took a step forward. "And…"

It all happened in a flash and Slay was down on his knees, holding his stomach, the captain standing next to him, her mechanical limb angled before her. "Don't you fucking get in my face again."

She left Farrah staring at her disappearing figure.

Everyone began breathing again, mutely acknowledging they had just avoided a catastrophe. Aslor stooped beside Slay and said, "Are you alright, chap?"

He nodded, feeling sick and blinked up at the renegade leader. "Sorry, Farrah," he mumbled.

"I'm not angry," she replied, looking thoughtful. "Though it would be best not to provoke her again."

Slay inclined his head in agreement. He was not only sorry for looking stupid, but he had also made an enemy out of one of the people he admired the most. That was not only a blow to his ego but a hit to what dreams he was harbouring regarding his future on the *Celestial Dragon*.

All this for a girl, he thought.

Chapter 7

Oros had been right: The lands due west had revealed a dusty desert. As they neared the volcano, the air they breathed became thicker and before long, a stifling veil of ashes had submerged the galleon. Thankfully, the wind sensors kept most of it outside the ship's perimeter.

The captain had grasped the wheel, her expression sullen. She had been shouting orders to the crew in preparation for their arrival. Seeing as the weather created risky flight conditions, all the men and women had taken positions around the vessel, readying themselves for just about anything.

The *Celestial Dragon* was now roaming the sky at lower speed as it neared their destination. The corsair directed it over a large mound sticking out of the sides of the mountain, shrouded in smoke. With the help of Master Kerok, they had analyzed the bearing of the galleon and had decided on a drop point close enough to the top. Though the renegades would have to trek the rest of the way up, the captain had thought this plateau a safer landing area.

She ordered the grappling anchor thrown in the middle of the rocky platform, opting to maintain the ship suspended in flight mode over it rather than setting it down. She had then approached the little group who had spent the better part of the last half-hour getting ready for the excursion.

They had prepared their weapons and found thick bandanas

to nestle around their noses and mouths. Though the wind sensors prevented the mist from passing through their invisible barrier, the air outside the *Dragon* would undoubtedly be suffocating.

The pirate went to Aslor's side, her stare on the volcano. "I can't get you closer to the top; the terrain is too dangerous. Here will be a good enough spot to initiate your ascent." Her voice was neutral though her eyes were sharp.

Aslor followed her gaze, looking nervous.

They didn't know what to expect out there, nor had they even had time to process what they were about to do. It seemed that all they had been doing lately was reacting to events unfolding before them. It was as though their quest had flown of its own accord without need for their input.

The only certainty they had was this: They no longer had the luxury to waste time on doubts. Thinking was an obstacle standing in their way.

Farrah drew up to the captain's side. "Thank you."

"I'll wait for your return," the pirate answered. "You have until nightfall."

"Then you'll leave?"

"Then you'll be dead. No use waiting around."

"We can't give you the money if we're dead," Farrah replied, repressing a frown.

The captain's dismissive gaze hovered from one renegade to the next. "You people are like cockroaches." She strolled off, voice carrying over her shoulder. "You always come back."

The group glanced back at the void beneath the vessel, then, one by one, began their descent.

The air below was asphyxiating. The ashes had enveloped them inside a dense smoke that threatened their vision as they made contact with the mountain's burning ground.

"Which way?" asked Essan, voice muffled by the fabric on her face.

There *had* to be an entrance that led inside the volcano. Humans were bound to have come here before. In conjunction with their gods, they had built the deities' shrines a myriad of eras before.

Thorick beckoned towards a winding path ahead and they followed the big man up a trail of sorts caught between draconian slopes of rocks. Already, the soles of their shoes had begun to burn and rivers of sweat were pouring down their faces.

"Stay together, and walk slowly," said Farrah, coughing as she opened her mouth and the smoking cinders travelled inside it.

Their heads dizzy and eyes stinging, they gathered close to each other, keeping in clear view of the person before them. As endless minutes of this arduous ascent endured, it was hard not to question the feasibility of their enterprise. Or its very nature.

The further they went up, the denser the air was turning, enveloping them callously inside its scorching mist. By the time they reached another plateau, they could barely see anything in front of them.

"Ouch!" Slay yelped, tripping on a crater and hovering on one foot, body tipping over, arms flapping like a bird.

Thorick gripped the man's shoulders, catching him just as he was about to plummet. Recoiling, they both looked down at the islander's feet, their eyes wide with shock, staring at a river of burning magma crawling underneath.

"Oh shit, volcano fluids!" Slay called out, regaining balance with the knight's help before hopping around the narrow opening. "Better be careful where we step."

Glaring now at their feet, they forged on into the thick shroud, their pace further diminished by this news, eyes pouring uncontrollable tears and lungs bursting out of their chests. As the lava craters increasingly became fewer between and larger in size, they began to wonder whether the scorching liquid would make the rest of their ascent impossible.

"*Hack, hack,*" went Essan all the while, coughing like a lifelong pipe smoker, an odd sound coming from her.

Farrah put a hand on the younger woman's back, worrying over her friend. "We need to hurry!" she told to the others. "At this rate, it will be the mist killing us!"

Her own head felt hazy and her vision was fading by the second.

If one of them fell unconscious now, everything would be lost for the rest of the group. The effort required to bring that person back would be enough to steal what little energy they had left. The ship would depart once the night turned up and they'd be on their own.

They had not been prepared for this.

What foolishness to even have come here, grasping at straws. They were risking their lives for what, tales of an old blacksmith? For all she knew, Slay might have been right. Maybe the man *had* been suffering from hallucinations.

As she was about to redirect their group, Farrah looked up and noticed something likened to blazes, flaming through the heavy clouds in the distance.

"This way," she cried out, dragging Essan along with her, invigorated by this sight.

They headed towards the doorway of light and began to see the outline of an opening, hoping for something, anything other than this dreadful smoke.

They came into view of the entrance and stepped inside it, the ashen shroud evaporating as they did. But though their vision had cleared, the heat felt more excruciating than before.

They proceeded inside the abyssal cavern, huddling close together.

Natural granite rocks of cooled molten lava covered both the walls and ground; the grains of sparkling minerals of pink and red, black and gold shimmered at the passage of their feet.

The cave was empty, save for a pearlescent, bronze-coloured pillar towering near the middle, right before a drop that fell into a magma cavity.

Essan gasped. "Is *this*...?"

It was evidently, or rather *inconceivably*, the shrine they had been looking for, layered in mysterious glyphs that Farrah recognized from some of her books.

The language of celestial beings.

"By the gods," muttered Aslor, growing pale.

She walked up to the monument, feet wobbling on the uneven floor of the cavern and gazed up at it in wonder. "Aslor, do you know what these symbols are?" she asked, heart thumping.

The gentleman trod closer and examined the designs. "I'm sorry, Farrah, but I cannot decipher their meaning. I doubt any human ever could. These are not meant for our comprehension."

The others drew nearer, coughing still. "Maybe we need to read them?" said Slay, voice raw. "Reveal the incantation?"

She further eyed the symbols. "I don't know what sounds they're supposed to make."

Farrah lifted her arm and ghosted her fingertips against the smooth-surfaced pillar, feeling the soft indentation of the engraved words. "Perhaps if…"

Instantly, the characters began to glow and the cavern to shake.

Their hands flew to their faces, shielding their eyes from the darting orange light emanating from the glyphs, threatening to blind them.

Dust fell from the walls as a swirling mist started to gather before them. The ashen-coloured cloud grew larger as it took the form of a contained tornado, absorbing rocks, dirt and lava from its surroundings and becoming streaked with layers of reds, greys and blacks.

"Farrah!" yelled Essan over the ruckus, looking panicked.

They clung to the ground as their bodies slid along its rough floor, the cyclone sucking them in.

"Hold on!" she cried out, fingers digging into the granite.

The twister raged and bellowed for a moment more before it withdrew its power and resolved in on itself, the subsiding fumes revealing the figure of a tall creature.

They stared wide-eyed at the god Ekhon, the Baron of Fire, his bascinet lowered as he surveilled them.

The deity was carved out of charcoal-coloured basalt rock. His naked feet and hands were bulging with rippling, polished muscles shimmering with the crystals of his mineral skin, and printed red glyphs covered his oversized stone body.

A blackened helmet hid his face, revealing gleaming slits where his eyes were, his fiery hair blazing under the helm of the bascinet. He wore a simple emblazoned loincloth around his groin area, forever engulfed in eternal flares, and two enormous cleavers encroached on his back.

None of them had expected this sight. None had thought this possible. Except for Farrah.

"*Who has stepped upon my domain?*" inquired a booming voice, echoing from the cindery-coloured helmet.

She went forward.

Though her body had moved, this unfathomable apparition had numbed her mind and Farrah felt as if she was going through the motions of a lucid dream. "We have come seeking aid in these times of need, Lord Ekhon. We are those who would wage war against chaos and bring justice to the people of these lands," she declared, her voice clear and eyes large.

The blazing figure contemplated her, immobile in his strapping presence. "*You are not the first to seek out my help. Why give it to you when I refused the last one who came?*"

She lifted a look of strain on him. "Who came to you before, Lord?" she asked, already knowing the answer.

"*A man who longs for power for himself and destruction for the rest.*"

"Then surely you speak of Daromas, the daemon," she replied, fingers closing in a fist. "He has acquired such theurgy and now governs Iscar, shaping it into a state of ruin!"

A shallow sort of sound resembling that of a toned-down growl reverberated through the helmet. "*In this dwelling of mine, though I am far from the dealings of humans and their affairs, I have felt the man's hatred and darkened soul,*" he said. "*Which of my siblings has given hand to such a vile creature?*"

"Daromas is Israthel's wielder, Bearer of the Night," answered

Farrah passionately. "His seven commandants each wield others such as he."

This time, a low rumble echoed underneath the helmet. "*Corrupt devils of the underworld. Those who would see the ruins of this plane rather than its flourishing.*"

"Won't you help us?" Slay blurted out. "You can't allow this to go on. People are dying!"

The renegades turned to him. Ekhon drew a short humph. "*I am better left alone, far from the troubles of those who would depart from a presence of contemplation,*" the god answered in his cavernous voice. "*Though I am not on par with those of whom you speak of, my mind is best kept apart from such malicious intentions.*"

"We cannot do this on our own," implored Farrah. "You refused Daromas's plea because it threatened your ideals. Now, it is our way of life, our very existence, that is being threatened. We desperately need your help, Lord!"

Ekhon surveilled her for a while and it felt as though time had stopped and he was seeing through her.

Eyes burning, the deity finally said, "*I have seen into your souls and have led you to this place. Yours are of purity and truth. I also know of your battles and pain. Through you, I see the havoc that is taking seed inside these lands and it is true.... I cannot allow such destruction to come to this realm.*"

"Then, you *will* help us?" she replied, chest beating faster than ever before.

The god drew his hands behind his back and grabbed his cleaver swords, retrieving them one after the other. "*Your cause is true, but it will take more than that to defeat the behemoths of your plane. Only those who are strong enough may yet wield the power of theurgy. I will provide you with my strength...*" He lowered his arms, revealing weapons as big as Slay. "*... if you can defeat me.*"

He charged at them, swooping his cleavers of doom their way. Farrah dodged to the side and the sharpened metal fell against the ground, smashing it to smithereens, the floor receding underneath.

"Fuck!" yelped Slay, taking hold of his two axes.

Everyone scattered around the cavern, the cleavers slashing towards their flailing limbs.

She drew away from the tremendous blazing weapons and fired at the god. But the bullets ricocheted against Ekhon's basalt skin, a few of them grazing him like the superficial nicks on a marble statue that had withstood the test of time.

Aslor had fled to the back, pistols in hand, aiming at the deity and receiving similar results as Farrah had. Thorick had retrieved the enormous hammer from his back and was now lumbering towards the Baron of Fire.

One of the cleavers fell against the metal of his weapon. The knight blocked him, the blade's flames darting close to his face while the hammer captured the shock of the blow. The big man, usually so impressive in size, appeared tiny next to the deity.

Slay flew to Ekhon's other side and began to dance around the sword swinging to catch him, swivelling and throwing himself out of the way before jumping back on his feet. Unlike Thorick, there was no way he could parry Ekhon's cleavers with the weapons he owned and all he could do was lunge away from his attacks.

Slay rolled on the floor before getting up again and cutting the leg of the deity but to no avail. He had given Ekhon no more than a scratch. He jerked away as the tip of the cleaver collided where he stood.

Essan was scurrying around the god, casting rebounding fingers knives against his hardened skin while Farrah discharged her guns against the helmet that cloaked the Baron of Fire's face. Though the deity had reared his head backwards when she had, as before, the bullets had sprung away.

Her features covered by her shozoku mask, Essan made her move. She hopped and climbed aboard the god's back. Ignoring the heat of his burning membrane, she bounced towards his neck and slashed at his throat with her kunai knife. But the flesh was just as hard and her assault did nothing to damage him.

At once, Ekhon planted one of his cleavers inside the ground and brought a hulking fist over his shoulder. Essan jumped right off, ducked the grasping giant's clutches, and spun away from him. She rolled on the floor, her clothes burning where they had made contact with the god.

Using this as a distraction, Thorick wheeled around, avoided the blade that was coming for him and smashed his weapon against Ekhon's chest.

The blow shifted the god's weight and he slumped over. But the impact lasted only a second.

Ekhon grabbed Thorick by the head and yanked him up in one fell swoop. He then lifted his other hand and paraded his cleaver towards the big man's imprisoned form. The knight heaved in time to avoid the charge, legs swinging upwards.

Farrah abandoned her handguns and grasped her kukri swords. Running over, she sliced her blades against the god's abdomen, Slay joining in on her assault, both of their attacks yielding no results.

The Baron of Fire peered down at them and then threw Thorick away. The knight went bouncing against the floor while the deity stooped to catch the islander the same way he had done Thorick.

"By the gods, he's a beast!" Slay yelled, dodging away.

"His skin is too thick!" added Essan, now back on her feet.

They had dispersed around the god, eyeing each of his massive movements, wary of coming near him.

"We don't have the means to take this thing down!" Slay continued, and then tumbled out of the way, avoiding the next burst of cleaver swinging towards him.

Farrah retreated out of arm's reach, trying to figure how to get near the god and inflict a wound of some sort. "Everyone has a weakness," she muttered to herself frantically.

Basalt rock and fire moulded the Baron of Fire's body, all except for his helmet.

Metal.

"Metal can be pierced," she said out loud.

The god had moved his head back when she had shot at it.

Perhaps a different membrane made up whatever stood underneath the bascinet. Why even own a helmet when one's skin was as hard as onyx?

Occupied as Ekhon was with Slay, Farrah was free to sprint towards Thorick. The knight was retrieving his hammer from the ground, looking dazed.

"Thorick," she bellowed. "Can you take out his helmet?"

He turned an observant eye on the deity. His glare was serious, but he nonetheless said *yes* with his head.

"We'll distract him." She ran up to Aslor while Thorick readied himself.

The gentleman was reloading his pistols, his fumbling fingers making the task harder than it was. "Aslor! Thorick will remove Ekhon's helmet; we must focus our fire on his face as soon as he does!"

Aslor nodded, trying to appear more courageous than he probably felt. Farrah reloaded her guns as well, eyes following the deity's movement.

The islander seemed to be getting further out of breath as he avoided each of the god's attacks. "Slay!" she yelled. "We have to remove his helm!"

Slay glanced at her before quickly twisting back towards the weapon coming his way. "You," he huffed out, "got a plan?"

She did not. "Thorick?" she shouted, scurrying back as the swirling cleaver edged near her.

Thorick was contemplating the scene. He dropped his hammer before taking a step back, analyzing his momentum. He then broke into a stomp, and his massive frame stampeded towards the god like an angry bull.

He clasped his arms around his waist, back hunching as he rammed his shoulder against Ekhon's rear end.

The deity was propelled off balance and came tumbling forward on the palms of his hands.

"Wow, that's effective," gaped the islander.

"The helmet, Slay!"

"Right," he said and squatted before the god. He took the bascinet in both hands and began to pull on it with all his might.

Thorick was pushing his weight down on Ekhon's back, grappling him by the waist, face contorted by the effort.

The deity moved up a little and attempted to grab Slay. The god's hand tightened around him, fingers squishing his bones inside their crushing grasp.

He began to yell as the pressure intensified.

Farrah appeared next to him, swords striking the arm that was holding him.

"Fuck this shit!" He clutched one of his axes in both hands and drew it up.

He brought the weapon down on Ekhon's head, its blade creating a tiny dent in the metal. He let out a cry and began hacking the god's bascinet, his hatchet soon finding its way through and into the skull, the strain against his lungs intensifying all the while.

"Argh!" he roared as he pummeled on with brutal precision and a certain hint of despair until molten lava, red and scalding, poured out of the gaping wound.

The blood of a deity of fire.

He winced as specks of lava splashed on his hands and arms, burning his skin. But he went on and on, his axe viciously burrowing inside the gash long after the god's fingers had let go of him and released his bones.

"Slay!" said a voice, breaking his trance.

He stopped all movement and stared back at the others, exhaustion smearing his face. "I think we got him," he mumbled, the fumes exuding from the god's opened scalp tickling his nose.

Farrah was by his side, gazing at the vanishing deity. The figure was reverting into the smoke that had brought it along and was soon no longer anywhere to be seen.

"I think so," she muttered, her eyes round.

When Ekhon had all but disappeared, they banded together and surveilled their surroundings, searching for the vanquished god.

Farrah heard a sound that resembled a crackling fire pit and sought its source.

The mist was rising.

The tornado was taking shape, the lava joining its tempest as it uncovered once again the form of a god.

Less than a few seconds later, the Baron of Fire was standing in front of them, renewed and whole as if their battle hadn't taken place.

"No way!" gasped Slay.

They drew their weapons, stepping back as realization set in.

They had failed.

"*Enough,*" uttered the deep voice. Wary, they kept their weapons in position. "*You have won. I can see that you may yet hold the means to defeat the dark ones. I will lend you my help and restore balance.*"

Farrah dropped her lashes and lowered her head. Her mind was spinning as it processed what they had done. The miracle of this accomplishment seemed so improbable that she could only accept it for what it was.

The theurgy of the gods.

"Wait. How did you heal so fast?" asked Slay as he put his hatchets away.

"*This is not my true form,*" explained Ekhon. "*It is the image that you have defeated, not my real self. Close to my shrine, I can send as many of these projections as wanted.*"

"And when you are not near your monument thingy?" he went on, pointing at the altar.

"*My human will be the one conjuring the projection as needed.*"

Slay nodded in awe. "That's fucking awesome."

"*And it is you who shall be my wielder.*"

His mouth fell, his eyes growing as large as their sockets. "I'm sorry, what?" The others also gaped at him, all their faces turning his way.

"*You defeated me. The one with the bearing to bend my will was to receive my power.*"

Slay looked as though a boulder had hit him. He glanced around at Farrah. "I don't know how to wield a god; it's you who should have him!"

She shook her head, her stare strong. "He has chosen you. It is how it needs to be."

He tossed his hands aloft and blinked at the others, seeking their support. Thorick was nodding, nudging him to accept this great honour. The other renegades wore expressions that were as blank as his. "You can't be serious!"

"*Will you accept me?*" cut in the Baron of Fire, voice booming through the cave.

Seeing as no one was speaking, all he could do was return his gaze to the deity. In a daze, he stepped up to him and peered at the tall figure. "I guess it's you and me, buddy," he said, a skittish smile curling on his lips.

"*Then it shall be.*"

At once, Ekhon turned to smoke, his body dispersing into a squall before darting towards Slay's forearm. Against his will, his hand lifted up and the hurricane began to surround the arm as it entered the wall of his skin, the mist vanishing into his palm as its essence was sucked inside and merged with him.

He fell to his knees, an intense pressure clamping him down as the shroud broke into his skin, feeling its burn as though it were tearing his arm apart.

And then, Ekhon was gone, his existence now linked to Slay's.

Expressions concerned, the others surrounded his side.

His eyes caught sight of his hand. The flesh appeared whole and unharmed. No trace of the god was left but for a tattoo that lined the skin inside his palm. It was a rugged portrait of Ekhon's helmet. Its sharpened strokes had drawn a compact sketch of the Baron of Fire's head and its orange colour resembled a burn.

Though Ekhon wasn't there anymore, the deity's presence pulsed inside of Slay and he felt somehow different, his body no longer only his now that he shared it with another.

Aslor patted him on the shoulder. "Congratulations, lad. We've got ourselves a god!" he clamoured. The trader looked beside himself as though he couldn't believe what had happened but had no choice but to accept it for what it was.

Slay scanned around for Farrah. Her expression was impossible to read. "I'm sorry," he said. Surely, the leader of the renegades had not expected *him* to be the first chosen wielder of a god.

Her eyes softened. "Thanks to you, we now walk alongside a god. Whatever are you sorry for?" And the slightest smile she now wore on her bewitching lips warmed him.

"It was your idea to get the helmet off. It's you who should have had the honour of having him."

Farrah shook her head "There will be others. I couldn't have hoped for a better outcome today."

Slay answered her words with a smile of his own. It soon vanished and a frightened expression took hold of his features. "How are my eyes?" he asked, turning white.

Chin resting on her fist, Essan lowered her face and analyzed his. "Seem normal to me."

He drew a sigh of relief. "Thank the gods."

"Don't thank them so fast," replied Aslor. "If what they say is true, Ekhon's already begun the process of life absorption. *Your* life."

Slay shuddered and envisioned the image of a leech sucking on his soul. "You know, mate. You could have kept that one to yourself."

Aslor readjusted his glasses. "Apologies," he mumbled.

"Do you feel any different?" asked Essan, eyes widened as though she expected him to turn into a sunken-eyed monster anytime.

He shrugged. "Not really."

Farrah looked pensive. "The process is incremental; it won't happen in a day."

Their stares darkened with the notion of their future selves, half-human, half-corpse.

After a while, they rose to their feet and loitered around the silent cave.

"Guys!" Essan suddenly. "We defeated a god!"

They grinned and Slay clapped his hand against hers. It was an odd moment for them all. Unimaginable.

"With the assistance of a deity, we now stand better chances of recruiting others," added Farrah. "I know now that our path is right."

Aslor cleared his voice and drew his fingers up to his top hat, retrieving it. "Farrah, I must confess something…" The man looked dishevelled, eyes cast on the ground. "I didn't believe."

She smiled and said, "You had every reason not to."

"I, uh," he went on, "I never actually thought that we would confront the daemon. But now that we've acquired a god, I guess…" His voice trailed off.

Their goose chase had yielded a golden egg. What had first appeared improbable had become very much real.

Now that they had acquired a god, they no longer had a choice. It was their charge to rid Iscar of Daromas and his commandants. There was no more coming back from this fate.

"Aslor, I'm not forcing you to go on if you don't want to," Farrah said.

He put his hat back on his head and drew on a semi-insulted look. "Please. I said no such thing."

Essan tapped him on his arm. "Don't worry, Aslor. I think we all weren't sure what we were getting ourselves into."

Slay drooped his shoulders. "Does that mean that we're… gonna meet with the daemon again at some point?"

Essan went to him and repeated the same gesture on his arm though her own expression resembled denial. "There, there."

His eyes became very focused on some distant non-existent object.

"Perhaps we ought to be getting back," said Aslor. "We shouldn't make Captain Sadahl wait."

“Let’s hope the ship is still out there,” Farrah replied, looking somehow concerned it wouldn’t be.

They exited the cave and found themselves once again outside the volcano. All traces of smoke had evaporated. It appeared that when they had acquired the theurgy of the mountain’s god, it had lifted the deep magic that kept the volcano enshrouded in its mystical clouds.

They looked up vehemently at the giant vessel approaching them, its ladder wriggling in their direction.

“Our comrades have found us,” Aslor told Farrah, one hand held over his spectacles, staring at the galleon.

Essan grabbed the ladder first, soon followed by the others.

Slay waited around for Farrah while the others went up. “Do you think that was the full extent of Ekhon’s strength?” he asked her. “It seems rather improbable that we’ve defeated a god, doesn’t it?”

Her expression looked thoughtful. “Each deity owns a certain set of abilities, unique powers they can unleash once or twice per conjuring alongside other recurring ones.”

“Unique powers?”

“It’s a powerful attack that requires a lot of energy to muster. That’s why it’s usually seen once in combat—if at all. Every god has one. Take Shalowhith, for example. Do you recall when he first appeared?”

He shivered at the thought. “I couldn’t move anymore.”

“We were caught under his spell. This was his *unique* attack: the ability to stop an entire army in one glance for a short moment, sparing friends and focusing on foes. This was Shalowhith’s *Death Gaze* attack.”

“That’s why all bullets and people were frozen from further motion.”

She acquiesced with her head. “Yes. Then, you also saw Shalowhith’s other ability, the strands that shot out of his fingers? That’s a recurring power, the *Puppet Web* assault. He can use it as often as he likes though these attacks consume more energy compared to a normal one.

"His *Puppet Web* assault is similar to that of a spider's web that traps the people he seeks to capture inside its filaments." Farrah grabbed the ladder with one hand, Thorick disappearing in front of her. "Ekhon didn't do any of those. He only used normal attacks." She pondered this for a second. "I don't believe he wanted to kill us. I think he gave us a fair fight to judge whether we were strong enough." She started up the ladder.

"And we won," said Slay after her.

She stopped and looked back. "He *let* us win."

The captain and her quartermaster greeted Farrah when she clambered aboard.

"The mist evaporated not long ago," the corsair explained. "I believed this meant you had done something good, so we came looking for you." She had her usual tone of voice, both dismissive and self-assured at the same time.

Farrah stepped aside to let Slay climb aboard the galleon. "We did," she confirmed, wondering what the pirate was thinking.

After a few gasps, the crew members that surrounded them began muttering to one another. The captain, however, had not so much as stirred. "You obtained your god then?" she asked, her tone implying nothing more than faint interest.

Farrah turned to Slay. He raised his palm up and showed her the fresh mark upon its skin.

At this, the gossip surrounding them took a renewed fervour.

The pirate's eyes narrowed. "*You* got him?"

"I said it should have been Farrah," the islander replied, hand drawing to the back of his head. "But he wanted it to be me," he finished in a mumble.

"Slay defeated the god in battle. He deserved it," Farrah said in a strong voice.

The captain looked as though she was tiring of them. She was making that face she did whenever she was trying to appear polite but really thought they were wasting her time. "I see."

Maybe she didn't believe them.

"I couldn't have done it without you guys," continued Slay, eyes now gazing at her.

The pirate glanced at them both. "How moving," she replied, simpering something resembling a mocking smile. "And how do you summon this god?"

Slay opened his mouth and closed it again, his expression now blank. "Uh, well, I dunno."

"How useful."

"We'll figure it out," Farrah answered, unflinching.

"Of course you will. But first, you can figure out your next destination, can't you?" The corsair veered around and headed towards the upper deck. Farrah took it as a sign that she wanted them to follow.

"We were thinking of going to the research citadel in Mondos," she began, trotting to keep up with the woman's long strides. "Perhaps we'll be able to find useful information there. Unless," she added, "you happen to know the location of another god?"

The captain remained silent as she went up the stairs and leaned against the control board of her galleon, Kerok taking position by her side. "Not really," she replied, mouth looping upside down.

"Not really as in, you'll tell me in exchange for money?" she asked, squinting.

The corsair grinned her charming side smile. "Every time I tell you things, I get stuck another day with you people."

Farrah put her hands on her hips. "Then, you *do* know something?"

The pirate shrugged. "The citadel in Mondos is a good plan," she answered, gaze scanning the skyline.

Farrah wanted to press her on that but felt that this would be pushing her luck.

"Capt'n!" boomed a voice beside them.

They both veered towards quartermaster Kerok.

"What's wrong?"

"A ship is coming towards us." He pointed at the radar, eyes widened at the monitor.

The corsair squinted into the distance and hurried to the side, clutching a telescope in her hand. She then took the stairs down two at a time, her expression alarmed. Kerok followed her and when she offered him the device and he glimpsed inside it, they shared a darkened look between one another, and these stares meant trouble.

"Prepare the cannons, Master Kerok. I reckon we will be having a fight."

The quartermaster shouted orders and the men and women of the crew began activating themselves.

"Do you know this ship?" inquired Aslor.

"Oh yes," the captain answered sombrely. "It bears the colours of Commandant Trent, general of the Sky Navy."

CHAPTER 8

Feras had retreated behind the *Celestial Dragon's* controls. Though Trent's ship was yet in the distance, his galleon was gliding on full speed and they would have to pick up the pace if they hoped to outrun him.

Commandant Trent had been elected sheriff of the skies before Daromas had seized Iscar. His *Lethal Vulture* was possibly the only vessel that had the means to engage the *Celestial Dragon* on par. It was the daemon's finest warship and most impressive combat machine.

Trent's *Vulture* had never crossed paths before with Feras's *Dragon*. Their mutual avoidance had been forged by a silent agreement to leave each other alone, out of convenience for the both of them.

After her father's death, Feras had staved off any sort of dealings with Daromas and his lawful guardians. It had meant keeping herself and her crew safe.

Moreover, she had been awarded special standing at docks throughout Iscar due to her *good* behaviour and station as a corsair. As such, upon her passage, the placaters minded their own business and she repaid them with similar favour.

This was the status awarded to those with credible names in the pirating industry; that was the deal struck with Daromas.

It was the daemon's way of putting them on a leash by giving them scraps, all the while maintaining his position of master. It was a false pretence at freedom, and that had been good enough for her.

Not that she hadn't dreamt of killing Trent.

She had been there when Corsak had been executed, had seen the commandant stick his sword down her father's throat. She had narrowly escaped with her life back then and had vowed to kill him.

Of course, when that time came, it meant that she would be ready to die.

No one could defeat a commandant. It could not be done.

Considering the pace of the fast-approaching *Lethal Vulture*, she thought that perhaps this moment would arrive sooner than she had anticipated.

Feras's stomach tightened as a result of the disparate feelings this created in her—this desire to kill Trent and the need to protect her crew against the monster that he was. She knew which one she had to prioritize over the other.

She barked her orders and the *Celestial Dragon* started gaining speed.

Known as the *ship killer*, the *Lethal Vulture's* membrane resembled that of a stronghold. This flying fortress also harboured an army of its own and was believed to be impregnable. If *that* wasn't enough, Trent carried alongside him his most devastating weapon—the Wind Bender, Menthlos.

Feras had never seen this god with her eyes, but she had heard tales from countless others.

He was a creature of the sky, a soaring kraken. His head resembled that of a cobra, his rear end erupting in dozens of killer tentacles, any one of them powerful enough to annihilate the main mast of a ship. No one knew how that thing even stayed in midair, for he had no wings to show. Some said and believed that this was part of his unique set of skills.

They could not allow Trent to invoke Menthlos. The *Celestial Dragon* could survive some attacks, but Feras did not know how her galleon would fare against this mythological creature. She wished she would never have to bear witness to such a fate.

She glared from the corner of her eye at the renegades gathering around her. They were peering at the horizon, calculating the closing distance between Trent and them. Though the gallon was gaining pace, the *Vulture* was darting ever nearer.

In this instant, she felt like blaming them. If they went down, it would be their fault.

In the last few days, she had made a conscious decision to help them. Not because it would bring her fortune but rather because she had been faced with a choice.

These people had tried to assassinate Daromas.

When she had first met with them, she had been… afraid. They were bringing unparalleled trouble, and she needed them off her ship.

To the residents of Iscar, the daemon's killers were like the plague. When one hears murmurs of this infectious disease, they feel pity for those afflicted by it.

When one finds themselves face to face with it, however, the urge to flee is as urgent as one's arse catching fire.

And yet, when she had been faced with this choice, she had taken them aboard.

Why? Because their little act had made a difference. It had created something and the repercussions of their manoeuvre were still to unfold even though most of Iscar's citizens hadn't figured that out yet.

They had borne witness to people who yet had the courage to refuse their way of life, and that was bound to awaken something in them.

By showing the rebels' faces on repeat over the screens ever since, Daromas had done one thing: He had made them *visible*. Being visible meant that some would chase after them. Others would hate them like the plague.

They would become a symbol for the rest.

She'd really had only one choice. She could not, would not, be remembered as the person who had led the new emblems of hope to their deaths.

By the gods, who wanted to be the shithole that had sided with Daromas instead of the heroes who had defied him? They had doomed her the second they had set foot on her galleon even though they were fucking her over.

And now, she was considering that perhaps these people were something more than she had realized at first. They had acquired the help of a *deity*, which was already absurd.

It also was a complete game changer.

Maybe these renegades had it in them to move things.

Well, nothing was going to change if Trent got to them. It was now in *her* hands to alter this game.

"Ready the cannons!" she shouted, and the crew busied themselves on the gun deck below.

The trader startled. "We're going to fight them?"

"Oh no, Mister Aslor, we are running away. But that doesn't mean we won't get into a fight."

The leader of the renegades stepped up to her, looking alarmed. "Can we beat him?"

Feras briefly glanced her way. "There is only one ship I'd rather not cross paths with and it's on our tail. Care to ask that god of yours for help?" she added, raising an ironic expression.

The woman twisted to that brawler blond man as though struck by this prospect. She shortened the distance between them and took his hand in hers, eyes watching the tattoo on it as though she could have awakened its power with the strength of her stare. "Slay, do you have any feeling inside of you, *anything* that could make you summon Ekhon?"

His shoulders sagged. "I'm sorry, Farrah. I really don't know…."

The woman squinted in thought. Feras rolled her own eyes as she darted them toward the horizon.

The *Vulture* was almost in reach of their cannons. They were losing the race, and the *Dragon* had only just now gained full speed. The enemy was encroaching on them, and there were no more doubts in her mind that a battle would take place in less than a few minutes.

"We don't have time for that," Feras told the man. "You're going to have to figure it out on your own, *chump*."

The renegade leader worried a finger to her forehead. "I've seen it described as a parallel to contemplation, where one must be in a state of stillness and focus on their inner god to conjure them forth. Only when you've given up control of your mind can you reveal his light, and sustaining his presence will require as much dedication. Your attention cannot sway or else you'll risk losing him."

That islander guy was now scratching his beard, and it was obvious to her they had lost him the moment Farrah had mentioned the concept of *contemplation*, which had been many words ago.

"I ain't known for being the best when it comes to concentration and stuff like that," the man replied, tongue pulling on a half grimace.

"You have to try," the woman cut him off. "Come on!" And she dragged him by the arm.

Feras glared at them while Farrah yanked Slay into a corner behind her and sat him on the floor, guiding him through murmured advice. She raised her eyes to the heavens for the second time today.

By the gods, these people are useless.

"Capt'n, they've readied their cannons. They're about to open fire!" shouted Kerok, driving her attention back.

"For fuck's sake," she whispered, before making her voice louder. "Prepare the guns, I'm turning the ship! We'll open on them first!"

"Ready the cannons!" yelled Kerok into the intercom system.

Feras steadied herself. Things would soon get hectic, and a single mistake could mean their loss.

"They're almost on us," bellowed the quartermaster as he surveyed the monitors. "They'll enter our firing range in less than ten seconds, Capt'n!"

"Hard to starboard!" shouted Feras through the intercom as she pulled on the helm of the ship and the *Celestial Dragon* made an abrupt turn before coming up perpendicularly with the *Vulture's* nose. Everyone had taken hold of something and the moment they regained balance, she yelled, "Fire!"

Their weapons blasted away.

The *Lethal Vulture* had not wasted a kerosene-infused breath on their manoeuvre. Already, it was countering their move with their own and had begun swerving around, taking parallel position by their side.

Their cannonballs detonated against the hardened shell of the flying fortress, doing close to nothing to impact its advance. And it would now be the enemy's turn to show them what their guns were made off.

"Repeat fire!" shouted Kerok. The crew recharged the cannons below as the *Vulture* completed its course and prepared its riposte.

The burst was deafening. The *Lethal Vulture* had mounted rows of guns, all firing as one towards the *Dragon*, shaking the ship to its core.

Most of the projectiles exploded against the reinforced walls of the galleon, fashioned out of some of the strongest metal in Iscar. Yet, Feras knew they could not withstand many hits such as this one without taking serious damage.

"We must blow out one of their propellers!" she told Kerok. "We need them to lose speed, it might be our only chance at survival!"

"Right, Capt'n! The port rear rocket propeller is our best bet. Anything else will be too small a target or too far off," he indicated.

Feras leaned to the side of the galleon and stared at the tail end of the *Vulture*. "Take the wheel, Kerok," she ordered. "You'll have to position the ship at an angle as soon as we're ready to fire." She darted off without another word.

Feras glimpsed at the renegades huddled nearby, the man with the blond beard trying hard to keep his eyes shut in concentration.

She knew by now not to expect divine help any time soon.

She raced the length of the vessel and headed down the stairs that led to the gun deck. She jumped over the last few steps and ran to the end of the room, speeding past crew members actively filling up the rows of cannons.

A resounding explosion detonated nearby, and it threw her off balance. She landed on her shoulder, her temples throbbing and ears sizzling from the blast. She shook her head once and wobbled back to her feet.

"Capt'n, parts o' the hull be startin' to split 'cause o' them hits," yelled Dahara over the ruckus, appearing beside her. "Next time, it be right through 'em wall whar we be standin'!"

Feras nodded her understanding and sped onwards and past the last few cannons. She yanked a crew member aside, taking position behind the gun in his stead, and peered through the outside opening.

The *Vulture* was not as close as she had hoped. She could easily make out its gigantic rocket propellers, yet feared their distantness. At the rate of the enemy fire they were currently under, she knew she wouldn't get many opportunities to retaliate before the *Dragon* suffered extensive damage.

She lowered herself and adjusted her massive weapon to the desired angle. Kerok's manoeuvre came no more than a few seconds later.

Her ship sloped down somewhat, offering a clear view of the *Vulture's* propellers. She pulled the mechanism and the huge projectile sprinted off.

She saw the round shot make its way towards the enemy vessel and collide little less than twenty feet above where she had intended.

"By the fucking gods," she muttered to herself as she recharged the cannon.

She was propelled sideways when the wall to her right imploded. Smoke and pieces of wood catapulted in its wake and Feras only had time to lift her arms in front of her before the debris came soaring in around her. Cries of pain resounded as the explosion blew some of the pirates away.

Feras hoisted herself up on shaking elbows as dust settled in around her, coughed a few times and levelled her stare on the scene. Though most of the crew appeared well enough, she feared the damage her galleon had suffered.

She took a deep breath and cast her eyes through the outside opening that painted the not-too distant form of the *Vulture*. She slouched forward, gaze aligning with her target and felt her surroundings quieten as she nudged the nose of the weapon down.

She fired it.

Feras witnessed the projectile galloping away, and swore loudly as it detonated above her intended target.

She rushed to ready the cannon again, bracing herself for the next round of enemy blasts, which would inevitably arrive about now.

She peered up and noted how the *Vulture's* advance had somewhat lost composure. Feras glared at the propeller and saw smoke arising from it.

Though she had not destroyed it, it had apparently suffered certain damage.

That would have to do.

Feras hopped up when she heard shouts coming from the outside. The *Vulture's* cannons had discharged again and a definite explosion resounded as the hole nearby took a bigger shape.

She dropped to the ground as other pieces of wood and metal created a fusillade of projectiles that would have meant numerous stitches had she not moved.

Her head was surrendered to a deafening fanfare of confusion and mayhem. Her mind foggy and vision blurred; she looked up. Blots of blood were coming out of her left arm where debris had torn her skin open.

So much for those avoided stitches.

Feras straightened herself. Ignoring the cries of those around her, she bustled back up the stairs towards the main deck on unstable legs.

The uppermost part of the galleon was holding firm. Pirates were scrambling all around, quenching fires or taking some sort of action that would help them out of this situation. Further ahead, Kerok was mouthing words she could not hear.

She headed in his direction, all the while shoving aside panicked crew members standing in her way.

"We're gaining speed!" he yelled when she had drawn close enough.

Feras leaned over the bulwarks. The *Vulture* was losing pace, but they were still well in range of its cannons and the distance they had secured was too meagre for her taste. She noticed a man standing on its bridge, one she would have recognized anywhere.

Commandant Trent.

Her jaw tightened and she ran back to the wheelhouse. Kerok stepped aside to let her resume her position behind the helm. "Time to reach the heavens," she said. "We've damaged one of their propellers; they'll be having a hard time gaining altitude on us."

Kerok angled the wings and fired up their propellers. At once, the *Dragon* lifted its nose, heading towards the vault of the sky. The *Vulture* attempted to copy their movement, but it was losing speed.

Their cannons fired again, and the *Dragon* shook all over.

"Damages?" she shouted.

"They hit them lower parts o' the hull. The metal be sustainin' the damage and be holdin' strong, Capt'n!" answered Dahara's voice from somewhere below.

"We'll lose them in the clouds," she muttered.

The *Vulture* was readying itself for another burst of fire, unwilling to let its prey slip away. It blasted towards the *Dragon* again, but this time, the projectiles went under the galleon.

"We've got them!" she shouted, smiling ferociously.

The *Celestial Dragon* entered the firmament and rose ever higher. It left the *Lethal Vulture* in its wake, smoke erupting from its rear end though the rest of its shell stood otherwise intact.

Some time later, the *Vulture* had turned into a distant frame on the horizon. The fog had engulfed them, soon shielding their enemy from view.

Feras had left the wheelhouse to Kerok and went to the back of the galleon, eyes scanning the skyline, expression yet woven into worry.

Sure enough, the group of renegades had come to her side the moment she had.

"We've lost them?" asked that blonde girl who dressed like a ninja.

"Not yet," she replied. "They're still on our radar, which means that we're on theirs. Master Kerok will push the ship at full speed until they've vanished from view. He'll then change our coordinates."

"Does that mean that we're safe or…?" said that brawler guy.

"For now. Damaging their propeller will slow them only for a while. They'll fix it and we can bet that they'll be back for us when they do." She put her hands on her hips. "Next time, I'm not sure we'll make it." She then lowered her eyes and whispered to herself. "I don't get it."

"Beg your pardon?" inquired Aslor.

"Trent was there, I saw him on the bridge. He could have conjured Menthlos. Had he done so, we would have been finished."

"Who's Menthlos?" asked the islander and for the life of her, Feras could not fathom how an all-powerful god could have selected this man as his preferred wielder, an exploit whose veracity she now doubted but whose likely fabrication furthered these people's needs.

It was their leader who answered. "The Wind Bender," she explained, looking as lost in thoughts as Feras felt.

"My guess," she went on, "is that he wants to capture us. Menthlos doesn't leave survivors behind."

The islander gazed away. "At least we're alive."

She glowered at the man. "No thanks to you. How much time do you reckon it's going to take Trent to track and tear us down?"

The guy looked taken aback, but kept mute. If anything, his silence made her appreciate him for the first time.

"Is there somewhere safe we could go to?" asked ninja girl, eyes peeking up at her.

She thought over it for a while. "We can't go where there are placaters," she replied. "At least, not in the state the ship's in."

Feras was debating with herself. She *did* know a place, but didn't want to bring these people there.

She dropped her arms to her sides. "There is somewhere. It's deserted and less than two days away. It'll give us the opportunity to do some repairs on the galleon and disappear from Trent's radar."

"Where is it?" asked the renegade leader, frowning.

She smirked. "Our hideout."

The corsair informed Kerok of their destination and consulted with the ship's boatswain, the one in charge of the galleon's maintenance, an older fellow named Danguer. It had been difficult for him to appraise the vessel's condition while in midair, but he had nonetheless declared the *Dragon* fly-worthy. Still, he had supported the captain's urge to conduct repairs as soon as possible.

Slay was staring overboard, feeling gloomy, his chin and elbows resting on the handrail. They were making their way past infinite sequences of clouds, the galleon's wind sensors safeguarding them against the outside weather.

"You look like you're in a mood," said Aslor, propping himself up beside him.

Slay glanced up at the trader. The man's eyes were peering at him over his round spectacles. "Yeah, it's just… it would've been kinda awesome if I'd summoned Ekhon," he muttered. "I don't get it. I have this incredible power inside of me and I don't know how to use it." He waved at the sky. "I mean, we almost got killed! What's the point of having a god on your side if you can't even use him?"

The gentleman patted his forearm. "Patience, chap. You think Daromas and his goons learned how to harness their abilities in one day? No, it's not meant to be easy, but you'll get there. You just need more time, that's all."

He smiled without much joy. "Yeah, patience… not really my strong suit."

Aslor chuckled. "There's a first for everything, lad."

"I guess." He looked around and noticed Farrah a short way off, Thorick beside her, staring off into the sky just as he had been.

He never got tired of gazing at her. She, on the other hand, always seemed cloistered inside her own closeted world. He wished he could delve into her head and get to know her better.

Earlier, when he had tried to conjure Ekhon, Slay had superbly failed at the task. As they had sat there, millions of thoughts had burst through his mind. Farrah had been edging near him, and already that had been enough to hinder his concentration, her touch too warm and face too distracting.

He'd heard some shouting and had figured that the vessel was under enemy fire. So, he'd started thinking how absurd it was that they were sitting on the ground, doing nothing, while the pirates were fighting for their lives.

Then, his hand had throbbed somewhat, but that was all there had been. No Ekhon, no god to save them. He'd even began to wonder whether this whole deity business had been a crazy invention of his mind.

Eventually, the cannon bursts had come to a stop and they had escaped the battlefield. Though relieved by this outcome, Slay had been disappointed in himself. It was only a matter of time before Trent, or some other commandant, would find them.

He didn't want to fail them again. Especially not Farrah.

Not that she had sanctioned him. When he had been incapable of doing anything, she had appeared more thoughtful than disgruntled. Perhaps she too had wondered whether their encounter with Ekhon had been a dream.

In the end, he was just some guy from some island.

He'd always been that person who could turn everyone into a friend. Now, he wasn't sure whether he belonged in the company of these people.

Worse, what insanity had made a god choose *him* as his wielder? Maybe he *should* have refused the opportunity and let Farrah merge with Ekhon in his stead. He had no doubt that where he had failed, she would have succeeded.

"You ought to close your mouth, son, others might wonder," said Aslor, looking amused.

Slay gaped at him. "Oh, I was just thinking."

Aslor laughed. "Better to think inside your head than with your eyes."

"I'm no different from those babbling idiots, eh?" he replied. "I mean, it's hard not to stare sometimes." He winked and elbowed the man in the ribs. "You know…"

Aslor's face composed into a somewhat less demonstrative expression. He pushed his round glasses back along the line of his nose using the tip of his index finger. "My word of advice, chap. Let it go."

With that, he retreated, leaving a rather dumbfounded Slay wondering on the nature of those parting words.

Farrah gazed away, looking nowhere in particular. It was hard to see in these nighttime clouds, or perhaps it was those that surrounded her mind that made it difficult.

Heading out in search of the gods had seemed like the perfect idea. Acquiring one had confirmed that. But now that Commandant Trent had given them pursuit, her certainty had wavered. Even though they were on the only ship in Iscar that could yet resist Trent, they had escaped him by a mere inch. Moreover, when they had tried to summon Ekhon, they had been met with a lack of success.

Her knowledge of the gods had been accurate. Yet, a considerable gap of lost interpretation existed between theoretical material and practical application. What if they acquired the theurgy of the gods but never found the means to conjure them? Or worse, died before having challenged Daromas's commandants even once?

If it hadn't been for the crew of the *Celestial Dragon*, they would all be dead. The pirates had saved their necks more than once by now. Would they be able to stand on their own without them when it came time to go their different ways?

Whatever it was that they were missing, they would have to figure it out, and soon. They could not afford another skirmish such as this one. The crew of the *Celestial Dragon* did not need to die for them.

She left the stillness of the night and went towards the main deck. She noticed Slay staring at her.

The islander had appeared dishevelled after the fight. Farrah knew he blamed himself for his failure, but she did not.

They made eye contact as she passed him by and it felt to her that he had been on the verge of saying something but had thought better of it.

She headed down the stairs and found the person she had been searching for. Captain Sadahl was hanging over the side of the galleon, gazing overboard at the hull and talking with the boatswain, Danguer.

Danguer was a rugged-looking fellow with long, grey hair and a spectacular beard lounging over an impressive round midsection. He wore an actual pirate patch on his left eye and appeared to be a straightforward sort of man.

"We won't be able to replace the titanium o'er them gun deck. I can close them punctures usin' regular wood in juss about no time. It'll do the job till we can find the replacement parts for those that were broken durin' battle."

"How about the ship's propulsion? Any lasting damage?" asked the corsair.

"Nay, Capt'n. Them cannons made some big-ass holes that's fer sure but except fer some pricey inside renovations, no apparent lingerin' damages. As I said before, 'tis fly-worthy."

"Still, we'd better take our precautions." She patted the man on his shoulder and took her leave.

Farrah pulled even with her, the pirate spectacularly ignoring her approach. "The ship's going to be fine?"

"It would seem so."

"That's a relief…." she answered and then paused for a moment. "Would it be possible to know where we are heading?"

"Wouldn't you like to know?" replied the corsair and Farrah lifted her eyes to her but did not complain. "Anything else?"

Farrah waited another second. "I wanted to thank you."

The captain stopped, wearing an unconvinced expression on her face. "Did you?"

She decided to ignore the mocking tone. "Yes. Commandant Trent is on our tail because we're aboard your ship. The least I can do is thank you and the crew for saving us."

The pirate lifted an unimpressed eyebrow. "Indeed." She cocked her head to the side while looming over her.

Farrah felt something hinting at insecurity as the captain surveilled her. It was an odd feeling. She was not usually intimidated in the presence of others.

The pirate curved a smile that seemed, for the first time, genuine. "I appreciate it though," she replied before heading off again, leaving her behind.

CHAPTER 9

It was dawn when a member of the crew signalled their arrival. Farrah had walked up to the side of the ship and was staring at the stream of clouds coasting away to reveal a flying island. She gasped in amazement at the piece of land, floating upon the roof of the heavens.

Infinite groves of trees gathered upon its soil as rivers tumbled over its edges, their waters pouring out below and becoming the very brume that shrouded the grove's magical existence amidst the sky. It was a wondrous sight, draped inside its mysterious presence.

She understood at once why the pirates had chosen this secret place as their hideaway. Not many would have stumbled upon it.

Several islands floated throughout Iscar. These flying pieces of land had torn from the earth and had taken root in the sky. Some of them even had civilizations of their own. This one, however, stood alone, seemingly barren of human traces with the exception of the pirates who came and went.

The *Celestial Dragon* vaporously approached the semblance of a shoreline where the cascading river fell down the island's side.

The galleon anchored on the shallow cove. Its undercarriage, used for terrains that held no proper body of waters, greeted the ship's weight on its landing gear. The *Dragon* made a loud rumbling noise as it came to rest and Farrah noticed the shared look between the captain and her quartermaster before they exited the bridge.

Kerok disengaged the gangway and it drifted towards ground, creating an expansive pathway between land and deck. The pirates proceeded down and assembled on the rocky beach, looking up the galleon, assessing the damage.

Farrah's brow knitted at the sight of the sizeable hole that had been drilled inside the gun deck, carrying over to the crew's cabins. Visibly, some people hadn't had a berth to sleep in for the last few days.

"Danguer will be in charge of the operations," the corsair informed them. "We will begin the repairs on the morrow. For now, let us settle down for the night."

As one, the whole crew mustered towards a cave, lying in wait at the edge of the cove, right before the forest.

Farrah and the others followed after them. Apparently, they also would not be sleeping in their berths tonight.

The corsair rounded them up in front of the grotto whose entrance was sealed by a polished stone harbouring old dialects. She understood their meaning at once, for she had seen similar ones before.

In fact, they had witnessed some of them no more than a few days ago.

The glyphs of the gods.

The captain retrieved a pocketknife from her jacket and slit the end of her finger before tracing its bloody tip along the orifice of the middle character. The door sprung into motion and drifted aside, revealing the inside of a cave.

"What the hell?" gasped Slay, having come to a sudden stop.

Farrah clasped her elbows with both hands. "Blood magic," she explained as she eyed the symbols. "Hidden rooms and passages necessitating payment in the form of blood, allowing in those whose content it belongs to."

"Only one person has access?"

The pirates followed suit as their captain vanished inside the darkened cavern.

Farrah let go of her arms and went in after them. "Family members. Those bearing the required consanguinity may enter and leave at will. Anyone who doesn't share the same genealogy isn't given access. Sheer force cannot strike its entrance down, and so there it remains, forever lying in wait for those whose blood was meant to open it."

Slay kept up with her pace, and they fell in line behind the pirates filtering in through the doorway.

"How's it made?"

"Powerful people and their partnering gods created these a long time ago when their magic yet had a strong influence in Iscar."

"Meaning the ancient Sadahl family once wielded gods?"

Farrah frowned as they neared the entrance. "I suppose... or Corsak Sadahl's adventures led him to some secret discovery which allowed him access."

The islander let out a slow whistle, looking as delighted as he always did every time one of the Sadahls came into play.

The sound of Slay's pitch followed her steps as they entered the cave. At once, she paused and gaped at the pirate trove's contents.

The Sadahl family had no unfair reputation to their name. The grotto was furnished with treasures of all sorts: gold pieces, ornaments, objects of art, richly decorated furniture, filling just about every inch of the room. If the galleon had appeared lavish, this was the definition of the word. A man could lose his way inside this luxurious bounty and Farrah doubted that even a king had such material wealth accumulated in one place.

The renegades proceeded inside, following in the footsteps of the beguiled pirates. Crates of liquor had already been opened and fires lit as the treasure trove was transformed into a hall of rich festivities.

Slay, Essan and Aslor looked just as amazed as they wandered about, taking everything in with hanging mouths. Only Thorick had remained his usual composed self, his expression placid while he surveilled his surroundings. His eyes linked with hers for a brief instant, seemingly assessing how she felt, and Farrah nodded quietly to him before resuming her contemplation.

She set her gaze on the captain herself, holding a golden cup in her outstretched hand, filled to the rim. She had done away with her coat and hat, looking more at ease than ever, and was talking with a beautiful pink-haired pirate.

Her stare trailed along the litters of sparkling golds and silvers. She had no doubt that Captain Sadahl would make them pay for the ship's repairs. When all of this would be over, they would be left with nothing but the skins on their back. It would also be Aslor's life work that would provide payment for most of it. And that wasn't fair to him.

She brought her fingertips around the bump of the necklace she wore under her shirt. Pirates appreciated things of value; perhaps she could find a way to convince the corsair that gold could be replaced with something else.

"You coming, Farrah?" said a voice.

Essan was smiling up at her. They had scattered over a set of rugged limestone stairs. Aslor was displacing some of the gold items to make place for them using the back of his palms as though afraid of being branded a thief if he was caught touching the objects.

Farrah climbed a few steps and took a seat beside Essan.

"Would you imagine that?" Aslor said, arms overarching over all the treasures lying around.

Slay's eyes appeared larger than his head. "One percent of this and I could live as a rich man for the rest of my life." He hunched closer, a mischievous look on his face. "How about we take some and use it to pay back our debt?"

Aslor slapped him on the back of the neck. "I wouldn't try it, chap. We have enough enemies as it is."

Farrah shook her head playfully. "We'll settle our debt fair and square."

Slay smirked while rubbing the back of his neck. "I know, I know. I was only kidding."

To be honest, it was true that she could have had Essan take some of those gold pieces and no one would ever find out about it.

But that wouldn't be just to the captain, nor to any of the crew that had lent them such help.

A crate came crashing down in front of them, a grinning Dahara hunched over it, noises of clanking glass following her arrival. "It be time to have a good one, fellas!" she said, grasping bottles of hard liquor in both hands and shoving them inside Slay and Aslor's arms. "Drink up, lads! We be celebratin'!"

"What are we celebrating?" asked Essan.

Dahara squatted beside the younger woman. "Missy, we escaped battle with the *Lethal Vulture*. Do ye know how many times this has happened in the past?"

Essan shook her head and peered back at Farrah as if asking her the answer.

Dahara chuckled. "None. 'Tis why we be celebratin'! That was a huge victory we won back there."

Aslor and Slay blinked up at each other and grinned. The trader lifted the muzzle of the liquor bottle. "To our triumph against the daemon and his ghastly commandants!"

"Cheers," answered Slay and they clinked glasses together.

Dahara retrieved fresh new jugs and passed them around to Thorick, Essan and Farrah.

She glanced at it for a few seconds before a smile crossed her lips. Dahara was right. Though they had technically lost the fight, survival was a victory in itself.

She lifted her drink and took a sip from it.

"Feels nice to have people rooting for us," said Essan, head lowered and twisting the content of her tankard around.

"They hate us, don't they?" added Slay.

It was hard to forget the Tharanites' reaction when they had recognized them after their meeting with the blacksmith.

"They're afraid."

They all turned to Farrah.

Her fingers stiffened around her tankard. "For years, they've been taught to fear the daemon. We mean danger to them because everywhere we go his wrath follows us. This is what they know."

They hung their heads in silence, pondering her words.

"We were just trying to help…" whispered Essan. "Don't they get that?"

"The moment our presence could endanger their lives, they do not have the means to care about us nor our intentions," she explained. "Self-preservation is a strong and natural human mechanism. These people are frightened because we are threatening their existence. We are nothing to them but another reason to be scared."

"I saw some of the playbacks when we were in Tharan," said Slay in a low voice. "It's fucking terrifying."

Essan swallowed her saliva and Farrah knew that images better left forgotten had invaded the younger woman's thoughts.

"Sometimes doing the right thing means doing what is difficult. This is our path. Many won't understand it because—for most—what is right is what is easy."

"People liked us back in Letholdus," murmured Essan.

"Back then," replied Farrah, "we weren't defying the daemon."

"Well," said Slay, "we've got a god now. I think that might give us better approval ratings."

She smiled. "We do not act for the people's approval. We do what is needed. If changing the world means being abhorred, then let it be so."

"I hope one day they understand," said Essan, looking more childlike than ever.

"They will. When they'll stop being afraid."

By now, many of the pirates were singing drunkenly and dancing to the tunes of the music. Their cheerfulness reassured Farrah. Even the corsair, seated on a spectacular golden throne, seemed as enlivened as the rest of her crew.

"Ye be changin' ye mind, eh?" asked Dahara, catching Farrah's stare.

She offered a grin. "On any other ship, I doubt we would have survived this encounter," she admitted.

Dahara leaned on her elbows, legs sprawled open on the floor. "The galleon's a wonder, but be the capt'n who saved our asses back there."

"Is that so?" she answered with certain interest.

"Yeah, saw her meself. She got down on them gun deck and took it upon herself to damage their ship. With everythin' explodin' all aroun' her, she blew out their rear propeller, givin' us a chance to flee."

Farrah wondered how she would have felt if the corsair had died while trying to save them.

The captain had every right to be angry at them. They had burst into her life, endangered her crew and made them enemies of Daromas. Perhaps it was time to put an end to this alliance. These men and women did not deserve any of this.

After they took their leave from this island, they would make way to the research citadel in Mondos and, after settling payment, she would terminate their dealings once and for all.

"Dahara," she asked. "How does the crew feel about us?"

The woman snorted. "See it this way, doll face. Ye be still alive, ain't ye? And we fought off a commandant on yer behalf. I'd say ye be in good hands."

Farrah nodded slowly and added, "I'd understand it if some of the pirates were feeling resentful."

Dahara lifted both eyebrows. "Resentful?"

"You're all in grave danger because of us," she explained. "It would make sense that you'd…"

The pirate burst out laughing, spilling some of her drink down her chin as she did. "Dolly lass, what d'ye think we be pirates fer? Ye don't become one if ye don't expect some danger in order to get a chance at glory!

"The daemon's killers come aboard our ship, promise a sweet lil' deal, dispatch a couple o' placaters and annoy some commandants along the way. By them gods, that be a pirate's fortune fer me, innit!" The woman giggled some more at Farrah's serious expression. "Believe me, doll face, this be a normal life fer us, to be sure. Ye ain't nothin' much different from what we be used to."

"I'm glad to hear that," she answered, grinning slightly as she took another sip from her jug and something inside her chest lightened up.

They drank some more, the renegades enjoying the first downtime they'd had in a while.

"Dahara, won't you tell us more about this place?" asked Aslor, eyes gleaming with curiosity.

The pirate scratched her neck. "'Tis the Sadahl booty trove. It been their hideaway fer I don't be knowin' how long. Can't be tellin' ye much more than that, except that not a lot o' people come in these parts o' Iscar, and even less be knowin' o' the existence o' that treasure."

Essan inched closed. "What's this place called?"

"Dunno the real name," answered Dahara, shoulders lifting. "We call it Prism Cove but that be us."

"It's definitely something," replied Slay, eyes still bulging.

"Yeah. As long as ye keep to the beach."

"What do you mean?" asked Farrah, head turning towards them.

The woman lowered her voice as though she was about to tell them the most scandalous secret she'd ever told. "Them woods beyond, they be as magical as this trove. We don't go there coz it ain't our place and we respect that. So the forest respects us in return."

Slay smirked. "Okay, that was disturbing."

The pirate smiled cryptically. "Juss don't go there. We wanna maintain that nice relationship we gots goin' on," she added, stroking her hands in midair.

Aslor angled over, voice lowered, following Dahara in all the secrecy. Although, Farrah knew that he was simply getting a bit drunk. "What's in that forest?" he asked, his polished accent tainted by the effects of alcohol.

Dahara drew her palms up. "Dunno. We juss been told to stay away. Sometimes at night, we can see them white figures far off in them trees. They say people that go there, they don't be comin' out."

Essan gaped at the woman, her eyes wide. "Got it, we keep away from the magic forest."

"You've been coming to this place for years and none of you have ever been there?" asked Slay.

"Nope. We respect it, it respects us, good 'nuff fer me."

"Seems like folk stories to me," the islander said. "It's probably all made up," he then added, looking at the others for support.

Dahara made a face while shoving a hefty finger in front of him. "Don't ye go and mock, matey! I ain't makin' it up. I saw them ghosts meself."

They all felt at a loss for an answer.

"Then, I ascertain that we should stay away from there," conceded Aslor.

Dahara nodded a few times, satisfied with the outcome of his remark.

But Farrah wasn't. She was thinking back on the blacksmith's story; the figure Oros had seen on the mountain he had climbed, the outline Slay believed had been an illusion.

The god Ekhon.

Ghosts of the forests? Or a magical presence from another realm? She chewed on the inside of her mouth while the others moved on to a new subject.

As the festivities of the night drew them into their exhilaration, Slay and Aslor joined in on the merry dance going around the room. Essan was singing along to some folk tune with Dahara, Thorick smiling contentedly by their side, sipping the drink in his hand.

Farrah had to give it to the pirates, it was intoxicating being around them. She was letting go more than she had in years and found it ironic that it happened to be while they lived lives of such peril.

These men and women were fascinating: fierce and blithesome and loyal to each other. Even though constant danger surrounded them, these pirates lived far better existences soaring the eternal skies away from all the pain of the lands below. Their lives weren't easy, quite the contrary, but they knew how to find joy in the darkest of times.

As she sat there, Farrah noticed the captain making her way out of the cave. She stared at her goblet for a while more before following her outside.

She found the corsair leaning against a clay boulder right outside the treasure trove, eyes trailing towards the nearby forest. She drew closer into the chilly evening air, arms wrapping around her waist. "So, this is the Sadahl family legacy."

The pirate glanced around, her face expressionless. "It is."

"It's impressive."

The captain contemplated her. "Was there something you wanted to tell me?"

"No, I just..." Farrah started but then realized that she didn't know *what* she was doing.

Perhaps she had wanted to inquire about the ghosts of the forest; perhaps she had wandered outside and went along with it.

Perhaps she had wanted to talk.

Well, whatever it was, the pirate was waiting, so she supposed she had to pick one. "Dahara told us how you fought off Commandant Trent. That was good thinking."

Feeling clumsy with her words, Farrah frowned at herself and drew her eyes to the water.

The corsair gave her devastating smile, the left corner of her mouth tugging to the side, upper lip lifting slightly to reveal a few teeth. "That's a compliment, then?"

Farrah blinked with confusion. "I, well... yes."

The pirate stared back into the woods and Farrah wasn't sure whether that was cavalier of her or humble. The crew would have said the latter. However, her impressions of the corsair's heightened sense of self-importance gave her the feeling that it was the former.

The silence hardened between them. She turned her gaze towards the woodland, eyes scanning its outline, somehow hoping for a spirit to appear.

She then readied herself for the words she was about to speak next, the reason she might have come up to the pirate all along. "Dahara told us of this forest." She looked back at the captain and added, "That it is haunted."

The corsair smirked and stared down at her feet, kicking a pebble with the tip of her boot. "It's not haunted. It's inhabited by creatures shy of humans."

"You've seen them?" she asked, feeling her excitement rising. And when the pirate pursed her lips and kept silent, she added, "Could... do you think...?"

The captain was looking at her as though waiting for Farrah to formulate into words the thoughts they both knew she was having.

"It's a god?" the corsair finally replied. "Yes, I do reckon there's one hiding in there."

Farrah's mouth parted ways with her lips. She stared more intently at the forest, all embarrassment now gone, her mind clear. "What makes you so sure?"

"Because I've seen him."

Her pulse had risen with anticipation. "Do you think we can attempt to talk to him?"

The pirate shrugged and stepped away from the boulder. "I doubt whatever I say would make much of a difference. I'm guessing either way you're going there in the morning, aren't you?"

Farrah contemplated her. "Why tell me?"

The corsair curved her side smile again. "At this point, why not?"

"You knew about this before. Why tell me *now*?"

She looked away. "This is our place. There's history here. It didn't feel... proper to give it to you."

Farrah felt thrown by her answer. "Why the change of heart?"

"You ask a lot of questions." The pirate adjusted the medallions around her neck. "You guys are good people; naïve perhaps, but good." She began making her way back towards the cave. "This god, I reckon he's good too."

She had soon regrouped with the others and turned over what precious piece of information she had received. Upon hearing this intriguing news, no matter what they had been told about this obscure place, the renegades had agreed to head out in search of this deity.

Even though the festivities had gone on late into the night, they had found a corner near the back of the room, hoping for some rest before they went on their venture.

The following morning, they had tried to gather as much information as they could on that forest but it appeared that not a soul, apart from the captain, knew much about it.

When they had questioned quartermaster Kerok, the man had gazed at them uncomfortably and kept mute. He had known something, Farrah felt sure of it, but they weren't getting anything out of him any time soon.

They had elected to depart after breakfast. The galleon's repairs had only just begun and these would require a few days to complete—if not more. Danguer had told Farrah they needn't worry about the pirates leaving them behind. At least, they didn't have to worry as long as they were back before said few days had gone by.

They were readying a few bags, provisioned with food and water, when the captain had made her entrance. She was wearing a beige woollen shirt and had fastened her plethora of weapons on her waist, shoulders and thighs. Her left sleeve had been rolled up around her bicep, revealing her tattoos, her other mechanical arm glistening in the sunlight.

"Ready?" she asked them.

"Yes, we're leaving. We should have returned by the morrow," Farrah answered.

The corsair arched her palm, showing the path. "Shall we?"

"You're coming with us?" exclaimed Essan, voice as surprised as Farrah felt.

The pirate smiled like a rascal. "Would you rather I not?"

The younger woman gesticulated with her hands. "Oh no, please do!"

"Then let us be off. Better to walk by day than by night," finished the captain and headed off into the forest, taking the lead of their journey, her pace urging them on.

The renegades glanced at each other before following after the pirate, feeling somewhat bolder walking into these haunted woods than they had been a minute before.

Farrah eased her way behind the corsair, wondering why she was coming with them. It was an unsuspecting turn of events to receive such freely given help from her.

They strode like this for a few hours, treading deeper along the shimmering rows of trees. It no longer appeared darkened to her as foretold in Dahara's gloomy tales. On the contrary, it was light and glistening, and though they had been walking forever, their pace was effortless. She felt almost serene, a feeling she seldom experienced.

She caught up with the pirate, whose expression looked collected. "You know your way around?"

The corsair shook her head, eyes focused elsewhere. "No, I'm waiting to be found."

Farrah peered at her surroundings. "By whom?"

The captain's face became bemused. "*Them*, of course. Maybe they won't bother though, but I think they will…" Her last words were distant as though she had been speaking them for her own sake rather than for Farrah's.

"You've been here before?"

The other woman slowed down to look at her. "No, they came to me."

Farrah smiled weakly. "You're being mysterious."

The captain chuckled and resumed her normal pace.

They went on like this for a few more hours. No one was talking more than a few sentences at a time, all as much in a trance as she was.

Out of the blue, she saw movement from the corner of her eyes.

Wind? No, a figure. It was hard to make out its shape.

The corsair had stopped and had put one arm on her waist,

waiting for something to happen. Farrah came by her side and everyone else gathered around, holding their breath.

"Don't move," the pirate ordered, engrossed by the same direction Farrah had been looking at before.

Bursts of foliage merged alongside whirlwinds of flowers, the leaves coming together, taking shape in front of them. Soon, they could distinguish flying silhouettes, laughing and twisting in midair. The delicate forms circled around them, and the renegades felt in awe, taken in by the uplifting appearance and charm of the floating figures.

One of them glided over to the captain and lips of petals soared to her forehead as they offered a gentle kiss on it, her eyes smiling as the corsair grinned, her gaze inscrutable.

Nature echoed back to them while soothing murmurs harmonized with their surroundings. Were these the ghosts of the trees the pirates had witnessed? Farrah now understood what the captain had meant before. There was nothing to be afraid of; these creatures were neither fiends nor enemies.

"Would you lead us to him?" The pirate had spoken in a tone of voice that was so subdued that it caught Farrah off guard.

At once, the floating figure that had approached them drifted into the woods, beckoning their group forth. They started off after her, the other silhouettes following them in an escort of sorts, twirling their soaring dance.

It seemed to her that that they had not found these creatures through sheer luck, and that their purpose all along had been to bring them somewhere.

Where, however, was yet to be discovered.

CHAPTER 10

"What are they?" Slay whispered to the captain.

"Nymphs, the guardians of the forest. They are at one with nature and have a soul of their own," answered the pirate as they followed after the soaring creatures.

"All the things I'm discovering with you guys," the islander replied while shaking his head.

"Where are they taking us?" came Essan's low voice from behind.

"To him."

"Would you like to elaborate on that?" tried the younger woman, looking worried by this *him* person the captain kept on referring to.

"I'm not even sure myself, but you mustn't be afraid."

Essan did not look much reassured.

The spirits soared on around them and soon others of their companions had joined along for the ride. Another hour or so had passed and they now had a convoy accompanying them.

Not only were there nymphs but animals had also begun to walk amongst them. It felt to Farrah that even the trees were clearing the way, extending their branches to reveal a path that was reaching out to them.

What was summoning these beings? Were they all part of a convocation? That same one they were responding to?

Aslor was gaping at the animals, barely paying attention to

where his feet were taking him. Essan was acting like the young girl she was, hopping and swirling alongside the nymphs, while Slay looked befuddled by this unfolding tide. As for Thorick, the man appeared right at home in this mythical place of eternal depth.

Farrah peered last at the captain. The corsair didn't seem anxious, but something in her gaze felt wrong; it was hard.

They eventually fell upon the remains of some ancient ruins, relics of a past era, lying in shambles owing to the passage of time. All that was left was scattered rubble on the grass, covered in moss and leftover vestiges of buildings and rooms from long before.

"What do you reckon happened here?" muttered Slay, glare scanning the ground as they walked amongst its embers.

Aslor dropped on his haunches and caressed the crumbling stones with his fingertips. "People used to live here."

"Or gods," whispered Farrah.

They proceeded along the rubble, wondering what these might have looked like thousands of years ago. In this eerie place of deference, it seemed to her that humans did not belong and she felt privileged to have the opportunity of even just passing through.

They next entered a clearing and as if a transparent curtain had surrounded them when they had set foot inside it, both animals and nymphs became still. Their heads had simultaneously turned in the same direction, faces drawn to some invisible focal point.

Farrah followed their gazes and, though her sight betrayed her, she felt a stirring on the inside. Her pulse began racing; her eyes trailed towards the middle of the clearing.

Rising amidst a patch of vines was an unmistakable pillar.

It held a strong resemblance to that of the shrine they had witnessed inside Ekhon's mountain. Unlike the Baron of Fire's blazing colours, however, the glyphs on its wall were ivory white and this more humble version rose only a few feet above ground.

It was unequivocally the altar of a god and though they had not touched it, this one was already shining.

He was here.

As if mirroring her thoughts, she began to feel, to know, that something was coming. *He* was coming.

The Warden of the Forest.

She scanned the clearing, her eyes focusing on a single drop of sunlight piercing through the trees. It had settled atop an alabaster ruin a few feet behind the shrine.

A hoof stepped into the light, followed by hind paws and the body of an enormous elk, its reddened pupils gazing at them.

His fur was a ensemble of coarse hair, green moss and pieces of trunks. Here and there, pink orchids flowered on his back and spiked vines curled around him. He was a superb animal of the earth and as large as Ekhon had been. He looked like an intersection between a deer and a beast, his antlers forming a complex crown of polished darkened wood on his head.

The energy emanating from this god felt different from Ekhon's. The Baron of Fire's presence had been focused and untamed. This deity radiated stillness and peace and Farrah's whole self was ensconced inside his serenity.

"*Children of the land, you have come carrying great burden,*" said he.

The voice resembled the deep reverberation of the wind returning to them and though the mouth of the creature had not moved, his eyes were staring at them. "*I can feel the weight that you heave with your every step. It is leaden on the ground and grim to my ears.*"

She wanted to talk but felt as though she ought to wait for permission to do so. The beast's muzzle started up, air breathing into its lungs, taking in all of them.

He then hovered his benevolent stare on the humbled-looking corsair standing by Farrah's side. He gazed steadily at her and it was as though they were having a silent discussion amongst themselves.

After a while, the god began to move, his front hoofs and hind paws drifting to the soil of the earth as he approached the pirate and lowered his majestic head near hers.

The captain lifted her eyes to the creature and they stared at each other some more, the woman wearing an emotion Farrah had yet to witness on her face before.

Was it reverence?

"I have seen into these people's hearts as I delve into yours now. I know what you have come for," continued the warm voice. He drew his head upwards and looked at them all. *"There is darkness in these lands, a despair that would engulf everything in its path. I see the world dying, the creatures of this earth crying out in pain."*

His stare glided to each of the animals, humans and beings that surrounded him, swelling their cores with hope as he did.

Endal.

That was his name. Farrah had not known before, yet now somehow knew. He was a deity of profound tranquility, a guardian of life.

This Warden of the Forest was one of nature's gods. Many had partaken in the creation of the lands, and this one had helped infuse vitality in them. He was a healing spirit, a benevolent being of renewability and conservation.

She dared a few steps towards him, and he gave her the courage to raise her voice. "An impostor who would destroy us all has massacred the ancient family of Letholdus," she began. "Thousands have died, thousands more will if we do not stop him."

The noble head lowered near hers, eyes gleaming with kindness. *"I have dreamt of anguish and have awakened to dread. A rotten presence has infected the beauty of this world. I have been waiting, offspring of the land. You have come to me that I may give myself to you and restore balance."*

Something poignant gripped her insides and with it came a sudden urge to cry though she let none of her tears invade her eyes.

At this, the corsair had withdrawn from their conversation and the Warden of the Forest had followed her movements when she had. The pirate's gaze was directed to the ground. She had slanted the back of her foot against a tree, arms folded on her chest, ignoring Endal's intent stare.

After a while, the god returned his attention on Farrah, breathing in, his muzzle coming to her. She felt a tingling throughout her body. *"Your journey will not be an easy one, but do not be afraid, child,"* the voice went on. "*The light of the moons will always shine through even in the darkest of nights.*"

In this instant of profound quiescence, she had no more hesitation in her heart. "You're coming with us," she said and it was a statement, not a question.

Endal bowed his head to her. "*Only through oneness may the fragile scales of fate be returned to their rightful position.*"

Her hand no longer hers, Farrah lifted it up and when the tips of her fingers touched the velvety mane of the deity, a poignant power coursed through her veins. Her eyes fell into the eternal depths of his own and unbound galaxies materialized inside their vermilion bottomlessness. "Please…" she asked in a whisper. "Tell me, what it is that we must do?"

The Warden of the Forest's features softened, and the fur on his back glistened. "*Your doubts, you must leave them behind. They are restraining you in the tasks ahead.*" His form began to emit a radiant light, mesmerizing in its incandescence. "*Worry not, children. Everything will be revealed as long as you keep faith in yourself.*"

The light intensified as Endal's body became translucent, disappearing before their eyes into shining particles that disintegrated his form. "*I will be here with you. Do not look for me, and I shall be found.*"

Endal's figure was no longer clear though his last words still resonated through them. The particles moved onwards, enveloping Farrah with their touch. They lifted her palm up and engulfed her.

His power raced through her with such intensity that for a brief moment she could see nothing but stars.

Endal touched her deeply in some unknown part of her that she had always had but hadn't known about until now. He was coursing through her as they became one, an ally forevermore by her side.

Hovering on her knees, she allowed a single rebellious tear to wander down the length her cheek. She drew a finger up to quench its path and then peered at her hand. Endal's shining white tattoo emblazoned it, the elk's head and antlers emanating from it like the radiance of the sun.

And just like that, it was over.

Farrah's mind buzzed with the revelation of what had just transpired. Was it all fortunate accidents or fate tracing its pathway before her?

Her destiny unravelled before her eyes while Endal's astral energy enveloped her, uncovering what had been meant to happen all along.

He had been waiting for them. They were answering their calling and all she had to do was follow the flow of the current as it led to their destination.

She heard the footsteps of the others hurrying to her and Essan's face appeared in front of hers. Her hand was still throbbing though the light surrounding it was dimming.

The animals and creatures who had borne witness to this unbelievable feat had started to leave when their warden had vanished, heading back to the place whence they'd come.

"Are you okay?" asked Essan, looking far too worried considering how Farrah felt.

All she could do was smile while her emotions remained trapped inside her throat.

Slay put a comforting hand on her back. "That was awesome, Farrah."

She looked into the gentle faces of those around her, her own becoming a reflection of theirs. She then searched for the corsair's and found her close by.

The pirate was staring at her, a nymph standing by her side, the same one that had accompanied them from the start.

Farrah rose, legs wobbling like a mess of meek sponges. Essan and Slay each took an arm, steadying her as she got on her feet. "I'm fine," she said, recognizing their anxious expressions.

All had returned to silence as though something unthinkable hadn't just occurred, except that they all felt a little lighter and two gods now walked beside them.

They felt rejuvenated as they headed back. It was as though they hadn't walked for most of the day already and these were their first steps inside the forest. The corsair kept to the back of their party this time around, looking elsewhere, and it was the nymph who had taken the lead.

"The sun is setting," Aslor said at some point, peering up at the sky.

"We should set up camp," Farrah had replied. "We'll walk the rest of the way tomorrow."

They had started a fire, ate ponderously, and talked little. The nymph had left them. They knew not whether she would return the next day or not so they had said their thanks and goodbyes when she had.

Even though it had turned to night, the forest did not appear more threatening than it had been before. It felt radiant in the darkness, ever so glistening, as though some magic made the trees glow and the insects become infused with fervent colours.

Essan had taken first guard; next followed Thorick and then Slay. The islander had woken Farrah when it had come to her turn. She had sat beside the fire, caught within the clutches of her awakened reveries.

She lifted her hand and contemplated Endal's symbol imprinted on it. Every time she did, something she had done quite a lot in the last few hours, it had given her a sense of courage.

She closed her eyes and burrowed deep inside her soul, the part of her unaffected by everything happening in her life. She knew it was there somewhere, yet found it hard to cast out images of her scared past and fears for the future.

The shell she had built around herself so long ago.

She spent the next hour or so searching. A presence lurked there, caught inside its slumber, but as soon as she'd tried to grasp it, it had gone.

She sighed and looked up at the moons. She could hear the howl of an ancient beast growling inside of her soul as it cried out to the sky, and it made her smile.

She got up on a whim and went towards the corsair.

The pirate was lying on her side, her back facing her. She dropped on her haunches and set a hand on the captain's shoulder. The other woman rolled around, looking dazed.

"It is morning?" she asked, her bloodshot eyes wavering in and out of focus.

Farrah shook her head. "We have a few hours before sunrise."

The corsair seemed annoyed. She fluttered her eyelashes with obvious difficulty and began rubbing them. "I thought I had taken last turn?"

Farrah's mouth twitched. She stood back, giving the pirate space as she pulled herself up on her elbows. "I didn't know that. There's still Aslor left, so you'll have another hour of sleep."

In truth, she *had* heard the corsair say that she wanted last turn, but had wanted to talk to her privately.

The captain growled. "I don't do going back to sleep. I already hate tomorrow now." She leaned on her back and started to stretch, eyes looking up at the stars, arms lifted over her head. After a while, she drew her stare to Farrah. "Don't worry. I'm not going back to sleep."

She smiled weakly and went back to the other side of the fire and sat down with her knees bent, waiting for the pirate to join her.

The captain got up and stretched some more. She then came over and took a seat on a broken log, her ankles crossed before her. "I thought the purpose of waking me up was so you could rest?" she said, her tone sleepy.

"He wanted to be yours."

"What?"

"Endal," Farrah explained. "I think he wanted you to be his wielder and I believe that's why you left."

The captain shook her head a few times and threw a branch into the fire. "For this to have been the case, it would mean he places me as one of you, a worthy defender of Iscar." She was wearing a smirk, her face mocking. "He chose *you*. Don't make it into anything other than what it was."

"Maybe not his wielder then. But I think you left because you're afraid that everything you just said is true and Endal saw that in you."

The captain plastered a smile on. It felt more like a patronizing gesture than an abdication. "As much as you'd love for this to be the case, I am not one of you people."

Farrah glanced back into the fire and scowled at its flames. "It's not about me," she said. "I know what I felt even if you're trying to deny it."

She allowed the silence for a few seconds, but the pirate did not add anything on the subject, apparently done with this conversation. She looked up and spoke the other thing that had been on her mind. "Endal mentioned that he had been waiting for us and you brought us to him."

The corsair sighed. "Your point?"

She pulled her knees closer to her chest, her arms embracing her legs. "It doesn't feel like a chance meeting to me," she muttered.

"It was," the captain replied curtly. "I didn't even want to show you this place."

"If Endal had been waiting for us, it meant he knew we would come. Who else but you could have brought us here?"

The corsair drew up her hands. "I don't know! My meeting with the Warden of the Forest in the past had nothing to do with this. I don't see how both could be related."

"What if your encounter happened so you could bring us here one day?" she insisted.

The captain smirked and appeared just about to answer before she stopped herself short and opted instead to remain silent, eyes lowered towards the fire. When she spoke again, her voice was softer than before. "Endal saved me.… You mean to tell me that he only did so because he needed me to bring you people here?"

"Or he saw something inside you that was worth saving." Farrah glanced away. "I'm not saying that your existence was instrumental to our coming here.… Maybe he saw what you could accomplish by staying alive."

"Are you trying to convince me again that I'm one of you?" the captain said, grinning her crooked smile.

Farrah felt coy. "No, I think there's something more to this. We're dealing with gods after all."

"Well, I suppose," the pirate answered before turning quiet once more.

She waited a few minutes, all the while peering at the other woman from the corner of her eye.

The corsair caught her stare. "Was there something more?" she asked, arching an eyebrow.

"How did Endal come to save your life?"

The captain let out an exasperated sigh and crossed her arms. "Don't you want to sleep?"

"After you tell me."

The pirate chuckled. "You're a bold one," she replied, but it didn't feel like a reproach this time. She rather looked amused. "Why do you want to know?"

Encouraged by the captain's last comment, she said, "Endal has become a part of me. I'd like to know more about him."

"You'll be disappointed," the pirate answered. "The story is more about me than him."

"Then I'd like to know more about you."

Farrah prevented her leg from twitching by placing a hand on it while keeping her expression neutral.

The captain stared at her as though debating whether she felt like telling the story or not. Or whether Farrah was worth it. "It happened after my father's assassination many years ago. You've heard of that?"

She inclined her head. "Killed by Commandant Trent in broad daylight in Racketeer Bay after Daromas had acquiesced to certain of his requests."

"My father was, at the time, the only person that was putting up any kind of resistance to the daemon. So, Daromas set out to exterminate him and all that he symbolized." She smirked. "Not unlike you guys it would seem."

The captain was right. About ten years ago, when Farrah had not yet begun her own insurgence, she had heard tales of this sovereign. The pirate's motivations had been somewhat debatable, but what had inspired her back then was the man who had single-handedly confronted Daromas.

Corsak Sadahl had done a lot to inspire a part of what she had become. Both rebels and pirates had revered him for the way he had stood up to oppression.

When she had realized they were going aboard the *Celestial Dragon*, that fate had brought them on the one ship that had also defied Daromas, Farrah had been amazed. "He was a great man," she answered and the corsair seemed to appreciate her sentiment.

"Back then, the commandants had yet to set foot in Racketeer Bay. They knew of the fragile peace between them and the pirates, and kept watch from afar. But on that day, Trent came into town with a militia to back him up.

"A fight broke out. We were just a dozen, me and my father's most intimate members. My father engaged Trent, but there were too many soldiers, their numbers were swamping us. They crippled him with their bullets. Those sons of bitches never gave him a fair duel."

She shook her head in scorn. "In the midst of the fight, Kerok tackled me out of the way and tried to reason with me. He had known from the start that we stood no chance and wanted me to flee. No one rises before a commandant and expects to live.

"The moment I saw my father's throat being cut open by Trent's rapier, I understood there was nothing else I could do and followed Kerok. Corsak had been the target, not us the pawns. We left, gathered the rest of the crew and took off."

Farrah did not need to imagine how the pirate must have felt. She already knew. "I'm sorry you had to bear witness to your father's death," she said, feeling something resembling kinship. "It can't have been easy."

"It wasn't," the corsair answered, grimacing. "Anyway, we didn't know whether Trent was after us or only him. We decided not to take the risk and fled to this island. Turns out that some of the crew did not want me as their captain." She chuckled without much joy.

"I had inherited everything by my father's death: his galleon and legacy. But some felt that the eighteen-year-old daughter of their deceased captain was not the leader they deserved. My closest allies had been killed by Trent that day, so I was left to deal with a crew I barely knew. A grave mistake, one I will never repeat. It's a fool's notion to believe themselves worthy of respect when they've never taken the time to get to know those who can award it." She sighed. "They ambushed me and threatened to kill me unless I relinquished the treasure."

Farrah grinned. "You told them no."

"Without a doubt," the pirate replied, scoffing. "Though I made them pay for their treachery, I soon could no longer engage the numbers being thrown at me. They pierced open my leg, so I could hardly move anymore, and skewered my chest."

She tugged on her shirt's buttoned-down necklace and showed Farrah the wound over her breast. "And that scar." She pointed to the cut below her eye. "They left me for dead on the shore." The lines of her mouth became thin. "And then they came for my arm."

Farrah's chin drew back, lips parting at this. "Your arm?"

"You've noticed that the trove unseals only by my own blood?"

She nodded and began to understand.

"They went back to the cave," continued the pirate, "carrying my arm, trying to get it to open. The joke was on them; the limb must be attached to a live body for the magic to work."

The captain's expression became mocking. She tossed another twig into the fire. "By that time, I had bled out so much that I was no longer conscious and may have pretty much been dead. At least that's what they believed." She pondered the flames for a moment. "Although… their departure might have been precipitated by the appearance of the *ghosts of the forest* when they came back for me."

"The nymphs," muttered Farrah.

She nodded. "The nymphs came and the pirates thought that my deceased father had cursed them for what they had done to me. They left the treasure behind and flew away."

"They came for you?" she asked in wonder.

The captain shrugged. "It was Kerok who did. When the fight had first broken out, he had rushed to my side, alongside a few faithful others. But they were soon as outnumbered as I had been. They restrained him as they tore me down and abandoned him on the island to fend for himself."

The pirate started making circles in the dirt with the tip of her boot. "When the *Dragon* lifted away, Kerok came to me, the nymphs by his side, thinking I was dead. They whirled around in the night, their bodies glowing and I regained consciousness. I believe it was their power that awarded me the strength to open my eyes even though my soul had begun to leave me." She gave Farrah a knowing look. "That's when *he* appeared."

Endal.

"To be honest, I don't remember most of it," she went on. "I only recall his face near mine, and a flurry of emotions I can no longer describe. He told me this one thing though that I remember still." She grinned and looked up at Farrah.

"Yes?"

"That it was not my time to go."

The corsair rearranged her posture and tugged on her pants. "I believe this meant that I had a part to play in this world." She smirked. "And I believe this is where you tell me that my part was bringing you here."

"You can make fun all you like. To me, it all makes sense," Farrah answered.

The pirate looked up to the sky mockingly. "Whatever makes you feel better about bringing me into this."

"I don't feel good about bringing you and your crew into any of this," Farrah argued quietly. "I know we got off on the wrong foot, but I am truly grateful for everything. We *will* get out of your way as soon as we can and I hope we can repay you one day in more than just the money owed."

The corsair's face softened. She stretched some more and said, "You guys may be going about without much of a plan, but I can't say that you aren't some of the most courageous people I've met. And your motivations are noble." She smirked. "I guess it makes me a noble person too, for giving you a hand." She winked and Farrah knew that things would be better from now on between them.

"What happened after?" she asked and the captain gave her an inquisitive look. "After Endal saved you?"

The pirate scrunched her face. "My wounds had closed, but I wasn't completely healed. My body had gone through a lot and I was exhausted and aggrieved. Kerok took care of rehabilitating me. I had to learn to go around with one arm, not to mention that we were stuck on a floating island. We went about like this for a few weeks, living off the land until a ship came over.

"It was, thankfully, not the *Dragon* but a merchant's vessel. Few ever fly to these parts, and this one had been searching for a place to refuel their food supplies.

"Kerok greeted them. They were suspicious at first, but when he offered them a nice amount of money to buy passage for himself and a friend, they changed their minds and welcomed us aboard. They never found out about the treasure. To them, we were only stranded adventurers willing to pay a hefty sum to get out of here."

Farrah marvelled at the corsair, this charismatic leader, daughter of one of the most famous men of the last century. She had taken his place, faced mutiny, been saved by a god and was now one of the best-known pirates in modern days. "How did you get the *Dragon* back?" she asked, wanting to know more.

The corsair muffled a yawn. She brought a hand to her mouth and closed her eyes drowsily. "I think that's enough for now, wouldn't you say? At this rate, my turn will be over and you'll have missed any opportunity of sleeping more." She gave a thin smile and Farrah understood that the pirate would say no more this night.

"Thank you, Feras," she said.

The captain cocked her head to the side. "For giving you a chance to sleep?"

She was also aware that she had used Feras's first name and didn't know whether the corsair would feel offended or whether she would appreciate her familiarity. Not many called her by anything other than her title, even Kerok.

She motioned with her chin. "For telling me this. I have the feeling you don't often recount this story."

The captain dropped her shoulders. "I blame this mystical forest," she said before adding, "and your stubbornness."

Farrah smiled and lay on her side, looking up at the stars.

She thought that Feras and her weren't all that different after all, and that the pirate may yet not be as uninterested in their cause as she made it seem.

CHAPTER 11

That morning, Feras opened her eyes to a feeling of grogginess. Short nights spent on roughened dirt floors were quite different from her late awakenings inside her cozy bedroom.

After she had finished her watch, she had awoken Aslor but had barely slept for the remaining hour of the night. They had set out after breakfast and were now walking down the path they had taken the day before.

Her body stiff and eyes burning, she followed the others as they climbed over a fallen tree trunk. She hoisted her leg up and boosted herself with her mechanical arm, catching Farrah looking over when she balanced her movement.

Though it was sometimes uncomfortable, her golden limb had been more than an improvement from her previous one. At times, she was even glad that Endal hadn't mended her arm. She somehow knew he could have but had preferred not to.

When she had seen him the day before, it had been akin to walking through a dream and being greeted by a long-lost friend. Odd emotions had come soaring up and when she had stared into his eyes, she had delved into his powerful presence.

He had conveyed thoughts to her mind, had sent his will to her. The renegade leader had not been wrong.

Endal had had expectations for her.

Communicating with a god was a difficult task to put into words. It was clarity muffled in water. Things became known though it could not be explained how someone came to know it. It just was.

The notion of disappointing him had felt crushing. Overwhelmed by this, Feras had abandoned his side.

Perhaps Endal had wanted to communicate his feelings; maybe he had wanted her to become a member of the renegade team. For many apparent reasons, she could not have accepted that, so she had removed herself from the equation. Be that as it was—she simply had nothing to do with their quest and Feras didn't understand why Endal would even consider that she did.

Soon, she would be as far as she could from these people, attempting to mend the lost grounds she now faced with the daemon.

Something caught her eyes in the far distance, a scintillating flurry of leaves. A nymph?

Even though she had returned to this island countless times in the past, this was the first instance she had reunited with the wind creatures and the Warden of the Forest.

Maybe this entire place *was* under the spell of the mystical forest and she had been an active participant of its intentions. If this was the case, it meant that the gods were still engaged on this plane, more so than the last thousand years had led them to believe.

This notion felt troubling. She did not appreciate feeling like a puppet without charge of her own life. If one's path had already been made, what was the point of free will?

Was everything just chance meeting or improbable reunion?

Well, no matter what it was, Feras had done her part. How the renegades would fare without her help wasn't her concern anymore.

She drew her eyes up and saw a few rays of sunlight piercing through the trees. Their trek was coming to an end.

"Nearly there," said Aslor encouragingly.

But Feras did not feel encouraged. She had stopped in her tracks and grown still.

"What's wrong?" asked Essan from behind her.

The big man had also frozen in place, his expression searching hers. He'd understood the meaning of their halt even before she had. Everyone's movements became as still as theirs. They had heard it—the unmistakable shouts and noises of battle.

The crew was under attack.

She darted off and flew past the last fringe of trees whose magnificence meant nothing to her anymore. When she escaped the shelter of the forest, she found a dreadful sight.

The *Celestial Dragon* was no longer the only vessel docked in the shallow waters of Prism Cove. Another ship had landed next to it, and there was no mistaking this metal fortress.

The *Lethal Vulture* had found them, and the placaters had engaged the crew of the *Dragon*. Some of the men were battling on the beach while others had boarded the galleon and were fighting on deck.

In the far distance, she could make out the figure of Commandant Trent aboard the *Vulture*, looking down at the scene. Blood boiling, she retrieved her shotgun from her back and flew towards the beach.

She was reminded of days long past. The vision of placaters assaulting her crew sent her right back to her father's murder. This time, however, she would not flee. She would kill Trent and end his tyranny of the skies.

Or die attempting it.

She blasted the placaters that stood in her way, her shells piercing fist-sized holes into their blood-coloured helmets. Soon out of ammunition, she parted with the weapon and grabbed her blunderbuss pistols. She sent their bullets flying into the flesh of the soldiers standing in her path with their swords raised.

She spotted the ship's boatswain fending off an enemy nearby and sprinted towards him. "What happened?" she shouted and fired defensive rounds around them as Danguer parried off his attacker.

"They juss came out o' nowhere! Took us by surprise while we were workin' on the repairs!" he cried back.

The sight of the red-armoured placaters was overflowing her vision. If she allowed things to continue this way, they were bound to encounter defeat.

She sped off and made for the *Celestial Dragon's* gangway, all the way to the galleon's topside and through the midst of fighting soldiers and pirates facing each other in deadly battle.

"What are you doing?" Farrah yelled out to her from behind.

Feras glanced over her shoulder. "You want to help?" she replied, grabbing her cutlass in her left hand, her other one still holding onto her pistol. "I'll take care of him." She pointed to Trent. "You will provide cover against the other attackers."

Without waiting for an answer, she headed towards the gangplank that created an improvised pathway between the *Dragon* and the *Vulture*. She sped across it and hopped on the spar deck of the enemy's fortress, parried a few placaters and shot one squarely on the chest while piercing another. She abandoned the leftovers for the renegades to finish, setting instead her sight on her target.

Trent.

She ran the length of the gigantic promenade deck, all the while taking out soldiers that stood in her way, her rage a fuel for battle. Feras aimed and sliced while dashing up the stairs of the forecastle deck and only stopped when she neared him.

The commandant wound around to face her.

Trent was at least a head taller than she was, large-shouldered and as straight as a column. His face was square, with a clean-shaven jaw and light-brown mutton chops that covered the sides of his tight lines. His features were as stern as she remembered; though now, those sagging unyielding orbs had become more skull-like and rotten than ever before.

"Captain Sadahl, I presume?" he declared in a bleak tone of voice.

"Commandant Trent," she replied, her own filled with distaste.

"You are under arrest by order of the daemon," the commandant continued in his mechanical way of speaking. "You are to hand over your weapons and surrender yourself, your men and the fugitives you are harbouring."

She drew her sword forth as her answer.

Trent's eyelids fluttered and this tiny detail could well have been interpreted as surprise. "You would fight me?"

Farrah and that islander had joined her side while Aslor and the knight had remained behind, fending off the placaters that had boarded the *Vulture*, coming to their commandant's rescue. Ninja girl was nowhere to be seen; she had disappeared into the shadows, taking out unknowing enemies from the cover of invisibility.

"Very well then. I will provide justice with my own hand." Trent retrieved the rapier from his belt and went onwards, greeting her with the tip of his weapon.

"He's mine," growled Feras without looking at the others.

She holstered her pistol and proceeded to meet with the general. They readied themselves in unison and sprung forward.

Farrah had never seen the captain use her cutlass before. Striking technique and dexterity infused her movements. She was as fast as one could be, easily parrying blows that would have ended the life of another.

Feras swayed and twisted like an animal prancing around its prey. It was a dance of blades, enthralling to watch and elegant in its application. She defined talent and reapplied the function of skill to sword fighting. It was no wonder this pirate had such a revered reputation. Who would dare challenge her?

Perhaps only a commandant.

And this general was one of the few people who could stand up to her. As the *Vulture* had clashed with the *Dragon*, their captains met in a melee worthy of songs.

Each of Trent's movements was precise and calculated, poised as a dawning storm. Feras, on the other hand, seemed motivated by a surge of emotions, driving her sword passionately against her opponent with unconfined ferocity.

Though Trent was as much of an accomplished fighter as she, he was up against the daughter of Corsak Sadahl, and she had come carrying vengeance.

Farrah tore her eyes from the duel and watched the masses of placaters swelling the deck, multiplying out of nowhere. Feras wanted to make certain that no one would interrupt her fight. That was something they could give her.

She rushed to the side of the ship where the soldiers aboard the *Dragon* were lowering down gangplanks, creating improvised bridges between both vessels. Slay had taken position at the top of the stairs and was fighting the placaters that had slipped from the others' grasp and were aiming to meet up with Trent.

She shot bullets into the compact armour of the enemy making their way above land, sending some of them plummeting into the shallow waters below. When the first one of them made it through, she throttled him with her sword.

The soldiers were issuing forth on all sides like mice escaping a boiling pot. She allowed none of them to approach the captains' duel.

Feras's pulse was beating violently to the images of her father's demise, underlying her every swing, her feelings echoing to the sounds of their skirmish. Her rage was an answer to dismay, and her arms carried her to the tune of unbound rancour.

She parried Trent's rapier and jolted aside, hitting the commandant in the face with the pommel of her cutlass, his nose pointing upwards in a flash of blood, eyelids closing on impact. At once, she came back around and slashed through his perfectly washed coat.

The man tottered back a few steps, his stoic expression now vaguely disapproving as he eyed the blood that plastered the hand he had brought up to his nostrils. At this, his brow crumpled somewhat.

"I have underestimated you, pirate," the commandant declared. "But no more," and a turquoise light ignited on his palm. "I've no time to waste with the likes of you."

Feras sprinted towards him, but a flare had erupted and a rift was taking shape. The skies ripped apart to allow a giant beast to emerge from its otherworldly realm.

The enormous kraken, Menthlos.

He looked precisely as she had pictured him: a two-armed creature equipped with countless tentacles that flew out of his splitting tail. He was almost a quarter the size of the *Lethal Vulture*, which was saying something considering the ship's bulk.

His rearing, snake-like head was watching them from above, his powerful claws grappling the sky as he held his mouth open, exposing teeth as long as claymores.

Farrah stared in disbelief at the monster's tentacles, flying up, and darted out of their way when they dove back down with unavoidable speed. The sound was deafening when they made contact with the polished deck as though an explosion had detonated, forcing Feras out of Trent's reach.

The commandant was now glowering at the corsair like a man in complete control of his surroundings.

The placaters had also understood the implications of this threat. She heard their screams of panic as they retreated from the huge monster, pushing one another in their hurry to flee.

"Slay!"

The islander searched her gaze and she found dismay in his eyes. His features took a turn of understanding when they stared at each other. If ever there was a moment to conjure a god, *now* was the time.

Farrah rushed past the tentacles rising upwards again but stopped midway as part of the kraken's tail came crashing in front of her, blocking her path. She drew her arms before her face, shielding it from the debris that went flying across it while the deck around her receded.

She stumbled away from the crumbling planks of wood and noticed Feras's outraged features. Grounded on her two feet, cutlass in hand, the pirate was contemplating the gap between her and the commandant.

The corsair suddenly craned her head to the side and caught

Farrah's stare. She whipped around, the kraken's tentacles rising in her wake and hurried past her, blocking her way to Slay.

Feras planted her eyes inside Farrah's, fingers manhandling her elbow. "We cannot defeat Menthlos!"

She searched around for the islander.

"No!" barked the captain, yanking on her arm. Farrah looked back, not understanding. "Not *him*," urged the corsair. "*You* must summon the god." She drew nearer, their eyes locking. "Trent's death will mean the disappearance of the kraken. I need an opening so I can face him. This is Endal's territory. He's all around, find *him*!"

Farrah felt a stirring on the inside. Feras let go of her and spun back towards the huge monster.

The tentacles were lifted in the air, his gaze set on them.

"Go!" the corsair yelled over her shoulder.

They separated. She sped towards Slay while Feras went the other way. Not a second later, the tentacles dropped, the wooden deck underneath collapsing further on impact.

The pirate soared through the giant arms of the beast, blunderbuss clutched between her fingers and fired rounds at the tentacles, her body twisting between two of them.

She rolled down on the ground, avoiding another blow when Menthlos came back for her. She then jumped to her feet and lifted her sword up, clanking it against Trent's rapier, who had been awaiting her arrival.

Farrah grabbed Slay's hand the moment she made it to him. They were alone near the large staircase, all placaters now gone from sight. Far below, they could see the others yet fighting, but up here they were trapped with a monster and two captains having a skirmish that would inevitably end with one of their deaths.

"Can you conjure Ekhon?"

The islander made a face and shook his head. "I've been trying, I swear, but I don't know how! And right now…" He gaped up at Menthlos and said no more, his expression conveying the necessary words.

"Then I need you to protect me."

"Whatever you require, Farrah," he answered, his stare set.

She flitted one last glance towards Feras. The pirate was having a difficult time battling Trent. The kraken was soaring above them, attempting to trample her whenever she gave him an opening, looking wary of stamping on his wielder by accident.

This might have been the only thing keeping her alive.

Farrah drooped on her knees and sat her palms against her lap. She lowered her eyelids and tried to silence herself, seeking the connection with her god within.

Trent had brought forth Menthlos. His hand had ignited and the kraken had appeared, which meant that…

She heard a yelp and opened her eyes.

Feras had been tossed up into the air and had collided on the deck close to them.

The pirate quickly retrieved her blade, nostrils flaring, her expression a mixture of pain and hatred. Already another tentacle was coming down for her. Now that she was away from Trent, Menthlos apparently no longer had scruples sending his limbs her way.

Feras lifted her sword with both hands and caught the full blow of the kraken's arm. The creature yielded a sound of agony when the cutlass pierced his tentacle, flattening the captain under it as it fell on top of her.

Menthlos took his tail back up, looking enraged but already Feras was running towards Trent.

"Slay!" she cried out to the motionless islander. The man blinked around. "Help the captain, she can't do this on her own!"

"That will leave you defenceless!" he objected.

"Feras is battling a god and a commandant, she *needs* assistance!"

Slay stared at the scene and seemed to fathom what she meant. "If anything happens, I'm coming back for you," he replied.

"Go!"

The islander sped off and lifted both hands in the air. "Hey, monster thingy! Hey you, I'm here!" he yelled at Menthlos.

The kraken noticed him and swivelled around. Slay darted out of there with a resounding "fucking hell!" when the murky tentacles drew towards him.

Farrah closed her eyes again. In the dimness of her mind, she tried to recall how Endal had imbued her with his strength.

Feras was charging Trent, the commandant weakening under her repeated assaults, the lines of his mouth thin as he took many a step back, avoiding her thrusts.

"Menthlos!" he bellowed to the skies. "*Luminous Ray*!"

The giant creature reared his head back, and the snake-like face opened its sharp jaw.

Gathering inside Menthlos's ribcage, a concentration of blinding energy made its way up. It illuminated his whole body, building along the scales lining his stomach. As the light became more intense, it turned into a radiating ball amidst the belly of the beast, its shine transpiring through his skin.

Feras gawked up as Slay ran up to her side, palm lifted over his eyes. "The fuck's going on?" he yelled, voice drowned by the scorching noises of amassing power.

"It's Menthlos's special attack," she replied over the ruckus. "The *ship killer*!"

Without a second look, she sprinted in Trent's direction. As long as she remained near him, the kraken would not dare shoot his energy bolt on them. The head of the monster was now following her every movement, waiting for a chance to fire the moment Trent drew out of her reach.

She kept the pressure on the commandant, the man now doubling his efforts to stay away from her. But she could not afford to let him go; she bridged the distance between them every time he fluttered away from her.

Trent suddenly withdrew a pistol from his belt and pointed it at her. She bolted to the side when the gun fired and went bumping to the floor.

"Now!" the commandant shouted at Menthlos as he retreated from her.

The god discharged his nova and rays exploded from his tails, curled in her direction, their beams galloping towards the ship.

Feras drew herself halfway up and jumped overboard.

She fell down the side of the *Vulture* and crashed into the shallow ground of water below, cushioning a dive she might not have survived had she landed in any other way than she had.

She sank inside the cove, body hurtling through the cold liquid, her heavy equipment dragging her down. Pushing with all of her might, she swam to the surface, gasping for air and paddled closer to the beach, chest heaving.

Feeling dizzy from the drop, she peered up and witnessed fires blazing on the upper deck of the *Vulture*. Though she couldn't see much from her vantage point, the deck appeared to have exploded as a result of the blast she had narrowly escaped.

She lifted her gaze further and found Menthlos, soaring above, his glower setting on her at the same time she found his. Shrieking in fury, the creature zoomed towards land, arms reaching out from his main body, jaw opening.

Feras stumbled away from the monster and threw herself on the side just in time to avoid the grasping claws. But the mouth came twisting around and its teeth clamped shut.

The tip of the fang caught her left shoulder blade, scratching it painfully. She lost balance and toppled back to the ground as the impact drove her forward.

She whirled around and faced the kraken hurtling down at her, took her blunderbuss in hand and aimed it up. She pressed the trigger and a bullet escaped its nozzle.

The snake reeled back, bawling, his shrilled cry a chilling sound that reverberated down the length of her spine, green blood spurting out of the eyeball she had blasted.

While the creature shrieked and squealed, Feras darted back towards the galleon and went up the *Celestial Dragon's* main deck, the furious kraken rushing behind her. Trent was no longer on the forecastle deck of the *Vulture*, left severely destroyed after the Menthlos's attack.

A flicker in the sun caught her eyes. She spun around and lifted her blade, preventing the commandant's rapier from striking her down.

Trent's expression had taken a turn for the worse. It had shaped itself into a maddening mask of infuriation. His lips were quivering, the veins around his orbs were sticking out, his dark pupils screening the depth of her soul.

Clenching the cutlass with two hands, her muscles shivered as the swords screeched against one another. Trent levelled his vulturous gaze with hers. The skin of her left shoulder was crying out in pain though she ignored its pleas.

The kraken had come to a stop and was hovering above the scene ominously.

"Menthlos will destroy everything once I'm done with you, pirate!" snarled Trent. "I will have all of your men killed, your ship taken and rebuilt into the finest of the daemon's fleet!"

As if on command, the creature opened his mouth and energy began gathering inside his stomach's cavity, preparing for his master's permission to fire.

Feras upheld the man's pressure, their stares competing with each other. One mistake and she'd be facing an enormous mass of scorching light that would undoubtedly annihilate her this time.

But then, the land started to bristle, and pieces of water, wood, leaves and sand began to twirl around, taking form as they connected to each other, becoming one. The wind blew as the powerful current streamed over their heads, turning into a sphere. She heard a howl into the distance as the orb spun upon itself and transformed into a beast.

The Warden of the Forest was taking shape before them, soon the solid figure of Endal materializing on the starboard deck of the *Dragon*. His gaze was challenging Menthlos, confronting his kin with the strength of a thousand creatures.

Feras gaped at the apparition and so did Trent's widened stare over hers, swords yet raging against one another.

Over the flaming bulwarks of the *Vulture* emerged Farrah, raising a shaking, glowering hand. She was wearing a fierce expression, her beauty savage in the blazing light of the fires.

"Now, Menthlos!" yelled Trent.

Endal rushed forth, leaving a swirling mist of flowers and leaves in his trail, his pounce high and omnipotent as he came to meet with the lowered head of his foe. His body was akin to a bullet charging towards the kraken, the might of the woodland driving him onwards.

The Warden of the Forest smashed into Menthlos as the ray of energy came bursting out of him, creating a deafening explosion rancorously enveloping both deities.

Menthlos reared backwards and crashed on the sand. The embrace of land welcomed the kraken as he crumpled onto it. Smoke was rising out of his tails, and his remaining eye had closed.

The god Endal had all but vanished and Farrah had faltered on the floor of the deck.

The commandant was looking confounded by these events: a significant emotion for this soulless creature.

Feras turned her sword sideways and angled herself to the right. Trent went staggering past her when her cutlass balanced itself out of their duel.

Her mechanical arm flew up and the man's jaw broke as it greeted her uppercut. Blood dribbling down his chin, he jolted back to avoid her next blow to the head.

The earth growled below as Menthlos awakened from his short rest, and began to rise out of the mayhem of the fumes his body exuded. The scent of burnt flesh flared inside Feras's nose as greenish fluid oozed from the pores of the creature's scales.

The kraken would retaliate and she could no longer afford to give him such an opportunity. Her cutlass clashed again with Trent's, and she felt his posture weakening, the light fading from his wielding hand.

He was losing control.

Menthlos was rising behind Trent, the monstrous form darkening her vision. She waited for the commandant's rapier to come her way before she lifted her right arm to meet with it.

Trent opened his eyes wide as the powerful grip took hold of his weapon and unyielding metallic golden fingers grasped his sword between their palm.

She roared triumphantly while Trent yanked on his rapier, attempting to retrieve it from her clasp. She drew her mechanical limb backwards and the commandant's sword flew forward, his body following as she simultaneously raised the tip of her cutlass and pierced his soft neck.

The rapier fell to the ground.

Feras shoved her blade deeper, tearing flesh and nerves from Trent's throat, his expression a mask of bewilderment.

From the corner of her eye, she noticed Menthlos disappearing into non-existence. His master had lost power over him, and he was retreating from this world.

She retrieved her sword, her opponent's veiled eyes gawking as she tugged on the neck and his corpse yielded to the floor. She drew herself up, breathing hard, glowering at the collapsed form of the commandant.

Farrah was leaning against the bulwarks of the *Lethal Vulture*, its deck burning behind her. That brawler guy was beside her, arms held high in celebration. Feras gave them a nod, repaid in kind by the renegade leader when they crossed gazes.

She walked up to the front of the *Dragon*.

Both placaters and the men and women of her crew were rooted to the spot, their mouths agape. The kraken's banishment had stopped all combat. Feras had won and Trent was dead. Her victory symbolized the enemy's immediate defeat.

She looked down into their solemn expressions, and a flare swelled inside of her. She hoisted her golden arm up and shouted out for all to hear. "Trent is dead!"

They lifted their own fists up amidst a profound silence that spoke of her accomplishment.

Her chest heaved chaotically while she gazed at her crew. She wanted to cry and yell at the same time. So much was happening inside of her that it was hard to define how she felt at all.

Tears leaked into her dead-set stare.

She had brought down one of the seven commandants. This triumph was imbued with meaning, a meaning bound to forever change everything.

The remaining placaters had thrown down their weapons and been put to their knees.

Aslor was slouching over Trent's body, expression mesmerized. The islander was clapping the hand of ninja girl and the big man was clasping his arms behind his back, torso covered in blood that was not his.

Farrah approached her, her face solemn. Unlike the tears that were threatening her vision, she could have sworn she had seen unshed ones in the renegade leader's eyes.

"That's one fewer for you to deal with," Feras said. Farrah smiled and though she appeared weary from Endal's invocation, she was holding herself tall. "You found your god," she added.

"It's as you said; I felt him all around," the woman answered. "It was lucky for us that we were still on this island."

Feras chuckled and shook her head. "You would have found him either way."

She saw something genuine in Farrah's face and knew the words she had spoken to be true. The renegade leader emanated a presence that was hard to define but that simultaneously transmitted will, purpose and fierceness.

She felt as though the woman had wanted to say something more but had been incapable of talking at the moment.

Feras understood exactly how she felt.

No time and energy would be spared getting back at them now.

They were officially a menace and a force to be reckoned with. A commandant and his god had been defeated. Daromas would go berserk upon hearing this news and they could bet others would soon be gunning for them.

They would need to be prepared when that moment came. War was on the horizon, and only a few actors had a role to play in it.

She went down the gangway and joined her crew on the beach. "Capt'n," muttered the pirates when she walked past them. She strode on amidst the deferent gazes. Hats were pulled while bodies cleared a path for her.

Silence accompanied their endless devotion to the woman that had brought down a man thought untouchable, a man of the daemon. If anything, she had surpassed even her father.

Captain Feras Sadahl, the *commandant's executioner*. She would be the first person alive to wield such title and perhaps the only one.

She lifted her chin and pressed her lips together.

She had signed her death warrant. She had signed all of theirs, and it was too late to ask for forgiveness.

Kerok's eyes glinted as she came to him, his face imbued with softened emotions. He grabbed her by the arm. "Now he can rest, and we can as well."

Feras took a hold of his shoulders and embraced him.

They stayed as such for some time, feeling the bond they shared through a mutual past of adventures and losses. An enormous burden had been heaved away, leaving sadness in its wake.

Corsak was avenged and they were alive. Everything would be different now, for better or worse.

CHAPTER 12

Night had begun to fall when they'd assembled on the beach, the orange skies crying with the blood of the day's battle. Farrah had sat on the sand, the renegades gathering around her.

"You did it, Farrah!" cheered Essan, grabbing her hand between her palms.

She smiled softly. She *had* done it, not that she could explain how she had.

In the midst of the fight, she had remembered that as long as she focused on her fears, she would find nothing. She had instead listened inwards, steadied herself as she had sought to locate a sense of Endal.

Her exploration had led her to him and the world outside had closed itself to her and its sounds had turned into background noise. Not that she could no longer hear anything, only that everything wasn't as prominent anymore.

Her connection with the Warden of the Forest had grown, becoming almost palpable. She had begun to make out his form, not physically there, and yet, present all the same. Something had unblocked within her, and he had been there, waiting.

Farrah had heard his voice, soothing her worries with whispered words, showing her the way. When she had opened her eyes, her sight had revealed a hand engulfed in light.

She had risen and the Warden of the Forest had appeared. Though her connection with him had lasted only mere seconds, it had been enough to give the captain the opportunity to kill Trent.

When her deity had vanished, she had collapsed in a weakened state, feeling the toll exerted.

Farrah had wanted to say *thank you* to Feras but had not known how to convey her thoughts in the aftermath of this momentous event. It had dawned on her that they could achieve it all as long as they stood by this corsair's side.

Feras had killed her father's assassin. This was bound to have awakened something in her.

Perhaps more than one person had gained something of value today.

"We did it," she said, her voice soft.

Slay beamed at her. "You summoned a god, that's fucking crazy!"

"Look at us now," Aslor added. "No longer simply defying but actually defeating them!"

"More like, Farrah and the captain defeated them," Essan reminded him. "I still can't believe it. The commandants are untouchable. None of this makes any sense to me."

Slay was shaking his head, mouth hanging, waiting to speak. "Guys," he told them, "I touched *them.*"

Essan pulled on a half-traumatized expression and Aslor said, "Please tell me that…"

"The eyes, I touched the *eyes*!" clarified the islander, turning bright red.

"Yuck," replied Essan, sticking her tongue out.

Trent's corpse had been dropped onto the *Vulture's* flaming deck. The pirates had been afraid that, unless nothing was left of the man's body, he would somehow return to them from the grave. No one had wanted to touch him though, so Thorick had done the work on his own.

"What was it like?" Essan whispered, her eyes large.

Slay grimaced. "Spongy and hard at the same time. The veins were rock-solid, but the skin was sort of soggy." Though his voice was queasy, the man was grinning like a schoolboy. "I could feel the skull protruding."

"You're disgusting."

"Come on, no one's ever touched them before!"

"I bet you were shitting your pants when you were."

"Fuck yeah, I was. Scared shitless," he answered with a shudder. "Might as well know what we're in for," he added, tone becoming serious.

"Can you please stop reminding us," muttered Aslor, a finger gliding up to his temple.

"What about you, Farrah?" said Essan. "Do you feel… normal still?"

She narrowed her eyes. "I don't feel any different than before," she replied.

"No vitality gone?" asked Slay.

"I was pretty worn out afterwards, but my energy's coming back to me now." They were all staring at her as though concerned she was going to lose her mind any second now. "I really *am* alright," she repeated.

In fact, a mounting excitement had taken root within her though she somehow felt apprehensive about letting it out. "Anyhow," she added, "we still have a long way to go, but I am certain now that we have what it takes to defeat Daromas."

"You'll have to teach me how to do it," said Slay.

"We'll help each other." She looked around. "All of us."

An impressive bonfire had been built upon the beach, the pirates singing and dancing to both its flames and their victory. The prisoners had been led aside, guarded by members of the crew taking turns.

The *Lethal Vulture* was yet ablaze, its fires consuming it ever so slowly. Her shoulder bandaged up, Feras had looked at it and decided to do nothing. "Let it burn itself out," she had said. "Let it rot there, never to fly again."

Deserting the others, Feras had made her way inside Trent's ship.

Most of its interior was yet intact. The strong metal and size of the vessel would prove its burning an agonizing and ponderous affair. She would have more than enough time to make her exit before the flames got near her.

She had walked for almost half an hour amongst the creaking, stern chambers of the *Vulture* until she had found what she had been looking for.

The commandant's quarters.

Trent's office was as barren and strict as he had been. Faded coloured walls and simple trinkets decorated the room that was kept otherwise spotless.

She stood there for a minute or so, peering at its contents.

Sure enough, there it was, levelled above Trent's desk on the far end wall. She crossed to the other side and recovered her father's sword from its perch.

It was as beautiful as ever.

She found it odd that Trent had kept the cutlass in such condition, considering he had not been using it. Perhaps it had something to do with how impeccable the room was, a reflection of the personality of its past owner.

She retrieved the blade. Its pommel was painted gold and burgundy, adorned with jewels collected during her father's travels. It was a considerable cutlass, its balance unequivocal. Her chest took a silent heave, feeling moved by this last remnant of Corsak's legacy.

She put it back inside its scabbard and turned around. There was nothing for her here. Parting ways with this place was like leaving her past behind while she headed in a new direction.

Before she could exit, however, something caught her eye and she rounded on Trent's desk where work orders and leaflets had been left behind. She lifted an eyebrow when she witnessed the scribblings of a few recognizable names written on a scarlet paper.

Her own stood amongst them.

She grasped the files. Orders for the arrest of Captain Feras Sadahl, Aslor Borough, Thorick Clandestan, and two other nameless criminals.

She gazed calmly at the sight of her face on that red sheet, marking her as one of them.

She foraged through the papers. Her warrant and Aslor's were filled with particularities of their lives. She scrolled through accurate descriptions of past dealings, names of her family, crew and clients. And while the gentleman's file may not have been as elaborate as hers, it was apparent that the enemy knew more than was necessary about his antecedents.

Like them, the knight had a few lines annotated next to his name. These told stories of his earlier life as King Redamastys's royal guard and his flight from the Anemas prison later on.

Farrah and ninja girl also held similar pages, yet theirs remained unidentified and only brief details of past arrests and unlawful behaviours were written beside their faces. It seemed that these two had no apparent previous lives to talk about.

As for the islander, he was nowhere to be found. The man had escaped recognition.

Feras lowered the warrants. Trent's pursuit had confirmed that Daromas knew she was harbouring the criminals. It was something entirely different to witness her own picture on that red sheet, listing her as one of the topmost wanted people in Iscar.

She dropped the palms of her hands on the desk, leaving sweat marks on the shiny cherry wood.

She and her crew would be forced to live out in hiding. As long as the daemon breathed, they would be chased down the same way her father had been. Not to mention that Trent's death would add heavily to her list of crimes.

Feras lifted her chin up and exited the office, expression determined.

She would buy as much time as she could.

She strode out of the ship and walked up to Kerok "There's something we need to do," she muttered to his ear.

The man rose to his feet and Feras beckoned at the group of pirates gathered around him. They followed suit without question and made their way towards the prisoners.

The placaters were on their knees, hands tied behind their back and armour stockpiled nearby. They lifted loathing expressions when Feras drew up in front of them, the other pirates soon forming a human chain of warriors behind her.

She glanced at her crew's curious faces and then flitted her gaze about, noticing the renegades coming her way, their leader's features appropriately concerned.

Feras thought it better not to wait for her arrival. "For our dead brothers and sisters," she told Kerok.

"May our enemies remain forevermore vanquished." The quartermaster grabbed a pistol from his belt and pointed it towards the nearest placater.

The soldiers' hateful faces turned to apprehension and panic erupted in their ranks. The other pirates retrieved their own pistols and also aimed them in the placaters' direction.

"Stop!" shouted Farrah, now breaking into a run.

But she was too late.

All guns fired as one. Smoke burst out of the weapons as the soldiers fell on their backs, blood spattering around their skulls, Feras staring placidly at the massacre.

Farrah bumped into the pirate's chest, hands gripping her shirt. "What are you doing?" she pleaded. "Stop it!"

The corsair stared above her head, her eyes hollow, as the last placater fell back on the sand, bathing in his fluids.

Gasping, Farrah grew quiet while her outburst subsided. Her gaze drew to the scene, and turmoil sought her expression.

A hush had draped over them. Their depraved task done, the pirates had begun retreating from the slaughter, leaving only Feras, Kerok and the renegades behind. As they did, one of them, the attractive pink-haired pirate Farrah had seen before, gave her a look bordering on disgust.

She chose to ignore it.

Her chest tightened with the sight of the butchered soldiers, she jerked back to Feras. "Why did you do that?"

The corsair seemed unperturbed by her display of emotion. "I'm buying us time."

"Buying us *time*?" she repeated. "Their ship is being consumed by its own fires as we speak. They were going nowhere!"

"I'm not leaving any of this filth alive to roam my hideout until we return and are given another opportunity to kill one of my men!" Feras answered.

"We could have found a way!"

The corsair's expression filled with bite. "There was no other way and you know it! The daemon is going to do everything he can to annihilate us, especially when he hears news of Trent's death. We could not allow them to go free, could not afford to take them with us and could not leave them here.

"Every placater we take out is one fewer enemy for you to fight and one more chance at survival for those you love." She stared Farrah down. "I did what you could not." She then peered around at the other renegades, her expression tainted by distaste. "As I always do."

Bitterness took hold of Farrah's tongue. "By killing them, we are lowering ourselves to the level of Daromas. We're better than this!"

Feras's face became mocking. "You are. Not me." She towered over her. "I'm a pirate. Do not take me for anything other than that. If you don't like it, then get the fuck out of my way. There's a ship right there if you want one!"

She gestured towards the *Vulture*, engulfed in blazes. After one last look of scorn, she stormed off, leaving them amongst the cadavers of Daromas's soldiers.

The placaters' remains were left there. When Farrah had asked whether they would dig graves, the pirates had begrudgingly moved the bodies but only to keep the smell of their rotting corpses at bay.

She had felt grim as she had dug through the sands of the shore. Darvis had once been a placater and she knew the pressure to obey the daemon had forced more than one to partake as a member of his defending armies.

Many who worked as the *guardians of the peace* had not become so out of duty but rather out of inescapable fate. Like everyone else, these men and women had families, hopes and dreams.

She had no doubt that more than one of them secretly wished that someone would free them from the daemon's clutches alongside the rest of Iscar. Though they were yet in the service of Daromas, Farrah could not believe that they deserved such pointless deaths.

It wasn't that she had scruples when it came to fighting them. But killing a foe on the battlefield rather than whilst they lay defenceless in front of you wasn't the same.

One death was honourable, the other was not. Oppression should never be fought with oppression.

Well, Feras *was* a pirate. Perhaps she had forgotten lately.... This was a reminder that she was not like them. She would make a note not to forget it again.

No funerals or words were said. Farrah had recited a short poem in her mind and had wished the spirits good luck on their journey while Thorick had made the sign of prayer with his hands, both palms straight up, little fingers lightly entwined.

She wondered whether someone, somewhere, was hoping for the return of these poor souls. She was hoping they wouldn't wait too long. Waiting was often worse than knowing.

Afterwards, the renegades had tried to help out as much as they could while the crew had worked on the galleon's repairs. Danguer had told Farrah that they would be ready to set sail by the end of the following day. She was eager for that; something had stained the island's beauty.

They had not talked to the captain. Feras had appeared distant, and that had been fine with her. She had not wanted to speak to her any more than she had.

The next day, the ship had been prepared for lift off in the afternoon. They had boarded the *Celestial Dragon* and Feras and Kerok had worked around the controls, making certain that everything was functioning as it should.

Then, they had gone, leaving the mystical island behind.

Farrah cast her gaze overboard into the infinite skies. Unless Daromas established communication with Trent, it would be safe to assume that no ships were yet on their tail and they needn't be wary of being chased down again anytime soon.

"Whatcha thinking about?" asked Slay, forearms resting against the bannister.

"I'm thinking of our next move," she answered him vaguely.

"Anything yet?"

She bit the inside of her lip. "We should be able to find some sort of clue in Mondos though I cannot say how dangerous it will be."

Slay seemed pensive when he turned to face her. "I was thinking that we could practise, with the gods and all."

She nodded, glad at the change of thought.

They made their way towards a bench nearby on the promenade deck and sat down. "It's hard to put into words," she began. "When I summoned Endal, I was focusing on how much I wanted to save everyone. I also knew that as long as I remained fearful of the outcome, I would get nowhere."

She explained how she had steeled herself before heading out in search of Endal and found him reaching out to her. How he had established a connection, and how exhausting it had been to prevent the link from shattering.

They talked for a while, Slay asking questions, Farrah doing her best to answer him on what felt like a very esoteric subject. They had then closed their eyes and attempted to make their gods appear.

Nothing had happened.

This time, however, Farrah felt that she'd had a better grasp on her shared link with the Warden of the Forest. In their moments of need, surely it would be easier to connect with the deity because of the purity of her demand.

As for Slay, the man had been uncertain whether he had felt anything.

"Keep on trying," she'd told him.

Their session came to an end when the crew had gathered the tables around the main deck and took out their evening feast. They found Aslor, Essan and Thorick already seated, waiting for the rest of the meal to arrive.

"How did it go?" asked Essan, grabbing a piece of bread and placing it on her platter.

"What?" answered the islander.

"You guys were trying to invoke the gods, no?" she replied, looking now at Farrah as though feeling uncertain.

"Oh yeah,' said Slay. 'I think I'm getting there. Just not… there yet."

Aslor took a bite out of his dish. "I wonder when we'll be arriving. Mondos is quite a distance from where we were last."

Farrah was also filling her plate when Essan queried to her, "Didn't the captain tell you?"

She shrugged. "We haven't spoken since that other night."

"You're still angry," Essan remarked.

"What is done is done," she answered, glancing away as she continued piling food on her plate.

Essan put her elbows on the table. "I like her," she said before looking back at Farrah out of the corner of her eye.

Farrah's lips curved. She wasn't surprised by this. In fact, she appeared to be the only one who had a problem with the pirate.

"I hope she joins us," she added, encouraged by Farrah's gentle expression.

"That would help, but I don't believe she will, Essan."

"That's regretful. I think she fits with us."

"You think so?" she answered, amused.

Essan inclined her head in acknowledgment, wearing an honest face.

Farrah wished she saw others the way Essan did. Liking people was not her strong suit. She found the world a harsh place, its denizens acting far below what they had the potential to be. Essan saw the best in them and believed in that.

That must be nice, she thought.

"At this point, she's already red-listed, so might just happen that we'll stick together," answered Slay with his mouth full.

Farrah's forehead crinkled. "She's red-listed?"

"Yeah, Dahara told me earlier," explained Slay after swallowing his mouthful.

She grew silent for a while, gaze lowered to the table. "This will make things difficult for her and her crew.... Was only Feras added?"

Slay looked 'round and located Dahara nearby, talking with other pirates. "Hoy, Dahara! I got a question for you!"

The woman turned around, searching for the person who had called out to her. She noticed the islander waving and came over. "Yeah, I got an answer," she replied and put her hands on the back of their chairs.

Aslor moved back and craned his neck towards her hovering figure. "Any chance that you know which of our names have made the Red List?"

Dahara lifted a palm to her chin. "There be ye, mister trader. Doll face, big man and blondie lass be on it too. Juss birdie here that ain't on the radar."

Slay looked taken aback. He fluttered a hand up to her. "Wait, am I birdie?" he asked, pointing a finger to himself.

Farrah ignored him. "Aslor's on it too?"

The gentleman startled. "They must have investigated my hovercar back at the docks and found me out."

"Why am I birdie?" Slay continued, everyone now pretending not to hear him.

Dahara kept her eyes on her. "Sorry, sweetheart. With the capt'n on it too, the *Dragon* be now the first thin' they be comin' fer."

Farrah shook her head. "No, I'm the one who's sorry. It will make life a hassle for you and the crew."

The pirate chuckled. "Nay, I told ye, don't go thinkin' 'bout that no more, dolly."

Farrah smiled apologetically, worry piercing through the emotion.

Slay was now gesturing with his hands, seeking Dahara's attention. "Birdie? Really?"

"Do you know how soon we'll be arriving in Mondos?" Farrah went on.

"Mondos?" the pirate replied. "Dunno 'bout that, we be off to Racketeer Bay and be there by the morrow."

"Racketeer Bay?" she exclaimed. "Since when?"

The woman's expression painted into one of confusion. "Since we left, obviously."

Farrah drew her glare onto the captain, seated at the end of the table. Dahara looked uncomfortable as she followed her gaze and began to lean away.

Farrah got up and stormed over to Feras. The corsair was talking to a woman sitting next to her, that pirate with long, strawberry hair. They both turned their expressions on her when she stepped in front of them. "We're heading to Racketeer Bay?"

Feras sat back with one leg against the table's edge, chest open as she tipped her chair back and forth. "We are."

She shifted her weight to her other foot, refraining from lifting her hands to her waist. "When were you going to tell us?"

"When you'd come to ask," the pirate answered, the corner of her mouth twitching up. "I didn't feel like talking to you before."

Farrah exhaled through her nose. "And I presume this will be our final destination with you?"

"Don't you want to find out *why* I'm taking us to Racketeer Bay?" the corsair replied, her shoulders angling back.

"Why?" she asked and realized at once that had played right into Feras's game.

The captain smirked. "Because you'd be nothing without me."

"Pardon me?"

Feras's crooked smile broadened as though she was enjoying

the situation. "I know a man there, an adventurer, that I'm certain you'd like to meet. In the past, he's told me fantastic tales of strange encounters." Her eyes grew larger. "Are you getting it?"

The captain glared at her and her stare felt unsettling. The attractive woman next to her was wearing the slightest grin, but Farrah could not read her expression. She suddenly felt incredibly silly standing there in front of all these watching pirates.

"You still want to go to Mondos?" asked Feras. "Or you want to go to a man who's seen gods?"

"Why do you do that?" She sighed.

"Do what?"

Farrah knew the captain had understood her meaning but thoroughly enjoyed making her talk. "Right, we're going to Racketeer Bay," she agreed before retreating, relieved to get reprieve from the pirates' glares.

She was feeling something she had not felt for a long time; like a teenager being scolded by patronizing adults. It was an inference that she was less than what she was. It was as though all that earned self-esteem was naught under Feras's mocking stare. How difficult it was to journey with such an inestimable ally who made her feel this way.

Farrah reclaimed her seat, hiding her emotions from the others. She wanted to be a symbol of stability and could not allow her moods to get in the way of her mind.

"We're going to Racketeer Bay," she declared in a balanced voice. "The captain is taking us to a friend there who may have details on the whereabouts of certain gods."

Though the others appeared taken aback by her news, Essan seemed ecstatic. "See, Farrah, I think the captain's got our back!"

She preferred not to tell the girl how condescending Feras had been about it. Her self-doubts were her own; it would serve no one to admonish the corsair in front of them.

Slay looked just as excited by the announcement. "By the gods! We're heading to the epicentre of the pirating world!"

"Arrr! We are!" Essan agreed, and both pulled their heads together, talking of the prospect of going to, in Farrah's opinion, not much of an agreeable place at all.

"You don't seem happy," said Aslor, contemplating her expression.

She worried her lips. "I'm just unsure of what we'll find there. It's a lawless region, after all."

Essan pointed to the corsair, still conversing with that pink-haired woman. "We have Captain Sadahl with us. I doubt any of those pirates will trouble us."

"I hope you're right."

"We'll have much improved prospects there," added Aslor. "Racketeer Bay may partake in Daromas's regime, but his rule is mostly symbolic. Most of the town, aside from the northernmost frontiers, is empty of patrolling placaters. After consideration, we are probably safer there than anywhere else."

Farrah had to agree with him. Racketeer Bay *would* be a good place to go, considering all things. Maybe she just wished that Feras had told her about it. "We should be there soon enough," she finished. "I guess we are yet in our dear captain's favour after all."

CHAPTER 13

They began their descent near the end of the afternoon the following day. As the galleon drifted towards the crescent moon of sand that harboured the docking waters of the pirate town, they witnessed the buoyant mix of this exuberant city's colours.

Bright reds, flamboyant yellows and cyan blues garnished both houses and shops, all draped in the livelihood of its residents. Though they hadn't anchored yet, already they could hear the boisterous rambles of Racketeer Bay's citizens.

Feras had dressed up for the occasion with her full attire, her mid-length pirate coat and hat, and Farrah noticed that not one, but *two* cutlasses, now sat in a cross between her shoulder blades.

"Alright, fellas," said Feras to the pirates as soon as they had docked amidst the bay. "You're free to go wherever you wish. Master Kerok will round up the crew by tomorrow evening by which time he will provide information on our next destination."

The renegades followed the corsair, Dahara, the quartermaster and a few other pirates inside the tender that would take them to land.

"You've got a home here in Racketeer Bay, Captain?" asked Slay, gazing wide-eyed at the approaching town.

Feras leaned back against the boat's ledges. "My home is my ship. Let us say that this is my…" She squinted and tilted her head to the side. "Vacation haven."

She grinned and Essan chuckled. "I can already smell the debauchery."

The corsair winked. "I may just make a pirate out of you."

Slay blinked at both, stare going to and fro between them. "I've always wanted to be a pirate."

Feras's face became as blank as a canvas, utterly failing at hiding her dislike. Slay dropped his head between his shoulders and returned his sulking expression to the town, Dahara looking as though she was feeling sorry for him.

They hopped off the tender, and Feras led them down the street. It was apparent that everyone knew who she was. Many were tipping their hats as she passed them by. Others were raising a bottle of hard liquor upon her passage, the crowd parting ways while she advanced regally on the mud-encrusted path.

Feras was half-grinning all the while. She did not appear exactly haughty. She rather looked as if she appreciated the sentiment but found it tiresome.

"Death to the daemon!" shouted a man and some of the pirates cheered him on.

It dawned on Farrah that they were not only staring at the corsair but also at the rest of them. Some were nodding while others were gaping at them warily. They did not run or hide like the citizens of Tharan had.

"Capt'n! Ye on the side o' the daemon's killers now?" said a voice.

"I don't take sides but my own," answered Feras breezily.

"Aren't ye carryin' them aroun'?" asked another.

"Ah, Mister Henick. Only for a little while more."

A flock was forming around their group, wanting to get a good look at them.

This was a sight she had not expected. In this most unusual of places, she walked amongst people expressing their political beliefs without fear of condemnation. *This* was most unexpected.

"Ahoy, little lassie," said a man to her, "when be the next round with skull-face, eh?"

A few of the pirates cackled.

"It would seem that some are growing fond of you," remarked Feras, looking over her shoulder to her.

Farrah had no words to share; she was muted by this sight. She had presumed that Iscar's citizens would have some sort of recognition of their group by now. But to be endorsed by them was something else.

Pirates may not have been her chosen type of crowd and yet, here were some of these brigands, supporting their rebellion.

"You know, when you think about it," continued Feras, "you guys are a bit like pirates." Farrah stared up, brow creased. "Welcome home," the corsair added with a smirk.

They soon came to a halt near the entrance of a tavern called *The Captain's Wench*, Feras glancing at it appreciatively.

"Is this where we'll find your friend, Captain?" asked Slay, pausing by the pirate's side.

"Not at all," answered the corsair with a malicious grin. "This is our hard-earned meal, drinks and beds for the night."

Feras craned her neck around and silenced Farrah with a palm as she was about to open her mouth. "We're meeting him tomorrow. We deserve a break tonight."

"This is a whorehouse," declared Aslor, chin nudging back.

"This is a tavern," replied Feras, looking falsely wounded. "It just might happen that women be here as well." She patted the gentleman on his shoulder, dragging him alongside her. "You may even meet one, Mister Aslor." The trader slid his round glasses up his nose, expression mortified.

They followed the captain inside the busy pub where pirates and merchants were chugging their drinks while quick violins played in the background. Some men and women dressed in provocative clothing were going around the room and sitting on sailors' laps, laughing with them.

Farrah sighed. It was a tavern, alright, but the *pirate* sort of tavern.

People glanced up when they made their entrance. A burst of delight erupted and the pirates lifted their glasses up at Feras, who had opened her arms as though embracing the room.

"Welcome back, Capt'n Sadahl!" said one of the nearest man.

"Good to be here."

There were a few gasps. "Are these…?" said another voice, sounding alert.

"By the gods!" spluttered a third one. "The daemon's killers!"

The whole tavern exploded in a fanfare of excited mutterings, all gazes now fixed on their group.

A sudden flourishing of fabric leaped up and a girl went flying into Feras's arms. Her legs wrapped around the corsair's waist, lips closing in on her mouth, fingers talking hold of her face. The pirate's eyes drew shut as she caught the blonde woman and kissed her back.

The girl leaned away, a blistering smile illuminating her features. "Captain," she began in a petulant voice. "I've missed you."

Feras grinned and put her down. "I've missed you too, Quinsey."

The girl giggled some and lifted her hands up to her mouth, a corner of her lower lip pulling back, her upper teeth tugging at it. "Me more," she replied, dancing at her side.

Farrah looked at the scene, feeling disconcerted. The woman was a good head shorter than Feras, with fair tresses and sweet, attractive features. She appeared youthful, possibly in her early twenties. She was twisting a lock of her hair, her stare going up and down the pirate's figure, and Farrah had a sense that she was not the most chaste person.

"Are these your friends?" asked Quinsey, her big, round eyes watching the renegades.

The captain peered around as though noticing them for the first time. "My investments," she explained. Farrah gave the corsair a look, and Feras smirked. "Get them drinks, would you?" she added while cupping Quinsey's cheek.

The girl blushed, or made it seem as though she was, and headed behind the counter. Feras beckoned over and their group made their way towards a table at the other end of the tavern, peeling away from the pirates seeking to get their attention.

After one last look around, Farrah went after them, all eyes following her movement as they retreated from the main crowd.

Conscious of the pirates' gazes on her, she sat her back to them and turned to the captain. "Feras, could you tell us more about this man…"

The corsair silenced her with an annoyed expression, an index finger outstretched in Farrah's direction. "Later. We can talk about work after we've had a drink."

Farrah frowned a little but respected her wishes, having learned by now that arguing would get her nowhere.

Slay was grinning as he leaned closer to the corsair. "So, Captain, who's the girl?" he asked as if he was an old acquaintance inquiring.

The pirate simpered. She positioned an elbow behind the back of her chair, sitting with an open posture. "Quinsey, the owner's daughter."

"Friend of yours?"

"From time to time."

Slay nodded with amusement while Farrah felt like shaking her head. It was odd to see Captain Sadahl going for a flirtatious bird with a pretty face. She had somehow imagined her being with a woman more *distinctive*, for lack of a better word.

Recognizing Dahara's expression, it felt to her that the pirate was of a similar mind. The woman was glancing at Quinsey with a longing stare that conveyed how much she wished she were in the waitress's shoes.

This did not take away her natural cheeriness when she looked around at them. "Welcome to our favourite tavern, gals and lads!"

"This place seems fun!" Essan replied, hands clapping to the rhythm of the violins.

If life on the galleon was one of almost constant drunkenness, this tavern embodied the spirit of it and most appeared to be rejoicing in the company of these pirates. All except Aslor.

He was avoiding making any sort of eye contact with the half-naked men and women going around the room.

"Calm down, gramps," said Slay, catching the gentleman around his shoulders. "They ain't gonna attack you with their snuggles."

Aslor coughed into his palm, looking out of place while Dahara snorted out loud at his embarrassment.

Alcohol arrived in the company of Quinsey. She first gave Feras her tankard, the pirate smiling sideways as she did, and then passed around the rest of them.

"Thank ye very much, ma lady," said Slay, clutching his grog in both hands before chugging it down. The girl giggled and went on.

Farrah took her drink and thanked the barmaid as well. When she was done, Quinsey sat down on the captain's lap, grabbing her by the neck and chuckling when Feras said what was apparently the funniest thing she had ever heard.

She drew her attention away from them when Dahara proposed a toast and they raised their drinks.

Not long after, the corsair had left with Quinsey to sit at the bar. The man behind the counter had caught Feras's arm with familiarity when they had and Farrah had presumed that it was the tavern's owner, Quinsey's father.

Both seemed to have engaged in some important discussion, Feras waving back at their group here and there, underscoring things she had said.

Dahara dropped into the seat next to hers, shouting over the loud conversations that were drowning their voices. "Ye don't approve, doll face?" she asked, leaning on one elbow.

"What do you mean?"

The pirate laughed. "Yer eyes be assessin' that lass ever since we first came in."

Farrah became rosy-cheeked and she hoped the dim lighting would show none of her colours. She didn't like it when people got a sense of her thoughts, especially when she directed these towards another. "I'm surprised that's all. My expectations were different."

The woman cocked her head. "Oh yeah? I mean, good fer her. The lass has got the capt'n in her pants with them doe eyes." She fluttered up and batted her eyelashes about while Farrah laughed at the failed imitation. "Well," the pirate went on, looking back at the pair, "she be just instrumental."

The waitress was now making those exact same eyes Dahara had done.

"Instrumental?" Farrah asked after a few seconds and then took another sip from her tankard.

The woman nodded. "The Capt'n comes and goes. I don't reckon there be somethin' goin' on between 'em but attraction. In truth, even Quinsey ain't enough o' a bright light to figure anythin' more with the capt'n. I think she believes she be lucky to be a chosen night fuck on the way. Good 'nuff arrangement fer 'em both.

"The lass sleeps aroun' all the time, and the capt'n don't mind it as long as she's priority when she comes." She looked at the pair again, shaking her head. "And their game be playin' on."

Farrah drank some more. "Feras doesn't care for her?"

Dahara had jumped slightly at the familiarity in Farrah's words but did not comment on it. "Not that she don't care. More like, she don't want nothin' more than them bouncin' buttocks and firm lil' tits all o'er her whenever she be aroun'." She snorted again and tilted her head to the side. "Instrumental, ye see."

She nodded slowly. She'd never quite understood the whole notion of sleeping around, nor had she ever had a mind for romantic pursuits, or time for it. In the past, her encounters had been brief, not to mention somewhat pointless.

She had never felt anything more than physical attraction for someone, thus terminating her few relationships hastily. Early on, she had figured that bedding a person was not worth it unless emotions were involved, something she had yet to experience.

It might have been that she was also tired of the attention she often received from uninvited others and found it maddening how many had blamed her when she had denied their feelings. Ego was a terrible thing, and she already had enough going on in her life that she had no time to deal with fragile ones.

By now, she felt almost estranged from the idea of romance altogether. Maybe she'd had no time for love because of her consuming work, or maybe she hadn't found the right person for her.

Maybe she had closed herself up to the possibility of pain.

Looking now at Feras, she thought it regretful that the pirate had taken for a lover someone that in no way resembled her, nor what she embodied.

Caught off guard by their train, she drew her thoughts to a stop.

It was not usually in her personality to pass judgment on a person's choices or their character. What had the maid done to deserve such prejudice? And since when did she hold Captain Sadahl in such high regard?

Maybe those two *were* good for each other; it wasn't for her to decide.

She stared down at her empty tankard and wondered whether it was the alcohol doing the thinking. Dahara had filled the drink in her hand once or twice by now and she was taking another swig at it.

It felt good to let go a bit.

Farrah noticed a waitress filling up her glass to the rim shortly after and wondered how many drinks she'd had. It wasn't so much that the alcohol was getting to her head, but rather, it was untying things better kept tied.

Slay emptied his fifth jug and wiped his mouth with the back of his hand, stealing a glance at Farrah. She was sitting on the other end of the table, looking distant and apart. As she often did, she appeared lost in thought, drinking on her own.

He felt a jolt in his stomach whenever she stared at him. Her presence was hypnotizing; the mere sound of her voice enough to send devotion flirting his way. By now, he was ready to give his life for her and knew that the others would do the same.

He also desired something more and was starting to crave for an opportunity to be alone with her.

Farrah was manifestly not entangled with anyone, which meant that she was free. It also happened that, between him, Aslor and Thorick, *he* was the obvious choice. The knight was a father figure to her and the trader was probably too old.

Sorry, chaps. Not that this meant anything but still, the competition was in his favour.

He hadn't forgotten Aslor's advice. True, Farrah was one heck of a woman, but he wasn't so bad either. He'd always acted on the things he wanted in life and he happened to have a clear idea of what he wanted right now.

"What is it with ye people starin' at unsuspectin' others all the time?"

Slay startled up and craned his head around, grinning when he saw the person who had addressed him. Dahara had levelled behind his chair while he had been peering at Farrah over his tankard. "What can I say, the eyes go to what attracts them."

"Nay, ye fancy her?" Her tone felt mocking. "Nay a soul had noticed." She then punched his shoulder though not in a mean way.

Slay drew his eyelids to a slit. "What's that supposed to mean?" he asked. By now, the alcohol was clouding his mind. And speech.

The pirate rolled her own. "Ye eat her out with yer pupils every time ye look at her." The woman lowered herself closer. "And ye do that *a lot*, lad."

Slay's mouth fell open. "I don't do that," he replied, thinking that the drinking had made his tone a bit dramatic.

"Yeah, big time," replied Dahara.

He drank some more, reckoning that by now, he was probably tipsy. "Did she notice?" he asked in a whisper.

"Chap, do ye even know her?" she answered, shaking her head. "Listen, birdie. I wouldn't be too anxious; I doubt she did. That woman, her mind be elsewhere, believe me."

Slay pouted. He wasn't sure whether this was an answer he liked or not. He didn't want Farrah to acknowledge him as one of those stupid perverts. But the notion that she hadn't noticed him, when others had, meant that she paid little attention to him. And that was not good.

Dahara offered a sorry expression. “Don’t ye worry ’bout it. Ye’ll get o’er her.”

At this point, Slay had drunk far too much alcohol to *get over her*. “No, no, wait up. Dahara, you love girls, right?”

The pirate inclined her head suspiciously. “Yeah, I like women.”

“Help a fellow girl lover, would you? I gotta try, otherwise I won’t be able to live with myself!” He gazed some more at Farrah. “I mean she’s just… wow.”

Dahara followed his stare and shrugged. “Sure, she be quite a catch. But that’s just it, innit? That lass be somethin’ else. Some birds, ye know’, too big to fry, eh?”

Slay nodded, but a plan had already began taking form inside of his blurred mind. “You could help me out.” He nudged the pirate, waggling his brows up and down.

Dahara’s expression resembled sympathy. “Listen, imagine how awkward it would be if she rejects ye?”

But he had gone off into his own daydream. “What could I say to her?”

“All them moments ye’ll be havin’ with her, constantly reminded o’ yer dejection.”

“Should I go with strong and confident, or maybe sweet and caring?”

“And she would give ye them judgin’ eyes.”

“I feel that she’d appreciate both.”

“Ye’ll be cryin’ yourself to sleep.”

“By the gods, it’s decided. I’m doing it!”

Dahara burst out laughing. “Darn it, lad! Yer really into this, aren’t ye?”

Slay took his fingers up to his beard and caressed it. “Come on, help me out?”

Dahara shook her head. “Listen, fella. Women like that, they be impenetrable. Juss be yourself and tell her how ye feel. It’d be either an aye or a nay. End o’ story.”

He looked at her as though he'd been drinking her every word. He really hadn't. He was simply drunk. "You think I stand a chance?" he asked, more or less having caught only a part of her last sentence.

Dahara made a face. "Oh, birdie, that ain't a question ye wanna ask me."

"Okay, I'm going in." He got up and stumbled over to the bar.

He ordered a set of drinks, and waited for them to arrive. The captain was nearby, talking to Quinsey. They had both apparently also drank a lot and were laughing and flirting with each other.

The corsair was such a charmer. He bet she could get any girl she wanted with a snap of her fingers. Slay glimpsed at her posture and began to imitate it, leaning his elbow down on the bar, trying on a side smile. He felt ridiculous doing it and hoped that no one had seen him when he had.

As he peered back at them, he noticed the waitress's hand languorously going up the length of the pirate thigh. He looked away.

The captain was very attractive in her own way even though this was one woman he did not want to think of in such a manner. Her feral beauty was part of all that presence she had about her. He admired her, and it felt wrong to even begin to see her in any other way.

Quinsey was darn attractive too.

He slapped his palms against the tabletop. *Okay, too many thoughts. Focus, Slay. Just keep your head in the game.* He gazed back at their table and stared at it in disbelief. Farrah had gone.

Fuck! He searched through the crowd, picked up both tankards he had ordered and started pacing around the tavern. He soon found her emerging from the ladies' bathroom.

He took a breath. It was a good thing he had drunk so much; he felt that much more courageous now.

Or that much more of an idiot.

Farrah was heading back to her seat. By now, she had consumed too much alcohol for her liking. She did not like the idea of her thoughts going out of control. She peered towards the bar and noticed Feras and Quinsey in close proximity to one another.

As she pushed through the crowd, Slay stepped in front of her, holding two tankards.

"Wannadrenk?"

"Sorry?" she replied. "Didn't get that."

Slay blew oxygen out as though he hadn't taken a breath in a long time. "Oh, I asked if you wanted a drink?" He quivered a grin.

She smiled thinly. "Thank you, but I've had enough."

He nodded and Farrah could have sworn she had seen thoughts flashing inside his eyes.

"Right, so two for me then!" He took a sip from both glasses.

Farrah chuckled and said, "That's good."

She glanced behind him. Feras and Quinsey were heading towards them. The waitress was clutching the corsair's hand, dragging her onwards.

Slay was staring at her expectantly. Had he just spoken?

"Sorry?" Farrah asked again, her eyes now moving back and forth between him and the captain.

"I asked if you wanted to… sit with me?"

"Would you excuse me for a minute?" She left him behind, holding his two bucks.

Farrah pushed through the crowd of pirates and interrupted Feras as she was about to go up the second floor. "Can I talk to you?" she asked.

The captain widened her eyes, clearly wondering why she was being accosted. "Why?"

In truth, she had no idea why she was keeping her from going up those stairs. "You haven't told us the plan. You said we would talk later," she explained. "After your drink?" she added as a reminder.

Feras offered Quinsey a look. "Give me a minute," she said and returned to Farrah. "Tomorrow will be dealt with tomorrow. Good?"

Her interior clenched and she felt like hunching her shoulders and curling up on herself. "Right."

She heard Quinsey saying something along the lines of "she's cute" before they left together, the pirate glancing one last time at her with a look of contemptuous confusion on her face.

Farrah returned to her seat, feeling flustered. She had crossed her legs underneath the chair, her left foot wriggling up and down against her other ankle. She pushed her tankard away and frowned at it.

"Are you alright?" whispered Essan's bright voice. The girl was leaning close to her, her expression concerned.

"Yes."

"You got into a fight again with the captain?"

She pursed her lips and attempted a feeble smile. "No, I'm tired that's all. I should go to bed."

Essan did not appear convinced.

Farrah retreated from the boisterous dining room and noticed that Slay had looked up as she'd passed him by.

Oh, that's right, he had wanted to ask her something. She figured that it could wait until morning; she wasn't in the mood for a conversation.

She started up the stairs, wondering whether she would stumble across the captain on her way. But Feras was nowhere to be seen. Nor was Quinsey.

Farrah dove in her own rented room, alcohol buzzing inside her ears. She wrestled out of her clothes and slipped into bed, eyes glaring up at the ceiling.

Against her will, her mind began to picture things she didn't want to imagine, but the more she tried not to, the more the images flew across her vision. She swallowed, pulse drumming inside her head.

She folded her hands on her stomach. Blaming the alcohol was easy; it had only pointed her towards thoughts that were a part of her unconscious psyche.

Though she probably knew what it meant, it didn't matter. She ought to go to sleep and forget about this altogether. Whatever she was feeling, it was not important, and she did not need to waste another moment on it.

Tomorrow they would be meeting a man that would lead them to a god. Tomorrow, their quest would be furthered.

This mattered.

CHAPTER 14

The next morning, Farrah glanced up from her plate when Feras entered the dining room, looking tired and not fully awake yet. Quinsey had made her entrance a bit earlier and Farrah had no doubt that both women had emerged from the same bedroom.

She wished she had opened her eyes and had memory lapses from the night before. Then she would have forgotten the odd twinge she had felt, but it seemed that her mind had other plans.

She stared back at her porridge when Feras sat beside her. The pirate yawned and peered around, waiting for service to come. It soon arrived in the form of Quinsey, who sat a coffee in front of her, winking as she did. Feras made a coy smile and took a few swallows before turning to Farrah who had been ignoring her gaze.

"We're at tomorrow."

She drew her eyes up. "Yes?"

Feras took another swallow. "Today can be dealt with." She inclined her head in acknowledgment and grabbed a bite off the platter Quinsey had set in front of her. "You had questions for me?" she went on and leaned her forearms against the table.

Farrah felt taken aback by this attempt at conversation. The captain would usually expect her to extract information rather than offer them of her own accord.

"I wanted to know the plan for today," she explained, somewhat fleeing her stare.

"Not much of a plan," Feras replied between two bites. "We go meet my guy. You see if he's relevant to your quest thing, and then we'll figure out what comes next, I suppose."

She noticed that the pirate had not mentioned banks of any sorts or settlement for their payment for that matter. She felt like saying this but decided against it. Instead, she nodded and took another spoonful of porridge.

Feras glimpsed her way. "Anything else?" she asked, looking suspicious.

"No, that's all."

The corsair seemed nonplussed at that. Lifting an eyebrow up, she apparently elected to respect Farrah's silence and resumed eating.

Slay was next to join them at the table. He did not appear to have had a good night of sleep. He was hanging his head in the palm of his hand, his puffy eyelids half-closing on their own.

"You don't seem well," said Essan looking him over from Farrah's other side.

The islander massaged his temples. "Drank too much," he grunted.

Essan chuckled and gestured to a waitress, asking for some coffee. Slay attempted a grateful smile but drew his eyes shut instead, fingers soothing his throbbing head. "You all look way too fine," he said after a while.

"I stopped right in time," Farrah answered with an amused expression.

Feras made a face. "I sure could use more sleep."

"Oh yeah, we all pity you, Captain," Slay replied.

The pirate grinned at the implication but did not answer.

They soon finished breakfast and left the tavern. Feras had said her goodbyes to Quinsey, the girl kissing her off with a seductive smile. Kerok and the others had remained behind, and only the renegades and the corsair were now making their way down the cobbled road towards the residential part of town.

They followed the captain through alleys of vendors and goods stores, the pirates never tiring of lifting their cups up to them as they did. News had apparently gotten around that they were in the city because many seemed to have been out only to get a glimpse at their group.

Most were whispering and pointing upon their passage. The expressions on their faces could have well described the whole range of possible emotions: from awe to fear, worry to surprise. Though Farrah couldn't figure the general feeling, the one that came closest to mind was *febrile.*

These people were scared for sure, but they were also excited. Things had begun to change.

Eventually, they entered the upper suburban area where they encountered fewer pirates along the way. It was a relief to be away from all those inquisitive stares. Farrah felt much more at ease in the intimacy of those she knew.

"Could you tell us more about this person were going to meet, Captain?" asked Aslor at some point.

Feras walked on blithely. "The name's Leos Stein. He was another friend of my father. This one though, they flew together. He was the captain of his own ship and has gone around Iscar countless times. He's more of an adventurer of fortune and explorer of hidden treasures than a merchant.

"Most of his findings were unearthed from Iscar's outer regions and uncivilized locations he's wandered to. He retired some years back. Many a few did, after my father was killed. Roaming the skies is not the same when you've got chains on your wrists."

"Is he a good pirate like you?" asked Essan, looking up at Feras.

The corsair chuckled and lowered her teasing expression on the girl. "I'm a good pirate, then?"

"Of course you are!"

Feras's smile grew larger. "Yes, he's a good pirate. To be truthful, the title of adventurer would suit him better than that of pirate. But it would appear both get confounded."

Essan pouted. "I think pirates are misunderstood people," she said, and her tone was so genuine that the corsair laughed in the face of such innocence.

"That's very considerate on your part," Feras answered. She turned to Farrah. "Wouldn't you agree?"

She grinned. Feras was picking her brains, yet something felt gentler about her approach than it had been before. "I think Essan meant to say that *pirates* misunderstand *people*."

The captain's expression became wounded. "Don't listen to her, Essan. She's just skeptical." Farrah shook her head, grinning some more. "You've never thought of joining piracy?" continued the corsair.

"Oh! You believe I'd be good at it?"

They began talking of possible futures for Essan in the pirating world. Farrah found it endearing to listen to them. It felt nice that Feras was showing more interest in them even though the reason behind her joyful mood probably had nothing to do with them.

Slay had not joined in on the conversation. He had looked unwell all morning, which was not usual for him.

Farrah fell out of line so he could catch up to her. "Feeling any better?"

"Every time I say I should drink less," he shrugged and attempted a feeble smile, "and then I go and do it again."

She chuckled and matched his dragging step. "You wanted to say something last night?"

The man scrunched his face. "Nah, I was just having some good old drunken fun."

Farrah nodded, unsure of what else to say. Even though the islander was a laidback person, she rarely felt comfortable around most people.

Thorick was closest to her, but it wasn't easy to make conversation with someone who couldn't answer you back. No matter how she felt, however, he always understood. He was the one who knew her the most; he'd known her the longest after all.

She liked being around Essan. She was like a sister to her and wanted to protect her and care for her as one. Essan also often knew what to say and how to be there for her. And yet, Farrah had never been able to relinquish herself completely in their friendship.

Or in anyone's.

She knew she closed her heart to most things. She had lost so much in her life, it was easier not to get within reach of anyone in the first place. Long ago, Farrah had shielded herself from most of her emotions and repressed them. Not that they were ever really gone.

When Darvis and Warwick had died, she had added their names to the long list of people who had been sacrificed for their goals. Had she not learned to harden herself, she wouldn't have had the strength to accomplish the work she had been doing all this time.

Farrah knew she was also different. She had no patience for frivolities and even less for empty talk. It sometimes felt to her that most lived in a different world than she did. She wondered whether theirs was brighter than hers.

Looking back at Slay, she realized how sudden the islander's appearance into their lives had been. In the span of a few weeks he had gone from stranger to a wielder of theurgy. But even after all this, she hardly knew him at all.

She made a mental note to remember to get to find out more about him. He was one of them now, and they were in this together.

"Here we are," said Feras.

Farrah gazed at the villa that had materialized in front of them. Though the house seemed as though it ought to have been expensive, its current appearance was frayed looking. Some might even wonder whether a person lived inside the shabby residence.

A limestone statue of a mermaid protruded out of the ill-kempt lawn and vines crept all over the aging façade, its fading rose-coloured walls a memory of its former glory. It was eerie and yet beautiful in hindsight.

Feras went up to the front door and knocked on it a few times with the confidence of a person who had no doubt that someone lived inside this desolate place. She waited a bit before knocking again. "Open up, Leos, it's Feras!"

They heard a rumble on the inside, and the door jolted ajar. Before them materialized a man with ruffled white hair, a goatee and green eyes. He was slightly shorter than Feras and wore an expansive belly underneath his flowing untucked shirt. Though he looked dishevelled and somewhat flimsy, there was an undeniable mirthful energy about him.

His face brightened up and he drew his hands up to the heavens. "Feras!" he said in the strongest pirate accent Farrah had heard yet, apart perhaps from Dahara's. He took the captain in his arms, and the corsair responded with as much warmth. "What be ye doin' here, laddie?" the man asked when he retreated, his palms still pulling on Feras.

"Long story, Leos. Care to invite us in?"

"O' course, o' course." He contemplated the others and startled into a jump. "Blimey! These be the renegades ye've been carryin' aroun' I presume?"

The captain smirked and gestured at them. "My jolly crew of miscreants."

The man took them inside and through the rubble of his bedraggled-looking house. Bottles covered the ground amongst piles of dirty clothing, food leftovers and random trinkets. Amidst the mess, they could spot different artifacts of unbound history and Farrah figured these were the ex-pirate's findings, now piling up on the floor and bereft of meaning.

Leos shoved them onto dusty sofas and put a finger up to his reddened nose. Farrah could almost smell the alcohol breath from where she sat. "Capt'n Feras be standin' in me house, accompanied by the men and women who tried to assassinate the daemon. Let me guess, ye didn't come here fer a visit, eh?" he said, rolling his *r*'s to an excessive degree.

His accent clashed with Feras's fully rounded words and eloquent speech. It dawned on Farrah that the captain of the *Celestial Dragon* had more the allure of an aristocrat in conversation than of pirate. Was it her status that had awarded her a background in elocution?

The corsair curved a smile and folded her legs. "Cunning as always. We came for information."

Leos rested his palms against his kneecaps, obviously intrigued. Opening her mouth, Feras stopped short of speaking and turned to Farrah. "I never asked," she said, "whether you were comfortable if I revealed your purpose to others?"

Her eyes widened. She had not expected Feras to ask for her permission. She had expected the pirate to say whatever she wanted with or without their approval. "It would serve us not to be shy of information now."

The captain nodded and returned her attention to Leos, waiting on the edge of his seat. "We're hunting for gods."

The man drew his ear forth as though he had not understood her meaning. He then stared further into their serious faces and pulled back, his eyes as round as saucers. "Alright," he replied, nodding, apparently unable to conjure anything else in answer to such a statement.

Farrah's fingers clasped together. Feras had said *we're* and a *we* implied oneself.

"Naturally, we came to you, our worldly expert," the corsair went on.

Leos narrowed his eyelids to a slit and a smile crept across his lips. "Yer tellin' me that ye be tryin' to find gods, be ye now?"

The corsair rearranged herself in her seat. "Daromas is on our tail, in case you hadn't heard. How else are these lovely daemon killers supposed to make it without a little extra help?"

The adventurer pinched his beard at the level of his chin. "I see what ye mean, Feras. When I caught yer ship on the regime's screen, I thought to meself: Leos Stein, there's people who be knowin' how to live life! I would not have expected anythin' else from ye, the daughter o' yer father, I be tellin' ye!" And Leos seemed very proud. It was as if he were talking of his own progeny. A sparkle had illuminated his eyes; a passionate fire was burning up.

"And here ye are." He shook his head, beaming. "I'm a lucky

man, I say, to have the lot o' ye into me home. Never expected such excitin' company in me old days!"

"Thank you for receiving us, Mister Stein," said Farrah, feeling warmed by his words. "Forgive us for intruding. You see, danger follows us wherever we go. We wouldn't want to bring you any trouble."

The adventurer contemplated her and answered with somewhat more poise. "Don't ye worry, miss, 'tis an honour. Now, how can I be o' help to y'all?"

"Gods, Leos. What do you know about them?" repeated the captain.

The man seemed to reflect on this for a moment. "I've seen 'em, one or two methinks. But Feras, ye don't wanna mess with that lot, 'tis suicide. They be powerful bein's… One does not simply go and ask 'em fer a hand!" He chuckled to himself. "Do they even have hands? Oh, oh, oh!"

Feras grinned and nudged her head to the others. "Leos, these people have already acquired two of them."

The man almost fell off his seat. "Ye what?!" He gasped. "How did ye do *that*?"

Feras explained how they had found Ekhon and Endal, the renegades barging into the conversation once in a while to fill in the missing details.

The adventurer looked dumbfounded by this. "By them gods!" he exclaimed. "I thought to meself before that ye lot were somethin', but now…" He straightened up, searching for the right words. "Now, that be somethin' else, innit! I reckon ye could almost take on a commandant, eh!"

Feras smirked again. "Shall I tell him?" she asked the others.

To say Leos had seemed impressed was an understatement to how he looked now. After they had told him of their battle with Trent, the man had gotten up and begun prancing around, muttering to himself all the while. "This changes everythin'," he kept on repeating.

He went over to the captain, pointing with his index finger, his other palm steadying on her armrest. “Do ye realize what this means, Feras?” He walked around some more, hands grasping his full head of hair.

He paused, somewhere midway between the members of the renegade group. “I’ve decided, I’m comin’ with ye!”

The pirate jumped up. “What?”

“Aye, Feras. I’ve been waitin’ fer the last ten years fer an adventure like this, maybe all me life. Ye want me to show ye the gods? I’m yer man. I’ll take ye to them and help ye get us rid o’ that damned daemon o’ ours!”

Feras gaped at the man and levelled a palm in front of her. “Listen Leos, I’ve not been clear.” She gestured to the group. “I’m not *with* them. I’ll be off as soon as we’re done talking.”

Leos’s face dropped, looking insulted. “What, leavin’? Nonsense, Feras! We need yer ship to get to Neir! And time’s a wastin’, innit?” He slapped her on the shoulder Menthlos had scratched, Feras leaning forward as he did, her lips pursed in annoyance. He then scattered about the house, gathering things in his soon-overflowing arms.

The corsair stood there, mouth agape.

“Come on, Captain! It’ll be fun! At this point, what’s the difference?” said Essan.

She waved a hand. “Nice try but there’s a world of difference. Better for me and my crew to lay low for a year or two. As long as there’s alcohol and food, that’s plenty good for me.”

“Captain, we could really use you and the *Dragon*,” Slay added, eyes imploring.

“Flattery won’t help you.”

Aslor was next. “As sorry as we are for it,” he peered sideways, worried of catching her eye, “as red-listed criminals, it would be hard to expect a quiet life. Why not make the most of it?”

Feras crossed her arms over her chest as Farrah approached her last. “You too?”

Farrah kept her expression forceful. “Come with us.”

Feras waited a second longer before taking her eyes from hers, mouth rigid.

Leos returned into the room, now better equipped with a suitcase, clothes pouring out from all sides. “Feras, no time fer dally-dallyin’. Whar’s yer ship?”

The captain glowered at all their approving faces. Even Thorick was grinning and nodding when she did. “I don’t understand why I’m doing this,” she declared, tone disbelieving.

Farrah knew they had won and a sort of warmth had spread through her solar plexus.

Feras gave them her side smile and let her hands drop in defeat. “I’ll take you to your gods but keep me out of the fights. I’ll be your transportation for a while more, that’s it.”

The group cheered, the corsair hanging her head all the while, fingers massaging her temples.

Leos was watching the old clock on the wall. “Now that this be settled, how ’bout we be off, eh?”

Feras glared. “You haven’t even told us a thing!”

Leos gestured about. “I already told ye, didn’t I? We’re headin’ for Neir! I’ll be tellin’ ye the rest on the ship. Come on, let’s go!” And he was off.

They could do nothing else but follow the eccentric man out the door.

They made their way back to the galleon, Leos beaming and waving at the passing pirates, Feras shaking her head all the while, possibly wondering why she had agreed to any of this.

The townsfolk they met along the return trip kept asking, “Whar be ye off to Leos? Going with Capt’n Sadahl?”

“Off doin’ somethin’ with me life, laddies!”

“Was nice knowin’ ye, mate,” they replied, sniggering.

“Say hi to the daemon fer us and then, can I have yer house?” others were saying.

“Me, I want the mermaid. Can I have her now?”

Though the adventurer had gestured back at them admonishingly, he never stopped grinning the entire time.

The crowd's mirth had followed the renegades as they'd made their return trip to the ship. Their renown was rising. Perhaps not all, but many of the pirates had given their approval, regardless of how teasing it had been.

Their passage in Racketeer Bay had been worth something after all.

Farrah wasn't oblivious that Feras had a lot to do with that. The captain's blessing meant a lot to these people. From the instant that Captain Sadahl had aligned herself with them, the pirates had accepted the renegades as their own.

Brigands and rebels forming a common front. What an unlikely alliance.

Feras had broken off with them near the *Captain's Wench* tavern to reunite with the rest of her crew, Farrah glimpsing at her retreating figure when she had.

They had taken the first tender back to the *Dragon*, Leos smiling the entire way. "Ye'll have to tell me everythin'," he said, body wriggling in his seat non-stop.

Essan giggled. "Yes, Mister Stein."

He gestured a finger at her. "That be Leos. I may be an old adventurer, but keep me heart young, would ye?"

They went aboard the galleon, the man soon greeted by the pirates who apparently knew him well. They then made their way inside the saloon lounge while they waited for the others to board the ship.

Leos had requested that they tell him everything. The adventurer was of a curious nature and as they recalled their story, it was as though he was reliving it with them.

Farrah vaguely explained who they were and what they had been up to. The man was delighted to hear of their work and impressed that people had been fighting the regime in the past few years. She had felt his disappointment, and even jealousy, that he'd been stuck in Racketeer Bay while they had been having *all the fun*.

They had next recounted their assassination attempt, their flight aboard the *Celestial Dragon* and their adventures ever since.

He was an excellent listener, making sounds at the right moment, expressing emotions when relevant and asking questions whenever he wanted to know more.

"Fascinatin', absolutely fascinatin'," he kept on saying. "Did ye know people be talkin' about ye? The gossips say that the commandants be out trynna get yer heads. Some even be laughin' at Daromas." He slapped his thigh. "Laughin'!" he repeated. "At the daemon! Can ye believe that? They be inspired, I be tellin' ye.

"Some insurrections have broken out, people are revoltin' against the placaters. O' course, they be punished, but who cares, eh? When an idea grows, there ain't much that can stop it from spreadin'."

He opened his arms wide. "And by them gods have ye lot started an idea! I mean, killin' a commandant, that's somethin', innit?" He touched the tip of his nose with his finger. "Wait till people find out about this, they be rushin' to the streets to rise up as well."

"How magnificent." Aslor tilted his head in wonder. "I had not foreseen such unexpected outcomes. It appears that our enterprise has grown larger than what we had anticipated."

"Daromas can hunt us down or try to suppress us," muttered Farrah, "but as long as there's one person yet resisting, we won't be defeated."

"Hear, hear," chanted Leos. "Now, time for me part." His expression became mysterious. "I've been aroun', let me be tellin' ye. All the wonders I've seen, ye wouldn't believe me. In all me adventures, I recall meetin' one god and hearin' stories about the other.

"The first one be the Dragon Emperor, Baltos. The second be far more obscure and dwells in the lands o' the livin' and the dead, a creature by the name o' Thar. Ye will find Baltos's residence in the ruins o' the ancient city o' Neir. As fer Thar, she resides deep in the jungles o' Shandew.

"But a word o' warnin' to y'all. The villagers in these parts believe that she be a goddess o' ill omen." He looked at them ominously. "Which one ye wanna meet first?"

Slay lifted his hand at once. "I'm down for the dragon."

"I'd take anything over a dragon," replied Aslor, fidgeting in his seat.

"Either way, we'll have to find them both," said Farrah. "Let us be practical and go to Neir. It's a shorter distance from here."

"Thy thunder dragon it be, aye," Leos agreed. "Mind ye, he's the emperor o' the heavens. I don't reckon it'll be easy to persuade him."

"How do you know about him?" asked Slay.

"Long ago," began Leos, "I went on an expedition. In the depths o' the faded walls o' the sleepin' city o' Neir, I heard a rumble amidst the earth. As I closed in on its source, the sky darkened and clouds sheathed the sun. Flashes o' electricity came rampagin' down as an improbable guardian o' the heavens broke out o' the firmament, perchin' himself at the top o' the nearest pillar as rain poured on us callously.

"The Dragon Emperor stared at us fer but an instant, his gaze deep and unfathomable. His curiosity evaporated, he growled, a sound akin to that o' thunder, utterin' a warnin' and dismissin' us from his residence.

"I ain't the only one to have seen him, mind ye. He be probably the most recognized god aroun'. He be not as shy o' makin' his presence known, at least, to those who fly the skies."

"Oh, wait!" Slay had drawn his arm up and was bumping his fist against his head. "I heard about him!" he exclaimed. "I heard about him back when I was first learning about the pirates. You all know this story!" He leaned forward. "What is one of Corsak Sadahl's best-remembered accomplishments?"

Essan clapped her hands. "Of course! His defeat of the thunder dragon!" she recalled and recited, "As the sovereign's ship was drifting along the skies, the clouds began to cry from all around and a dragon appeared. Corsak and his men resisted the winged creature's menace, wounded it and emerged unscathed from the fog."

Farrah remembered it too. It was one of those stories they had heard when they were children. Back then, she had treated it as a mythical tale, not a true event. It seemed she might have been wrong. "How had we not thought about this?" she muttered.

Leos was nodding while they took this in, all smiles. "It bein' that story that led me to Neir. After Corsak told me of his encounter, I had to go in search o' the famed deity. O' course, I was no Corsak Sadahl, and when I saw the dragon in front o' me eyes, I ran fer it." He chuckled and sagged his shoulders anticlimactically.

Slay was twisting his knuckles against one another. "If he was defeated once, we can do it again!"

"Corsak wounded the beast, he didn't defeat it," Farrah reminded him. "And we're talking here of someone at the helm of a pirate ship, equipped with cannons. This time, it'll be us against the god."

"Not to forget," Aslor said, "this is a dragon, an immense creature of redoubtable reputation. Let us not grow too confident."

The islander looked discomfited by their rebuttal. "Come on guys, we're going either way.... Better to get positive about it."

"And we've got two gods on our side, that's twice more than what Captain Corsak had," Essan added, lifting two fingers and waving it in their faces.

Farrah's hand loomed around her necklace. "It's settled then, we're travelling to Neir."

Feras resurfaced not long after in the company of the crew. Leos had met up with her and both had retreated inside the captain's sitting room, talking all the way.

Farrah had sat against a wine barrel near the side of the sun deck.

A thunder dragon? Where have I seen this before?

She had heard this story long ago but also had a clear image of it in her mind. Still, she could not recall where she had sighted it. A dazzling black-and-gold beast fending off a galleon.

She looked up as a person approached her and was surprised to find quartermaster Kerok. He had a plate of food in his palm, his expression equable. "The Capt'n ordered we bring you all lunch, considering you had not dined before returning aboard the ship."

She took the plate off of his hands and noticed how hungry she was. She had not eaten since morning and with everything going on lately, she often forgot to eat. "Thank you, Master Kerok."

The man inclined his head and leaned over the bulwarks. Farrah ate for some time while he stood there, gazing away. She decided that he was the sort of man she could be comfortable sharing the silence with and waited for him to speak first.

"The Capt'n is happy she had the opportunity to kill the commandant," he began after a few minutes, tone of voice enigmatic.

She watched him. "I've no doubt it must have brought a certain peace," she answered slowly, gauging his intentions.

The robust quartermaster nodded. "Everything changed when Capt'n Corsak died."

Farrah dropped her plate on the ground and rubbed the crumbs from her hands. "She told me about the mutiny," she said and let the words hang in the air.

Kerok's nose crumpled. "Those people were cowards. Men like them get what they deserve."

She nodded a few times. "How did Feras recover the *Dragon*?" she then asked, wondering whether the quartermaster would be more talkative than the captain had been on the issue.

Kerok sized her up with his stare as though unsure she was worthy of the information. "After we left the island," he explained, seemingly deciding that she was, "the capt'n knew what she had to do. We found a mechanic surgeon to affix a new arm. Afterwards, she spent some time refining her swordplay and getting her health back. Along the way, more than one came to assist us, many a few men and women pledging their lives to the daughter of Corsak.

"We eventually located the thieves in Racketeer Bay at that tavern we were just at. They weren't too hard to find; the *Dragon* is not a ship easily kept hidden."

Kerok grunted and huffed out a brief laugh. "She entered the tavern, went to the nearest pirate she recognized from her father's crew, and aimed a pistol to his head. She pulled the trigger at them one after the other while they scurried around like scared little rabbits trying to ferret out a hole to run into.

"Her sight petrified them. It as though she had risen from the dead to slaughter them. Which she just might have," he added, inclining his head to himself. "They begged for mercy she didn't grant them with not a witness around to disagree with her sentence. No one crosses the Sadahl family." He shifted his gaze towards the skyline. "The capt'n compensated the tavern keeper for his troubles. We recovered the ship and lifted off with a new crew."

A smile drew on Farrah's lips. "I'm glad you found your peace."

Kerok gave her an inquisitive stare. "What you are doing now—is this what you need to find *your* peace?"

She arched both eyebrows, gaze becoming still for a second. She then looked away. "I guess… that's what it is, yes."

"That's good. Finding your peace is important."

She contemplated the rugged man. He reminded her of Thorick. In this instant, she knew that she could trust him and understood why Feras had felt it appropriate to award him the title of first mate. "Do people know this story?"

Kerok chuckled. "Aye, stories travel fast. You become someone only when they've wandered to enough ears."

Farrah looked down. Apparently, the only part kept secret was what Feras had told her about.

The quartermaster straightened up and gave her a nod before leaving her side.

"Thank you for the conversation, Master Kerok, and the food," she said as he started off.

The man waved back. "It is nothing, miss."

She glimpsed at her empty plate.

Tragedies darkened Feras's past, not unlike her own. Not unlike most.

Maybe flying the skies did not come with the freedom expected.

Chapter 15

Dinnertime was as flamboyant as ever. The whole crew had gained a heightened sense of confidence out of their descent into Racketeer Bay. Word was spreading around that the *Celestial Dragon* had become an emblem of resistance, its members caught in this coerced role.

This had brought Iscar's denizens back through time. Leos had told them that images of Corsak had begun resurfacing on the walls. Graffitis of the *Dragon* were being painted on official buildings. If anything, the notion that Corsak's daughter was harbouring the daemon's killers meant so much more than if any other pirate had taken them along; as though this part had been hers all along regardless of whether she wanted its implications or not.

There was meaning to be found in this. And meaning gives faith.

It could not be denied; something of a family cycle was taking shape in the hopes that this story's outcome would end differently.

Whether this newfound notoriety was a blessing or a curse did not appear to bother the crew. Instead, it seemed to have increased their sense of self-importance and motivated their desires to embody the personas people had conferred on them.

Farrah had been relieved to learn that the public knew nothing of their goals. Though word of their travels aboard the *Celestial Dragon* had begun to spread, most of these rumours were but speculation and hearsay, reports that would surely handicap their journey but not betray their venture.

Leos had sat by their sides at dinner, eager to find out more about their quest. Dahara had also elected to join the renegades, whom she was apparently growing fond of.

"If ye've e'er set yer eyes on it, Neir be nowadays a city o' desolate ruins," Leos was telling them. "Ain't nothin' there but the remnants o' an ancient place whar thy kin's and queens' o' old had erected their seat o' rulin'."

"Why did they abandon it?" asked Essan.

Leos made a frown as though perplexed that she wouldn't know the answer to this. "'Twas durin' them great wars and all, when them gods were yet active in Iscar." He grinned and leaned a forearm on the table. "And guess which protector god them kin's and queens' o' Neir wielded?"

Essan raised her hand at once. "Baltos!"

The adventurer nodded. "Aye, but there came a time when the city was bein' attacked by a foreign invader and their own godly powers. Neir was ravaged, its citizens forced to flee. They say that the deity that lived there ne'er forgot this and has since been weepin' tears o' stones, waitin' fer his ancient wielders to grant him the opportunity to redeem his failure in shielding these lands."

"I'd say we've got ourselves an emotional dragon," Slay sniggered.

Leos patted the table. "Oh, oh, oh, I wouldn't take him so lightly. Baltos be a terrible beast. When the invaders came with their own gods, it took five o' 'em to brin' down thy thunder dragon."

"Five gods to bring one down… and Corsak did so single-handedly?" Slay muttered.

Leos pursed his lips and crossed his arms over his chest. "Stories be stories, not facts, me lad. Don't be so ignorant to believe Corsak triumphed o'er Baltos. When a person escapes battle with a god, it be not because he was stronger." He lifted his index finger. "It be because the deity were bein' merciful enough to let 'em go. I think the Dragon Emperor saw a worthy adversary in him and allowed Corsak to leave out o' respect."

"How do you know that?" asked Essan.

Leos chuckled. "If ye don't trust me, ask Feras. She'll tell ye 'bout him."

Farrah stared at the man, eyes narrowing. Essan twisted back to glimpse at the corsair at a distance, her expression dreamlike. "Oh, I'd love it if she could recount her father's story."

Slay peered around as well but swivelled back just as soon. "I think our captain's otherwise occupied," he said, brows lifting a few times.

Not only Feras, but all the pirates had turned their gazes on the dancers that had appeared on deck. A few men and women were moving their bodies to the tunes of the musicians, accompanied by the audience's cheers.

Farrah recognized the dancers as members of the *Dragon* and the one closest to Feras was that pink-haired pirate.

By now, the performance had captured everyone's interest. Dahara was lifting her cup, spilling her drink all around her, whistling harder than all the other pirates. Slay was grinning like a teenager, and Essan was clapping her hands along the music. Even Thorick seemed content to sit back and watch the entertainment.

The strawberry-haired woman was dancing close to Feras, enjoying the captain's private attention and moving her hips at the level of her eyes. The corsair was holding herself with poise, the ghost of a smile edging on her mouth.

"Who is she?" asked Slay over the loud music, referring to the same woman Farrah had been staring at.

"That lass next to the capt'n? That be Alena." Dahara was smirking while she drank the rest of her tankard. "That one be always flirtin' aroun'." Though she had pursed her lips at that, her tone felt casual. "Mind ye, if I looked like that, I'd be doin' so as well."

Dahara snorted and Farrah glanced at the pink-haired woman again. She was right; Alena was a classic beauty for certain.

"Is there something going on between her and the captain?" asked Essan.

Dahara waved her palm up and down. "Nay, that lass likes lads. She's slept with about a quarter o' the crew. She be good mateys with the capt'n, but I don't reckon there's anythin' happenin' between 'em."

The woman drew her gaze to Alena and kept quiet for a few moments. She then shrugged. "Well, I dunno, maybe they be sleepin' together, maybe they not be. All I know be that Alena flirts with the capt'n and the capt'n does the same but that be their dynamic."

Farrah said, "Isn't Feras with Quinsey?"

Dahara laughed as though her question had sounded ridiculous. "As soon as she be exitin' that tavern, Quinsey be left behind. The lass ain't the only wench the capt'n visits and won't be the last."

Farrah looked back at Alena yet in the midst of dancing, the stares of the overly excited crew following each of her movements. Her eyes then travelled to Feras. She gazed down the length of the pirate's body and paused on something that had grabbed her attention.

Feras had a tattoo on her left arm that went from the tips of her fingers, all the way up to the side of her neck. From this far away, she could not distinguish any of the details but had discerned a flash of gold and black.

A dragon.

She wheeled towards the adventurer. "Leos, you said that Feras knew of Corsak's story, did you not?"

The man peered at her. "Naturally."

"Because he told her about it?"

The adventurer shook his head. "Nay, me dear woman, because she be *there* when it happened."

She remembered now where she had seen the image of Corsak battling Baltos; it was inked on Feras's arm.

"She was there?" exclaimed Slay. "But wasn't Corsak's meeting with Baltos a long time ago?"

Leos played some invisible instrument on the table with his fingers. "Aye, she would have been a sprog indeed. That bein' said, I doubt she participated in the fight."

"It would appear that our chance encounter with the captain keeps on getting more fortunate for us," said Aslor with a grin.

Farrah was watching her hands. "Why wouldn't she mention this before?" she muttered. "A god she's stumbled across in her past… that would have been a good place to start."

"Maybe she forgot?" tried Essan.

She pointed her chin to the corsair. "I doubt that. Look at the tattoo on her arm. It's that of a ship and a dragon. I'm guessing the scene is more than just a long-forgotten memory."

Essan shrugged. "It's not as if she hasn't been helping us. All the leads on the gods we've gotten thus far came from things she told us. She's offered us much more than she hasn't." She had finished with a timid smile as if realizing just now how little they had done on their own.

"Farrah's trying to start a grudge against the captain," said Slay with a sly grin.

She frowned. "I'm not. I only found it curious that she kept this from us only to bring us to a man who would do so in her stead."

Leos folded his arms, his look frank. "Don't hold it against her, miss. Feras holds her cards close, but she's not playin' ye. She does things when it be time they be done, that's all."

Farrah acknowledged Leos's words by nodding briefly. As the others resumed their conversation, she caught Slay staring at her.

"Something about the captain bothers you, isn't there?" he said.

"Why would you think that?"

Slay moved closer to her. He rested his forearms on the table, fingers wriggling between one another. "I don't know. Maybe because you've looked uncomfortable ever since we got on the ship."

Farrah arched an eyebrow. "We've had diverging opinions, that's all. Though I've come to see these as misunderstandings and nothing more."

Slay grinned further and played with his jaw. "I've seen the way you look at her."

She tensed up at his words. "Yes?"

"Your eyes glare disapprovingly."

She looked away. "I had not noticed I was making those eyes."

"I get it. You have this huge responsibility on your shoulders. You're no longer on your own turf and been forced to dabble in politics with a corsair. But I think the captain's genuinely trying to help us."

Her expression was a mask of neutrality though many thoughts were passing through in her mind. "I do find her impressive," she said. Though Slay nodded at that, he had dropped his eyelids midway. She fretted in her chair. "What's wrong?"

"Sometimes, you're kinda hard to read," he answered, now staring down into his tankard.

"You don't have to convince me that Feras is a trusted ally, Slay. I am well aware of how precious a person she is to our cause."

"Oh, okay. That's good."

The islander gazed longer at his drink. It dawned on her that he was making an attempt at conversation and that she was being a rather poor conversationalist.

She had never been the best when it came to small talk and didn't know how to make others more comfortable in these situations. In fact, Slay's apparent uneasiness only increased her own.

The dancers were now making their way around the tables. The music was loud and intoxicating, the atmosphere cheery.

That girl, Alena, was approaching their seats. As she drew nearer, she removed her sash and threw it around Slay's neck. She fluttered up and down in front of him and he seemed both abashed and delighted by her attention.

The dancer whirled next to Farrah and gave her a wink as she passed her by. She didn't know how to receive it but thought that it was better than a smirk.

As the men and women went around them and attempted to

get the attention of a spectacularly indifferent Thorick, she noticed Slay's eyes gauging her reaction to the scene. Farrah decided to ignore his gaze, which was beginning to feel wanting.

Though she was trying hard to look elsewhere, she felt compelled to glance towards Feras again. The captain was no longer paying any interest to Alena but was talking instead to Kerok.

As she pondered on the nature of their conversation, the corsair flicked her eyes towards her. Farrah blinked away, embarrassed that Feras had caught her staring.

She saw from the corner of her eye that the pirate had not averted her gaze and felt agitated by her scrutiny.

"So, Farrah," Slay continued, "I was wondering if you could tell me how you became the leader of the rebellion in Letholdus?"

She reflected on this question, unsure of what she was willing to share and what she preferred to remain hidden. "At first it was just Thorick and I. Our numbers grew afterwards as more and more joined our ranks."

He lifted a leg on the other side of the bench and straddled it between his thighs, facing her. "Yeah, I was told that you were, what? Sixteen or something?"

She smiled thinly. "Eighteen."

"What happened?" She gave him a puzzled look and he shuffled in his seat. "Come on, no one that young decides to start a revolution for no reason."

Farrah knew she was being conservative. It was not that she wasn't proud of her past. She simply didn't like to open up to others. His face, however, looked so hopeful that she felt bad not giving him at least something to go on.

"My parents were murdered on the daemon's orders when I was eleven," she began. "Thorick saved me from a similar fate and sheltered me in the home of a woman he knew. I spent the following years harbouring resentment for the person responsible for the loss of my family.

"Thorick eventually found me again and we headed off for

Letholdus when my training was complete. It took us years to figure out the underground passages, seal and reconfigure them to suit our needs. With time, we found new allies along the way to assist us with our mandate."

"I'm sorry," said Slay, the numerous wrinkles on his forehead showing just how much he was. "I didn't know about your parents."

"It's alright," Farrah replied mechanically. The only answer she ever gave.

"What were you guys doing back in those days?" Slay asked, chin falling into his palm.

"Anything we could. Helping citizens in need, jail-breaking people out of the control posts and preventing prisoners from being taken to the Anemas. We've even tried to assassinate the daemon a few times but nothing came close to succeeding. I doubt Daromas knew of our attempts."

"So, you began elaborating plans at the age of eleven?" He made an apologetic face. "Talk about a lost childhood…"

Farrah looked at her fingers, her features becoming harder. "No one's childhood exists in Daromas's world."

They both grew silent for a while.

"How about you?" Slay went on.

"Me?"

He nodded a few times. "Yeah, you told me what you did, but what was your life like?"

She cocked her head to the side. "I've been waging war against Daromas for the last eight years. This is what my life has been about."

Slay motioned with his hands as if he was moving something that wasn't there. "Yeah, yeah, but tell me about you. Any, I don't know, hobbies? Like, who are your friends? Anyone waiting for you back in Letholdus?"

At this, her brows became furrowed. "I'm sorry. I don't like talking much about myself."

She could understand Slay's wounded expression and how dry she must have sounded. She wasn't certain anymore what he wanted to hear and didn't feel like risking the implications of what her answers might reveal.

"Yeah, sure. No problem," he said, though she knew her flat reply had let him down.

She withdrew her gaze from the pressure of his disappointment and noticed Essan staring at them. She rose from her seat when she did. "Farrah, wanna come with me and watch the stars from the sun deck?"

"Sure," she answered quietly.

Both women went up the stairs and strolled towards the back of the galleon. They peered down at the emptiness underneath them as the ship glided along the clear darkened sky.

"You looked as though you needed help," Essan began with a grin.

"Was it that obvious?"

She giggled. "I've known you for a long time, Farrah. You're not as hard to read as you believe."

"That's not what Slay thinks," she replied with a sigh.

"What do you mean?"

Farrah rested her forearms against the ship's bulwarks. "Nothing. Don't worry about it."

Essan made a face and then looked up at the stars. "I think he likes you," she said casually though Farrah knew she was curious to hear her answer.

She lifted her shoulders. "I wouldn't know."

"You should just tell him."

"I won't create a conversation about my personal life unless I must." She sighed again. "Now is not the time for such trivialities. I don't want to have to take care of something like this. Besides, it's all speculation."

Essan offered a sly grin and said, "Honestly, he's all over you and there's nothing surprising about that."

"Is he?" she answered, feeling deflated.

Essan pulled her hand over her mouth, and her eyes narrowed

with a frank expression of gentle mockery. "Honestly, sometimes you're so much in your head that you become oblivious to the rest of the world."

Farrah felt vexed. She didn't want to appear aloof or unconcerned with others' lives. She wanted them to know that they could not only rely on her as a leader but also as a person. "I'm sorry."

"There's nothing wrong with being inside of your mind!" Essan took one of her hands in hers. "I'm just saying, I'm pretty sure that Slay's been… well…" She snickered some more. "… *slayed* ever since he first laid eyes on you."

Farrah let out another long breath. "We've almost never spoken."

"It doesn't really matter, does it?" She gave a quick tap on Farrah's shoulder. "Don't worry, I'll come to your rescue if you need me again."

She grinned and they stared some time at the endless vault of the stars, her head filled with many questions about an uncertain future.

It was daytime when Leos found her. She had been reviewing Feras's intimate library inside the captain's sitting room when he had entered the otherwise deserted parlour.

The lavish boudoir was a hidden treasure vault of knowledge, sitting on thousands of titles.

Farrah had found the captain a short while after she had emerged from her chambers that morning. She had waited for her to finish her breakfast before asking whether she could get her hands on some of the books of her sitting room.

"I don't recall having something that might be of interest to you, but be my guest," Feras had said before turning her back to her and resuming drinking the rest of her coffee.

Farrah had gazed for a few seconds more at the corsair's tattoo. She had not been wrong about the scene it depicted and had wanted to ask Feras about it. However, now might not have been the best moment considering the pirate's obvious desire to be left alone.

She'd set out for the sitting room and ignored the objects of valour that decorated it. Instead, she had brought her feet towards the numerous bookshelves that lingered against the parlour's sidewall.

Farrah had contemplated the immense stash of volumes, feeling overwhelmed by their number, and decided that she would have to rely on the titles of the works. Going through this collection would take more than a lifetime and she did not have such a luxury.

She began by pulling out any text that relayed an account on the gods, or rune magic, and started a pile to the side.

"What are ye lookin' for, me dear?" asked Leos's eccentric voice.

She wheeled round to welcome the man, half lifting a book as she did. "I'm trying to find any piece of information I can get my hands on. It may all be for nothing, but I have time to spare until our arrival in Neir and thought it was a good thing to do."

"Oh, oh, oh. Aye, ye told me that ye and the laddie have acquired the power o' a god."

She inclined her head. "We have been fortunate enough to come to wield such incredible allies."

The adventurer drew over and gazed at the titles she had retrieved from the shelves and ferreted through them. "Ah! *Iscar's Heritage*, this might be a good place to start indeed." He sat on the edge of the sofa and settled his palms on his lap. "Tell me, how did ye fare when conjuring yer god?"

Farrah rested her shoulder against the wall and grasped her elbows. "I've come to believe that summoning a deity isn't meant to be easy."

He hummed and said, "What ye need is someone to teach ye."

"Yes." She grinned. "But the only people who know about the gods are the ones that we are up against."

"Have ye tried askin' the experts?"

Farrah blinked at him. "The experts?"

"Aye, the gods ye've acquired! I'm guessin' ye've spoken to 'em, haven't ye?"

She narrowed her eyes. "You believe they could teach us how to convoke them?"

"Well, o' course, child! Wouldn't they be knowin' best, after all?"

Farrah beamed at him and said, "Thank you, Leos. This would indeed be a good place to start."

The adventurer gave a slight curtsy. "Aye. Now, I don't be knowin' 'bout Baltos, but I hear ye've come to befriend a spirit o' the forest. Perhaps he be a good one to ask."

"I would need to summon him first. In order to do so…" She let her sentence hang in the air.

Leos rose from his seat. "Or wait to question the Dragon Emperor. Whatever's easier." Farrah nodded, feeling thoughtful. Leos clasped his hands behind his back. "We'll be arrivin' in a few hours. I will be yer guide when we get there."

"That would be appreciated if you do not mind the danger."

He waved her off. "I certainly don't mind it and would love to see how one acquires the theurgy o' a god. It would be ma honour to accompany ye."

"Thank you," Farrah said and then asked, "Leos, what are we to expect in Neir?"

The adventurer's eyes glided to the side in thought. "I wish there were somethin' I could be tellin' ye that would help. What I be knowin' be that Baltos be a noble creature. Though, I cannot say what will come o' this meetin'." He tipped his head towards her, lifting an imaginary hat. "Happy searchin'."

The quest for gods was not an expected journey. Lately, they had been thrown inside a whirlwind they had little power over and yet was more crucial than anything they had done before.

Whatever was easier, Leos had said. If only she had the means to summon Endal, but he had only appeared for her once and hadn't since.

Farrah had tried to get in touch with her deity but to no avail. If she had a reason to contact him, to ask for his counsel, would that be enough to stir his rest?

Ignoring the pile of books she had retrieved, Farrah sat back and dropped her eyelids in concentration. She quietened herself and travelled to that place where Endal dwelled. It was a space where time got lost and her thoughts and feelings became still, in a universe of unbound depth.

She was not unfamiliar with this place. Tragedies in her past had forced her to find it early in life. It was the part of her she sought out whenever things became too much to handle, a space of strength and knowledge where her mind met and merged with her being. It had saved her from the madness of grief many times before and had helped her turn into the person she was today.

Endal, she began. *I ask for your counsel. Guide me to understand this power and how to use it.*

She groped at an answer she could feel there, so close, and yet, kept just out of reach.

Was there an answer? She felt as though there was and wanted to believe that a part of her could get in touch with it.

Was it Endal telling her this… or was it herself?

She jolted awake when the sitting room's door creaked ajar.

"You were trying to conjure your god?" Feras asked while making her way to her.

Farrah reached up, body relaxed though feeling somewhat uncomfortable she had been caught in a vulnerable state of mind. "I'm seeking answers."

The pirate smirked. "Books are easier to read when your eyes are open."

She looked down at the pile of works sitting nearby. "I was getting to that."

Feras began studying the titles that she had taken out of the library. "Anything useful?" she asked as she rummaged through them like Leos had done minutes before. Or was it hours?

Farrah shrugged. "I don't know yet. If you were wondering, I'll be leaving soon."

The captain continued on perusing through the books. "I don't mind." She looked up. "I came to tell you we'll soon be in Neir."

Farrah narrowed her eyes. How long *had* she closed them?

The corsair folded her arms on her chest, examining her baffled expression. "Did you have a plan in mind? Or you want me to drop you off in the middle of the ruins?"

They never had much of a plan when it came to gods because they didn't know what to expect from them. Leos had offered to guide them to Baltos's last known location and she had figured it would be up to them to convince him to join them. "Take us as close as you are willing to go, we'll walk the rest of the way."

"Which translates to a false sense of decision-making to make me feel bad if I don't take you far."

Farrah got up and put her hands in her pockets. "Think what you will. I'm not forcing you to come near the dragon unless you want to."

"It's basically the same thing again."

She shook her head. "I'm not trying to use you, Feras."

"No?"

Farrah stared on. "No."

The captain's eyes did not waver. "I'll ask Leos to guide the ship."

"I have a question for you," she said before the corsair could retreat.

Farrah took Feras's wrist between her fingers and peered at the image on her skin: a raging sky surrounding a galleon commanded by a tiny black-bearded pirate raising a cutlass, defying a dragon. "Why didn't you tell us about Baltos?" She lowered the captain's arm down though she kept her hand around it.

Feras had remained motionless the entire time. "What about him?"

"You were there when Corsak battled him. Why not tell us of his existence before?"

The pirate retrieved her wrist from her clutch and crossed her arms again. "I didn't feel like it."

Farrah felt somewhat wounded. "I thought you were helping us."

Feras plugged her index finger inside her ear and shook it. "I'm sorry, aren't I the only reason you've gotten this far until now? All I have been doing *is* helping you."

"I know." She scowled a bit. "I only meant to say that it doesn't make any sense to keep this information from us."

This time, Feras smirked. "But I *did* tell you."

Farrah drew her head back, confused and said, "No, you didn't, Leos did."

"Who brought you over to him?"

"Well, that's not the same thing!"

"But it is. Did you think I had any idea of Baltos's location? My father gone, I brought you to the one man who had met with him."

Farrah looked down and contemplated Feras's tattoo further. "Leos said you were there."

"By the gods, woman!" The pirate gazed up with exasperation. "You ought to stop questioning my motives when all I've been doing is proving you wrong." She widened her eyes. "I was five years old. Do you think I had any idea what was going on?"

She looked away and Feras seemed to approve of her silence. "All I remember," the corsair went on, "is what's on my arm. My mother was keeping me inside the ship to protect me from the dragon. I wanted to see him, so I fled from her embrace. I ran up on deck and witnessed this." She lifted her arm again.

"I heard my father speak a few words with it before my mother yanked me back to safety. Next thing I knew, we had escaped and the crew was yammering about how my father had confronted him and the dragon had allowed us through."

Feras sat a hand back against her waist. "There was no fight, he simply let us go. Nothing near the extravagant story being passed around."

Farrah glanced up at her. "I wasn't questioning you, Feras," she began. "I just…"

I just, what? Wanted to know more about you? She could see how she could have sounded mistrusting. The corsair was still waiting for an answer, so she supposed she had to give one. "I had noticed your tattoo. I wanted to understand."

The look Feras had in her eyes may well have been the one she reserved for the king's fool. "You don't need to control everything, you know."

At once, Farrah stiffened up a bit. "Right, I'll remember that."

She guessed the door that Feras had unlatched for her in Endal's forest had closed and she was not keen on opening it again. What rapprochement they had shared that night by the fire apparently no longer meant anything to her.

Was this how Slay had felt before, when she had refused him conversation?

"Better be prepared," said Feras, tone returning to neutral.

Farrah kept to her silence.

When the corsair tugged on the door, she called out to her one last time, wondering what impulse was making her do so. "What words did Corsak tell the dragon?"

The captain lifted her shoulders. "It was the dragon who spoke to him." Her gaze drew away for a second. "I believe he said that my father was not the one he had been looking for."

"What does that mean?"

Feras shrugged again. "I don't know, but he sounded disappointed," she answered before leaving Farrah on her own.

Had Baltos been seeking Corsak? If he'd been let down by his finding, then who was the dragon searching for?

She stared back at the pile of books sitting beside her. Her questions would have to wait. Although, she might find out soon enough. Neir was right outside.

As was the thunder dragon.

CHAPTER 16

Leos was guiding Feras as she stood at the wheel of the *Celestial Dragon*, dragging the ship through the ancient City of Kings. All that was left of it were miles of timeworn stones, most of them in crumbles. Pillars protruded from the decay alongside arches of old and degrading constructions, all reminders of a forgotten empire sitting amongst the rubble.

Feras was navigating the vessel below the city's skyline. It floated along the vestiges of a past great capital, now lying dead in the epicentre of Iscar. The sun was setting, its orange fluorescence piercing through the desolate remains, tarnished by time.

"I wonder where the people went when the land was destroyed," said Essan in a low whisper, chin levelled on her forearms, eyes peering overboard.

"They rebuilt themselves elsewhere," answered Farrah, a hint of sadness in her voice as she also gazed at it, feeling stricken by its sight.

"Aye," agreed Leos. "Almost three thousand years ago that was."

Farrah kept her stare downwards while she watched the passing ruins.

"Where did they go?" continued Essan, lifting her head to look at the old adventurer.

"They found their faith again, away from the ashes o' their past and rose up to build the great capital o' Letholdus, little missy."

She opened her eyes wide. "Wow," Essan exclaimed before glancing back at her. "The rulers of Iscar once lived here!"

Farrah smiled and Aslor gave a quick wink that only she could see.

Of course, everyone knew this, but Essan had lived in the slums. She had not had the luxury of an education and knew little of the world and its history. Glimpsing at the younger woman's wondrous expression, Farrah thought that no children should ever have to reside outside the comfort of a home.

"Yes, Essan, they did," she answered, looking back at the city, her gaze profound.

As the galleon glided through the never-ending skeletons of buildings of old, Farrah felt solemn in the face of these past relics. She tried to imagine what the former capital of Iscar would have been like back when it was yet breathing life.

Oh, how time was fleeting… everything inevitably going back to dust once enough years had passed.

"How far, Leos?" asked Feras's voice from behind.

"Keep on headin' towards that obelisk. 'Twere bein' whar be the centre o' the city. Right beside it, stands the ancient temple o' the gods, Ethelstar. I believe 'tis whar Baltos remains."

Leos pointed up towards a considerable colonnade, rising mightily amongst the rest. "'Twere bein' whar he perched himself when I last saw him, comin' out o' that temple."

"Does it have symbols on it?" asked Essan.

"Symbols, ye say?"

She brought her palms together. "All the gods have their own shrines, haven't they? Pillars made up of weird glyphs."

Farrah inclined her head in acknowledgment. "She's right. Both Endal and Ekhon had pillars enabling a projection in this realm."

"Gods can summon themselves insomuch as they remain within distance of their shrines," Aslor explained to Leos, stroking his beard between his thumb and finger as he did. "Their physical shapes are cloistered to these pillars from whence they can make an appearance in our world, that is, unless they are bound to a wielder. Only then can they freely move about Iscar."

Farrah dropped a hand on her friend's shoulder. "You're right. If we discover the shrine, we should find Baltos."

Essan put up a fist. "Okay! We're looking for a pedestal thingy with symbols on it!"

The adventurer scratched his shaggy hair. "Well, I be damned. What I believed to have been ancient Neir writin' may just have been yer godly pillar o' summonin'. I thought that Baltos had come from the temple, but he may have appeared because o' that pillar next to Ethelstar."

Aslor held onto his glasses as he scanned overboard at the approaching monument. "It's much bigger than the ones we've seen before, isn't it?" he said with a tinge of uncertainty.

"If that's not our shrine, the real one is bound to be nearby," Farrah replied. "Baltos hasn't got the means to travel away from his resting place."

"Who's to say the pillars all have to be of similar size?" answered Essan, and she lifted her hands up above her head, creating a picture of a column with her body.

"We'll know soon enough," cut in Feras. "We're almost there."

"Where are you going to drop us off?" asked Farrah.

Feras pretended not to hear her and maintained her gaze ahead, the ship gliding ever closer to their destination. Farrah kept her smile to herself as she returned her own stare to the horizon.

They cast their sights on the approaching pedestal. It was gigantic, one of the tallest obelisks they had ever seen. Sure enough, symbols covered it, impossible shapes of a language unknown to humans.

She turned to the captain. "Can we get close enough to touch it?"

Feras made a face as though insulted by her lack of faith. "Master Kerok, let's trigger the stabilizers."

The quartermaster pressed down on a few buttons and the corsair peered at the monitor displaying a two-dimensional representation of their surroundings. She nudged the ship nearer to the pillar and then lifted her gaze up, calculating the last few feet by eyesight. In less than no time, the galleon was next to the obelisk, hovering in place.

Farrah exhaled out while the others held their breaths in.

Leos came to her side and surveilled the writing. "What now?"

"We touch it."

"Right," said Slay, standing nearest to the monument. He angled across and pressed a full palm against the pedestal.

Nothing happened.

The islander drew his fingers up, frowning, and positioned them again on the cold surface. Nothing but the mute silence of an empty city.

"Perhaps this is not our pillar?" wondered Aslor.

"The writings are the same as those found on the other shrines," answered Farrah, teeth gnawing on the inside of her cheek. "I find it hard to believe that this isn't it."

"Maybe he doesn't want to be disturbed?" Slay replied, stepping away from the monument.

"How did Baltos last appear to you?" She inquired to Leos.

"He came out o' nowhere and perched himself on that column. His gaze pierced through me and I felt as though he were lookin' right at me heart. After a minute or so, he told us to leave."

"This isn't helping much," answered Slay. "Seems to me that gods sometimes materialize when they feel like it and at other times, they need a little incentive."

Farrah darted her eyes back to the obelisk, her surroundings vanishing as she contemplated it, pushing out the voices of those who stood beside her. As she did, she wrapped a hand over her necklace.

The dragon had risen on top of this monument. He had sent Corsak away, the person he had been looking for. The myths also said that Baltos had failed the kings and queens of old and had since remained here, waiting for a chance to redeem himself.

He was waiting for a time of reckoning.

Endal had also been waiting.

The gods knew boundless things about Iscar and the people in it. They only needed a channel to open between them. Maybe all the dragon required was to know they were here.

That they had arrived.

Feeling entranced, she lifted her palm and her breathing resonated with Endal's howl, infusing her with his presence. The theurgy of the gods flooded her core, showing her the way, unveiling deep truths and uncovering the path that lay before them.

Her body, left forgotten, was moving on its own. She was the messenger brought forth, the long-anticipated answer.

And then it wasn't Endal; it was the Dragon Emperor.

Baltos *had* been waiting for them.

Farrah found this clarity became evidence. It was as if someone had told her this truth in explicitly spoken words.

Her fingertips caressed the glyphs of the pedestal, and they began to glow a fiery golden colour, taking life along the length of the pillar. Its luminescence shone back into her eyes, illuminating the fading sunlight on the horizon.

Then she heard his voice. No, not heard, *felt* it.

Her surroundings withdrew from sight as visions of the past flooded her mind. She saw the abundant city of Neir in its bountiful youth, and its dragon protector, draped in nobility. She witnessed the rise and fall of an empire, the light of its life and the darkness of its ending. She saw a weeping god, framed by fire and death while a dynasty collapsed, and its people fled the misery of their fate. She felt the angst, the pain and the suffering of a ruined past.

She delved inside Baltos's heart, witnessed his melancholy and torment. The dragon had been waiting, waiting for those that would grant him one last chance, an opportunity to rebuild a wrong.

A time to rebuild a dream.

The images poured through Farrah as though thousand pieces of information had rushed her, revealing a story she needed to know and was now a part of her, a part of her own history.

The skies darkened and clouds gathered over their heads. A gleaming circle beamed down at them from out of the grey fog.

There emerged the Dragon Emperor, Baltos, crashing down from above, his powerful wings flapping in the wind. The air around them growled at its master's arrival and lightning ignited in a tempest of lights and shadows as the heavens were torn asunder.

Spectacular horns adorned his forehead. His chest was as golden as his shrine was. The rest of the skin on his back was as black as charcoal, his scales glinting like the armour of knights of old. Sturdy claws dressed the end of his muscular limbs, his sharp teeth revealing an unyielding jaw structure.

His aureate-filled eyeball surveyed them as he levelled himself over their heads, lowering his gaze to meet with their stunned expressions. "*I have waited thousands of years,*" he announced, mouth unmoving, his growl like thunder breaking against the ground. "*You have arrived.*"

Pirates and renegades stared awestruck at both Farrah and the dragon. She peered up at the enormous creature of the sky, her chin held high and hair flying in the wind. "I know," she replied, her voice unlike her own. "I have heard your plea. We have arrived."

Something incredible happened as the fading sunlight glowed upon the god's back, its form shaped by the dazzling beams.

He began to weep.

The dragon bowed his head, and giant tears fell from his eyes. Pearls of diamonds glittered the length of the shimmering scales before shattering like rain below.

This event halted the flow of time, this sight an impossible privilege for the humbled group of watchers.

Baltos lifted his face to gaze at the people gathered on the galleon's deck, looking unperturbed by the emotions that had seized him. The god's golden pupils penetrated Farrah's soul and he delivered her a powerful message, which no one else heard.

They were present and past intertwined in a future of possibilities, bound in their own mysterious world, where they kept each other.

While the others around marvelled at the pair, Feras approached Farrah, searching her eyes. Then, the pirate gazed up at the dragon, the celestial creature doing the same. It was as though he had called out to her and had been the reason for her approach all along.

Something in Feras's face was different. It felt involved. She had worn that expression when she had been conversing privately with Endal. She was now doing the same with the dragon.

Baltos's deep, scorching voice echoed again through their souls. "*I have waited for wrongs to be made right. I am your inheritance. You are my ancestor. We are perpetually linked, are one, and time is a mere obstacle to what must be done.*" Though he was speaking to all, Farrah felt the ripples of his words reverberating as though he were talking only to her. "*I will give you back your kingdom and you will rule your lands once more. I will offer you eternity that you may offer me legacy.*"

She looked up at the wondrous face of the dragon, and the creature pierced his gaze into her own. "*Take me, and free me.*"

Baltos was giving himself to her. She would need to refuse him. Endal was already hers, and she could not wield two gods. But somehow, he understood this.

She felt speechless. What could she tell him? What words of rejection could she speak to the Dragon Emperor?

A balm touched Farrah's soul, and it resembled the sound of music. He was the one giving it to her, calming her fears, soothing her worries. Endal was there too.

"*I cannot be yours,*" Baltos declared, sorrow tainting his asserting voice, "*but there is another I can offer myself to.*"

Farrah closed her eyes and the dragon's warm breath filled her heart with answers. There was another.

Only one other.

She turned around, her chest vibrating. She knew what she had to do, yet felt apprehensive of the repercussions. She was sealing unwilling fates.

Farrah was making a choice, and Baltos was aware of it too. He had known it all along because he had felt it before, though he had not yet understood it. The dragon had already found the person he would become one with. It wasn't the father but rather the daughter that he had been seeking.

Now was the reckoning of their meeting.

"You are the one who belongs with him." Farrah's eyes clung to Feras's hard face, the encompassing wind enveloping them both in its effervescence, freezing everything else around to capture them, only them, in this moment.

Incomprehension flooded the pirate's features and she kept mute. Nothing could deny what she also knew.

This was what was meant to be, and it could not be fought.

"No," muttered the corsair, but the word felt weak, a final attempt to counter a destiny that had been chosen for her.

Their stares did not let go of each other even as Baltos levelled his head with them, his golden pupils depicting an endless awareness of all things known. He was already a part of the pirate.

"It's what must be," Farrah continued.

A thousand feelings crossed the depth of the captain's eyes: apprehension and angst, understanding and knowing, denial and acceptance. "This wasn't my choice," she told Farrah in a whisper.

She smiled. "But it was."

Feras contemplated the dragon, both now conversing in Baltos's mind fortress.

The corsair began shaking her head, her chin lowering, eyes closing. And then, after a while, the lightest smirk appeared on her features. "I guess we've all known for a while that it would get to this," she muttered and then peered into the faces of the people around. They also knew it. "You're not going to tell me why we're meant to be joined, are you?" she asked Baltos.

The dragon's glare was absolute. "*Everything is forever revealed in its rightful moment. In its infinite nature, the world is unbound by time.*"

Feras's stare became harder. "You've been waiting for this?"

Baltos's expression, though ridged by harsh features, seemed to soften. "*This is the instance I return. When I am called forth to rearrange things as they are supposed to be.*"

"End Daromas's reign?"

The deity's face brightened somewhat, engulfing them in his sight. "*All the usurpers must vanish to reveal the path of those who have been dethroned and return everything to its rightful place. This is my duty as protector god of Neir's ancient seat.*"

"But Neir doesn't exist anymore," came Slay's voice from somewhere behind. A second later, Essan had rounded on his back and placed a hand over his mouth, hushing him up.

Baltos's eyes brimmed with sorrow, and sadness pierced through his next words. "*The land may be different, but its people are yet very much alive. I have failed them once. I will not fail them again.*" The venerable god looked to Feras. "*Will you accept my redemption, knight of the skies?*"

The corsair jerked her head down, her lips pulled tight. She seemed submerged by so many emotions that it was difficult for her to speak.

"It's okay."

Feras turned her gaze on her. "It's okay to be afraid," Farrah repeated, her voice reaching only the captain inside the intimate bubble they shared with the dragon.

The pirate's eyes widened at this.

"I sometimes get scared too," she added and gave Feras a smile only the other woman could see.

Feras swallowed hard and looked back at the god. She then lifted her chin and heaved a breath. Her mouth a narrowed line, she acquiesced.

"*So it shall be written.*"

Farrah tore her eyes away from the captain, her chest beating. "Before we part, there is something I must ask of you, if you are so willing to grant me an answer?" The dragon nodded. "How do we conjure the gods?"

His head moved imperceptibly to the side. He maintained the silence for a while as they waited for words that could change everything for them.

"*I cannot tell you how to summon us,*" he began and Farrah felt the immediate crush of disappointment at this. "*Because it is not something that can be voiced.*" Warmth started to emanate from him, filling them up with its brilliance. It was as though he were apologizing for his cryptic answer.

"*You can wield your god when you find it inside, child. When your eyes are blind and your soul opens its gaze to the truth. When your body is left behind and your mind expands. When everything is so still that you witness life bursting all around. When you are returned to nothingness and become all things.*" Baltos's face softened again. "*All can uncover it–if only they would stop searching.*"

She tried to transcribe to memory what he had told them. It was not the answer she had wanted to hear, but perhaps it was better this way. She knew Baltos had hidden the solution right in there. Or maybe he had put it in plain sight.

The dragon drew his beatific face back to Feras. "*It is time. Will you take me?*"

"Yes," the corsair answered and the voice felt like a pale echo of its usual strength.

Baltos's growl thundered. "*I will be beside you.*"

Feras's hand was lifted up, her features taut as she offered it to the dragon. A golden flash scintillated along Baltos's form, and his shape turned into particles of diamond stars reaching for the pirate's palm. She fell to one knee as he penetrated her consciousness, flooding her with his being.

He vanished alongside the last rays of sun disappearing into the night, sheathing the sleeping city in its shadows.

Farrah stooped by Feras's side and rested hesitant fingers on her shoulder. The corsair huffed, looking exhausted.

"Was this your plan all along?" she muttered.

Farrah smiled softly and shook her head. She grabbed Feras's mechanical arm and helped her back to her feet. She then noticed that all the others were gazing at them with odd expressions on their faces. "What's wrong?" she asked Essan, standing closest to her.

"Farrah," she whispered. "Are you not aware of what just happened?"

Slay stepped nearer, eyes gleaming. "Baltos and you had gone into your own universe. The Dragon Emperor was subdued before you."

Aslor bowed his head, his expression revered, his stare cast down. "I believe our dragon had been waiting all this time for you to come along…."

Slay threw his hands up. "It's like we were witnessing a great event of some sort, or a long-lost reunion!"

Leos's features looked cryptic, his eyes intent on her. Farrah searched for Thorick's reassuring gaze amidst this uncomfortable admiration. He shared with her a private look, the one he wore whenever he wanted her to know that he was proud of what she had accomplished.

"Gods… have a plan of their own. I guess I was a part of Baltos's," she answered fleetingly before turning to Feras. "And you were too."

The pirate's stern expression seemed elsewhere. She nodded but said nothing.

"Congratulations, Captain!" exclaimed Essan. She hopped closer to Feras and clapped her on the arm. "I knew you'd make a wonderful renegade!" she added with a wink.

"Welcome aboard *our* ship, Captain," agreed Aslor.

Leos finally drew his gaze from Farrah and grinned while he grabbed Feras by the shoulders. "About time, eh!"

The corsair simpered an ironic smile. "Is that so?" she answered and then cocked her head to the side, glaring at the man.

Feras then contemplated the faces beaming up at her and cleared her voice, making her tone louder for everyone to hear. "I cannot ask any of you to join me on this folly," she told her crew. "It would be much wiser to get off of this sinking ship as soon as you can. If anyone one of you lads wishes to be removed from service, I would not refuse them."

"Capt'n," said Kerok, standing tall amongst the pirates. "You think we'd let you keep the glory to yourself?" The man smirked and the other crew members chuckled. "We are with you," he finished, and the pirates threw their hands up for their captain whom they now—if that were possible—held even greater respect for.

"You lot of scurvy dogs! Don't come nagging when you're all dead." Feras grinned and watched them with an expression that resembled pride. "I guess our business here is done," she finished, looking back to Farrah.

She nodded as a poignant feeling warmed her inside.

Each day now, their path was removing all obstacles as though they were castles of sand overthrown by the raging sea they encompassed. She was following where the calling was taking her and every step of the way, she was being rewarded for it. For listening.

"It is."

Feras tossed her fingers through her hair. "Master Kerok, set a course for the jungles of Shandew. I believe this is where our next destination lies?"

"Aye, Capt'n," replied Leos at once.

The pirate glimpsed at Baltos's pillar one last time and retreated. Her abrupt disappearance released Farrah, the spell of their encounter with the dragon broken.

The rest of the crew resumed their positions and the *Celestial Dragon* hoisted off towards the darkened horizon, Kerok taking control of the vessel. Soon, the renegades and Leos were all that was left, their meeting with Baltos already a thing of the past. Or was it that all this running around for gods had become a natural part of their lives?

Slay was stretching his hands over his head, beaming. "Another deity in our arsenal and effortless to retrieve at that. I'm beginning to think that the universe is blessing our venture. The gods definitely are, it would seem."

Aslor had to agree. "The more we progress through this quest, the more I believe that they have scripted us a story, and we are writing its words." He bowed to Farrah. "And it would appear that you are its main actress."

She shook her head. "Baltos bonded with me, but it was Feras that was meant to get him."

"But how did ye come to be knowin' all o' this?" arose Leos's voice while he surveilled her with interest.

"I can't say." She squinted in thought. "I just did, or rather, I felt it. This is what Baltos wanted. For whatever reason, it had to be her."

"I'm glad it turned out this way," said Essan. "Not only have we acquired a god, but the captain is officially one of us!"

Aslor was shifting his weight from one leg to the other. "Let us pray that things remain this easy for the entirety of our venture."

Essan bumped her fist against his shoulder. "Don't jinx it, Aslor!"

"I wasn't! I was just saying…"

Farrah felt warm. Everything was coming together and Feras's change of heart only furthered that.

She caught Slay staring at her. The man drew by her side when she did. "Why do you think nothing happened when I touched the pillar and Baltos appeared when you did?"

She lifted her shoulders. She knew the answer, but it was not one she wanted to share. "Gods have a will of their own. I guess this is how it was supposed to be." She turned to Leos, hoping for a change of subject. "Would you tell us more about this Shandew goddess were about to go meet?"

"Aye," replied the man distantly, gaze hovering longingly on Neir's remains as if wanting to take in this moment longer. "She goes by the name o' Thar and I have ne'er seen her with me own eyes." He beckoned them over and they followed him inside the ship and into the saloon hall.

He took a seat on one of the couches, and invited them to do the same. "I had gone to Shandew in search o' lost treasures o' the Shandalew people, the natives who sheltered me fer a few weeks as I got to learn about their cultures. The goddess o' their jungles be called Thar, but it were rather unclear to me whether she were good or evil."

He made his voice quieter as though feeling anxious the deity would somehow overhear him. "She were thought to be a goddess o' life and death. Sacrifices and rituals in her name be still practised nowadays to keep them people in her graces, and they told me stories o' how she burnt and ate those who had infringed on her jungle and upset the balance in it. But it 'twere ne'er quite apparent to me whether it were all folklore and make-believe cemented by reality. Ye will find Thar there though I cannot say how she will respond to yer arrival."

Slay scratched the underside of his throat. "That's unfortunate."

Leos nodded a few times. "I will lead ye to this village and they can tell ye more about her. Maybe their input be more favourable than me own."

They fell silent, sharing a similar hope that Thar would be as willing to join their group as the other deities had been.

Farrah retreated to her cabin at some point later, carrying the pile of books she had salvaged earlier. She stacked them on her bedside table and grasped the copy of *Iscar's Heritage* while sitting back on her berth. As she scanned through the pages, she found her mind wavering.

She knew Feras had not expected their encounter with the dragon to resolve the way it had.

Days before, Farrah would have believed it impossible that the captain would join them. How was it that one of these lands' most influential players had allied herself with them?

Did Baltos think that without the captain of the *Celestial Dragon* their enterprise was doomed to fail?

Farrah herself was having a hard time understanding what had happened. Her connection with Baltos had appeared out of nowhere and had somehow created an entire story between his past and their present as it led them towards their joint future.

She set the book down, coming to terms with the notion that she would not be reading tonight. She slipped inside of her sheets and grabbed her pillow between her arms as she lay on her side.

Feras had looked conflicted when she had left them.

Tomorrow, Farrah would talk to her, and if she were feeling unsure, she would convince her to stay.

Chapter 17

Feras was leaning back in her armchair, a hand sitting on the desk in front of her, the other on her lap.

One moment she had been carrying the renegades to their destination, the next she had acquired the god they had been searching for, making herself a full agent of the rebellion.

Everything that had happened since these people had come aboard the *Celestial Dragon* had led her to this day. Farrah had been right; it *had* been her choice to be where she stood.

It wasn't so much that she had needed convincing; it was how things had panned out. She had simply been keeping her eyes shut to the changes that were operating inside of her all this time.

Her encounter with Endal years before had not been by chance. She knew that much by now. Meeting the renegades had not been by chance either. Every step that had brought her to this present seemed orchestrated by higher powers that were playing their cards at opportune moments.

When the dragon had appeared, she had felt a deep rousing. When she had looked into Farrah's mesmerized expression, she had felt like moving forward, drawn unwillingly towards the events that were unfolding.

Through the eyes of Baltos, he had transported her to past days, when she had first seen him. She had remembered vividly the reverent beast. Remembered that, even then, he had been seeking her.

Before the mind of a child could have made sense of this, her mother had brought her back inside the ship and the vision had vanished.

Feras grinned and shook her head from side to side. Her father had later named his galleon after the dragon. The ship she now commanded.

Oh, how fate was a strange and mysterious thing.

Throughout their peculiar meeting, she had felt drawn to Baltos. And yet, it was Farrah whom the god had first appeared taken with. Why had he been seeking *her* instead of the other woman he seemed bound to?

Well, no matter what it was, she couldn't turn back now. The renegades desperately needed the theurgy of the gods and though a part of her still felt like it, she could no longer abandon them.

She had come to believe in the rebels' quest. Against all odds, these people stood a chance of vanquishing Daromas. To refuse them her hand now would hinder their probability of success. She was not ready to let this happen even though she hadn't sought to be an active participant in this rebellion.

All she could do was accept this path and become the unsuspecting renegade she was bound to be. If she were to fail, well, she would be acclaimed as the pirate who had resisted the daemon as her father had before.

Yet, she could not ignore the cold that had grasped her chest at the thought of facing Daromas.

Yes, she was afraid. That much was true.

She loved life. Hers was bountiful; it had always been. She did not want to give it up. Yet, it had been fleeting through her fingers lately like an hourglass whose flowing grains were willing her ever closer towards a destiny she felt petrified of having while she held on to what remained.

Oh, Father, she thought.

Corsak would have never hesitated. He wouldn't have had doubts.

Feras could feel the god's unfathomable presence rumbling through her and was beginning to understand what it was like to become one with such a power. She stared down at the palm of her hand where Baltos's crest now decorated her skin, its golden shape glistening only for her eyes to see.

This was her legacy, her inheritance.

The dragon had found its rightful place, and so had she.

Shandew's jungles stood on the edge of Iscar's eastern perimeter and were yet unoccupied by the placaters. Though it was only a matter of time before the daemon would set his gaze on these territories and claim them as his own, as of now, they remained untarnished and untamed.

It also meant that it would prove a secure location for them to travel to. Unless another ship intercepted them, it would be safe to assume their road free of troubles. For now.

Considering Shandew was a few days away from their current whereabouts, Feras had decided to use this opportunity of time to their advantage.

She was pacing along the spar deck when she spotted the group of renegades she had been searching for. It was the beginning of the afternoon, and the rich sun was making its course above her head, the perfect weather for what she had in mind.

She drew herself in front of them and dropped the heavy leather bag she had been carrying. Watched by multiple inquisitive stares, she removed her coat and shoved it to the side before throwing her tricorn on it.

"Right," she began, using the tip of her boot to nudge the sack of gear she had brought. "Let's see what you lot are made of."

Slay rose to his feet and ferreted through the bag, soon salvaging a wooden sword from it. "Training equipment?" he inquired, eyes pointing at the weapon.

Feras drew a second wooden blade. "You'll be going first, then?"

He smirked, seemingly eager at the prospect of battling her.

They stepped away from one another and unto the wide-open deck space. She noticed the renegades standing up, ninja girl and

Aslor looking as excited as the islander was. Farrah had crossed her arms over her chest and was staring curiously at the scene, the knight doing the same by her side. Crew members had also begun to assemble around them, pausing their daily chores in order to watch the performance.

She drew her eyes to her improvised fencing partner.

The man was slouching a little, one hand wielding the sword up, the other held upright next to it. She did not bother to raise her own. These people were amateurs, at best.

Feras had seen them fight and found them *good.* But good was not good enough; she needed them to be *great.* They would not win the war against Daromas and his commandants if they did not become much stronger.

He sprung her way, attempting to catch her off guard before she could take action.

Feras lazily parried his sword, and he went stumbling past her. She rolled her eyes. It was a wonder how these people were still alive.

She trained with him for the next fifteen minutes or so, her blade finding its mark more than a dozen times over his soon-to-be bruised body.

It wasn't so much that the man lacked skills. It was rather that he was leaping all over the place like an enraged animal. There was no structure, no technique. He had the potential of a great warrior but required discipline.

The guy, Slay was his name, eventually drew a hand up in a gesture of peace and squatted on the floor, panting hard and unable to withstand her beating anymore. "I think I need a break," he huffed. "Someone else wants to have a go?"

Feras sat the tip of her sword down. "Ninj… Uh, Essan and Mister Aslor, you two are next," she told them, not offering them a choice in the matter.

The trader and ninja girl glanced at each other. Essan shrugged. "Ready, Aslor?" she asked in a playful tone.

The gentleman glowered at the bag of arms. "Captain," he began. "I'm not fond of close-range weapons."

Feras retrieved two short wooden blades from the sack and shoved them at his chest. "Then about time you learned."

Aslor took the swords between his fingers, looking unnatural holding them.

Essan giggled and lifted two timber knives from the bag. "Anytime now," she told the trader.

He sighed and coerced his feet onwards. "Be nice to me, Essan…"

As light as a feather, ninja girl jumped towards the man, making her way around him at incredible speed, body moving up and down. Aslor could do nothing but squirm away from her furious ambush, attempting to avoid her blows and missing quite a few times in the process.

Feras put her hands on her hips. Aslor was no expert when it came to close-quarter fighting but learning how to dodge attacks would prove excellent training for him. And who better than a martial arts fighter to teach him?

Essan was now swaying about, akin to a shadow soaring up from the ground, Aslor trying to stave off her incoming assaults to the best of his abilities.

She peered back at Slay's lowered figure, forearms resting on his knees, still recovering from their skirmish. She went his way and bent down on her toes, head hovering above his. "You rush in without thinking. Take your time."

The man gazed up at her. "That's how I learned to fight back on the islands."

"Then refine yourself and learn something new." She patted her mechanical hand on his shoulder before pulling him back up with a yank on his clothes.

She modified his stance and positioned his back straighter before readjusting both his offhand and weapon arm. She then made him practice some movements before changing his posture again. After a few tries, she gave him a probing nod. "Start with these basics and become habituated to them. Once you've mastered these, we'll add in new techniques."

Slay acquiesced solemnly and went off to train on his own, Feras watching him for some time before reconvening with the others, putting an end to the trader's sad skirmish.

"Mister Aslor," she told the gentleman. "You have a right to be scared when you fight. We all become scared when we duel against opponents who are stronger than us. But you have to learn to control that fear. It doesn't matter that Essan is a better combatant than you are, but controlling that fear may let you live a while longer."

Aslor took his foggy glasses off and began to rub them. "I'm not used to fighting like this."

"Then practice makes perfect. You'll never be the best at close-quarter combat. But that's fine, you're a good gunslinger; I've seen you work around that pistol of yours. Nevertheless, your enemies may yet breach the barrier that stands between you and them. If that happens, you'll need to fend them off before resuming your gunman position. We'll train with defensive stances with you and escape techniques."

She pointed to Essan. "She can teach you avoidance strategies. We'll look together at postures you can take using pistols."

Ninja girl trotted her way and thumped her fingers against her shoulder blade. "What about me?"

Feras shrugged. "You are your own specialist at what you do. You're fast and deadly. Just don't get caught. Someone like the big man over there would kill you in one blow."

Essan pondered this for a second. "So, I need to become even faster and deadlier?"

She grinned. "Precisely." She then set her sight on Farrah and Thorick. *This will be fun*, she thought wickedly. "You two, you're next."

They exchanged an entertained look between one another before leaning over the bag of equipment to take a pick at their weapons. The knight retrieved a long pole, while the renegade leader grabbed both short swords from Aslor's sweaty palms.

They took position, Farrah's back facing her. Feras folded her arms as they leaped onwards.

It was apparent that they had crossed weapons before. What should have been a clash of styles soon became an unlikely brilliant duo.

Essan came by her side and folded her arms just as she had. "You seem surprised, Captain."

She arched an eyebrow. "Okay, what's the story?"

Essan giggled. "Thorick's the one who taught Farrah how to use a weapon when she was young. They've fought together thousands of times."

Feras contemplated them. This was not hard to believe. It was as if each of them knew what the other was about to do.

Farrah was lunging around Thorick, who was using his weight and size to try to subdue her, each of them harnessing their talents flawlessly against an enemy that fought differently from the other. The duel seemed endless, Farrah fast and precise, Thorick strong and unbendable.

"Cheaters," she answered with a wink. Essan laughed again. "You can stop now. You've proven that you two can fight," she called out.

Both loosened their stance and grinned at each other. "Henceforth," Feras continued, "we shall make the odds less predictable." She pointed at the knight. "You can train with me next," and then to Farrah, "You can challenge Slay."

As the afternoon glided into hours, Feras skirmished against Thorick, who put up a nice fight before she brought him to his knees, her sword to his throat.

Farrah's duel with the islander had lasted just a while longer before the renegade leader, hard-faced and focused, had taken him down. The brawler guy had looked discomfited when she had, but Feras had awarded him an approving nod. "Better," she had told him.

Aslor had then practised with her defensive techniques using guns while Farrah had battled Essan, the renegade leader proving her expertise again.

One after the other, they had trained for as long as the firmament yet wielded light and only when the first moon had appeared had they stopped.

Feras wiped the sweat from her eyes, feeling worn out. She had not exercised for such an extensive period of time in a while.

She looked appreciatively at the group of renegades, spent and exhausted by the day's work. "I guess I can make something out of you lot. Tomorrow, we'll start again. Better sleep early tonight."

"Thanks, Captain," said Essan, hand massaging the back of her neck.

Feras took her leave of them and grabbed a cup of water at the nearest casket, gulping it down as the rest of them gathered around, grabbing their own share.

Even though she had guided these renegades through most of their undertakings, she still felt estranged by their presence. Theirs were two different worlds collapsing together.

And yet, there was something about them that was drawing her in.

She noticed Farrah, silently drinking by her side. That woman was a bit of an enigma. An air of mystery surrounded her, which most would have found enticing.

Feras found it rather dreary.

"Can we talk?"

Farrah was now gazing at her with a certain conviction.

"As you wish…"

They went up the forecastle deck, saying nothing until Feras drew her back against the bulwarks, elbows holding her against it. "I'm listening."

Farrah faced the other side, forearms sitting against the hard wood. She stole a glance her way and Feras wondered why the woman suddenly appeared reluctant when it came to speaking her mind.

"I appreciate what you're doing," began the renegade leader.

"Which part were you referring to?" she answered. "Because we could go for a while."

Farrah drew her expression fully on her. "I'm talking about your assistance," she replied, not taking the bait. "It was considerate of you, how you gave everyone advice."

She shrugged and grinned. "I guess acquiring the power of a god would do that. I'm involved now, whether I like it or not. Better to make the best of it."

The woman stared back at the sky for a minute or so. "What made you change your mind?" she asked, wheeling again to her rather forcefully.

Feras felt taken aback. It was a difficult question to answer. Well, maybe it wasn't. "At this point, why not? Everything that has happened in the last few weeks has led me to this, hasn't it? Or maybe my entire life…"

She pulled herself straighter and turned around, also facing the clouds. "Meeting Baltos as a child, Endal later on. Even *I* cannot close my eyes to it. I'm starting to believe that this *is* my destiny." She gave her a wink. "I guess I'm stuck with you."

"I agree," Farrah replied. "And I'm not saying this to convince you or anything. It just feels… right that you would join us. Having you at our side will make our enterprise that much more conceivable."

"So many warm thoughts for me," Feras answered, eyes opening in surprise. "I'll start thinking you're glad that I'm stranded with you."

Farrah smiled and looked away, leaning further onto the bannister. "I am."

She grinned teasingly but replied nothing as she watched Farrah's expression, which she realized, was honest. "Any breakthrough yet on how to conjure these gods?"

"Have you tried?"

Feras nudged her head to the side. "Something about discovering the deity within, that it?"

Farrah's lips moved imperceptibly, teeth catching them on the inside of her mouth. "I'm working on it."

"You've done it before, so it's doable. We'll figure it out eventually. Or perhaps there's nothing to figure out."

The other woman contemplated her. "What do you mean?"

She smirked and pointed to Farrah's forehead with her finger. "I think you spend too much time up there. Gods are not about head; they're about heart." She offered the renegade leader her side smile and left, deciding she didn't have anything more to add.

Leader? she thought as she retreated from her. Did this mean that Farrah was her leader now?

Not if she could help it.

She was the captain; this gave her final say on everything happening as long as they were on her galleon.

Feras made a face. What an awkward situation.

She proceeded to the main deck where the dining tables had been placed. *Good*, she thought. She was dead hungry and needed a drink after this day of training.

She noticed the renegades huddled nearby and squinched her nose to herself.

It wasn't that she didn't find them amicable; Aslor was an interesting fellow, and ninja girl was an uplifting character. It was that big man she liked most, but he was not one for conversation. That was regrettable.

She paused for a moment before heading towards them. As her new companions of fortune, it would serve no one to disdain them. She could learn from getting to know these renegades better. Even that awkward fellow, Slay.

"Join me at my table," she said while placing her hands behind Essan and Aslor's shoulders before retreating. She knew they would follow.

She sat in her usual chair at the top end of the largest table and hoisted a tankard of ale filled to border. Slay and Aslor took their seats on both sides of her while Essan took hers next to the islander and Thorick beside the gentleman. Only Farrah was missing.

"Thank you, Captain Sadahl, for the training today. Your help has been most fruitful," said Aslor.

Feras had always liked the trader's manners. So darn polite. She smiled cursively and grabbed a bite from her plate. She then noticed Leos approaching and invited him to take a seat with them, which he did, eyes groping at the food scattered on the table.

"Tell me, Mister Aslor," she resumed, "I thought you were a peaceful merchant, not an anarchist. How did you come to join this winsome group?"

Aslor chuckled as he filled his dish. "You would not be wrong. I, as well, often wonder what has taken hold of me to have made off with this venture." He cast his eyes around at the others' faces. "But I have no regrets whatsoever."

Feras stared at him, her drink levelled with her lips as he went on. "I am a trader, have always been as was my father. Back in the old days, our family's fortune was profitable in the service of our dear King Redamastys. When the daemon gained control of Iscar, our affairs took a turn for the worse and we were forced to flee court and work in otherwise less legal dealings.

"We became front merchants for the pirates and rebels who were resisting Daromas and prided ourselves on reaching out to anyone but those who stood under the daemon. As traders of the capital, we dressed under the banner of Daromas's Letholdus, hidden from his sight. This is how I met Farrah."

Aslor had smiled upon saying those last words. "I became her main provider and have been for a long time now. Though I've never taken part in her operations on the field before, when she came to me, I knew I had no other choice but to offer my assistance. It was my duty to her as it has been for many years."

What was intriguing to Feras was the twinkle that had illuminated the man's eyes when Farrah's name had risen on his lips. The way he had spoken of her, the tone of his voice, had been filled with such admiration. It was somewhat fascinating to see how every member of this impossibly small group appeared to hold this woman in such high regard.

"Incredible, isn't it?" she replied. "How our lives can take such improbable turns." She turned to the islander and emptied her tankard, staring at the man with inquiring eyes, still getting a sense of him. "What about you?"

Slay looked around and lifted his hands up in a shrug, smiling diffidently. "I'm new to this. I bumped into these guys just before the attempt on the daemon's life, and I went with it. Glad Farrah accepted me."

Feras blinked at few times. "Right," she answered, losing interest. What did he remind her of with his laid-back attitude and brawler-like behaviours?

She contemplated Essan next. "You've been along for a while, I presume?"

Ninja girl beamed, apparently happy that she had thought so. "Farrah took me in when I was a child, back in the streets of Lethol-dus. She kinda raised me, along with the others." She gave Thorick a grin. "I was officially the youngest member of the group and I've spent most of my life being a part of the resistance."

Again with Farrah. Something indescribable bonded them. They had been through a lot and it appeared that their leader had guided them through it all.

"What is it with you people and this woman?" Feras suddenly asked, eyes narrowing, wearing the slightest grin on her lips.

"Captain?" inquired Aslor.

"Your leader."

"What's your…"

"What makes her so special?"

All four of them seemed stumped by this. It was as though she had uttered something blasphemous. She folded her legs, curious to hear what was about to come out of their mouths.

"You don't know her."

She set her stare on the youngest member of the group and intertwined her hands. Though Essan looked abashed by the scrutiny, she sustained Feras's gaze nonetheless.

"Farrah has done more for us than any would have," she explained. "She never does anything for herself, she only cares about others."

"Ah, the self-righteous vigilante. This particular trope can turn into somewhat of a bore...." replied Feras, cocking an eyebrow.

"Not when hundreds of people owe her their lives," Essan answered, voice uncharacteristically firm. "Not when she kept a dream going when no one else believed anymore. If it wasn't for her, none of us would be here today, doomed to remain forevermore in the daemon's grasp." She raised her chin up and said, "So no, it's not a bore, Captain." She then hardened her eyes and repeated, "You don't know her."

Feras grinned. She was starting to like them. There was courage, yes, and friendship and loyalty. She was beginning to get a sense of the deep drive that led them. Yes, she could respect that; these people *were* worth her time.

"I wonder, is she willing to do the right thing, even when it means doing something difficult?" she asked.

Aslor shuffled in his seat and without looking her in the eye, said, "If you're referring to those placaters back on Prism Cove, Captain..." he began and Feras smirked. "Well, there are many interpretations of rights and wrongs. Different understandings of these concepts do not make a vision better than another." He wriggled his fingers nervously. "I dare say that she *is* capable of doing the difficult thing."

Feras contemplated him. "Good answer, Mister Aslor." She turned to Slay and said, "I'm certain *you* have something to add."

The islander's mouth dropped. "Uh," he began. "I mean, how she talks, it's, uh..."

"Captivating?"

"Well... yeah. Everyone just hangs on to her words."

"Of course they do," Feras replied, grin widening. "Anyway, you've convinced me," she acquiesced while opening up her arms.

"We have?" answered Slay.

"No better way to know a leader than through their troops, is there?"

She *had* heard enough. Respect was a hard thing to acquire. If Farrah had theirs, it meant she had been doing something good.

No one fucked with the daemon unless they had someone with a solid head on their shoulders to lead them.

Essan seemed satisfied by that, and Slay relieved that she was no longer teasing him. "What about the big man?" Feras turned to Thorick, sizing him up. "What's his story?"

It was Essan who recounted it. She told them how he had been a soldier of the royal guardian corps under King Redamastys before they had thrown him into the Anemas after the daemon's ascent to power. She explained his escape with the assistance of a now-deceased friend named Darvis, and how he had regrouped with Farrah to later create the renegade alliance.

"Regrouped?"

Thorick was staring at the younger woman, listening to her as she told his story, trusting her account and allowing her to confide in Feras.

"Yeah," replied Essan, also glancing at the knight but with a sudden reluctance. "Thorick helped Farrah flee the capital when the daemon… well…"

"When he murdered my family," finished Farrah, finally joining them for dinner and taking a seat next to ninja girl.

"Oh, yes…" mumbled Essan, eyes cast down at her plate.

Farrah placed a hand on her shoulder, silently telling her not to worry.

Feras tilted her head to the side. She was starting to get a sense of it all. If anything, revenge was a powerful motive. "I'm guessing that it was after this tragic event that you began harbouring plans to wage war against the reign of a mad daemon?"

Farrah's expression was indecipherable. "Yes."

She nodded. These people *were* engaging after all.

"So, me dear, ye've been doin' this fer a while?" asked Leos, now also staring at the renegade leader with an ardent gaze.

Before she could answer him, Slay did. "Yeah, since she was eighteen."

Feras watched the islander, a leering smile pulling on the corners of her mouth as she angled her neck to the side. Ah, yes, now she remembered what he made her think of: a dog wagging its tail. And this one was quite fond of its new master.

Leos bowed slightly, looking fascinated. "And how old were ye when ye lost yer parents ye say?"

Farrah answered him with a tone that felt contained. "Eleven."

"So young," the adventurer replied without removing his gaze from her.

Farrah glanced elsewhere. The woman was decidedly a closed book.

"It's impressive everything these guys have been up to," continued Slay, grinning at the renegade leader.

Farrah smiled, but it did not quite reach her eyes and Feras felt like snorting. The woman was looking so uncomfortable, it was incredible the guy had not noticed.

"You're trying too hard, lad," she said, resting the side of her head inside her open palm, her voice low enough so the others would not hear.

"Beg your pardon?"

"You're coming on too strong. Women like her, they don't appreciate it."

The islander glanced around. "Oh, I don't understand what you mean," he answered, returning to her.

"You don't?" Feras's face became blank.

Slay drew even closer, expression embarrassed. "Okay, yeah, I do. It would appear that everyone knows anyway."

"You could not have been more conspicuous."

"So it would seem…."

"That was your first mistake."

He squinted. "Yeah?"

"You shouldn't be too obvious with your feelings from the start. It takes away the excitement of the chase and makes you too easy of a catch, not to mention rather dull."

Seeing as she had his complete attention, she went on with a whimsical simper playing on her lips. "Your second mistake was speaking of it. It makes it seem as if you're telling everyone and that puts her in a delicate situation. Next thing, she'll start resenting you for placing her in a role she never asked to be in."

The guy looked as though her words were only increasing his confusion. The boy-man definitely had no game. "Your third mistake," she finished, "is being all over her. You're acting like an excited puppy rather than a steady prospect."

"You're a pretty direct person, Captain," Slay muttered.

Feras shrugged and filled up her tankard.

The islander peered around again and played the piano with his fingers. "So, what would you do in my place?"

She grabbed her utensils. "Nothing," she answered, before dipping her fork to her plate.

"Nothing?"

She drew her eyes on him. "Oh yes. I like to be flirted with. I don't go for impossible catches. Far too troublesome and energy consuming."

"You think she's impossible?"

She wiped her mouth, chuckling. "Believe me, friend, don't go for women like her. Go for someone easy. You're complicating your life for a person who won't make you her priority."

The islander looked down, frowning. "You're making it seem as though she can't love anyone."

Feras grinned more gently this time. She didn't like bursting his hopes. The guy was obviously taken with his leader and had no idea that he had no chances with her.

"No one chooses to be with a woman such as her; *she* chooses the person. All you can do is wait to be the one. Or better yet, find someone who'll appreciate you as much as you like them." She peered at him with a quasi-feeling of compassion. "Cheer up, lad, plenty of mermaids in the sky."

But Slay did not appear too cheerful anymore. He was looking rather sullen. "I don't want to give it up."

Feras shook her head. "Do what you must," she answered and lifted her jug. "Who knows, perhaps I'm wrong?"

She stared at Farrah who gazed back when she did, then drew her fingers higher, bowing her chin a little. The woman took her own drink in hand as did everyone else.

"To our new alliance," she bellowed.

They drank in good spirit. Well, most of them did.

Chapter 18

Farrah parried Slay's sword, dodged sideways and brought her other hand up, hitting the islander in the stomach.

Slay seemed elsewhere this afternoon. More than once, she had won their match mostly because he had been looking at his feet rather than at his adversary. *Her*, in this instance.

Feras had been practising with Aslor today, teaching him the basics of a sword fight. Essan and Thorick had been going at each other's throats in a peculiar duel resembling the portrait of a lethal insect attempting to sting a bear.

After her conversation with Feras the day before, Farrah had felt relieved. The corsair had decided to embrace her new role as a vital player in their rebellion, and this meant a lot to them.

All that remained now was to conjure their gods.

Following her encounter with Baltos, she knew that she held the key, but was simply missing the door. Though Farrah did not know *how* she would do it, when the time came, she felt that she would.

She noticed Feras making her way towards the water barrel, her skin flushed in the afternoon sun. She stared back at Slay, whose chest was heaving and his hands were on his knees. "You need a break?"

He responded with a quick, appreciative nod and she caught up with the captain while she was retrieving a cup from the casket.

"Did you want to train with me?" she asked her, somehow holding her breath as she did. She had been looking forward to fighting the pirate ever since they had first started training.

The corsair opened her mouth for a second, before answering a flat *no*.

"Why not?" Farrah replied, confused by her refusal. She had been practising with everyone except for her.

Feras grinned and she was relieved to see that her expression was not mocking. "You're a pretty good fighter," she explained. "It's apparent that you've been training hard for many years now. But you're not skilled enough to beat me."

She knitted her brows as Feras gestured towards the others and said, "They admire you as their leader. Duelling against me and losing would serve nothing but to weaken your status. Although they know I would win, somewhere inside of them, they believe you capable of miracles. And when I inevitably defeat you, that would affect them."

"Not at all!" she objected. "They wouldn't mind."

Feras leaned against the barrel. "No, they wouldn't *mind*, but they would be disappointed. Trust me, I've been captain for a while now. You must appear strong at all times—even when it doesn't matter. They rely on you for strength so that when they fail, they know *you* won't." The pirate's eyes delved into her own. "You must not falter. When all things seem lost to them, your steadiness will give them hope, and that can be a powerful motivator."

She held Feras's profound gaze. "I've failed them before," she replied with a hint of pain in her voice.

The corsair made her privy to her charming side smile, a glint shimmering in her eyes. "Then don't do it again."

Farrah nodded. She had carried this weight most of her life and it appeared that Feras knew of this burden all too well.

They began walking back together, the pirate's hands clasping behind her when they did. "Made any progress with your god?"

"I… think I'm getting there," she answered, head inclining a little. "If it works, I'll share with you my insights."

Feras smiled and so did she. The corsair wasn't as impatient anymore with them or bothered. This made her feel *good.* If ever there was a word that could describe how the captain made her feel, she guessed this particular one came closest.

It felt important now, the way they appeared in Feras's eyes even though Farrah would rather it didn't.

They returned to their training and continued for a while more before heading for dinner. Slay had not talked to her all evening and had elected to sit with Dahara and other members of the crew, while the rest of them had joined Feras's table once again.

Essan had taken her seat next to the corsair, regaling her with stories of her past while Farrah had kept mostly to herself. That was, until Essan had asked a question that had drawn her eyes away from her meal.

"Were you brought up on the ship, Captain?"

"I was even born on it," the pirate answered.

"Your mom was a part of the crew?"

"She was, out of love for my father. Leaving a heritage of nobility behind, she raised me on the *Dragon*, following him on his every adventure. They wanted to be together and be there for me. As such, I spent most of my life in the sky."

"What happened to her?" inquired Essan, expression compassionate even though Feras had yet to give her an answer.

"She got sick." The corsair made a face. "But that was a long time ago."

"That must have been hard," Farrah said quietly, the others turning to her as she spoke for the first time of the evening.

The pirate glimpsed her way. "It's never easy to lose a parent."

Farrah nodded with understanding. They all knew about it too well.

"Capt'n Corsak talked of her until the day he died," came Kerok's voice. "I hadn't met her, which is regrettable. I know she was an incredible woman."

Feras smiled crookedly. "Now, now, enough with the sad stories." But Farrah had noticed the way she had readjusted her stance when she had. Grief was a hard thing to forget.

Essan contemplated the quartermaster. "When did you become part of the crew, Master Kerok?"

"The capt'n took me in after she set me free, back when Capt'n Corsak was yet of this world," he answered. "Placaters had captured me in the city of Trasq and were dragging me to a control post for immediate execution."

"Immediate?" she gasped. "What had you done?"

Kerok simpered, but there was no joy in it. "I killed the placaters who stole my daughter's life."

They were muted by this, all glares now intent on him. He looked ahead. "It was an accident. They drove their hovercar over her while she was playing outside and abandoned her there.

"They didn't care how precious she was to me. They didn't even apologize as I stood there, holding her body in my arms. They told me to leave or else I'd suffer the same fate. So I delivered them said fate. After I did, others came and arrested me."

He gestured to Feras. "The capt'n had witnessed the entire event, and freed me before they could take me to the post. When all of them placaters lay lifeless around us, she reached out to me and said that *there's no greater victory over those who have wronged us but to rebuild ourselves and live fiercely*. I went with her and have since been in her service." He grinned softly. "This I remember well. It was thirteen years ago."

Farrah had been eyeing the corsair's expression while listening to the man's story. From the look on their faces, she saw how much they cared for one another, and the pirate was no longer her usual smirking or haughty self.

"And I found a precious companion," finished Feras.

"You must have been pretty young when that happened, Captain," said Essan, who had looked both saddened by this story and delighted by Feras's role in it.

She squinted somewhat. "I was sixteen, I believe."

Farrah began imagining Feras at such a young age, defeating her adversaries with a swing of her sword, taking down placaters and saving the lives of those in need. It would seem that this pirate was not as disinterested in their cause as she had first appeared.

It felt to Farrah that Feras had always had it in her to rise against Daromas but had been pretending not to care. Every new discovery about the corsair only made Farrah value her as an ally that much more.

"I am sorry for your loss, Master Kerok," she told him and made a fist with her hands. "Though we cannot change the past, we can try to make things better for the future. I want to make certain that no one else suffers as you have."

Kerok had pursed his lips, and she could see his Adam's apple working underneath his thick beard as he swallowed his emotions. He inclined his forehead to her. "It is a noble wish indeed."

Shortly after, she had retreated to her cabin, exhausted by yet another day of training and alcohol beating inside her head.

Pirates never stopped drinking if they could help it. Feras and Kerok had drunk twice as much as she had and had appeared well in control. Farrah thought that she ought to work on her tolerance if she were to voyage longer with them.

She sat on her berth and lifted *Iscar's Heritage*, deciding that she should have a look at it before going to sleep.

She opened the first few pages and scanned through Iscar's renderings. She noticed the greyed-out territories that went beyond the known parts of the world, kept out of reach and cut away from them by the impenetrable veil that separated the different realms.

Many times in the past centuries, the veil had been breached and foreign enemies had come through. But it had been at least a thousand years since that had last happened, if not more. The deep magic could not be unravelled except in the presence of otherworldly rupture.

Sometimes, she wondered whether Daromas would one day set

his sight on these other realms. Part of her felt that he would never flee the comfort of his own closed-down regions. The totalitarian regime of Iscar seemed to be enough for the tyrant for now.

She went through the next few pages until the introduction started. It was a heavy sort of book, filled with names and different language complicated for the common folk.

Farrah read through the history she knew and had mastered long before, searching for any piece of information that might have slipped her studies.

Sure enough, many gods appeared throughout the text, but there was no mention of their resting places. Some were so old she believed they no longer even existed in their current modern world.

She sighed and closed the volume. Fatigue was misting through her mind, driven by the ale she had drunk. Books could wait for the morning. Sleep would serve as a far better ally for now. Her father had taught her that a long time ago.

She flicked the lightswitch of her bedside table and leaned back, searching for Endal, the deity now akin to a consoling presence she could always turn to.

The next day, Slay had come seeking her guidance with his own god.

"Shouldn't you ask the captain to join you?" Aslor had said.

Farrah wasn't convinced that Feras would be a willing participant and somehow had trouble imagining her in a meditative stance. It would probably bring about a sharp reply just for asking.

She had nevertheless agreed and they had found the pirate mulling over the ship's control.

Feras glared up and down at them when they arrived, looking bothered by the interruption. "Yes?"

"Would you like to join us?" said Slay. "We're going to practise theurgy."

Feras grinned, staring at them both far too teasingly in Farrah's opinion. "Oh, I'm sure you two can work at it without me."

This time, she definitely did not appreciate the implications she was hearing in the pirate's voice. "You also have to train."

"I don't believe this theurgy stuff is about practice," she answered, looking blasé. Feras reminded her of a student who'd rather stay out of school.

"I can understand why you'd feel that way," she replied. "I also think that you are right and to be honest, our current goal has more to do with figuring it out."

Feras stood back against the wall. "Meh, looks time consuming."

Farrah stared at her, feeling now the responsible mother persuading her child to do their homework. "I promise to let you go after you've tried, and that it won't take too much of your time. Whatever it is that you need time for right now."

"My time is always precious." She pouted. "But… I guess I can relinquish a few minutes of it, if that's important to you all."

Feras grinned and she did as well, all the while shaking her head. She was beginning to enjoy the captain's snobbish sense of humour, which was more pretending than actual beliefs. She was making herself appear difficult when she really wasn't.

Feras gallantly beckoned with her hand, inviting them down the stairs before leading them inside her sitting room and taking a seat on a sofa armchair, fingers lifting behind her neck. "I'm all ears," she told her, forcing enthusiasm Farrah knew wasn't there.

She sat her palms against her legs, wondering how to even begin explaining any of this whilst under the pressure of the corsair's profound stare.

She started with the state she put herself into whenever she tried to summon Endal. By the expression on Feras's face, it looked as though she was getting what Farrah was attempting to convey. Although she might have simply been pretending to listen.

Her eyes did appear rather glassy.

Slay, on the other hand, seemed motivated but as lost as he had been when they had last practised.

"When I concentrate," she told them, "I can pinpoint Endal's presence inside of me. I think this is our goal for now so that, when the time comes, they will materialize to us."

"You want us to get a sense of our god, that it?" inquired Feras.

"It's a good place to start."

"By emptying our minds?" Slay went on.

Feras looked at the man, her eyes becoming larger, and Farrah had the feeling that she was conjuring a cunning comeback.

She decided to answer before said remarks could pass the corsair's lips. "Can you try that?" she asked and Slay did so upon request. She then turned to Feras, who had yet to do so. "Would you like to as well?" she added, feeling unsure.

"I don't need to."

Farrah narrowed her eyes. "Why is that?"

"I've already felt Baltos."

"You have?" she retorted, doubting the veracity of her words.

"Did you think I'd acquire the theurgy of a god without attempting to seek said power?" replied the pirate. "Of course I've tried to find him! To be honest, having something like that inside of you is hard to ignore." She folded her legs somewhat regally. "I am the wielder of a mighty creature. Naturally, my goal is to become the best dragon summoner there ever was."

"Well… that's good, Feras," she answered, dumbfounded.

Slay was looking discomfited and she could understand his vexation. He had been the first one to acquire a god and had yet to get a sense of him at all. She herself hadn't had that much difficulty finding Endal and apparently, neither had Feras. What had they figured out that held the answer? "Would you feel confident summoning him during battle?" she asked.

The captain shrugged. "Not until I've done it. And I'm not saying that I will when it comes down to it."

"Then I guess…"

"You don't require my presence anymore?" Feras replied, looking satisfied with herself. She stood up. "I'll leave you to it then, won't I?" And she was off in less than no time.

Farrah followed her movements as she vanished through the door, eyes scrunched, wondering whether the student had just tricked the teacher to get out of class. "Right, shall we begin?"

They spent the following hour or practicing theurgy. All the while, the man avoided making eye contact anytime she would talk to him directly, further increasing the building tension between them that she kept trying to ignore.

On a few occasions, Slay had believed he'd got a sense of something and Farrah had encouraged him on, explaining that she'd felt the same at first.

After a while, however, he had put his hands down, declaring that he didn't think he'd be going any further today, and she had accepted this. Summoning gods could not, and should not, be forced or coerced.

As soon as they'd made their way outside, Slay had rushed off and left her alone. She had watched him leave, feeling perplexed.

"We'll be arriving shortly before noon," Feras told them at breakfast the following day.

The previous night, everyone had gathered their weapons and filled their bags with provisions for the upcoming trek. Owing to the ship's substantial size, it would be unsafe to set anchor near any of the villages without taking the risk of damaging the vessel amidst the dense jungle. This meant that they would have to walk.

Leos had been looking considerably cheerful to be leaving on this escapade. He had been the first that was ready to go and had spent a few hours eagerly awaiting their descent behind the galleon's figurehead.

When Shandew had been in sight, Feras and Kerok had begun searching for a patch of ground within its abundant jungles, wide enough to greet the ship's massive frame.

Conscious of their surroundings as they lowered the vessel, the *Celestial Dragon* landed with a thump, all four stabilizer legs holding its weight on their feet.

"Master Kerok," said Feras while she sat her chest pistol holster in place, "take care of the galleon while we are gone. I believe a few days are in order."

"Aye, Capt'n."

She gestured to the renegades. "Shall we?"

They made their way down the ship and into the dense and humid jungles.

This tropical forest was different from most of the woodland found in Iscar's other parts. Its vegetation was thick and convoluted, making their advance arduous whenever their limbs entangled themselves inside hanging lianas or their feet got stuck amidst saplings. And more than once, they were forced to create a passage through the foliage by slicing it open with their weapons.

Feras was glad she had left her jacket behind; she was already sweating underneath her clothing, and humidity had coated her eyebrows with pearls of water. Behind her, the big man was carrying the bag that held their provisions as if it were nothing though the perspiration glistening on his forehead definitely betrayed his body's reaction to the weather.

"You do know your way around, don't you?" she asked Leos while keeping up with the adventurer.

He grunted. "I can't say I be knowin' them jungles by heart, but as long as we follow a path, we'll get to a village."

"I hadn't noticed we were on a path."

Leos chuckled. "I wouldn't exactly call it one. Ye can spot the vegetation be disturbed here and there. Others have been through this place before."

"You're the expert," she replied, lifting an eyebrow up, not seeing what he meant.

Feeling bored, she had soon fallen behind next to Slay, slouching somewhat as he walked. "Why so bent out of shape?"

He drew his face to her. "Oh, I'm good."

"Of course you are. Go on."

Slay gauged her ironic expression and pointed his chin towards Farrah, some ways ahead of them. "It's hard being around her and pretend not to care."

Feras stared at the renegade leader's back for a while and said,

"I get it. You like her, but maybe this isn't the time to sulk on it." She trudged around a dirt puddle and made her tone sarcastic. "We are *heroes*, after all. We have a mission to accomplish."

"Darn it." He had stepped right into the puddle she had just avoided. He hopped on one leg while shaking the water off his other foot. "I'm just kinda confused. I'm not sure what to do anymore."

"Just be yourself," Feras replied. "Whatever happens, happens."

She jerked her head around and paused.

"What's up?" Slay asked, half bending forward while he crumpled the fabric of his pants.

She did not answer him but was staring instead at the renegades ahead who had grown still. In the front, Leos was looking concerned, eyes trailing their environment.

Something fluttered behind a bush, and a man meandered before them, a bow lifted in front of him. As he approached them, others rose all around, also pointing their arrows at the renegades.

Leos put his hands up. "Do not grab yer weapons!" he told them in a hurry. "And follow me lead."

Feras let go of the blunderbuss's hilt she had clutched from around her leg and drew her arms up, a scowl on her face.

The man who had blocked their path uttered something in a language she could not understand. Leos burrowed inside his front pocket and retrieved a worn medal. He pulled on the strand that held it and showed it to the Shandalew man. The hunter, eyes glaring, took the bronze piece between his forefingers.

He inclined his head before disarming his weapon and telling the others to do the same. He then gestured at them curtly and dove back inside the jungle. The hunters gathered around their group as they followed after him, forming an improvised fence of sorts.

Feras walked up beside Leos, Farrah also joining them, her expression worried. "You know these people?"

Leos glanced her way. He had a serious look on his face. "Aye. They gave me this medal so I would be granted passage amongst the Shandalew and be welcomed in their village."

"You speak their language?"

The adventurer shook his head. "Not a word! But some o' their leaders be knowin' the common tongue. It be with them I have spoken with in the past." He lowered his voice and Feras noticed the anxiety in his hushed tone. "It be odd though. They did not have such guarded dispositions when I last came."

Farrah did not look surprised when she said, "Many things have changed in these past fifteen years."

Leos gazed at her and nodded.

They proceeded along the never-ending rows of trees and plants, light piercing through feebly to guide them.

Farrah stayed close to the captain, wearing her usual look of thoughtful consternation. She wondered whether these Shandalew were as peaceful as Leos remembered them.

Their faces seemed hard and unwelcoming to her.

She peered up at Feras's grave expression, gauging whether the pirate was feeling as concerned as she was. Probably not; the corsair had a way of making everything appear as though it was going to be fine.

Farrah stared longer than she had intended. She pulled her eyes away, hoping the captain hadn't noticed.

Feras was—for lack of a better word—handsome.

Sharp and chiselled, even the scar that ran the length of her face hung with the details of her features. The sly smile that crossed her lips from time to time only added to her considerable charm, not to mention her self-assured stance.

Farrah found her very attractive.

It was hard to admit to herself that she was drawn to Feras. It was perplexing, in the sense that she had always been so committed to her mission. How absurd it was that, in such a period of uncertainty, she would feel enticed by this famous captain. Not only was the timing poor but she was also feeling enthralled by possibly the worst person in Iscar for her to be attracted to.

If anything, Feras was a lover. She did not appear the type to settle down nor to partake in romance. Dahara had described her behaviours well enough by now that Farrah needn't know more about the sort of person she was with other women. She also knew that she could never be with someone like that.

Moreover, Feras had demonstrated anything but interest in her. The pirate *tolerated* her presence. When far too many were encumbering her with their overbearing adoration, Feras made her feel as though she barely existed.

Farrah felt bothered that now, as much as she buried it on the inside, every time the corsair gave her some attention, it felt as though it were of value. And the more she attempted not to pay heed to it, the more it mattered.

Feras was famous for a reason, and Farrah hated the notion that she was another one of those women, charmed by the honoured Captain Sadahl. It made her feel insignificant. Mostly because it was clear by now that nothing would ever come of it.

It was becoming a virus seizing hold of her. Every passing day, as hard as she tried to fight it, it was taking root, and she was getting apprehensive of the scale it could amount to.

It wasn't like her to have her feelings get out of control, even less having her mind stray the way it had lately. She *needed* to get a hold of herself, at least for the reminder of their quest. Then, it wouldn't matter anymore. Feras would leave, and things would be over of their own accord.

The pirate could never know. Farrah would hate to see the look on her face if she found out about her affections. She didn't mind the humiliation, but she couldn't handle the pain of rejection, and could not afford to get sidetracked with such flimsy emotions. Not now when their future was at stake.

"Such a long face."

She tore her stare from the laden floor of the jungle and looked into Feras's clear, golden eyes. Being noticed by the pirate, when having such forbidden thoughts, disconcerted her, and her pulse quickened as a result. "It's nothing."

Feras appeared skeptical but did not press her further.

"Did you really feel Baltos?" she asked her, taking advantage of the open door for conversation.

The corsair appeared offended. "You're doubting me?"

Farrah shook her head sideways a few times. "In case you had been trying to get away from our lesson." She smiled, showing her that she was not being tight about the situation.

Feras grinned smoothly. "I would have said *no* from the beginning if I didn't want to. Besides," she went on, "I think Slay needs it more than me."

"With time, he'll get it."

"He's not a bad guy, just kinda…" She was looking as if she was searching hard for a word. "Let's just say that he's the underdog," she finished.

Farrah glimpsed at Slay, pacing some ways behind them. "He's a truly good ally."

Feras gave off another of her playful expressions. "Oh yes. I'm certain you can teach him."

The captain's tone somehow annoyed her. Again, it felt insinuating. She reminded herself that it really didn't matter what the corsair thought. This was not her mission.

They eventually headed up a slope that led towards a palisade made of wood bordering around a village. It was convenient they had fallen upon these hunters by accident. Though they had walked for many hours, Farrah doubted they would have found the town this easily otherwise.

The lead hunter guided them towards the open wooden gate.

Some of the residents gaped down at them from the top of the stockade as they passed by, Leos looking like someone trying hard to control his excitement.

"Welcome to the Shandalew village!" he declared.

Chapter 19

The Shandalew village had a quaint atmosphere. Houses were made of wood and animal skin. The villagers wore thin pieces of clothing adapted to the jungle's weather and were going about their business, living in quiet contentment.

For a second, Farrah envied them. As she looked into their carefree expressions, she felt that these people knew and understood life.

How she wished for a peaceful existence like this.

Not one of them averted their gaze when they entered the village, some glimpsing at the little group with interest, others with uncertainty as they followed the lead hunter.

"They're takin' us to the chief," muttered Leos, staring ahead.

A mass of townspeople had surrounded their sides, their children running around them, seeking their attention. Farrah painted a relaxed expression on her face when they did though she was anything but calm.

They came in front of the largest tent in the village where an older man with greying brown hair and a ragged beard of the same colour greeted them. The only thing that distinguished him from the other villagers was a noticeable leather headdress adorned with flamboyant animal feathers sitting on his head. An aging woman was standing beside him and so was a youthful man wearing stern features.

The elder surveilled them guardedly before he peered sideways to share some words with the lead hunter. The warrior gave him Leos's coin, and the chief studied it. He then glanced up at Leos, eyes blinking. "It has been a while, my friend. Welcome back to Shandew." His smile shone through a thousand wrinkles.

The adventurer's uncertain expression turned into a beam. The elder went forward and took his forearm into his.

"It be good to be back, Chief Yandu," replied Leos, wrapping his hands around the other man's.

The chief kept his fingers around Leos's arm and tugged on it, urging them inside his tent while the villagers craned their necks to get a last glimpse at them.

The lead hunter and both Shandalews who had been standing with Yandu accompanied them inside and took place beside the elder. He took a seat upon the carpeted floor, inviting them to do the same. "Forgive me if Atana was rude to you. Times are troublesome and we no longer know who we can trust."

Though he was speaking the words with a heavy accent, his perfect understanding of the common tongue surprised Farrah. Not many in these parts of Iscar would have found it useful to learn this language.

Leos waved it away. "O' course. I believe these troublesome times ye are talking about be the reason why we have come seekin' the help of the Shandalew people."

Yandu's expression turned grave. "I remember a man investigating the mysteries of Shandew long ago. Have you returned yearning for more?"

"Chief Yandu," Leos answered darkly. "Perhaps ye be aware o' what's been goin' on in Iscar?"

The elder lowered his eyes to the ground, his features becoming upset. "I have heard many tales of *he* who would destroy our ways, claiming a title that is not his to wear. He has sent his blood-coloured armoured dolls, asking for our lands, grasping at our trees, and wanting to eradicate all that we hold dear. They have promised to return and we have been dreading it since."

Leos drew closer in indignation. "Have they done anythin' to hurt yer people?"

Yandu sat up straighter, tone of voice sour. "They have humiliated us and treated us like animals! They have no respect for this place. They have threatened us, demanding our surrender, warning us of the days to come under the ruling of this… *Demon.* I fear that when they return, they will do more harm, and I am not certain whether we will have the means to stop them."

"I'm sorry to hear o' this, Chief," answered Leos with a look of dismay. "But ye must know that this be what has already happened to most o' the rest o' Iscar, and I also fear that yer people are gonna be the next victims' o' these atrocities."

He turned to Farrah, giving her the reins of the conversation. "Daromas, the daemon, is our enemy as well," she continued. "We have come in search of a great power to stop him, that he may no longer bear any harm to these lands."

The elder intertwined his fingers, his poised demeanour undermining none of his apparent sullenness. "I have heard of the terrible abilities he wields and been frightened for my children ever since. If you seek to stop this man, then Shandew and you are mutual friends in this affair. We simply wish to be left alone and continue living as we have always done."

Farrah breathed a sigh of relief. "We do not want to implicate your people in our quest," she explained. "We only need certain information that would point us in the right direction."

The chief nodded and glanced towards Leos. "I have known this man long ago and remember him as one who has walked with us. What do you require?"

She inclined her head gratefully. "We want to acquire the theurgy of the gods. Only then can we hope to fight on equal footing with the daemon." She heard a gasp and witnessed the shocked expressions of the people in the room. "Leos mentioned the goddess who resides in these jungles," she went on though less comfortably than before. "Could tell us about her?"

The Shandalew's eyes had narrowed with apprehension. The adventurer lifted both palms in front of him. "Ye have told me o' Thar before, Chief," continued Leos. "We come not to defy her but only to ask fer her help."

The elder quieted the others with a minute gesture of his blemished hand. Although like them, he appeared just as stunned by Farrah's words. "Thar is no friend of the humans. Though she is the one who takes care of these jungles and we celebrate her, we do so from afar.

"She lets us roam her forest because we respect it. As long as this treaty remains, she allows us to live in peace." He gave them a look of warning. "You must trust my words. Nothing good can come out of those seeking to bother her retreat. Our legends speak of terrible tragedies dispensed upon those who have trespassed on her domain."

"What kinds of legends?" asked Slay.

The chief inclined his head ominously. "Tales of demise and disappearances. Those who chase after Thar never return. That is why we leave her be."

"So many ghost stories surrounding gods," he muttered.

The elder gave him a look of caution. "Thar is not just any deity. She is called the Mistress of the Underworld and is our goddess of life and death, rebirth and ashes. She creates and annihilates in order to fulfill the required balance and believes humans are the contagion that plagues this world.

"It is said that Thar was brought into being to punish those who do not respect these lands. We are the source of this suffering, the sickness that's destroyed the natural order. She gave birth to the jungles of Shandew, hoping to sustain a semblance of wonder in this dying universe. That is why we honour her, because we know of the earth's marvels and seek to preserve them. She's allowed us to remain here because we follow the deep understanding of life."

Yandu glared at all the faces across the room. "We also fear her. Because if we ever step out of balance, her wrath would befall us.

That is why I worry for you, foreigners, who have not known our ways, and I must caution you against braving such an exquisite and destructive power."

Farrah had heeded the chief's words but could not let them stop her. "Yet, we have no other choice but to meet with her. We *must* find the means to convince Thar that her jungles won't survive long if Daromas comes here."

The elder's expression was cut from stone. He blew out a breath, his face painting with sorrow. "I will have one of my hunters lead you to her, but I must discourage you from such enterprise again. Though I believe your cause just, it saddens me to send you to a place you might not return from."

The atmosphere around the room darkened and Farrah noticed her friends' fearful expressions. None of them were prepared to face something like this. "There is no need for all of us to meet with her. I'll go on my own."

"That's rubbish," Slay intervened at once.

She shook her head. "I have Endal by my side, I…"

"For gods' sake, Farrah."

All faces turned to Aslor. The trader had stood up a little, his glare unfamiliarly ferocious. "There are a thousand reasons for us to go together and none to leave you alone, except to make us look like cowards."

He rearranged himself in his seat and added, "I'll admit it. This whole enterprise frightens me, and I've had my share of moments when I thought I was about to die. But if we step back every time a threat confronts us, then, Farrah, you'll be on your own this entire journey." His face softened and his lips drew into a smile. "I know you want to protect us, but in reality, we're not that important."

Farrah's eyes grew harder, but Aslor stopped her before she could speak. "We dove into this quest fully aware that we might not survive it, and that's fine. The role I'm playing is greater than the *me* participating in this. If my death means bringing Iscar closer to becoming alive again, then it's worth it."

He sat his resolute glare on her. "You, Farrah, you have to *use* us. We're the tools supporting your journey. You're more important than any of us and we need you. So, enough with these shenanigans. If anything, *we* should be meeting with that god while you remain here."

The gentleman took off his glasses and inspected them briefly before putting them back on his nose. "Alas," he finished, "I know you won't accept that. So let us do what we do best and stand by your side. And no more reckless talk in regard to your life, a life worth a hundred of ours."

Farrah couldn't speak. She felt moved by his words, even more so considering the man who had said them was no warrior at heart.

She watched the expressions around the room and found in them that same glimmer that had appeared in Aslor's.

Only Feras's was different. The corsair was contemplating them as though she were an observer on the outside making sense of a portrait. When she finally drew her gaze on her, however, a grin formed on her lips.

"We'll go together," Farrah said. She gave Aslor a look that spoke of her gratefulness and he bowed a little.

"Now that this is settled," he finished, "let us resume this briefing."

Chief Yandu had also been staring at their exchange with an expression of curiosity. "If this is your decision, then I will respect your wishes. But know that my people can do nothing for you if you get near Thar."

He turned to the hunter and spoke a few words to him. He also nudged the younger man behind him, and both of them nodded.

"My son, Mirka, and Atana here will guide you to Thar's domain," Yandu said. "Mirka knows the common tongue and will be able to show you the way. May our blessings follow you."

They had re-entered Shandew's flora, this time accompanied by their guides trudging rigidly in front of their group. Both men seemed watchful as they meandered about the forest, fearful of approaching Thar's cloister, a feeling Farrah also shared at the thought of their soon-to-be encounter with this ambiguous goddess.

The others were looking just as concerned. Considering the villager's reactions when they had brought up their desire to meet Thar, it wasn't hard to imagine why. If anything, this deity appeared sinister.

She was called the Mistress of the Underworld, and this alone was enough to inspire dread.

"Yer lookin' like ye need a cheer up," said Leos, wrenching her from her thoughts.

Farrah stared at the man and grinned. "I wouldn't mind that."

Leos was perhaps the only person who seemed unperturbed by their ongoing excursion. His face was a depiction of ease, his features relaxed into a gentle expression.

How simple it must be not to worry so much about everything.

"Are you okay with this?" she asked him.

Leos chuckled and said, "Again troublin' yerself, are ye? I thought that friend of yers had made thin's rather clear back there?"

She glanced back reservedly. "I don't know you all that well. I wouldn't want to presume your position on the matter."

The adventurer surveilled her, his expression turning serious. It wasn't the same gaze men usually had when they ogled at her; it resembled the stare of someone trying to delve into her soul.

It was questioning.

"We may not be well acquainted, me dear, but I see how the others look up to ye, and how they speak yer name. I think I be standin' exactly whar I should be. If this be the way to go out, then all the better. Me life has been a great adventure and I want it to finish the same way."

Farrah grinned, relieved that the withholding gaze had come to an end. "I hope you'll tell me more about these adventures of yours when things settle down."

Leos beamed. "Oh, I would be delighted." He then cast his eyes around the jungle. "Now, how 'bout we learn a thin' or two from these new mateys o' ours, eh?" He winked at her and took a few strides forward, looking far too eccentric for the stern hunters. "Excuse me, lads," he began. "Me and the lass here were wonderin' whether ye could be tellin' us more about Thar?"

Atana gave Mirka a look of confusion. The chief's son spoke a few words before his stare returned ahead of him. "You turn back is my advice, foreigner. Thar not welcome you," he said in a broken version of the common tongue.

This did not discourage Leos. "Aye, I think we got that part already. But seein' as we're still goin', it would serve us better to learn a thin' or two, wouldn't ye say?"

Mirka's mouth looped upside down. The man was obviously not taken with their group. "Thar is Thar. She is Goddess of Underworld. You go to her, she not be pleased. You be strange people from distant lands. She not welcome you here. You different and bring polluted ideas."

Leos tipped his head back without the others looking, showing Farrah a grimace. "I hope we can demonstrate to our dear Thar that we be not as bad as ye believe us to be."

Mirka pouted at Leos's words. "I not say you bad, only misguided."

This time, Leos laughed heartily and patted the man's shoulder. "Oh, ye'll be a good leader one day."

The glimmer of a smile appeared on Mirka's face, and he seemed to loosen up a bit afterwards.

They walked on for another hour or so before Atana lifted a hand to stop their advance and dropped to the ground. He beckoned them forward again and shortly after they reached a meadow that opened up to a greyed-out ashen hill.

This discovery stunned Farrah.

Death and rot had struck the jungle, its trees and vegetation left to moulder for aeons.

"What happened here?" she asked, a knot tightening her insides.

Mirka glowered ahead. "This is delimitation, big circle where everything dead. It means warning; we arrive in Thar territory."

"That's inviting," muttered Feras, joining them, hands on her hips.

"We come no further," said the chief's son. "Is sacrilegious to enter here."

Taken aback by this abrupt end to their partnership, the members of their little group gazed into the unknown.

"As long as we go forward we'll find her?" said Slay.

Neither of the men answered, and the silence deepened between them.

"Thank you for bringing us to this place," said Farrah to the both of them.

Mirka nodded. "We wait for you until night, after we gone. If you no come back before, we know you dead."

Feras smirked. "You're the cheerful one of the village."

Farrah gave the corsair a look and began forward. "Reminds you of someone?" The pirate snickered as she left after her, Thorick on her heels.

The others hesitated for a second more as though expecting the canopy to pulverize them the moment they reached inside Thar's domain. Seeing as nothing terrible happened when they stepped foot onto the cinders, they soon followed after Farrah, Feras and Thorick.

The leaves creaked as they strode along the broken route of fallen trees and rotting bark. Apart from their ridiculously noisy footsteps, they could hear no sounds in this place void of meaning amidst the emptiness of festering putrescence. Their very passage upon its soil felt blasphemous, the presence of life a transgressive sight to be kept at bay.

Soon, the air began to catch in their throats and the essence that filled their being began to flee from them, seemingly drawn from existence within this land of breathlessness. Their steps grew heavy with the pull of mortality, their bodies soaked into the earth on which they walked.

Surely this was what the siphoning process must be like, what both Daromas and the commandants were going through year after year since they had merged with their gods.

Was this what it would be like for them in a few years?

This was a thought that never strayed far from their conscious minds. That the road they were walking on only led to this one destination.

The rot and decay of an empty shell sacrificed in the name of power.

After they had ambled around for some time, a row of blossoming trees had suddenly met with their path, emerging like a wall of existence.

They hurried towards the light that pierced through the jungle, a beaming ray of hope instilling life into their shrunken cores.

The weight lifted the moment they passed through the barrier of the living and entered a new area.

This one was brimming with vitality. It was as though the rotten vegetation of its predecessor had served only to discourage any from stepping inside this glorious display of vigour. Or perhaps, to encourage the growth of this zest.

The trees appeared fuller and more colourful. They noticed plants they had never seen before and insects that radiated vividly. It was a place awash with vibrant life and yet, surrounded by death—odd and beautiful at once.

"Would you look at that," said Aslor.

"It's amazing," whispered Essan.

Farrah had yet to witness such display of different hues in her life. Endal's forest had been mysterious and awe-inspiring; Thar's jungle was vigorous and eccentric. As they pushed ahead, she felt disappointed that they could not linger and enjoy this wondrous painting of existence, kept out of sight of their human world.

Slay gaped at the strange vegetation, wondering how it was that places such as this existed and they knew nothing about them. He tried to suppress the nervous sensations that had pitted his stomach ever since Yandu had spoken of Thar. It was odd that he would feel both mesmerized by this canvas whilst being worried by the goddess that had created it.

He blinked away from the splendour of his surroundings to stare instead at Farrah. The pit in his stomach tightened as he did and he knew it was no longer his fear of Thar that acted upon his gut.

He had never been a man shy of approaching women. Girls found him charming—in his own way. It was a new and intrusive feeling to be so dejected about a person he liked.

But, Farrah, she was something else.

Not that it was his style to withhold his attraction because of the opinions of others but he knew they were right about one thing: Farrah's first love was her mission.

He didn't mind that. He didn't need to be some picturesque lover to her. He just wanted to be with her.

Swallowing, he coerced his feet to go up to her. "What do you think we'll find out when we get there?" he asked.

Farrah caught his glance. She was looking alert. "I can't say, but I am apprehensive of the possibilities."

She was so darn attractive with her perfect features and inviting form. For all he knew, they could all soon be dead. To think he hadn't even told her that… "You're beautiful, Farrah."

His heart accelerated. "I mean, for a girl."

You. Fucking. Idiot.

Farrah was looking as though she was trying to ignore his gaze. He swallowed harder than before and his palms became clammy. He covertly attempted to wipe them against his pants.

"Thank you."

A *thank you* was good, but this one wasn't. It was a cold thank you. A thank you devoid of warmth.

"Slay…" she began, turning to him. Her expression seemed almost pained.

He knew it would do no good to let her speak now. He averted his gaze, feeling like a complete mess, and pointed to a pink-coloured palm tree. "Wow, that's also fucking beautiful!"

She peered at the place he was gesturing at and was gracious enough to smile weakly and nod. His pulse began to slow down as he focused his eyes everywhere except in Farrah's direction, hoping she wouldn't notice his mortification.

Feras was staring at Farrah and Slay. The boy-man had summoned up the courage to talk to the renegade leader and both of them had been walking together for a while now, Slay gesturing around at the plants like some overzealous tourist.

Who knew, perhaps the guy *would* find the means to impress the tough leader. Feras waved her head, smirking. He was motivated. She could give him that.

She peered down at the ground. It was perfect as though no human had ever set foot on it before, healthy and untouched.

"Amazin', innit?" murmured Leos, tone of voice offering deference to the forest.

"It is," she answered, imitating his pitch.

She realized how silent they had gotten. Apart from a few words she'd overheard here and there, it seemed as though the eerie jungle had quietened them.

The calm before the storm, she thought.

They eventually reached a large expanse opening up into an archway leading to the epicentre of Thar's territory. The absence of a road had forced them to follow an improvised linear path towards its centre and from the looks of things, they were nearing their destination. Feras knew, not so much because she had seen it, but rather, she had *felt* it.

Something was different, and that something was telling her to leave, making her every step uncomfortable. As she glimpsed into the others' frowning expressions, she knew she was not the only one who'd had a change of mood.

She paused behind Farrah's unmoving form.

As stone faced as always, the renegade leader asked them, "Are you ready?"

"Ready to meet a goddess that supposedly brings death?" answered Slay. "Oh yeah, definitely."

Farrah grinned. "You can turn back if you'd rather not come."

The islander lifted both of his hands at once. "Stop right there, I've had enough of Aslor's monologue for one day. Wouldn't want to get him going again."

The gentleman readjusted his glasses. "I could go on for hours."

Essan grabbed his forearm and hoisted it up. "Hurray for Aslor, the speaker of truth!"

"I guess I have my answer," replied Farrah, grinning some more. "No matter what happens in there, stay together. If things get out of hand, run. There's no need to forfeit our lives if the cause appears lost."

The renegade leader exhaled and drew her gaze to Feras, her expression seemingly telling her "I'm counting on you." If it came down to it, she was possibly the only one who could hold Thar at arm's length while the others fled.

What the bloody hell had she gotten herself into?

Feras opened a hand, showing the way forward. "Shall we?"

They crossed the archway and stepped inside the sweeping orchid field of Thar's domain.

Chapter 20

Feras saw her as soon as they stepped forth on the bed of flowers, Thar's pillar of summoning residing in its faraway centre. The glyphs on the goddess's pedestal were glowing a foreboding muddy yellowish colour, and its mistress was standing in front of it.

Straight away, she knew that something was about to go wrong.

Amidst the vast field of white and pink orchids, the atmosphere became dense and the skies darkened though it hadn't turned into anything other than its normal shade of blue.

"*Creatures of the broken world, ailments of the lands, have you come to be purged?*" said she. The tone was scorching, voice irreparably filled with hate. It sounded dangerous, imbued with a desire to slay.

This sinister sight was at least fifteen feet tall, her emaciated waist slouched on itself. Her black limbs were elongated and gaunt-looking, her body resembling that of a hybrid between a bird and a werewolf. Her slender legs ended in honed talons and the long, sharpened clawed hands were that of the wolf though their fragile bones were that of the bird.

Her head resembled that of a crook-beaked raven. Her greyed eyes were bulging out of their sockets, the skin around them pink and riddled with wrinkles that poured across the shallow face. A crown of metallic feathers emerged from behind her neck and rose well over her head like a choker of death.

A murky pulsation exuded from the goddess's body, killing everything around her. The flowers folded upon themselves at her passage, becoming darkened and lifeless.

Something about that stare reminded her of *him*.

Those ravenous eyes.

The daemon emanated quietus the same way Thar glided somewhere between the living and the dead. Like Daromas, she was a sickly sort of entity, a hollowed bird of mortality, and Feras had no doubt that they were in grave danger.

Farrah stepped forward, the cavities of the creature's blurred eyes following her every movement. "Goddess Thar, we have come seeking your help, we..."

The deity bellowed a shriek that sent shivers running through the jungle and their chilled bones. "*You are the disease!*" she screeched, her words hissing inside their aching ears. "*The planet is sick and you are the ones causing the infection! You cross into my haven and contaminate the precious life I create with your filthy souls!*"

Thar threw her arms and fingers into an open embrace. The pores of her skin opened, revealing needles that littered her frail body.

"You must listen to me!" Farrah pleaded. "We want to abolish the powers that destroy life, we seek..."

The high-pitched sound squealed again and Thar jerked her trembling beak towards the sky, her chest heaving up.

"Farrah, get down!" Feras slammed into the renegade leader, and both of them fell to the ground.

The needles fired from Thar's body in a fusillade of steel thorns. Caught as they were amidst the canopy of orchids, the darts went flying over them.

Feras lifted her head and helped Farrah back to her feet.

They stared at the goddess wide-eyed. Thar was rushing their way, petals scattering upon her passage as she did.

They would have to fight the Mistress of the Underworld.

"Everyone, disperse!" yelled Farrah.

Sharp fingers came raging down on them and Feras dodged to the side in order to avoid their sting.

She rolled out of the way of the creature and Thar unlatched her elongated beak, squawking in anger when she missed. At once, she rounded back on them and initiated a successive wave of attacks.

Damn, she was fast! Those sword-like hands were thrusting at them with amazing speed, and they barely had the means to contain the relentless assault.

"Thar, you must listen!" was imploring Farrah, all the while circling around the goddess.

She'll get herself killed, thought Feras. "Stand back!" she growled to Farrah and went past her, clutching both cutlasses she now possessed, her own and the one Trent had stolen from her father.

Farrah fell back a few steps while Feras initiated a duel of death with its messenger, scarcely stopping any of her blows every time the deity's arms lashed out as her.

From the corner of her eye, she noticed the others speeding to her help. "No!" she shouted at them, panting hard as she avoided yet another hit. "Essan!"

The younger woman didn't need to hear it twice. She dashed towards her target, her small frame cowering inside the blanket of flowers.

Farrah had initiated firing at the goddess, alongside Aslor and Leos, pistols in hand. Their bullets did naught but graze Thar's body, the projectiles turning her skin to ashes as it dropped from her like scraps of dust. If anything, the enraged deity was growing more restless with each of their renewed attacks.

Caterwauling, Thar sprung up on powerful talons and knocked Feras down before smashing inside the circle Aslor, Leos and Thorick made.

The big man immediately covered the others with his bulk, taking the assault head on.

Thar ripped the metal of the knight's armour to shreds. Blood came gushing out from where her long fingers had run through.

Chest painted red, Thorick made the first sound Feras had ever heard him make.

It resembled a beast's roar, arising from somewhere deep inside the cavity of his profound lungs.

He knocked his hammer down the length of the creature's limb, and a howl of pain erupted from her throat. The slim frame of the goddess's arm splintered on impact, the brute strength of the knight's attack shattering her fragile bones.

Essan was now dabbing pocket-sized, narrow knives all over Thar while the deity lay folded on herself, holding her arm.

Emboldened, the younger woman sped closer and hopped on Thar's back.

With a yelp of pain, Essan withdrew and plummeted down on the jungle floor, her fingers clenched against her chest, smoke erupting from her gloves. "Her skin is poisonous!" she yelled to the others.

She rolled on the ground when Thar came around for her, avoiding the claws of the deity's remaining arm.

Thorick was drawing himself behind the creature, hammer in hand, readying another hit. But the goddess threw her head back in a horrid fashion and twisted her neck towards the knight at an impossible angle, her fast beak catching the big man's leg. Swivelling, she spun Thorick out of her mouth with incredible strength and propelled him away.

"Thorick!" Farrah cried.

Leos used this opportunity to empty his magazine on the head of the bird-like monster.

As the petrifying face came around, Feras's heartbeats quickened. "Move away, Leos!" she barked and barged in on the deity's assault, Farrah on her heels, covering her with her bullets.

Feras diverted the creature's attention from the adventurer and both resumed their impossible waltz, Thar fencing now with one only arm as the other hung by her side.

Aslor and Leos's rounds soon joined Farrah's ammunition,

while ninja girl emerged here and there from the field of flowers, throwing her stilettos on their foe.

As for that islander, he was nowhere to be seen.

Slay had kept back the entire time, both of his axes in hand. Not that he had no intention of joining the battle.

He was at a serious disadvantage in this fight. He wielded no long-range weapons like Aslor and Farrah, and he was not as fast and deadly as the captain or Essan.

To no avail, Farrah had been trying to reason with the creature. Seeing as things had gotten out of hand, it had dawned on him that he was the only person who could summon a god to come to their aid.

For the first time in his life, Slay had willingly avoided a fight. He had stood back and concentrated, the way Farrah had told him to. He had not closed his eyes though, he had wanted to witness the struggle, the danger, the fear of this horrible melee.

Ekhon, buddy. You seeing this? he thought, stare fiercely surveilling the battlefield.

By the gods, she's fast, thought Feras, catching the hand right between its fingers with her blade. The steel scarcely made an incision on the rotten skin and cinders scattered around it the same way the bullets had done before.

Even though the knight had broken one of Thar's arms, she was still struggling against the scorned deity.

This fight wasn't auguring well.

Thar had gone berserk. Thorick was wounded, and it appeared that their weapons had no will to inflict much of anything on the creature's decaying skin, apart from further decomposing it.

"Watch out!" cried Essan.

Feras parried to the side as the beak closed down on her, her cutlass grazing the iron-firm bone of her neb as she moved past it.

Ululating, Thar folded her able arm upon her chest and leaped up, retreating from them and speeding now towards the centre of the field. She swivelled around and scowled ominously as the pillar behind her began to glow with foreboding intent.

"She's preparing an attack!" yelled Farrah. "We need to stop her!"

Feras sprinted as fast as she could, but before she could reach her, Thar slammed her hand inside the jungle's soil and a rumble reverberated as the earth started shaking.

The forest came alive.

The orchids began clawing at their feet, their petals sharpening into chops that gnawed at their boots. *Swoosh* the trees went as they whipped their branches around while long vines broke out of the jungle's floor and flew to their limbs.

The land was outraged.

It became everyone for themselves. Feras swung her cutlasses about, cutting offshoots, ushering her feet around every time the flowers tried to immobilize her.

Farrah had retrieved her kukri swords and was following Feras's lead. The knight, back on his feet, was pummelling the ground around him, limping as he did, his chest drenched in blood. Essan was scurrying in every direction, doing some acrobatics to avoid the plants.

Aslor and Leos were having a hard time. Both men were attempting to shoot the flora, but the mass of foliage was overpowering them.

From the corner of her eye, she witnessed Farrah rushing to their aid.

She hesitated.

The goddess had burrowed her hand deep inside the ground. With no other arm to defend herself, she would not have the freedom to act as long as she concentrated on her lethal attack.

She was vulnerable.

Teeth clenching, Feras forced a path through the raging blossoms as they tried to block her advance. She swivelled around them, cutting the hard wood and yanking on the long vines. Step by step, she closed in on Thar while the leafage clamped down on her.

She heard a gasp and witnessed Aslor flying up into the air, entwined in a massive row of creepers wrestling with his body. Farrah and Leos were shooting the branches holding him, looking wary of hitting the trader as they did.

She focused back ahead and saw the hideous goddess's gaze on her. It suddenly felt as though the slaughtering jungle was doubling its effort to prevent her from continuing onwards.

Come on! she raged as the flora's embrace made each of her renewed step near impossible.

She heard other cries.

The death snare had also entrapped Thorick and Leos inside it. Worse, Aslor was beginning to appear non-responsive.

Cursing, she pinned her swords inside the ground, took hold of her shotgun and decided that she was near enough her target for this endeavour.

As vines started to twist around her ankles, she triggered her weapon. It fired not towards Thar's face but rather on the fragile bones of the arm caught inside the earth.

The goddess shrieked and dust collapsed onto the dirt.

The look she served Feras was now deadlier than dead. It was the underworld assembled inside a stare, a thousand crying souls seeking to feed on hers.

"Argh!" she roared when the vines grasped her midsection and wrenched her off the ground. They burrowed inside her skin and twisted around her waist while she struggled to keep still.

When one of them circled around her neck, Feras lifted her shotgun again. She gritted her teeth as her body hovered about, the muzzle of her weapon tilting from left to right. She wrestled her mechanical hand away and as the wicked creepers darted back towards her fingers, she fired another round.

The goddess's arm jerked sideways. The hit severed the bones and tendons, and matter exploded inside the nightmarish ashen-coloured skin that had nevertheless held on like a rubber wall.

Feras was dropped. The vines clutching her regained a will of their own and Thar's assault rescinded.

As nature's fury dissolved, Feras rose back on her feet, glancing behind her as she did. Aslor was on the ground, unmoving; so was Thorick. Farrah was speeding towards her, mouthing words she could not hear.

But when Feras witnessed the woman's fearful expression, she leaped out of the way, Thar's head snapping where she had been a second before.

She looked up. The goddess was now looming over the swords she had abandoned, leaving Feras exposed.

She drew her blunderbusses and began shooting as Thar bolted towards her. Though both of her arms were no longer of any use to her, Thar's terrible beak was enough of a weapon on its own, and so was her unnatural speed.

More bullets merged with hers when Farrah arrived by her side, soon backed up by Leos. Under their assault, Thar shielded her face from view and collapsed forward, her back bending over itself in a grotesque sort of posture.

They fired at the creature until she apparently had enough of it and sprung her beak back up.

A guttural sound emerged from her throat and she bounced on her considerable long legs, her pounce carrying her all the way to the top of Leos. Feras and Farrah both went stumbling away from the powerful collision.

Leos yelled in pain as the nib delved into his stomach and shattered the skin of his midsection. Feras sped towards them. Without thinking, she grabbed the lower part of the creature's mouth with her mechanical arm and pulled on it.

She drew the neb away from Leos's shredded organs and Thar's beak came lunging for her instead. She fell backwards, holding the mouth as it attempted to rip her own intestines apart.

At once, Farrah flew to her side and shot a bullet into Thar's open nib. The projectile imploded the back of the creature's head and thick, viscous blood resembling liquid tar spurted out.

Thar recoiled away. Another furious, guttural shriek followed and the cursed needles began covering the goddess's body again.

Farrah yelled something that had to do with getting down. Those still on their feet did so at once, but Thar was not going to make the same mistake twice.

She leaped up and opened her core, whisking her chest forth. When she reached high enough off the ground, she let go of the steel darts.

They flew off in an array of murdering bolts, creating a discharge of needles that would spare no hiding places.

Feras could do nothing to stop it when one of the projectiles dove into her sternum, her breath leaving her as it did, body stumbling backwards.

She tried to get back on her feet but felt a sharp pain across her chest. Clutching a fist where the thorn had hit her, her vision became hazy and the air around her turned sparse. Her head pounded and she collapsed to one knee before yielding to the comfort of the ground, her pupils shielded by the weight of her eyelashes.

And there was only darkness left for her.

Farrah drew herself up and hurried to the unconscious pirate. "Feras!" she bellowed, cupping the back of the captain's neck.

She looked up. Essan had rushed to their side. "She's coming!"

The creature was now making its way towards them, more deliberately this time, though this sinister walk wasn't any less frightening than her previous quick movements had been.

"Essan, leave now! Find Slay and take the others away from here! I'll distract Thar for as long as I can!"

"I'm not leaving you alone!" replied Essan. "I…"

"Go! Not for me, do it for *them*!"

Essan hesitated for a brief moment, doubt filling her expression. But then, her stare hardened with resolve. "No! Our mission is to get Thar to join us! We're doing this!" She veered around and ran towards the goddess.

"Essan!" Farrah yelled after her. She bolted back to her feet, trying to ignore the fear that had grasped her.

Many were unconscious and she didn't even know whether they were still alive. Essan could be next and she couldn't allow that happen.

Essan was charging Thar on all sides, avoiding the beak each time it came for her. She was sliding on the ground, jumping back on her scorched palms before leaping up, a pocket knife chasing away from her fingers into Thar's neck.

Farrah came face to face with the angry deity.

Thar pushed her head to the side, peering at her with one eye, animosity filling it as she sized her up.

She lifted her swords.

"You do not deserve these lands," Farrah told her, her voice now quieter amidst the mayhem that ensued around them.

The creature opened her mouth, a squawk ululating from her rotten core as she threw herself on Farrah.

A flaring light ignited out of thin air. Blazes were born from its flicker, and smoke smothered her vision. It gained altitude, becoming a raging firestorm before revealing a form emerging from the ashes.

There stood Ekhon, the Baron of Fire with both of his cleavers drawn.

Thar's eyes swelled with surprise when Ekhon shoved his weapons inside the goddess's beak, holding back the ferocious nib as it was about to tear down on Farrah.

At once, the god pushed Thar back with his cleavers, their fire consuming the interior of the creature's mouth while scales of darkened dust ate at the beak.

The Mistress of the Underworld stood paralyzed, her expression confused, eyes round with shock as Ekhon confronted her.

The god let go of his swords. As the blades tumbled from the goddess's mouth, he yanked his fingers on both sides of her beak and began to pull it open.

A grotesque splintering sound cracked. The lower part of the creature's jaw broke and collapsed under its own weight.

Thar moved away from the Baron of Fire, nib hanging loose towards the ground. Her arms and beak rendered useless, she appeared now the shattered remain of what she had been before. "*You're helping this filth, Ekhon!*" her raspy voice bellowed.

"*These humans are special, Thar,*" answered the god, abandoning his fighting stance to resume a standing position. "*You must listen to their pleas for we are on the same side.*"

"I am defeated," Thar replied swelteringly. "*Taken down by fiends!*"

"*You must listen!*" he cut. "*If what you hold dear is in these lands, then you have no other choice but to join them!*"

He drew a hand against Thar's temple, and energy began shooting from his fingers. Farrah realized at once that they were exchanging information.

The trade-off lasted less than a few seconds and as soon as Ekhon had pulled his arm away, he began to vanish in a puff of dense smoke.

Slay had done all that he could.

It had been enough; he just might have saved them all.

To her surprise, Thar disappeared as well, following the other god into their dimension, her body disintegrating like a corpse aging at incredible speed.

Farrah spun around and rushed to the sides of those who had fallen. Slay was also running towards them, looking weak and stopping a few times in his tracks to recuperate from the cost of conjuring.

Essan was already next to her. "Essan," she said. "Go and check up on Thorick and Aslor, and make sure they're alright."

She then dropped beside Feras and Leos. The pirate was feverish and pale. Though Farrah did not like the look of things, the captain was yet alive. She would have to wait, she told herself as she bent over Leos's gaping wounds.

An alarming puddle of blood had amassed around the adventurer. His breathing was fast and shallow and his eyes were wide as they stared at the white clouds above.

Farrah knew at once that nothing more could be done for him.

Her throat narrowed. She lifted his upper torso and cradled his limp form in her arms. His eyes focused on her face as she looked down into his.

Though others urgently needed her care, she could afford him one last moment of warmth knowing that his time would soon be over.

"Did we get her?"

"We couldn't have done it without your help," she answered quietly.

The adventurer replied with a skewed smile, his wrinkled features pulled taut.

How many times had she been through this?

Her hands now reddened with blood, she resented how she had grown too accustomed to goodbyes.

"Yer lookin' like ye need a cheer up."

She grinned. "I wouldn't mind that," Farrah murmured, trying on a warm expression for him. She had learned that, in these moments, it was strength that made their deaths a bit easier.

Smiles over tears, fondness over grief.

"Don't be sad, ma dear, this be what I wanted. Oh… what an adventure that was."

"Forgive me." She lowered her gaze. "I didn't mean for anyone to get hurt."

His fingers wrapped around her own. "But, ma dear, ye can't expect to win this enterprise without any losses."

"Yet, I still find it cruel…."

He attempted a laugh and his breathing grew laboured and sullen. "Ye'll have to look past this," he said. "Ye need Thar on yer side. I don't mind dyin' if it means ye go and take down that darn daemon. Ye make me a promise now."

Farrah steadied herself. "Yes?"

He smiled and life began escaping from his eyes, his features whitening with the embrace of imminent death. "Ye leave me here.

Not just me body, ye leave yer sadness. Ye leave me and go on… ye go with Thar."

Farrah could no longer speak. If she were to, she wouldn't be so strong anymore.

"Promise," he said, gaze steadying into hers.

She felt the prickling of tears endanger her resolve though none of their rivers would yield to her cheeks. "I promise."

He smiled and drew his eyelids shut. "It was a privilege, to fight by yer side…"

He was gone.

Farrah inhaled. Another dead friend, another day she lived on.

Others were yet breathing and every second she spent holding Leos against her chest was a second wasted taking care of someone else needing it.

She laid his head down on the canopy of orchids and thought it oddly perfect that this old adventurer would find his last resting place amidst this mysterious and beautiful land.

Farrah drew her fingers against his forehead and muttered, "Thank you."

She peered up and noticed Aslor staring at them both. The trader stooped down beside her, looking stiff. He placed a hand on her shoulder but said nothing. She knew that what he meant to say was: "It's going to be fine."

But when had things been fine since her parents had died? When so many had given their lives for this cause, sacrificed for an ideal?

This was the sin she would have to carry. Her burden.

They both startled at the sound of a low chirping sound. Farrah jumped to her feet and retrieved her swords, fear washing the pain away.

Thar was standing over them, her body regenerated and her gloomy eyes looking down at them. "*Life and death,*" she rasped.

She slouched forward, and Farrah wasn't scared of her anymore. She somehow knew that she no longer wished to hurt them.

Her long fingers brushed Leos's lifeless form and the flowers near the adventurer began to shift positions and came to a delicate rest upon him. Soon, the orchids had blanketed his body, hiding the wounds, obscuring the blood. Only his face remained untouched and it wore a mask of quietude, freed from the turmoil of this world.

Farrah gazed inside the Mistress of the Underworld's darkened pupils. She could not conceal the hate in her glower in the knowledge that so much hurt could have been avoided if she had listened to her from the start.

And Thar knew how she felt.

Their stares competed with each other, Farrah fighting the impulse to lift her weapons against the fiend's charred skin. How bitter that acquiring the theurgy of a god had meant losing the life of an ally.

Was this the price of power?

Loathing rushed through her every fibre as her glare competed with the creature's. But this was Farrah thinking—the woman, not the leader.

The leader knew that this was worth it, knew that casualties were sometimes unavoidable to achieve a greater purpose. The leader was also looking into Thar's eyes, and seeing a necessity. They needed her. The woman wanted to refuse her; the leader could not afford to.

Another burden to bear.

"*Ekhon has shown me the state of the world and has demonstrated the madness,*" Thar told her, oblivious to her angst. "*As I look into your souls, I look at despair. As I see into the future, I see death. I will help you restore balance.*"

Farrah restrained a breath. "Then let it be done," she replied coldly.

"I will take her."

Aslor drew himself beside her, stare fixed on the Mistress of the Underworld. "You will never bear to look at her and I know how hard it will be for you to fight by her side," he said. "I won't allow Essan nor Thorick carry this hateful charge, but I can. And let us remember the sacrifices we are ready to make for our cause every time we summon her."

He turned his gaze on Thar and stood his ground, both fists lowered. "I may not be physically strong, nor the fastest, but if you'll have me, Mistress of the Underworld, I'll take you."

Thar inclined her head to the side but did not seem to mind the man's proposal. She appeared now subdued in contrast to her previous self.

Maybe it was her way of apologizing for what she had done, though Farrah had her doubts. She knew this goddess of rebirth and ashes had no scruples when it came to taking a life. She had shown only neutrality in the face of the tragedy she had been responsible for.

Farrah looked away, unable to stare any longer at the deity's sagging expression. She nodded to Aslor and retreated from them while the trader chanced a foot forward.

"I accept you, Thar."

Without a moment more, the creature's body began to decompose and Aslor's hand started to emit a bright yellowish colour. He fell on his knees when her light came diving through him and he became her host.

"Farrah!"

She turned away from both man and goddess mutating into one and set her sight on Essan. She was leaning close to Feras, eyes narrowed with agitation. Farrah rushed over and crouched beside them.

"We must get her back to the village, I think she's been poisoned," said Essan.

Farrah looked down at the pirate's pale features and placed a hand against her forehead. It was burning. "We need to leave," she agreed. "How's Thorick?"

"He's gonna be fine," Slay said from behind her.

He was half carrying the huge man. Thorick was smiling weakly, and Farrah knew this was the face he made when trying to reassure her that he was better than he appeared.

Which meant that he wasn't well at all.

He was limping on his leg, and the red stains on his armour looked larger than before.

Farrah got up, concerned by the sight of blood pouring through the holes of his metal chest piece. "We need to bandage the wound."

Thorick heaved a hand, making a forward motion with it, his eyes set. "You're hurt," she argued. "Let us wrap up the lacerations and be on our way!"

He drew his arm away from the support of Slay's shoulders and walked on his own, limping towards Feras's unconscious form.

She stopped him, annoyed by his stubbornness while admiring his courage. His motivations were selfless; the man would die before putting himself ahead of the needs of another. But they simply had no time for this. "You're in no condition! I know Feras requires care. So *please*, let us dress up your wound and hurry!"

Seeing as things were going nowhere, Slay came to her help. "Leave with the captain. I'll take charge of Thorick and we'll catch up with you guys." He glanced into the knight's stoic face. "Good?"

Farrah nodded and scowled at Thorick. The man hesitated for a few seconds more before yielding to her gaze.

"Thank you, Slay," she told him and headed back to Feras.

She moved around, grabbing the corsair's things and giving them over to Essan for safekeeping, knowing the pirate would make her hear about it if she dared leave her weapons behind.

Aslor was kneeling on the ground close by, panting hard, eyes glaring at the palm emblazoned with Thar's tattoo, a flavescent, long-beaked raven head.

Farrah felt sorry he'd had to endure this critical moment on his own whilst they had tended to the others. "Are you alright?" she asked, coming to his side.

He winced up at her, looking nauseated. "I'll be fine, not to worry."

She gave his shoulder a squeeze. "I fear I must ask for your assistance," she hurried on. "I know you're not feeling well, but I need you to help me carry Feras."

Though pale, Aslor nodded at once. "Of… of course…" He drew himself on weak knees and took a few wobbly steps towards the others.

Essan had positioned the corsair's weapons in their correct scabbards and was waiting for them. She was holding her hands close and Farrah noticed how singed her palms were. "We'll mend you up when we get back," she told the younger woman, briefly grasping her fingers with concern. The poison had melted the gloves she had removed and some of the fabric had burnt into her skin.

"I'm okay," Essan answered bravely.

Farrah leaned over Feras and picked up an arm while Aslor lifted the other. The captain was heavy enough and she knew their strength would not last forever. They needed to bring her to the hunters at once.

They pulled the corsair's hands around their shoulders and began the return trip as fast as their load allowed them, Essan opening the way.

Time was forgotten and apprehension guided their feet. They rushed through Thar's jungle, both faltering under Feras's weight. Aslor was having difficulty hauling the corsair. As much as Farrah was trying to be strong for them both, they could not afford to walk around like this for hours.

The pirate had not uttered a sound or made a movement ever since she had collapsed, her skin rendered wet by perspiration and fever.

Worry hijacking her thoughts, Farrah placed every last ounce of energy she had left into carrying Feras as swiftly as she could back to the village, hoping that its people would have a cure for whatever it was that was affecting her.

Regardless of the bleak powers of her surroundings, when they re-entered the scorching lands, Farrah felt optimistic. Mirka and Atana ought to be close by and that thought was more potent than the despair that had clung to her bones at the contact of the air's putrid smells.

"Farrah!" she heard the familiar voice calling back to her. Essan had run ahead and reached the hunters first to explain them the situation.

She tried to ignore her growing annoyance that both men still remained outside the limits of Thar's domain, waiting for them to step through its border before giving them a hand.

When they finally did, Atana pulled Feras from their grateful shoulders and drew the pirate on his back. Readily, he broke into a jog towards the village, carrying the captain as though he were holding a bag of potatoes.

They left after him, Mirka beckoning her over, his face hard. "Your friend is cursed," he told her. "We go to witch doctor, Telawui."

Farrah nodded, trusting that he would know better what to do than she would. "This woman, she can cure her?"

Mirka did not grace her with an answer.

Her chest tightened as she pondered his silence. "We still have people behind, Mirka. One of them is gravely wounded, they'll soon be coming out of Thar's jungles!"

The hunter glimpsed over before uttering a few words in Atana's direction. The other man responded with a grunt, preserving his strength for the rest of the trek.

"I go for friends. Follow Atana, he take you to village," answered Mirka, before halting mid-track and heading back to the meeting place.

He was soon out of sight and as she stared back ahead, Farrah hoped they would arrive in time to save Feras.

Chapter 21

Atana had taken Feras to one of the largest tents in the village, the bypassers watching with interest as the little group made their way inside the darkened room.

A middle-aged woman was waiting for them, hands folded before her as though she had been expecting their arrival. Her head was shaven, her face and skull painted with foreign white symbols. Her eyes were a deep, bottomless green and she had strings of jewelry sticking out from her ears to her nose and down to her bare breasts. A boy of teenage years was sitting on his knees next to her, awaiting her command.

"This woman is cursed," remarked the healer after a single glance at Feras.

Farrah went up to her. "Can you help her?" she asked, tone betraying her concern.

Telawui gave the captain another look. "Put down," she ordered and waved at the hunter so he would understand.

The man deposited the pirate on the lively coloured blankets layered on the floor. The young assistant brought a few pillows over and pulled them under Feras's head.

After he had lowered the corsair to the ground, Atana had left them. Farrah had thanked him when he had, inclining her chin in his direction when he had gone.

Telawui was glaring at the pirate, a sharp-nailed hand floating above her form. When her fingers hovered over Feras's sternum, they halted. "Remove things," she said before rising to her feet and heading towards a cabinet at the back of the room.

Essan had already begun taking Feras's scabbard off. Farrah hesitated a second more before pulling on the pirate's leather sash, unfolding the belts that tied it across her abdomen. She slipped a hand under Feras's back and heaved it before retrieving the rest of the garment.

Feeling a blush coming, it crossed her mind that this had not been the way she had envisioned talking Feras's things off. To be honest, she hadn't imagined she ever would, and her pulse quickened at the notion that she now was.

Essan had finished taking away the weapons and armour that hung on the corsair's chest and had begun lifting her shirt. "Help me." She winced, clutching the fabric tucked inside the captain's pants and Farrah remembered that Thar's poison had burnt the girl's hands.

She scolded herself for letting her embarrassment give her pause when Feras needed urgent care.

She ushered her thoughts aside and pulled on the pirate's shirt. As she did, she wondered whether Feras removed her mechanical arm before putting on her clothes or whether she forced the fabric on each time.

She opted to tug the shirt over the limb's metal frame, not knowing anyway how to remove it in the first place.

Her eyes raced over the corsair's exposed abdomen before setting them on her sternum, the wrinkles on her forehead returning when she did. A black hole was nesting right above Feras's small bust, veins darkened and bulging around the wound, spreading across her chest, imbuing it with poison.

Both women shared a look of concern.

The witch doctor was coming back, her assistant taking place on her other side when she drew down. "What is wrong with her?" Farrah asked.

Telawui ignored her gaze and dropped her own to the gash, her hand settling palm over it. "That is curse by Thar to purge life. Your friend poisoned, and virus is being bigger and bigger inside her. It kill her slowly."

Farrah's stomach grew cold. She pursed her lips, keeping her emotions under control. "You can help her?" she asked for the second time, hoping for an answer this time.

The woman glanced her way, and a faint wave in the corner of her mouth twitched. "This woman strong, her body is taking out poison. If she survives night or not, I don't say. But I purge toxins."

Farrah stared into Feras's face when the healer left their sides again. As she gazed into her chiselled features, she decided that the pirate would live. They needed her.

No, perhaps she was the one who did.

Endal, she thought.

She lowered a hand against Feras's thigh. For the first time, she didn't want to hide anything from herself. She didn't care about her feelings implications or whether she even understood them.

Healing spirit.

"I'm certain she'll be okay," murmured Essan. She was obviously trying to sound hopeful, but Farrah heard the stress in her voice.

Farrah tightened her jaw, unsure whether she felt upset, confused or frightened. She was only now beginning to comprehend and come to terms with the way she felt. It was that much more perplexing to think that she might lose it all before processing what *all of it* meant.

Help Feras as you once did.

The captain was, in all probability, dying, and unless that witch doctor had the means to mix up a cure, she would not survive the night. "She's going to be fine," she declared in a low voice, not answering Essan, but rather addressing her own thoughts.

Let her be fine.

Telawui returned with her assistant, carrying a host of different ingredients for the remedy and proficiently crushing bright-coloured orange seeds inside a stone mortar using a pestle.

She leaned over Feras again and passed the bowl to the young man, instructing him to continue the grinding. She then buried audacious fingers inside the corsair's wound and pressed it between her thumbs.

Darkened blood poured out of the incision.

"What are you doing?" Farrah asked.

"I retrieve dart, so no more giving body poison," answered the healer in a neutral tone of voice.

Her nails buttered with gore, Telawui spun around and grabbed a knife. She placed the tip of the metal blade inside the lesion and began opening the skin surrounding it. More blood spurted out when she did.

Farrah watched in disbelief as the woman shoved her hand further inside the gash, searching for the steel thorn.

"Give me towel," Telawui told the young man without taking her eyes away from her work.

The assistant got to his feet and came back holding a piece of cloth. The healer wiped the fluid from her fingers and briskly cleansed Feras's chest to take a better look at the wound. In Farrah's opinion, it appeared far worse now than it did before.

The healer grasped the blade again and burrowed it inside the slit some more, tearing the skin apart as though the tender tissue mattered little.

She finally retrieved a strand, sticking out from between her thumb and forefinger and contemplated it for an instant before shoving it inside the cloth.

She gave it to the assistant and said, "Burn. And bring me other one and water."

After she had cleansed her hands and the wound once more, Telawui grabbed the grinder jar and drove some of its content into the open lesion. "This take out poison and stop it going in body," she said without looking up. She then disappeared for a while more at the back of the room.

Farrah appreciated that the healer took the time, if only in a few words, to explain whatever it was that she was doing. It made her seem in control of the situation and this, if anything, prevented Farrah from interrupting the witch doctor's work because of her own fears.

Each of Telawui's movements was precise. Though Farrah may not have known what the woman was doing, she had no doubt that the healer did. Though her expression always stayed blank, her eyes were sharp and competent.

Farrah stared at the irritated incision, now shielded by the unusual seedy paste that would absorb the poison. Though these were no longer spreading, the blackened veins yet coloured Feras's chest, which meant that the curse was still festering on the inside.

Telawui came back and muttered some words in the Shandalew language before drooping down. "I told Mesaï to make steam stones. Is good for purification of body. Mist help get rid of toxin." She showed them the content she was holding. "This is remedy I make. Now that dart out and infection stopped, we force darkness outside."

"What will become of her?" asked Farrah, unsure of what this meant.

Telawui brought the cup closer to Feras's mouth and lifted her head. "Everything come out."

She went on to coerce the thick brown liquid down the corsair's throat. She had to pour a bit of it at a time so that none of the remedy would be wasted. The witch doctor then sat back with her hands on her lap. "We see reaction. If not work is because body not have strength to fight curse. If does, we continue treatment until rid of poison."

They waited in silence for a while, Telawui muttering words they couldn't understand. Farrah had crossed an arm over her chest while her other hand had come to rest on her lower lip.

Essan looked as troubled as she felt. She couldn't stop moving. In the span of a minute, she had gone from sitting cross-legged to bringing her knees up, to lifting herself on all fours, head surveilling Feras, eyes round.

Suddenly, the pirate's stomach contracted, and so did her expression, her features morphing into a mask of quiet agony.

Farrah didn't know whether the captain's reaction was a good sign or whether the sharpness her face now depicted was one of ill omen. She placed a palm against Feras's lap and could feel the tensed muscles of her thigh.

"Turn on side," said Telawui, her voice as emotionless as ever as she grabbed Feras's hand and drew it up.

Farrah helped the woman position the pirate by sliding an arm under her back. She noticed that Feras had begun to shiver and her stomach was flexing in and out in short bursts.

Telawui took the cloth Mesaï had brought and placed it under the corsair's left cheek, laying it on the ground before her. Sweat was pouring down her forehead, and her breathing had grown laboured.

She was reminded of an animal suffering from overheating and wondered whether it was the curse or the remedy that was affecting her this way.

The panting suddenly became somewhat heavier and a whistling sound came wheezing out of her lungs.

She looked from Telawui's stony expression to Feras's pained one, her discomfort rising in accordance with the pirate's apparent torment.

The corsair's back rounded into a fetus position, her breathing worsened and she began to whimper. She drew her eyes shut and cramped lines painted over her already wrenched face.

It seemed as though any second now could be her last, and the tightness inside Farrah's chest came to prove how much she was not willing to let this happen. All she could do was watch as one of the most powerful people she had met wept like a wounded infant.

Her hands trembled.

She was confounded in the face of this sight and how it affected her. It was as though all of her repressed emotions were coming back to her at once. Not only those she had disavowed lately but those built up from years of denied feelings had returned to haunt her.

Part of her felt like blocking them out. Another part wanted to plummet down their abyss and let herself be drowned by their flood.

A warm mist entered her vision. Mesaï had brought in the steam stones and was preparing them in a corner. He then carried over a bowl filled with water and more cloths, which he settled next to the pirate's face. After he was done, he sat back, his frightened eyes mutely gazing at the scene.

Telawui chanted muffled words the entire time while she moved a palm over Feras's body, getting a sense of her energy. Essan was holding her knees up to her chin, her expression resembling Mesaï's, and Farrah wondered whether the girl had the nerves to sit through this. Even though she no longer was a child, it sometimes felt to her that she was still so young.

Abruptly, darkened liquid gushed out of Feras's mouth.

Her body jerked in and out with every repeated hurl while tears began flowing the sides of her tight-shut eyes. The lines of her face were now so drawn that the veins of her neck were bulging out.

Farrah fretted in her seat and turned an anxious stare on the healer. "Telawui?" she asked, worry obvious in her tone.

The woman appeared at rest. A slight smile crossed her lips while the shivering pirate continued spurting out the venom that was afflicting her. "Body is rejecting poison. That is good," she declared, nodding.

It seemed more to her that Feras's gasping form rather looked as though it was fighting its last battle. The corsair's fingers had grappled her chest, clawing at her skin as though wanting to tear it apart. Her lungs searched for air as blood and vomit were coming out of her lips every few seconds or so.

After a few minutes more, the purging appeared to settle down somewhat and stabilize.

"How long will this last?"

"For as long as curse still inside," answered Telawui. "I prepare more medicine. This not enough." As she was about to make a move, Farrah grabbed her wrist. The witch doctor's eyes travelled back not to her but to the corsair. "Treatment alone can kill if body not support it."

Telawui stared down at her. "But this is good start." She gently removed her fingers from Farrah's trembling grasp and motioned at Mesaï. "Change cloth and give new one. Burn it and wash hands."

Though he did not seem to speak the language, Mesaï appeared to have understood her meaning.

The young man drew closer, looking nervous as he did. It was as though he was afraid the curse would affect him if he came near the pirate. By now, the dark liquid had drenched the entire piece of fabric under Feras's head and was threatening to spill onto the floor.

Farrah leaned in and helped the poor assistant who didn't know where to begin. She grabbed Feras's neck with one hand while her other one pulled behind her hair. She gave Mesaï an expectant look as he stood there, gaping at them.

He reached out for the rag, flipped it in folds and improvised a bag of it in his fingers. He then threw it into the fire.

They watched as the flames crackled and feasted upon its content.

Farrah clasped a fresh cloth and placed it down before lowering Feras's sweat-riddled face on it. Though she was still trembling, she had quietened a bit.

She drew a hand against the pirate's mechanical shoulder, feeling the cold metal against it, wondering whether she could sense it when people touched her there.

Her face rose to Essan's, whose frightened stare was teary-eyed. "Essan," she began. The younger woman did not turn to meet her gaze. "Essan," she repeated. "Are you well?"

The girl nodded. She was gazing at the captain, looking shaken. "Is she going to be alright?"

Farrah lowered her eyes towards Feras's pained expression. "I'm certain of it," she answered. "I'll stay with her tonight. I want you to take care of your hands. Thorick and Slay should be back by now and will need your support." She had made her voice as reassuring as she could.

Essan nodded some more, looking somewhat out of it, and Farrah knew this was a lot for her. "Thank you."

Essan's expression saddened as she stared one last time at the pirate. "Are you going to be okay too?"

"Of course." Farrah gestured her forward. "Go on now. The others will be waiting for an update on the captain."

That was, if they had found their way back to the village. She pictured Thorick's bloodied armour and felt a pang, hoping he was alright.

Essan let out a snivel before exiting the tent, her movements tight as she did.

Telawui stole the girl's seat, a jar resting between both of her hands. "Give this in two hours," she explained before placing it down. "Until no poison left."

Farrah inclined her head. "I can take care of her."

The woman did not budge. "I know. That is why I say what to do."

It didn't cross her mind that Telawui was getting bored with her task. She somehow felt that she had wanted to leave her alone with Feras.

"Change cloth and keep steam going. No touch wound. Paste take out what left during night." She rose. "If need help or anything bad, get me. I am next tent and be back in morning."

Farrah nodded again, her voice feeling stuck.

Telawui and Mesaï exited the room. At this, a crushing fatigue swooped down on her. She set it aside and switched position in the hopes of making herself more awake. She peered at the pirate and tucked away the hair that had pasted to her gaunt-looking cheek.

Feras's stomach contracted some more. She yanked her head to the side and regurgitated more darkened blood on the cloth Mesaï had brought.

She began gasping for air and appeared as though she was trying to evacuate something more. Nothing else came out. She broke instead into a coughing fit, and her constrained expression turned into a look of anguish, her eyes receding. She was shaking all over.

Farrah didn't know what she could do to bring a semblance of peace to her, also unsure of how much she was willing to do.

She glanced down at Feras's mechanical arm, still holding on to her chest, her body so stiff that it was akin to a block of shivering cement.

She leaned over her, ignoring how her closeness was making her feel, and trailed her hand alongside Feras's metallic limb, tracing her fingers inside hers. She drew her other hand over her temple, and her body locked in around the pirate's. "It's going to be alright, Feras," she whispered.

Though the agony held on to her features, Feras's shivers settled down when she did, if only a little.

She wrapped her palm against the mechanical arm and lifted it up, removing the claw-like grip from her raw chest. Though Feras's limb felt tense inside hers, she let Farrah move her arm away from her chest.

Feras's body contracted against hers and soon, she was retching more poison. She kept her fingers in the corsair's hair, holding it back while she whispered soothing words into her ear right up until she had calmed down again.

Feras's life energy was leaving her. Farrah's own painted look of wariness deepened as she felt the captain's clammy skin against hers. Teeth gnawing on the inside of her mouth, she let go of the hand and slid towards the other end of the pirate's body.

She removed her leather boots and set them to the side. She then leaned over her and drew her on her back. Except for the harsh wheezing that never ceased, Feras made no sounds as she did.

She moved up and unbuttoned Feras's pants with fingers that were far from still. She attempted to steady her nerves and tugged on the fabric, palms gliding over and under the corsair's thighs as she pulled on her trousers.

Feeling rosy-cheeked, she contemplated Feras's lower body, admiring the tattoos that stretched the width of her legs.

She ghosted her fingertips along the colourful tapestry of ferocious beasts intertwined in a fresco of delicate needle pricks. She looked at it for a minute or so, taking in the details of the lively scene depicted on the corsair's svelte legs.

She then noticed the scar that slit Feras's left thigh, and the other ones that raced here and there across her figure in a canvas of ancient wounds.

She drew her eyes up the rest of Feras's form and marvelled at her deepening attraction for her.

Farrah couldn't help gazing at the firm lines of her body, the designs that adorned it and the power she radiated, even now, in this weakened state. She was ensnared by the enticement she felt burning inside, confused by this feeling of lust she had kept out of mind for most of her life.

She lowered her stare, unable to keep at bay the guilt that was taking hold of her. The guilt that she was getting carried away, not only in the face of her mission but also in the notion that when Feras was left unaware, she would transgress her intimacy in such a way. Were she in the pirate's place, she would have hated the idea of someone's eyes lurking over her. She shunned herself for doing it when she had scorned others for acting the same in the past.

She grabbed one of the blankets that littered the floor and pulled it over the captain's legs, ignoring how the sight of her briefs increased her flutter when she covered her crotch region.

She chuckled softly, wondering what sarcastic comment Feras would have said had she caught Farrah gazing at her the way she had been just now.

She lowered her eyes to the blackened, pulsing lines of the pirate's torso and her desire washed away as worry surfaced up again.

She fetched another cloth from the pile nearby and dipped it inside the bowl of water Mesaï had brought. She came closer and wiped the residues of darkened liquid that had clung to the corsair's mouth.

Feras was beginning to appear waxy and from the look of things, there was nothing left in her stomach.

When the pirate's abdomen relented to its renewed contractions, Farrah drew her to the side. Panting hard, Feras recoiled tightly unto herself and an odd thought struck her.

She seemed almost childlike.

Though this sick woman was not the captain she knew, she softened at this image of her and discovery of something she hadn't believed possible: that Feras could get hurt and needed others for care.

She was touched that she could be this person.

As she held her near, Farrah allowed her emotions to increase in a moment of authenticity where it did not matter what consequences were entailed. She wanted to stay like this, unwilling to share in words how she felt but able to live a chance opportunity at tenderness even though this was only possible because the corsair was unconscious.

How ironic, she thought, that Feras had needed to be on the brink of death for her to permit herself to *feel.*

She soaked a cloth in water and dabbed the captain's forehead with it. She then drew her nearer and cradled Feras in her arms as though holding an infant.

As her body embraced the other woman, she felt a sort of closeness she had never experienced before.

And she felt sad.

At some point in the evening, Mesaï had returned to check in on the steam stones. He had also brought food and water, which Farrah had gratefully taken from his hands, realizing how famished she was.

To her relief, Feras had quieted down in the last hour or so, having fallen into an unsettled sleep and though yet harsh, her breathing had evened.

The young assistant had pointed to the potion jar, indicating that it was time to give Feras the remedy. When the man had left Farrah to her unpleasant task, she had clutched the cup Telawui had used and filled it with the thick liquid.

She heaved the corsair's body into her arms and hung Feras's head on the corner of her elbow. The captain felt fragile in her embrace, and her own lips grew worried.

"I'm sorry," she muttered.

She emptied the cup's content inside the pirate's limp mouth. Soon enough, the corsair's wheezing had turned tortuous again, her stomach making waves, the medicine having its desired effect on it.

Feras's hands flew up to Farrah's elbows as she held her close to her breast. Her fingers dug into her skin as though clutching onto life. When her breathing grew rougher, Farrah guided her to the side.

Feras resisted when she brought her down, her back retreating further into her embrace as though afraid she would let go. Farrah girded her arm around the corsair's chest, her other hand caressing her hair away.

The pirate's features twisted in pain, and she retched against the cloth. Farrah drew her hand against her stomach and grabbed her upper body with the other, holding her a few inches above ground.

Feras yanked her fingers on the floor, steadying herself. Though her eyes were closed, tears swelled underneath their lids as the pressure of the gagging pulled them down. Her good hand was still clutching Farrah's arm while she muttered soothing sounds to her.

After a few more spews, Feras calmed down and rested against Farrah. Thinking the worst had passed for now, she drew the corsair on her back and removed the dirty cloth before throwing it into the fire as Mesaï had done before. She placed another one in its stead and returned to Feras's side.

She had never felt more keenly the longing to lie down next to a person and take them into her arms. She lowered her stare to her hands and saw them trembling as she made fists with them. She pressed her lips together; her eyes gazed without focus.

Sighing, she pulled the blanket over Feras's shivering form, hoping it would bring the warmth her body would not.

Hours flew by.

By now, Farrah had poured the pirate another cup of the remedy. When she had lifted her up, the blanket had fallen back and her stare had dropped to the wound on her chest.

She gazed in awe when she witnessed the faded darkened veins that had appeared above Feras's breasts. The cursed vessels had diminished considerably in size and looked paler than she remembered.

A wishful smile grew on her lips and she drew her eyes shut, holding Feras against her. The poison had stopped spreading and was receding. The potion was working.

Exhaling, she bent over and brought the cup to Feras's lips. The corsair moaned and her expression hardened. She turned her head imperceptibly to the side, refusing the drink. Farrah tried again, and pressed the liquid more firmly this time to the pirate's mouth.

"No…" The sound was a whisper, a ghost taking the form of a two-letter word.

Her voice rendered Farrah mute, conflicted that she had to give her the remedy but would have to force it upon her. "Please, Feras," she said. "You need to drink this. It will help…."

She hoisted the cup once more, and misery crossed the lines of Feras's skin. She did not refuse this time and when the thick liquid fell inside her mouth, the pirate's resistance abated.

When she was done, the corsair dropped her head back, her body resuming its shivers.

Farrah cradled her in her arms until the gagging returned and she had to turn her on her side. Both of the captain's hands came crashing to the ground, holding herself up as she ejected the poison while Farrah gripped her midsection and stabilized her shifting weight.

When Feras crumpled up again, Farrah dabbed her mouth before throwing the stained cloth into the fire.

For a brief instant, Feras's reddened eyes opened before shutting once more. Several tears slid out of them and she slitted them ajar a few more times. It seemed as if she was fighting the pressure that brought them down, her haggard expression turning to confusion. When she next opened them, Farrah witnessed the hurt they conveyed.

She had the look of a person who wanted to get it over with, someone no longer able to bear this agony.

Farrah placed her fingers against the corsair's cheek and caressed it. Feras was stretching her neck back and forth, her teeth rubbing against one another, moaning softly, but at Farrah's touch, her cheek had retreated into her palm, seeking its comfort.

After a few minutes had passed, Feras was gone again, and Farrah thought it much better that she remained unconscious for the reminder of the treatment.

Sensing the weight of her sleep-deprived self, she lowered to her side, not far but not close either. She drew her hands under her head and stared for a moment more at the woman lying next to her, her back facing her.

Feeling overwhelmed, Farrah knew she wouldn't have found rest had it not been for her exhaustion. The sun would soon rise and Telawui would be returning shortly.

Feras looked calmer now. Her form appeared softer and her breathing more even. She glanced one last time at the pirate's sleeping figure and allowed herself to let go.

Chapter 22

When Farrah next awoke, she noticed the witch doctor by Feras's side, her knuckles kneading against the pirate's chest.

She drew halfway up, body stiff and too aware that she hadn't slept much. Telawui did not look her way when she came to sit beside them, fingers rubbing her eyes, ridding herself of the sweeping fatigue she still felt.

"Your friend better," said Telawui after a fleeting glance. Farrah could have sworn she had seen the hint of a smile over the woman's neutral features.

The healer had changed the paste over the pirate's wound and she was relieved to see that the cursed lines had further dampened and wore more of a greyish tint now. "That's good to hear," she replied, her chest growing warm.

Telawui nodded briefly and resumed her examination. She lifted the captain's hand and felt it against her palms, her expression turning to one of concentration. She then began poking her finger over different regions of the corsair's body, Feras unmoving all the while.

The pirate was yet pale looking and her eyes were just as sunken. Though she had been in a continuous dormant state, the toxin was exerting a toll on her. "Should we give her water?"

"Only potion," Telawui answered. "Water come back up. As

long as poison go out, nothing stay in stomach. Only damage organs more."

She nodded her understanding, her concern taking precedence again. The treatment would cure Feras from Thar's curse, but her body could yet surrender before the end. As she looked into the corsair's hollowed features, she had no doubt that this was still a possibility.

Telawui brought the cup to the captain's lips, who did not resist this time.

They waited a few minutes before something happened. The healer arched an eyebrow when Feras jerked to the side and ejected the liquid, her breathing becoming rattled again.

Farrah put a hand on her back and caressed it. Sweat was glistening all over the pirate's skin, and she was shivering under her fingers.

Soon, the gagging settled down and Feras returned to a quiet repose. Telawui nonetheless appeared satisfied by these results. "Good," she said before picking up the dirty towel and moving to her cabinet.

The healer was right; the same drink she had just given Feras made up most of the spew. The poison was almost out.

A short while after, Essan had thrown open the curtains of the large tent and sat beside Farrah, her eyes worrying over Feras. "How is she?"

She sighed and said, "The remedy is working, but I'm afraid her body is having a hard time."

Essan tore her glare away from the pirate's pallid features. "She's going to be alright though, isn't she?"

Farrah hesitated a brief instant before answering, "Yes."

No use in alarming the younger woman more than she had with the fears and doubts that clouded her own mind.

Essan didn't look as though she needed to hear more. Her expression depicted a similar concern as hers. "Is there something more we could do?"

Telawui came up from behind them. "Anything to detoxify body is help but not much. Like steam stones. Hot water good too, though not cure, only alleviate symptoms."

Essan exclaimed, "Like a bath!"

The healer nodded. "I ask Mesaï to bring tub and fill up for you," she said and left them alone with Feras.

Farrah rose questioning eyes on Essan. "How are the others?"

Her face turned into a grin. "You have nothing to worry about. Sure, Thorick is sorta bent out of shape, but the villagers are taking care of him and everyone else is fine."

"That's good to hear." Her insides had felt cramped and compact since the day before and if only for a second, her breathing became easier.

Essan pulled a hand around her arm. "Have you slept at all?"

She glanced away. "A few hours. It's enough for now."

"Farrah…" replied Essan. "I know you're strong, but you still need to take care of yourself. I can watch over the captain if you want."

She shook her head at once. "As long as there is yet a chance that she may not make it, I wish to stay by her side."

Essan stared on, her admiring eyes gleaming in the damp lighting of the room. "You know it's not your fault that she got hurt… right?"

Farrah whirled around, her heartbeat drumming louder as she watched Essan whose own expression was imbued with compassion. She pulled her lips together and her throat tightened.

She had been trying to ignore her throb at the thought of her friends' wounds—that one of them had perished and that Feras may yet not survive this endeavour.

Farrah was also trying hard to fulfill Leos's last request and not think of his passing, trying to ignore her angst at the notion that Feras was barely holding up.

She knew that some part of her was scared of leaving this tent, fearful of the scrutiny the others might bear down on her. And here was Essan saying that it was not her fault. What a wonderful, beautiful person she was.

She softened her expression though her features remained stiff. "Thank you…"

Essan threw her hands around her and pulled her into a hug. "Please stop torturing yourself! You're not responsible for any of this."

She glanced away. "I'm your leader. Everything is my responsibility."

Essan drew back and took her fingers in hers. When she did, Farrah noticed the bandages that went around her palms. "My life is my own and so are my decisions to follow you and be a part of this quest," she said. "We're with you to the end, whether the end is tomorrow or fifty years from now and our eyes have turned all dead-like."

Farrah's chest heaved silently as she composed her face. "I will try to become better," she answered, voice collected.

"Please don't," Essan chuckled. "You already make it impossible for us to walk in your footsteps."

She squeezed her friend's arm, feeling a wave of appreciation for her.

"Right," continued Essan, turning to the pirate. "Let's take care of business. The captain needs our attention and it's much more helpful than our worries!"

Farrah nodded as Mesaï came inside the tent accompanied by Atana and another wary looking villager, both men carrying a wooden tub half-filled with water. They settled it down while the assistant went to retrieve some of the steam stones from the fire and busied himself with the bath's rising temperature.

Essan eyed Feras's mechanical arm. "Should we… take it off?"

Farrah peered at it, stare narrowing. "I guess it would be better. But I am not sure how to."

She leaned over the pirate's limb and grabbed it, glancing at the apparatus of its intricate pattern. She noticed a nook near the armpit and lifted the lever that slotted tightly into the arm and triggered the components. Farrah had to wrestle with it harder than she had expected, all the while hoping she wasn't damaging anything, before they heard a flicking noise and the mechanism released.

She handled the golden bicep between both palms and pulled on it. The arm loosened from its hinges, uncovering Feras's side where sat an intricate metal plate connected to her nerves. It was etched right into her skin at the level of her shoulder where the rest of the limb was attached, forever fastened over her missing part.

Farrah contemplated the design that anchored the arm to the body and figured by its complex display that the implant wouldn't suffer from a quick shower.

She found it rather awkward to be holding Feras's hand into her own and placed it down to the side, surprised by its weight. It had been fashioned out of quality materials and she had no doubt that the aureate pieces that covered it were actual gold.

She grinned. Feras wouldn't have gone for anything less.

Essan was glancing over her shoulder, looking amazed by the craftsmanship of the mechanism. Mesaï made his way to them and nudged his chin towards the tub. The bath was ready.

He then left as quickly as he had arrived. The boy was evidently shy of nature.

"How are your hands?"

Essan pulled her palms up. "Telawui came to see me last night and gave me an ointment. They're much better."

"Can you help me with her?"

Essan bolted up on her feet and stooped over Feras's legs. "Ready!"

Farrah drew herself over the pirate's shoulders. She tucked her hand under the corsair's armpit and across her chest while her other pushed her up so she could get a better grasp of Feras's torso. Her cheeks warmed as both of their faces came near and their heads folded unto each other.

She avoided Essan's gaze as they pulled on the captain and lifted her above ground, midsection dangling between them. They then made their way towards the tub and lowered her limp figure into the water.

Farrah dropped down at the same time, keeping her arm around Feras, making certain that the lifeless pirate would not slip into the bath if left unattended.

The water went up to her breasts, her bent knees sticking up awkwardly over its level. Farrah could feel its heat rising to her face. Or was it her emotions that scorched her flesh?

Feras's features appeared subdued now, and the skin on her drawn expression revealed smoother lines.

Farrah glanced at her side and noticed a blanket and a kind of plant left behind by Mesaï. Frowning, she used her other hand to lift it up.

"What's this?" asked Essan, elbows resting against the edge of the tub.

"I believe it's what they use for soap," she answered before dropping it into the bath and rubbing it between her palms.

When the root made contact with the water, it generated foam. Farrah began to massage it gently over Feras's chest and washed the leftover traces of blood.

Essan let out a small cry of excitement as she lifted another root but then glowered when she realized she could not rub it against her bandaged fingers. She put it back down, looking disappointed.

Farrah caressed the foam across Feras's upper body, feeling embarrassed whenever she came near her breasts. She peered sideways when she heard a light whisper, her face edging dangerously close to Feras's.

The pirate's head had slid to the side, her worn-out features drawing against her renewed lines. Her eyes had opened, her gaze as confused as it had been the night before.

Farrah's grip tightened across her chest as she stared into the woman's wan face. Feras was now closing her eyes and pulling them open, seemingly meaning to stay conscious through the exhaustion.

She hoisted her hand and cupped it against Feras's cheek. The captain did not flinch, her gaze remained focused on some far distant point, looking bereft of life.

She felt a surge of pity as she watched the struggling corsair trying to remain awake, her pupils glassy amidst a world of pain. She held her close, comforting her the only way she knew how.

Feras's face eventually softened into a mask of sorrow. She began to drift and dropped her eyelids one last time, her body relaxing against Farrah's.

She stared at the pirate's resting features for a minute or so before tearing her gaze away, still cupping her cheek.

Essan was watching them both, her mesmerized expression also one of understanding. Her mouth had hinted into a smile, the faintest glint of wondrous curiosity lighting up her eyes. "You like her," she said, tone betraying her amazement.

Farrah glanced away, unable to lie, yet unwilling to agree. Feeling heavy hearted, she tightened her lips. "It matters not."

Essan got up a little, looking astounded. "Do you?" she asked, more intently this time.

Farrah's stare came in contact with the younger woman's. "Yes." She found the word strange in her mouth. It was filled with sorrow and ache as if telling Essan this meant that she was opening herself up to disappointment.

Confiding in Essan had lifted part of the pull on her heart. Accepting that she liked Feras somehow helped free her from the burden of her denied emotions. She knew that she could trust her friend with this secret and was glad she had someone to depend on whenever she felt the weight of her feelings become too heavy.

She turned her anguished expression on Essan, shy of her reaction. But the other woman was smiling, her face depicting a sincere softness. "Farrah, I am so happy for you…." she began.

At once, she shook her head. "Please, think nothing of it," she replied. "I do not intend to dwell on these feelings. I will beseech you to refrain from telling her any of this. Feras must never know."

Essan was looking confused now. "Why?" she asked. "Why wouldn't you want the captain to know?"

Farrah lowered her eyes to Feras's pulled features and grinned rather sadly. "Because it cannot be between us."

Essan frowned and fought back. "What are you talking about? The way you were staring at the captain just now… I have never witnessed such tenderness inside your eyes. I have known you for most of my life and have yet to hear you speak of feelings for another. Why would you ruin your chance at love?"

She searched for the right words. How could she explain how she felt? That every day that went by, her growing attraction for Feras was taking her over. That this desire pulling her away from her mission was consuming her.

How could she explain that she was afraid that Feras would reject her? Or worse, that she be allowed a glimpse of happiness by her side before the object of her affection shunned her for a more willing participant into a game of love and loss. "It's not that easy…."

"Of course it is!" Essan shot back. "By the gods, Farrah, no one would refuse you! I don't know of a single person who wouldn't dream of receiving a quarter of the warmth your eyes just gave the captain! Why ever would you be afraid?"

Farrah's heart sank as she prepared herself for what she was about to say. "Because I cannot bear the idea of rejection." She smiled without much joy. "Feras barely tolerates my presence. When she isn't baiting me, she admonishes me. I fear that if I do not even fall into her good graces, what chances are there of getting her affections? You've seen the sort of women and relationships that she desires. I am not one of these pompous, lustrous objects nor do I have care for false impressions of devotions. I will not be the shelved prize of a brief trip."

Essan glimpsed back at the corsair, biting her lower lip as though considering Farrah's words and seeing some truth in them.

"Feras needs me and I will not be shy of my feelings," she continued. "I will tend to her but will relinquish my role as soon as my work is over. I *must* stay focused on our quest and have no time for foolish romantic chases." She made her expression softer. "You must understand, Essan, that drowning in these feelings is taking away from the responsibilities I have towards you and the citizens of this land. I do not have the luxury of wavering, or else risk losing everything. I must erase myself if I am to be the leader you need."

"You of all people deserve the most love." Essan was looking at her now with a chagrined expression. "I hope one day you can realize this and let yourself be free of the barriers that encumber you."

Farrah gazed into the opaque water and whispered, "Maybe one day."

"For what it's worth," she continued, eyes gleaming, "I think the captain and you would be great for one another. Though I will respect your wishes and refrain from speaking a word of this, I won't stop believing in that."

She swallowed, feeling the strain like never before. She could only nod as she returned to her task of washing Feras, closing the door to her heart.

They had lifted the pirate out of the tub and sheltered her inside the blanket Mesaï had left behind. They had then plopped her back on her bed of fortune and covered her once more.

Farrah tried to remember the last time Feras had eaten as she poured another glass of the remedy and brought it to her lips. The corsair was consistently losing what little energy she yet held and was beginning to appear more like a corpse than an actual living human being.

Both women waited as minutes trickled by, the captain's breathing almost inaudible to their ears.

Farrah's concern had flared up as she wondered whether Feras was on the verge of releasing what vitality she had left. Essan had twisted towards her but said nothing as if afraid of what her words would sound like if spoken out loud.

They glimpsed up when Telawui entered the tent and came beside them.

"We gave her the potion," explained Essan in a breath, "but she isn't moving anymore."

Telawui's brow creased tighter. She pulled the blanket away from Feras's torso and glared at her. The sight of her lifting abdomen somewhat soothed their worries.

The witch doctor pressed her fingers along the pirate's chest and around her wound. The dark veins had all but disappeared; so had the paste she had applied earlier.

She cocked an eyebrow. "Nothing happening because nothing else need out. Poison gone."

Farrah closed her eyes, lips quivering.

Glimmers of happiness had flooded Essan's. "Thank the gods," she whispered and she squeezed Farrah's hand.

She breathed in, fighting back her emotions. "When will she awaken?"

Telawui went on inspecting the corsair's condition. "I know not but not soon. Woman is weak and need water. Food wait until she wake up."

She rose and headed to the door, calling out to Mesaï. When she did, Farrah's vision blurred and exhaustion declared its toll on her.

Essan grabbed her by the arm, as if realizing how fragile Farrah's state was, and said, "You need to sleep."

Though it pained her to admit it, now that she knew that Feras would live, she could afford to rest for a while. She also wanted to see the others and check up on them. "Will you stay by her side while I am gone?"

Essan squeezed her hand again. "Of course I will."

Farrah plunged into Feras's pale expression before pulling herself up on her feet.

She took her leave, wondering what would happen now. She couldn't walk away from her feelings anymore. Though the situation had coerced them upon her, she knew it would only have been a question of time before the strength of them invaded her heart.

She would have to hide these as well as she could. As long as

Feras wasn't aware of them, she felt that she could cope with this situation.

"Farrah!" She heard the cheerful voice call out to her and noticed Slay waving and trotting her way, Aslor behind. "How's the captain?"

She grinned slightly, her fatigue evident on her drawn face. "The healer announced that Feras is rid of the curse. She's in a fragile state but will recover."

She explained what had happened since the night before in more details, their expressions hardening when she recalled the corsair's agony.

"What a relief," said Aslor. "What a bereavement it would have been if we'd lost her."

Farrah nodded absentmindedly as she peered around the dirt road. "Where's Thorick?"

Slay indicated a tent not far ahead. "He's recovering." He only had time to say these two words before she sprung in his direction.

She entered the tent, discovering a heavily bandaged Thorick propped up against a canopy of thick pillows. He gave a weak grin the moment she came in and she smiled fondly. "How are you?" she asked when she had sat by his side.

He waved it off and inched towards the edge of the improvised bed to demonstrate how fine he was. She grabbed his forearm between her fingers and pulled him back. "Would you just stay down," she replied impatiently, Thorick grinning good-naturedly when she did.

She stared at his gentle expression for a moment more before telling him what had been on her mind since the day before. "I'm sorry I didn't come to see you sooner."

Thorick frowned, and it meant something along the lines of "what are you sorry for?" He pursed his lips, gesturing again with his hand, shoving her apologies away.

She wrapped both hands around his massive fingers. "I'm happy that you're recovering."

"He's tough, that guy," said a voice behind her.

She turned to find that Slay had followed her inside. "What's his condition?"

Slay explained that Thorick's wounds had been alarming enough but not life threatening. Telawui had given him some ointment that should accelerate the healing process and she expected a healthy recovery.

Farrah felt admiration for this woman and wondered whether Feras would have survived if the healer hadn't been there. "I'm grateful that you're alright," she told him.

He smiled and then frowned, pointing to his sternum with a finger, his other arm gesturing to the outside of the tent.

"The captain's unconscious, but she should be safe now." As she had done with the others, Farrah explained what had transpired since the night before. Relief was also evident on Thorick's features when she finished.

She stayed with them for a short while more before promising Thorick that she would come back soon to check up on his health.

Slay accompanied her outside where Yandu, the village chief, and his son, Mirka, readily greeted her. Both men inclined their heads to her, wearing kind expressions on their faces. "Mirka alerted me of yesterday's events, and so have your friends. I want to tell you how sorry I am for your loss."

Farrah's features became taut. As much as she had tried not to think of Leos's death, it was coming back to haunt her. At this, a hand pulled on her shoulder and she realized it had been Slay's.

"Leos was a brave man," he answered, looking not at her but at Yandu. "His sacrifice will be remembered and we honour him as we continue our quest."

Farrah's gaze did not waver as she inclined her head at the chief. Though he had not been talking to her directly, she knew what Slay's intentions had been—that she would not feel responsible for Leos's death and that they were willing to carry forth on their journey.

"Thank you, Chief Yandu. We are in your debt for the help

offered by your people. Without Atana and Mirka, our situation would have been much graver. And had it not been for Telawui, I believe more losses would have been mourned today."

The elder's expression became aggrieved. "Were it only that we could have assisted you further.... If there is anything we can do, do not hesitate to ask. Shandew will forever welcome Thar's equals. It will be our honour to serve them."

He wheeled to the side and stared forcefully in Aslor's direction. The trader was sitting off in the distance, caught in his own thoughts.

Farrah wondered how much the villagers knew of their encounter with Thar. She was conscious of the wide-eyed expressions the people were giving them. They were somewhat reverent but also... apprehensive-looking.

"I..." she began. "I do not believe we are her equal, rather that we are blessed with her support." The words seemed bitter inside her mouth as she recalled the sickly looking creature, her anger rising at the mere thought of it. "If you wish to speak further, Chief Yandu, I am at your service."

The man bowed and left them. As soon as they had disappeared, Slay showed her to a tent where she would be allowed to lay down.

"How much do they know?" she asked him.

He shrugged. "We told them most of the story. How Thar attacked us but we were able to reason with her in the end, and that she agreed to accompany us on our quest." He lifted both eyebrows. "Let me tell you, that really dazzled them." He glanced around at the villagers, still gaping at them, and lowered his voice. "It's as though they think we're gods or something."

He had said it with a hint of innocent pride, and Farrah couldn't help smiling. "We were lucky to receive their blessings." Slay nodded sheepishly before she added with a changing tone, "I never got a chance to congratulate you."

The islander pulled his hand to the back of his neck, a grin drawing on his lips. "You mean Ekhon, eh? Well, I guess I had the means to invoke him because I had a pretty darn good teacher."

She shook her head. "Take the credit, you earned it. Without you, all would have been lost back there. You and Ekhon saved the day."

"Oh well, you know, I'm just glad I was able to summon him."

Farrah agreed and said, "We'll talk about it some more later. I guess I ought to catch some sleep." Her head felt dizzy and her eyes had begun to prickle with the threat of dryness.

"Oh yeah, of course. Good night," he replied, shoving aside the curtains to her tent and grinning as she entered.

She headed towards the pillows and fell into them like a log, her entire body craving rest.

With everything that had happened, she hadn't had the chance to celebrate their victory. Not that it was a celebration per se, considering the pain they had suffered. But it dawned on her that they were one god closer to their goal, and that was important, no matter what.

When Farrah next awoke, it felt as though she hadn't slept. She extended her arms and legs on the ground and stayed there for a few minutes more, enjoying the stillness. That was until yesterday's events came to mind.

She headed outside and the setting sun told her that she had not rested as long as she had hoped. She made her way towards Slay and Aslor, both sitting around a fire and eating from some wooden bowls.

They gave her a serving when she grabbed a seat beside them and ate in silence while they waited for her to finish. She took her time, staring absentmindedly into the fire, making sense of her thoughts.

After she was done with her meal, she looked at Aslor. "How are you feeling?" she said, remembering that she hadn't asked him yet.

His eyes twinkled. "I have nothing to complain about," he replied. "But how are *you*, Farrah?" he added, assessing her over his spectacles.

"I'm fine," she answered automatically. "Have you been feeling alright in regards to Thar?"

"I have not sensed her if that is your question. Slay has been telling me all about the summoning. I believe time will be my ally in this enterprise, but I am motivated, have no doubt."

Farrah was glad the islander had taken over the conjuring lessons. Her mind had been drawn to Feras since she had awakened, and she'd rather forget about the Mistress of the Underworld for a while if she could help it.

"If there is anything you want to talk about, don't hesitate to tell me," she nevertheless told the gentleman, aware that they were both avoiding the subject at hand: that Aslor was now carrying the burden of summoning the deity that had killed their friend and hurt many others.

They had conversed for a short while afterwards. Slay had recounted his exploit with Ekhon and how the villagers had been treating them with admiration ever since. She had then checked up on Thorick before her feet had brought her over to the one place she wanted to be.

When she approached the tent, she heard screams of excitement coming from it right before Essan emerged from its den.

At once, she pulled Farrah's hands inside hers. "The captain is waking up!"

She then called to the others, waving at them, and they all rushed to the tent, Farrah's pulse making ripples as she dove inside it.

Telawui and Mesaï were sitting next to the pirate and Essan dropped on her knees by their sides, a beam painted on her face. Aslor and Slay looked uncertain whether they were allowed in but shoved their embarrassment aside as soon as they witnessed Feras's opened eyes and gathered around her.

Farrah made a motion to join them, but her feet weren't moving anymore.

Feras was grinning weakly, her eyes yet hollowed but wide now, and staring at them with a strained expression.

As Farrah gazed at her, her elation vanished and was replaced by a well of emptiness.

The veil lifted and her smile began to fade.

Now that Feras was getting better, she could no longer stay by her side, could no longer care for her.

Could no longer afford to have feelings.

She stepped forward, her feet guiding her beside Aslor, partaking in their enthusiasm while her insides collapsed. She despised the cold that had taken hold of her. When she should have been celebrating with the others, she felt instead like being alone.

She composed her face as she denied herself.

Feras had not even looked at her yet.

"How you feeling?" asked Telawui, ignoring the beaming expressions of the people around.

The pirate's raw voice answered her. "Like I died and came back to life."

The healer went on to explain what had happened to her, making sense of how she had arrived at this place and what her body had gone through. "You rest. You weak and need food," she finished

Feras nodded, looking tired again after listening to her. She turned to Essan who was closest. "Is everyone else alright?"

Essan's grin faded. She glanced at Farrah but it was Aslor who saved her from an answer they all believed was better not to share in this instant. "Rest, Captain, now is not the time for conversations." He glued his palms together. "Good to see you coming back into shape."

Feras allowed her lashes to drop, the pressure of keeping them open dawning on her eyes. Telawui placed a kind hand on her forearm. "You eat first before you sleep."

"We'll see you soon, Captain," said Slay with a beam, and he turned around and exited the tent, leaving her to her intimacy.

Farrah followed after him, Aslor behind. She felt Essan's gaze on her back when she did, her confused expression burning like a whip between her shoulders.

She had no strength to face it now.

She breathed into the night air and retreated to her own tent. Though she had not awakened long before, it was getting late anyway and she ought to sleep some more.

She sat on the floor, numbness running its course. Her stare became immobilized while her insides stiffened. Though she had allowed herself to slip for a little while, it was time to return to what mattered.

As she lay on her side, she knew that things would not be that easy but that she had no other choice.

Feras was alive. It was enough.

CHAPTER 23

It was the morning after when Feras awoke again. Essan was standing close by, whispering with Telawui near the tent's entrance. She felt as though her body wasn't her own; it was in such a weakened state that it scarcely responded to her wants and needs.

She lifted herself and came to the realization that her right arm had been removed. She tried not to think of the way it made her feel. She usually never took it off in front of others.

She dropped back against the floor, deciding that her missing limb was probably not as important as the fact that she had just escaped death.

Feras had but few memories of what had come to pass ever since their fight with Thar. When the goddess's dart had pierced her, it had carried her into a state of nightmares and shadows, walking on the brink of a crater hailing her incessantly. Right up until she had awoken, she only remembered fragments of torment better left forgotten.

"You're up!" called out a cheerful voice. Unmistakably ninja girl's.

Essan came into her line of sight. "Let me bring you some food. You need to start eating, so you can gain back some of your strength." She flexed her bicep and revealed what little muscles the tiny arm held.

Feras's stomach hurt so much that the idea of eating felt painful. She watched the girl going around the tent before returning, carrying something that resembled oatmeal. Telawui, the one they said had cured her, came to check up on her while Essan began spoon-feeding her.

"How you feeling this morning?" asked the healer.

Feras shrugged. Though she was more awake than she had been in some time, she nevertheless felt crumpled by lethargy. She glowered at the approaching spoonful of gruel Essan was shoving her way. "You tell me," she replied in a hoarse voice, trying not to make eye contact with the soaring utensil about ready to drip over her.

The corners of Telawui's mouth drew up, superbly also ignoring Essan's valiant efforts. "Better I say. I give you more ointment for wound," she answered before heading to her cabinet.

Feras took a swallow of the food Essan was forcing to her reluctant lips, her throat narrowing when she did.

"I'm glad to see that you're recuperating," said the girl.

She formed a grin on her own worn-out features. "Thanks, Essan. I appreciate you looking out for me."

Ninja girl shrugged. "No problem. But you know, it was mostly Farrah who did," she replied, glancing sideways as she put down the bowl.

Feras arched an eyebrow and said, "Is that so?"

"She never left your side from the moment she brought you here right up until we knew you were out of the woods."

"The apathetic leader, holding my health in such high regard?" she answered mockingly.

"She's not apathetic," Essan replied, her tone now sounding upset. "Farrah is warm and caring. You should know that about her."

Feras's smile vanished. It was the second time she had seen Essan looking annoyed. She remembered that the first instance she had, they had been talking about that same subject.

Though she had intended it as a joke, she was sorry she seemed to have offended her. "I only meant to say that I'm surprised," she rectified. "Forgive me, that was uncalled for. I am grateful for her care."

Essan beamed and resumed feeding Feras her meal. “She was scared. We all were. Really, Captain, that thing you went through, it looked awful….”

Feras tried to ignore the throbbing recollections of the last few days. As she relieved the misery, she couldn’t fathom how she was still alive. And *Farrah* had been the person to take care of her through it all? Why, she had hardly spent a minute with her when she had awakened.

Still, in some dim memory, she recalled tender arms holding her and soft words whispered, echoing distantly through her agony. She remembered how it had comforted her even though a dreamscape of pain had muted the presence.

Yes, there had been someone by her side, and though it was faint, it had breathed life into her while she was losing it.

She contemplated the idea of Farrah being this woman. Perhaps the renegade leader was even more of a peculiar person than she had thought.

Feras smiled a sort of smile she recognized as being the same one the members of the group shared. “What happened after I became unconscious?”

Essan shifted and placed the food down again. “Oh, maybe I shouldn’t be the one to…” she began.

“Tell me, Essan,” Feras muttered, making her tone harder.

The inner corner of the woman’s eyes drew up. “Oh, Captain…”

Essan gazed at the ground as she recalled Thar’s demise and started quivering when she described the extent of Leos’s wounds. She then took a pause. At this, Feras’s chest had tightened though not because of the curse that had afflicted it.

When she had mentioned the adventurer’s name, Feras had known. As Essan recounted the rest of the story, she had drawn her stare to the ceiling, waiting for the inevitable, which had come cruelly.

“There’s nothing we could have done.”

Tears swelled inside Essan’s eyes when she told Feras how he had died in Farrah's arms, breathing out a last message of hope as he did. "I am so sorry for your loss," she finished, watching Feras's empty gaze.

She took her time paddling into the emptiness. Somehow, she knew that her friend had not been meant to survive their quest and that it had been his moment to go after the drawn-out life he had had. Yet, she would miss him.

It wasn't until Essan had gone from her side that she had allowed her tears to fall, alone into the depth of her grief, knowing that when she next awoke, she would also fulfill the promise and leave him behind.

Never forgotten but cherished as a memory.

Two days more had passed before Feras had been able to stand on her own again, making progress on her recovery and becoming stronger.

After she had reattached her missing limb in its socket, she had taken Telawui's forearm and given her an earnest expression. "Thank you for everything," she told the witch doctor.

The healer smiled cryptically and inclined her head. "May blessing of gods accompany you."

Feras exited the tent, taking unhurried and controlled steps, breathing in the outside air.

A voice called out to her, Slay coming her way. "Glad to see you're up on your feet."

"Believe me, I'm the happiest," she answered him before glancing around for the others. "Where is everyone?"

Slay pointed at a huge form walking steadily. "Thorick's an hour ahead of you out of bed. He's rehabilitating his leg and Essan's helping him. Aslor is somewhere in the fields trying to figure out the whole god thing." He gestured last behind them. "And Farrah is, you know…"

"Worrying?" finished Feras, looking at the hunched figure of the renegade leader, cleaning her handguns around the fire pit. She clapped him on the back. "See you later," she said before moving in her direction, taking her time.

Farrah peered up when she saw the captain approaching, her walk controlled and one hand holding her abdomen. Her breathing hastened when she noticed the smirk on the pirate's lips.

She had been hoping that Feras had not been aware of her presence during the night she had spent by her side and been avoiding her ever since. As the corsair neared her, she wondered whether she was about to have a discussion on an event she wanted to pretend had not happened.

"Hello," said Feras, coming up full length in front of her. "Can I sit?" she asked, indicating a wooden log next to hers.

"Of course," she replied, her tone quiet.

The corsair's face still appeared paler than usual, but her familiar poise had returned. "Essan told me you took care of me when I was sick." Farrah's fingers twitched and Feras added, "I don't remember much to be honest, but I wanted to thank you for being there for me."

She found her voice again. "Don't mention it," she answered. "You're a part of the group."

The pirate smiled her cocky sideways grin. "I feel so privileged," she replied. "But really," she went on more seriously, "Essan told me how you barely slept until I was out of danger. I appreciate it."

Farrah felt awkward, not knowing how to answer her instead of the things she wanted to say. "Of course," she said with reserve.

Feras stood a bit straighter. "You know," she continued, looking around some more before gazing back into Farrah's direction, her stare piercing into hers. "You're nicer than I thought you were."

Farrah's mouth became slightly agape. She gave a brief laugh when she recognized the captain's playful expression. "Well, you're also nicer than I first thought, Feras," she replied.

The corsair lifted both her eyebrows and wriggled them. "Gosh, aren't we likeable people?"

Farrah grinned and then looked down at her hands. "Feras..." she whispered. "I'm sorry for Leos."

The pirate's eyes went out of focus for a short instant before a forlorn smile took form on her lips. "Is there a better death than that for an old adventurer?" she asked, even though it wasn't really a question.

Farrah hung her head, holding the corsair's gaze. "I feel that this is my fault."

What she had meant to say was "Are you angry that I got you and your friend into this mess?"

Hearing no answer, she withdrew her eyes from the pirate's sight.

"Does a moment go by in your life where guilt is not a part of it?"

Farrah looked up. Feras drew forward and lowered her head, levelling her intense gaze into hers. "Enough," she said and grinned far too charmingly before turning round and walking away.

Farrah followed her disappearing form, a sigh passing her lips.

They left the day after. Thorick and Feras had not completely recuperated yet, but the pirate had been eager to return to her ship, and the group had agreed that they had already stayed too long in Shandew.

Farrah had spent some time with Aslor, teaching him the ways of theurgy alongside Slay, whose fervent practising held a renewed sense of purpose now that he had convoked Ekhon. They had gathered their things when Feras had asked if Thorick felt capable of making it back to the galleon and they had said their goodbyes to the villagers.

Farrah had taken Telawui's hands in hers and thanked her for everything. She had then done the same with Mesaï, Atana, Mirka and lastly, Chief Yandu. The elder had sent them off with his blessings, chanting a traditional Shandalew farewell.

They felt a certain nostalgia when they left the peace of this harmonious people, knowing they were returning to a far more troublesome existence, and wanting one day to travel back to this place where time was no longer stringent and people lived in unity.

Essan was clearing the walk behind Atana, who had offered to guide them back. They took their time on their return trip, strolling leisurely amidst the jungle's feral beauty, admiring its essence.

Slay remained by Thorick's side the entire trek, making certain he would not fumble his step upon the wobbly, uneven soil.

Feras had often appeared out of breath and Farrah had been afraid more than once that she was on the brink of collapsing. But the captain had held her ground, her walk stiff and forehead glistening.

The *Celestial Dragon* was a welcome sight. They had gestured their farewell to Atana, the galleon's worried crew just as soon greeting their return.

Kerok had placed a stabilizing palm on Feras's sweaty back when she had set foot on the spar deck and ushered her off to her stateroom. Dahara had also brought Thorick to his cabin, patting his hand all the while, telling the knight that they would take "good ol' care" of him.

The rest of them had headed inside the ship, feeling tired after their long walk.

Slay had collapsed onto one of the burgundy sofas in the main lounge and raised his fingers over the top of the couch, yawning. "So, what's next?"

Farrah had been thinking about that ever since Feras had been out of trouble. All in all, things were going well for them. They had acquired four deities and defeated one of the seven commandants. Though their quest would surely meet further misfortunes along the way, up until now, fate had been on their side. Mostly.

"The research citadel," she answered. "It was the plan all along. The library in Mondos is the largest one in Iscar. We'll be able to find clues that could point us towards other gods."

"I concur," said Aslor. "The research citadel is our best bet, though we are bound to encounter resistance given that it's one of the biggest cities in Iscar."

"I fear that once we leave Shandew, the sky as well as the land will provide constant menaces for us," Farrah agreed.

"Right," said Essan, squirming in her seat. "If you ask me, we're turning into a real threat. As long as we keep on becoming stronger, we should be fine with everything that daemon throws at us."

"Hear, hear," cheered Slay.

"It'll take a few days before we make it there. Let us recuperate and figure out a plan before we arrive," she finished.

After they had cleaned themselves and washed away the dirt and sweat from their clothes, they had reconvened outside in the setting sun and met with Feras on deck.

The corsair had been staring at the dusk and did not turn when they came by her side. "Where to?" she asked, somehow knowing it had been the renegades who had approached her.

Farrah said, "The research citadel in Mondos."

The captain nodded. "We'll have to leave the ship a good distance off into the fields outside the city. It will be impossible to get near Mondos without painting a huge target on our backs."

"Do what you think is best."

Feras eyed her. "Aye, aye," she replied, voice mellow, before stepping up the bridge's staircase. Her coat was resting on her shoulders, looking fearless as her fingers grasped the wooden wheel between her hands, regardless of the dark circles she was wearing under her eyes. "Master Kerok," she said, her tone commanding. "Input our coordinates; we're going to Mondos."

They hoisted away, leaving behind the jungles of Shandew and headed out to the horizon.

That evening, Slay had taken a seat beside the corsair when the long tables had been placed and the feast had started. The captain had been glaring at the tankard in front of her as though analyzing its content.

He grinned. "Wondering if it's poison?"

Feras gave him a smirk. "Oh no, I want to drink but am unsure whether my stomach can fathom alcohol considering what it's gone through."

Slay chuckled and grabbed the sides of his own jug in a full fist. "I don't envy you." He glanced around for a while, seemingly just for the sake of it, but searching for one person only.

He ended his exploration when a woman came to stand beside the captain, placing a rather possessive hand on her shoulder. He recognized her as that pink-haired girl who had been dancing some time ago, Alena.

"How are you holding up, Captain?" she asked in an enchanting, yet concerned tone.

Feras shrugged, still looking at her tankard. "Whatever. I just want to drink."

Slay grinned, trying to think of something to say, feeling that this was the type of person he ought to impress. "Yeah, it's good ale," he agreed, motioning to his tankard.

The woman raked her gaze over his body. The tension rose in his lower belly when she did, and further when he realized that Farrah had just sat on his other side.

"Yes… not bad," answered Alena, making a simper.

"Fuck this," said Feras, and she took a swig out of her jug. She drank it and clanked her tankard back on the table. She breathed in as though waiting for a reaction and then looked up at Alena. "Think I could have some of those pills? In case alcohol turns out to be a horrible idea. Which it will."

"Of course, Captain," she replied, delight painted over her face. "Anything you need."

Slay sat his drink down. Farrah was watching them, and he could almost feel her touching him. "Pills?" he inquired.

The corsair lifted her shoulders. "For the upset stomach. I'm not sure what they are. I make it a thing not to ask questions."

Alena gave a little tap on top of Feras's head. "Nor should you. I don't like my patients to doubt me."

Slay looked at them both. "You're her… patient, Captain?"

Feras stared at him as though she found the implication in his tone oafish. "Yes, Slay. Alena is the ship's healer. Haven't you two met?" she added, glancing up at the woman.

Alena gave a leering grin. "Not officially."

"I saw you before, but we didn't talk," he answered, realizing right after how creepy those words must have sounded.

The woman giggled, her fingers covering her mouth while Feras rolled her eyes. Slay witnessed Aslor's blank expression in front of him and Farrah's neutral face.

He shifted in his chair.

"Alena, please stop whatever you're doing to this poor man," said the captain.

"I'm not…" he began.

"I'm Alena," cut in the woman, drawing a confident hand forward.

He took it hesitantly. "Slay," he mumbled back.

Feras pointed to the others. "This is Aslor." The woman tilted her head in his direction. "And Farrah."

Alena's grin wavered only briefly, eyes scrunching a little before she tipped her chin to her as well. Farrah returned the gesture, but it felt restrained to him.

"We've met before," said the renegade leader in a casual tone.

"Have we?" answered the other girl while cocking her head to the side.

Farrah smiled and this time, the chill in it was definitive.

The captain appeared to have lost interest in the conversation. She was looking at her empty drink, seemingly wondering whether she should fill it up again. Alena had her hand on the corsair's shoulder still but was making eyes at Slay.

He peered at Farrah's expression, but she was more taken with her own plate at the moment. He did the only thing that felt normal and took another swallow of his drink.

"I forgot to thank you." Slay blinked around at Farrah. "After our battle with Thar, you stayed behind with Thorick," she said. "That was really considerate of you."

"Oh, you know, was the right thing to do."

Here was the thing.

Ever since Slay had blurted out to Farrah that he found her

beautiful, he had decided that taking a step back would help his cause. And though they hadn't talked much since, he had felt a growing appreciation on her part following Ekhon's intercession.

Sure, yeah. She would probably have thanked anyone for assisting a friend in need, but maybe, just *maybe*, Farrah had bourgeoned a certain fondness for him.

And perhaps it was the alcohol talking, but it felt to him that Farrah didn't like this Alena girl much. He also knew for a fact that the strawberry-haired woman had been flirting with him just now.

He gazed back into the renegade leader's perfect features and took another sip from his drink.

She smiled. "It was."

Considering he hadn't consumed anything yet, Slay thought he ought to slow down on the ale.

Alena was whispering some words in the captain's ears, and the corsair was grinning rather maliciously while she continued eating. Then, both lifted their stares on him.

Uh. He shuffled once more.

The woman drew herself up and began walking away, brushing soft fingers along his neck as she went past him. "See you later, Slay," she said before disappearing into the crowd.

His back jerked straighter, body coming to attention.

Feras was now wiping her mouth with a handkerchief, smirking. "Don't let her get to your head, friend."

"What?" he answered, feeling trapped.

The pirate rolled her eyes for the second time. "She does that to all the guys she meets. Don't fall for it."

"Oh," he replied, voice slightly bemused. He stared back at the others, who had all been paying attention to the conversation. "I wasn't falling for it," he told them, but Farrah was ignoring his gaze and was looking instead at Feras.

"And Alena gets jealous of every woman she finds beautiful," added the captain, staring now at the renegade leader. "It's nothing personal, just a competition thing… I think."

Farrah tensed almost imperceptibly by his side and Slay felt a renewed sense of confidence as he pondered her reaction.

And as he took another drink.

Farrah moved her shoulders back. "I wouldn't want her to believe that I'm competing with her."

"Oh, I know that," the corsair said with a short laugh. "But I don't think she can help herself."

Farrah did not answer. Though her expression had not changed, Slay noticed her fingers had twitched under the table. She smiled and resumed eating her dish.

He was going crazy. How many weeks had he been unable to be himself around her? He was getting headaches overthinking this situation all the time.

He just wanted to tell her about his attraction and get it over with.

Slay looked at Farrah, feeling decisive, or rather impulsive. But, whatever. "You don't like her, eh?"

She seemed taken aback by his statement. "I don't know her. I cannot judge," she answered in a neutral tone of voice.

He grinned in a boyish way. "You don't have to be so politically correct." He winked. "I'm beginning to know you."

Farrah drew her shoulders up. "I don't think we're similar people, but there's nothing wrong with that."

Slay's gaze lowered to her wonderful mouth and lips before he wrenched it back up. "No comparison there."

Farrah's face became blank for a second. "Alena sure looked interested," she continued, grin returning.

His alcohol-ridden brain went into override as he considered her statement. "Oh," he began. "You think?"

"I believe that was obvious," she answered in both a tone and expression that implied it.

Slay tried to focus. He had never been the best at reading others and this could go in too many different ways. He laughed. "Well, the captain did say she does that to every man."

Farrah grinned and again, resumed giving her attention to her plate. She was moving away from the conversation, but he didn't want that anymore.

"You wanna go for a walk?" he asked, trying to sound casual even though he felt anything but.

Farrah stopped eating and watched him.

"I wanna talk to you about something," he continued and his leg began twitching out of control, foot tapping against the floor.

Farrah's stare looked calculating. "Of course," she answered in a low voice.

When they went up the stairs, Farrah tried to disregard Feras's penetrating eyes as they made their way towards the quarterdeck.

She knew what was coming and couldn't help feeling nervous as they separated themselves from the rest of the group and headed away into the night, alone.

Slay was looking so anxious that he appeared about ready to crumble under the pressure.

A part of her had wanted to say "no" when he had asked her for the walk. But when it had come down to it, she hadn't figured how to refuse him. She couldn't deny his request to talk, nor should she.

Farrah could no longer go on pretending that this situation wasn't making her uncomfortable and knew she had to be honest with him.

They drew to a stop at the rear end of the galleon and she turned to face him, waiting for him to begin.

Slay looked down at his feet and cleared his throat. It took another few seconds before he gazed back into her expression. His fingers had clutched the handrail, knuckles becoming white. His eyes sparkled with such emotion that she found it hard to sustain them with the void of her own.

"Farrah…" he began, voice husky. He came a bit closer and she stiffened up as a result, body unconsciously rearing back a little. "I…" he went on, his hand sliding towards hers on the bulwarks. "I've been wanting to tell you something for a while now."

She waited as he collected himself, his gaze going from her to the ground, every second of it excruciating.

"Dammit. Why is it so hard to say?" He let out a sigh and lifted a pitiful expression on her. "I like you, Farrah," he declared in a whisper.

Her features morphed into a gentle sort of openness. She knew he was expecting an answer, and had no choice but to give him one. "Slay… I'm sorry…." she began.

She couldn't count the number of times she'd had to face this, and whilst it sometimes annoyed her, sometimes angered her, today, all she felt was compassion. He was a good person, and she hated wounding him.

He quivered a grin and mumbled, "I know. I'm not entirely stupid…. In truth, I think I only needed it said." He stepped back. "I'm not good enough for you and I'm sorry I made you feel awkward."

Farrah's expression softened. "Slay, you need to know…"

Slay chuckled dejectedly and drew an arm up. "Save the pity speech. I'll get over it."

She took his hand in hers and brought it down. "Slay, I'm attracted to women."

His lips parted. "Oh…" he answered, eyes drifting upwards, nowhere in particular. She released his fingers while he assimilated this. "Oh," he repeated. "I didn't know that."

She went on, delicate but firm. "Listen, I can't say if it would have worked out between us or not even if I *did* like men. Either way, my interests simply do not go in this direction."

He nodded a few times as if considering the information. "Since… always?"

Though she did not like the connotations implied in this question, Farrah tried to keep her tone bare and spare him her judgment. "Yes, Slay."

He nodded a few more times. "The others, they're aware?" he asked timidly.

She understood at once that she had made him feel silly, for not knowing. "It's not a secret," she replied. "I've no time for romantic pursuits and so had no use in sharing my interests. And though it is no one's concerns but my own, I am not hiding the information if that's what you're wondering."

She eyed his semi-confused, semi-saddened expression before adding, "Some people know, some don't. It's not important to me. But I don't want you to think that I've been leading you on, I…" She searched for the right words, figuring how best to put it. "I'm just trying to clear my head of this stuff, and I guess my secrecy has a lot to do with the notion that it's my personal life and I want to keep it to myself. If that makes sense?"

He gave her a half-grin. "Yeah, I understand," he answered. "You don't have to explain anything. To be honest, I don't think you've been leading me on at all. You've done quite the opposite." He chuckled at that, and his tone was lighter now. "Truly, I think I just needed to say it, so I could move on." He arched an eyebrow. "If that makes sense?"

Her features softened. "Yes, and I hope we can be friends."

"Yeah…" His smile widened. "Now, we can be."

They both stared back into the space below. Though Slay was trying to look composed, she could still see certain emotions lurking inside his eyes.

"So… does that mean we can talk about girls now?" he said, his habitual grin returning.

Farrah laughed and the tension dissipated between them. "I have a feeling that we don't have the same type," she replied, her expression amused.

He pouted. "Oh well."

Farrah knew they would be less awkward with one another now. She was glad. Not only because it would make things easier but also because she didn't want him to like her as a woman but rather as a trusted ally.

She wondered whether she would have this with Feras.

CHAPTER 24

When Feras had called it a night and retreated towards her quarters, her stomach far too queasy and head dizzy, she had seen Farrah and Slay returning from the quarterdeck. She witnessed their casual stride and smiling expressions, and when she looked into Farrah's face, she noticed something akin to ease. A rare sight.

She shook her head and moved onwards, wondering whether the boy-man had revealed his feelings, and though improbable, if this had brought them closer. She had a hard time imagining the renegade leader falling for a character like him.

Well, whatever it was, or wasn't, it was none of her concern.

While she strolled down the passageway leading to her chambers, she heard a cry from above and swivelled on her heels.

Feras ran back up the stairs she'd just gone down and emerged outside. Though many of the pirates were yet at dinner, everyone's heads had turned to Kerok, standing on the bridge.

"What's wrong?" she asked when she arrived next to him, eyes following his gaze on the screens.

"We've been spotted," announced Kerok. "A ship is coming towards us."

He pointed at the monitor where Feras figured the enclosing distance between the *Celestial Dragon* and a fast-moving vessel. She yanked an electronic spyglass from the counter and flew back down.

She strode past the tables and headed to the other side of the galleon, taking the stairs up the forecastle deck two at a time. She halted midway and darted an eye inside the telescope.

A shiver ran through her spine when she noticed the waving black flag of the approaching ship, its design flapping towards her mockingly. She clenched her teeth and lowered the spyglass.

It was bearing a hung skeleton.

"Feras?"

Farrah's voice lifted her out of her contemplation. She cleared her throat when Dahara said, "Capt'n, yer orders?"

"Stay on the course, and prepare the crew for our guests. I reckon we'll be having company."

The woman yelled her commands. Feras clasped her fingers behind her back, her expression grave. A soft hand touched her forearm and she glanced down into Farrah's expression, her face demanding answers.

"What's going on?"

Her own expression became uncertain. However, trouble was still evident in it. "I know this ship. Its captain is no… enemy of mine."

Aslor and the others had joined with them and were squinting at the approaching vessel. "Who's this?" asked the islander.

"This is Antwan La Faux's freighter, the *Red Skinner.*"

"A pirate…" said Essan in a low voice.

"Not just any," added Aslor, his brow also creased. "A merciless killer, a vile torturer of the worst kind."

"You all need to listen to me carefully," Feras went on, her tone as brash as her sudden turnaround had been. "We are acquainted, him and I. Though I do not enjoy his company, nor the person he is, it is of the utmost importance that we give him no reason to wish us ill-will." She glanced back at the freighter. "Especially in these troubled times," she murmured.

Farrah said, "You are uncertain of his motives."

She tossed a hand through her hair. "He is of a sadistic nature; this is what I know of him. I happen, however, to be in his good graces and believe me, you want to be on that side of him." She paused for a second, mixed feelings showing on her features. "Though I am not aware of his current motives, I intend on finding out soon enough."

"Could he be against us?" asked Slay.

She shook her head in thought. "I would not think so, but one can never know. Some men have… different goals in life. I would not presume to understand the workings of the mind of a lunatic." She put a hand on the bannister. The incoming vessel was almost on them. "I will take care of him," she finished, stomachache forgotten.

Farrah grabbed her arm. "Don't let him inside the ship, we don't know what he wants."

"I can't take the risk of angering him," Feras replied. "Turning him around would accomplish just that."

The renegade leader's expression grew alarmed. "If this man is a killer, it would be better to stay away from him, especially considering our already precarious situation!"

She yanked her arm away. "It's better to keep that sort of person happy, so he doesn't have a reason to retaliate," she answered and swiftly strode back towards the main deck.

At once, Farrah turned to Aslor. "Tell me about this La Faux character."

Anyone who knew a thing about piracy knew the names of the big players in their industry. Beyond the celebrated Sadahl family, Antwan La Faux was also an infamous participant in their world. Though Farrah was not well acquainted with the subject of pirates, she was aware at least this much: He was feared throughout the lands and was called the *Butcher of the Skies*, a man with the cruellest of dispositions.

"Oh, that's a name you speak, not a person you want to meet," Aslor began. "Though I haven't stumbled on him in the past, I've heard enough stories for me to abstain from ever crossing his path. People such as him belong in the company of our dear daemon, for his troublesome acts are no better than his."

The freighter was near enough now that Farrah could see the faces of those standing on its deck. Chills ran down her forearms; her stomach pinched. There was something hungry about those expressions.

"If he's friends with the captain, then everything's gonna be okay, right?" quaked Essan.

"I don't think they're friends," she replied. "Let's keep to ourselves in the meanwhile. I believe we can trust that Feras will take care of this situation."

"They're boarding," said Slay and he nudged his head towards the main deck.

The gangplank was being drawn between both vessels and Feras was waiting on its other side, her feet grounded, one hand sitting on her leg holster. She had armed herself with her plethora of weapons: twin cutlasses on her back and shotgun in the middle.

"Let's go," said Farrah and they merged with the rest of the crew glowering at the newcomers.

They found Dahara some ways behind the corsair, scowling at the *Red Skinner*. From up close, she could see the burgundy hue that painted the ship's hull as though the blood of La Faux's enemies stained it. Or rather, that of his *prey*.

Dahara eyed her when she arrived by her side, all the while sneering at the gangplank. "Trouble be brewin'," she declared darkly.

"You think he could be dangerous?"

The woman cracked her knuckles and spat on the ground. "Disgustin' piece o' human shit. It juss gives me them shivers when he be lookin' at me with them eyes o' his." As if compelled by her own words, Dahara shuddered at the thought. "Thankfully, we don't be crossin' his path too often. That fucker here ain't right in the mind."

Farrah glimpsed at the approaching figure on the drawn passage, arms opening wide at the sight of Feras.

Antwan La Faux.

"Feras!" he clamoured, grasping the corsair into an embrace. "How've ya been?"

He seemed young enough, possibly in his late thirties. Covered in black, he wore a long leather coat over his pirate garments and mid-calf boots. He wielded no other accessories but for a sword, sitting on his hip, and a curved jewelled dagger hanging on the front of his breeches, dangling over his manhood.

His almond-shaped eyes were brown and narrow, and his cleanly shaved jaw was molded in all the right places. He was an attractive man, with his centre-parted espresso hair falling just over his ears in a ragged frenzy that looked too perfect to be natural.

All the same, she understood what Dahara had meant. He had the stare of a weasel: a calculating steely gaze.

Had she not witnessed Feras's troubled expression a short moment ago, Farrah would have thought that she had been reacquainted with an old friend. Not a trace or hint of distress could be detected from the corsair as she greeted the man and responded to his embrace with as much enthusiasm.

"Antwan," Feras replied. "I have been well. Tell me, what brings you here?"

La Faux simpered, thumbs delving down his front belt, posture candid. "For fuck's bottom sake, Feras, y'all have been busy.... I had to come and see ya when I noticed yer galleon on my radar."

He grinned and Farrah was reminded of a shark. Perhaps she was imagining it but even his teeth looked sharpened.

A voluptuous woman was standing behind him, also dressed in black leather. Her hair was short and dark makeup hollowed her eyes. She had a distant expression, a ghostly reflection emptying her features of any warmth. If anything, she seemed devoid of existence.

A person who had gone through so much that she had already died while still being alive.

"Have you now?" Feras replied, and Farrah knew the pirate was trying to conceal her emotions. "Well, we are somewhat on the run, which means that we can't stay here for long and must get going." She pulled on an apologetic expression and intertwined her hands before her, one leg leaning back.

La Faux lunged forward, grabbed her by the shoulder and spun her around. He began walking her forwards onto her own ship. "O' course, o' course, but this calls for drinks! I want to know everything," he burst out, fingers tugging on her arm, the leather-clad woman following suit.

Farrah felt disturbed by the man's disregard of Feras's wishes. It somehow upset her as though it were her own dignity that had been shoved aside.

"Oh, and bring me them rebels of yers, so I can get a good look at 'em," she heard him say as they entered the saloon hall. La Faux obviously knew his way around the *Celestial Dragon.*

Farrah spun around to the others. Dahara lifted an agitated stare on them. "I think ye be about to find out what I mean," she said in a foreboding tone.

A few of the *Red Skinner's* crew were also making their way into the *Dragon's* main lounge. These men and women had a different presence about them, something that felt… dangerous.

A part of her wanted to keep away and let Feras deal with their lot; another wanted to know how things were going to unfold. "I'm joining them," she decided.

Dahara and the others shared uncertain looks before following after the rest of the group. They entered the saloon hall, where many pirates from both the *Celestial Dragon* and the *Red Skinner* had already gathered.

The crew's tensed dispositions augured nothing good.

La Faux was leaning back on the largest sofa, the leather-clad woman seated beside him and Feras in front, looking even-tempered.

Farrah caught her eye for a brief second before lowering herself on the couch beside hers, Essan sitting by her side and Slay and Aslor picking another sofa close by.

Her stare met with Antwan's shrewd gaze, similar to that of an animal having found its quarry. He drew his arm behind his head, opening his armpit, the slightest grin pulling on the corners of his mouth. "So, this be the fearsome rebels," he snarled in a delighted tone of voice, all of his teeth showing as the words simmered through them.

"Ah, yes," Feras replied rather dismissively. "But you know, the nature of a tale is warped the second it is told. People often blow things out of proportion, don't they?" She drew a short laugh. "Tell me, what ludicrous stories are being passed around?"

Antwan's eyes widened. "They say yer in open rebellion against the daemon. That ya killed Commandant Trent and are coming for Daromas next."

Feras's expression revealed nothing. "Yes, I killed Trent. We both know that had been on my list for a long time. As for Daromas, if the man's gunning for us, I wouldn't mind a good fight." She smiled, but La Faux's grin had wavered.

"I thought ya were being a naughty gurl," he replied, sticking his tongue out as if he'd eaten something sour. "That's not nearly as exciting as I'd hoped. I thought there'd be more killings involved." His shoulders sagged and he pouted. "I wanted to join ya."

Feras said, "Completely exaggerated." She made a theatrical gesture with her hands. "I guess this is what happens when you take a piss on the daemon. Alas, we're only fugitives. Nothing exciting about that."

Antwan scowled, wearing a moping expression, and Farrah got the distinct impression of a toddler having had his toy confiscated.

He soon lit up again, a sly grin covering his features. "Ya should know that Commandant Husar is in the area, looking for ya. His command post is in Mondos." He nudged himself forth, wriggling his eyebrows. "Wanna take 'im out together?" His tone hid something unbound and cruel.

Feras chuckled and drew her left ankle on top on her right lap. "It's probably better to keep our distance."

Farrah saw a flare cross Antwan's eyes, his features sharpening into upset. "We could slaughter 'im easily between the two of us: La Faux and Sadahl, bringers o' death!" he declared, rising as he did before crashing back down, legs soaring up when his buttocks collapsed against the sofa.

The corsair straightened up a little. "That sounds interesting. Let me think about it."

This seemed to satisfy the man. He sat both of his forearms against his thighs, back rounding. "Yer going to Mondos, aren't ya?" he continued, eyes glimmering.

Feras had paused for less than a second, but it was enough to convey her surprise. "What makes you say that?" she replied, her tone conversational.

Antwan let out a quick burst of laughter, his smile ferocious. "Come on, Feras, I've been around them skies for as long as ya have. I know what course yer on."

"Clever."

Antwan threw his hand up and snapped his fingers, his stare obstinately set to the side.

Many of the *Dragon's* crew members glanced around as he did, but he simply went on snapping until the person he had been calling turned to face him. He had a petulant expression on as though he was insulted by the time it had taken her to look at him.

Alena came in their direction wearing a bitter scowl, and Farrah couldn't help noticing the sudden unrest in the room.

The strawberry-haired woman stopped near Feras, eyes directed to the floor, jaw set. The corsair looked stern, her gaze shifting between Alena and Antwan, the veins on her hand bulging as it rested on her leg.

La Faux's carnivorous smile was fixated on Alena. "I'll take a cup of yer best wine, ma'am," he ordered, tone purring.

Alena slapped on a definitely coerced smirk and veered rigidly towards the bar. The hate that had filled her eyes was unmistakable and Farrah felt a newfound respect for the woman. She had half-expected her to flirt with the dark pirate, but her blatant unamused demeanour was something she had not foreseen.

Antwan returned his attention to Feras as though nothing had happened. "Always a pleasure to meet with familiar faces," he said, winking as he crossed his legs. "See what a good boy I am?"

Feras's mouth twitched in answer and everyone turned silent. Antwan began humming a song right up until the moment Alena came back. Though Farrah could not read the corsair's expression, she saw something behind her glare. Something like rage caged into a tightly shut box.

Alena returned, holding the drink she'd been ordered to fetch at arm's length.

Antwan made no move to take it. He looked instead with appreciation at her robust cleavage. She stood there, her body at an awkward angle, straining to keep away, all the while bringing the cup closer.

He lifted his finger and crooked it at her. At this, Alena turned far-less confident eyes towards Feras. The pirate was staring at the scene with the same contained expression Farrah could not read.

She cleared her voice. "Alena, would you give the man his drink," she said with a hint of impatience. "And then, won't you go and fetch me one as well? I'm certain the others are thirsty too and it's rude to keep them waiting."

"Yes, Captain," the woman replied and she shoved the cup into Antwan's outstretched hand before rushing away.

He leered at her as she retreated, eyes ogling her shape.

He then took a resounding slurp out of his drink, head scanning the room, his stare soon falling on Farrah again. Antwan threw a kiss her way and her stomach lurched with disgust. "I always find ya in such delectable company, Feras. What do you do to surround yerself with these adorable creatures?" He reached over and squeezed the corsair's leg as though she'd scored the biggest goal.

"I'm charming I suppose," Feras answered. Her tone had been playful though her eyes had none of the warmth they usually conveyed when offering a quip.

Antwan snorted and hovered back. "Can I borrow one tonight?" he asked, and though his face was light, his tone wasn't.

Feras looked mischievous as she put an arm up behind the sofa. "I don't like sharing, you know that."

Farrah tilted her head sideways, feeling like cattle that had just been claimed, though this was a rare moment when she did not mind.

Antwan leered once more at her and pressed his tongue against his lips. "Mmm," he said, mouth hanging. "Yer lucky I have such respect for ya." His upper lip curled up the way a smiling animal would.

Again, his tone had not suggested a jest, and from Feras's casual but tense body language, Farrah knew the pirate had also felt the implication behind the words.

Alena came back carrying their drinks, Antwan caressing his thighs languorously the whole time. As soon as she was done, she removed herself from their presence and exited the room altogether.

The man let out a long sigh, looking bored and glowering at Alena's disappearing form. "Anyone I can play with?"

The captain chuckled, eyes cast downwards as she did. "I don't take prisoners, too troublesome."

Antwan threw his head backwards and moaned. "No fun," he answered. "Ya should see the ones I've got on my ship," he continued. "Delicious."

The more the conversation was unfolding, the more uncomfortable Farrah was becoming.

More disturbed.

"I just love the way they scream when I tear off their fingers, one..." He emphasized each word, "by... one." He grabbed his genitalia with a hand and pulled at it, eyes bulging. "Or when I fuck a warm torso!" And he burst out laughing.

It was a chilling sound. It cut through Farrah as she went numb.

"Come on, I'm messing with y'all," Antwan continued, looking discouraged when he noticed that no one else was laughing along with him.

"Who were these people?" she heard herself say. Farrah only realized she had raised her voice the moment she had finished saying the words.

She noticed Feras's stare on her from the corner of her eye but kept her own on Antwan. This man did not deserve false impressions. He deserved every last bit of her judgment, regardless of what the corsair thought.

La Faux surveilled her. "I dunno," he answered, forgetting all pretence at humour.

She tightened her fists. "What had they done to you?"

He shrugged, appreciation growing on his features as he twisted her upset into an object of gratification. "They happened to be there when I happened to want to be entertained."

"They were innocent then."

Antwan laughed as though he'd found her question funny. "Well, o' course, ya little cunt! It ain't nearly as fun otherwise.... It's the way they beg fo' mercy that gives me the hardest boner." He chortled some more as though she was the biggest idiot for not knowing already.

At that precise moment, something became clear in Farrah's mind. She wanted this man gone as much as she desired Daromas dead.

As his laugh endured, she felt Feras's studying gaze on her. She had no doubt the pirate was as troubled as she was though she was definitely more skillful at playing this character game than she was.

Slay's mouth was hanging open and Aslor's wide-eyed expression revealed nothing but shock. Essan was looking mortified and Farrah discreetly placed a hand on her leg, feeling her tremors underneath it.

They were about to blow their cover or whatever it was that they were doing right now.

Feras cleared her throat and readjusted herself before standing up. "Why don't we go and talk in private, Antwan? I fear it has been too long and we've got a lot of catching up to do, haven't we?" She beckoned towards the entrance. "I would love to invite you into my parlour."

La Faux beamed at the suggestion. "I agree. Them people are not like us." He rose up and pretended hitting her a few times in the stomach.

They began making their way towards the exit, but Farrah caught up to Feras and held her back. "Can I talk to you? It will take only a second," she added.

The corsair apologized to Antwan. "This won't be long," and she grabbed Farrah by the elbow before shoving her near the bar where no one could hear them. "You need to calm down," she said in a hushed tone.

Farrah drew closer, her voice a tight whisper. "He's sick."

"Your point?"

"I don't think we should be spending one more moment in his company. He ought to be stopped," Farrah added, knowing that Feras would not agree to this.

The corsair scoffed. "He is dangerous, that much is true, and you know that I don't like him anymore than you do. But…" She raised a finger just as Farrah was about to interrupt. "But," she repeated, "we can't afford to make an enemy out of him when we already have the full fucking government on our backs!"

"I understand, but this man is a lunatic," she said staunchly. "We can't let him go around killing innocent people!"

Feras came nearer to her face, keeping her rising temper down to a murmur. "What he does is not our business. When Daromas is dead, you can be my guest and head out on another quest of yours to purge this land of its vicious residents. But as it is," and she stressed her next words, "we already have more than enough going on."

"He is right here, *right now*. We could be saving dozens of innocent lives if we stop him, Feras…"

"This is my ship, *I* decide," the pirate bit back. "I will get rid of him as soon as I can and then we can be on our way to Mondos. Is that clear?"

"No."

"Really, Farrah?" Feras replied pointedly, drawing her eyes up to the roof. "You want this guy as our enemy? Think about it for a second. Think about what he just said. Really, *think*." She waited for a few seconds, offering her said time to reflect on it. "What if it's Essan he's playing with? What if it's Aslor? You think about that and tell me whether you're willing to take risks when it comes to this man."

Farrah's resolve dwindled as gross images flowed through her mind and visions of carnage emerged before her eyes. "You're telling me he's stronger than us? When we're equipped with the theurgy of four gods?" She stared at the pirate. "And *you*?"

"I can take him on."

"Then, what are you afraid of?"

"I'm not taking the chance and this discussion is over." Feras spun around and retreated from her.

Farrah hated how she always left her in her wake.

Feeling concerned at the notion of Feras alone with that man, she went back to the others. They were now standing at the bar, away from the leather-clad woman still on the sofa. Her head was lopsided as though she were half-asleep.

Farrah motioned at them and they followed her back to her cabin.

"This guy gives me the creeps," said Slay, sitting on her berth.

Aslor had leaned against the wall. "What should we do, Farrah?"

She was hovering near the entrance, palms clasping her elbows. "I talked to the captain. She thinks it's best to leave La Faux alone."

"You want to take him out, right?" asked Essan in a low voice.

"I understand that Feras doesn't wish to anger this pirate but after what he just told us…" she went on, feeling conflicted.

They looked at each other and shuddered silently. "Let's get him," said Slay as though it were the easiest decision in the world.

Farrah shook her head. "Feras isn't on board and we can't do anything without her approval. And she's not wrong, we can't take any risks when it comes to men like him. Although, I won't deny that this sort of thinking is exactly the reason why things don't get accomplished. This world is afflicted by people minding their own business while others' lives are left abandoned to decay."

Feras could defeat Antwan in single combat if it came down to it, but this was not the pirate's fight, and Farrah would be using her to get what she wanted. If she were honest with herself, this wouldn't be the first time. She could ask no more of her.

She shook her head. "If Feras isn't on board, we have to respect her decision. But I make this promise: La Faux will not go unpunished. Once this is all over, I'm coming for him."

"No way we're letting this piece of shit go free," Slay agreed, fists flexing in and out.

Aslor was looking pensive, forefingers trailing along the length of his whiskers. "Perhaps we could convince the captain? It doesn't feel right to allow this man to go on doing his… business."

Essan drew her arms around her waist as if embracing herself. "He doesn't deserve to live," she whispered.

"Without the consent of the captain *and* the crew, we can't go forward with this plan," answered Farrah. "There's too much resting on it; on this point, I agree with Feras. We don't want a madman such as La Faux coming after us. I wouldn't be able to live with myself if any one of you were to become his next victim."

Slay punched his fist in his other palm. "Let that fucker try."

Truth be told, Farrah wanted to say the same thing but kept herself from it. "Let's just see how this plays out," she finished.

Feras was sitting in her favourite armchair inside her sitting room, Kerok guarding the door outside. She had motioned to her quartermaster when they had left the main lounge. The man had understood her meaning and followed behind. If anything were to happen, he'd be ready to jump right in.

"Forgive the woman, Antwan," she began, "she's a bit of a saint." She held the back of her palms before her in mock prayer.

La Faux laughed at that and shoved her words aside. "Most people don't comprehend my art."

A chill ran down Feras's back. She felt particularly uncomfortable now that she was alone with him. She had never felt at ease around him and presently, more so than ever, she wished him gone.

The man was deeply disturbed.

They had met some years ago while she had been out haggling and made a stop at Racketeer Bay. He had approached her, seeking to connect with powerful people. She had acknowledged his presence for the night, but the more she had gotten to know him, the less she had found his company desirable.

Throughout the years, she had learned more about him and had been perturbed by the man's actions. She had tried to keep away from him, but like vermin, he had cycled back to her every now and then.

But she didn't want to make an enemy out of Antwan La Faux. Honestly, Feras was glad he had taken a liking to her. It kept her and the people around her off his radar.

She had never encouraged their reunions and their casual meetings had been so far between that she had been able to cope with this *friendship*. But in truth, she had wanted him dead since the beginning.

As she stared into his deranged eyes, she felt like strangling him. Alas, things weren't that easy.

Antwan's associate, the leather-clad woman named La Bayonet, *his* choice of the title, was just as deadly as he was. Not to mention the group of maniacs that made up his crew.

The thing with a madman was that one could never know how they would react and that was dangerous. And a lot of those dangerous people were either aboard or a short distance away from the *Celestial Dragon* at this moment.

She understood how Farrah felt, but that woman did not grasp that sometimes the right thing to do was to do nothing.

Well, maybe not the right thing but the best thing.

"What are ya up to, Feras?" asked the captain of the *Red Skinner*.

She focused on him. "Up to?"

"Mondos," continued the man and his expression and tone somehow implied that he would know if she were to lie to him. In fact, it almost felt as if he already knew what they were *up to*.

She dropped her fingers on her lap, thinking fast. "As I told you, we're runaways. We've been hiding out, but it would appear that Daromas has eyes and ears everywhere. If we want to survive, we need to be strategic, don't we?"

La Faux's expression did not change, and his stare was beginning to make her uncomfortable. Her feet twitched and she said, "I guess we're going to Mondos because we want to…"

"Kill Husar."

Feras's mind raced, but she knew that the longer she waited to give him an answer, the more he would figure her motives. Men like him were disturbingly intelligent when it came to reading others. "Yes."

Better this than saying anything about the gods.

He clapped his hands, beaming as though he'd caught her into her games but not seemingly annoyed that she had tried. "I knew it! I knew it!" he repeated as if he'd won something. "How do we take that son o' a bitch down?" he asked while slapping her on the knee.

Oh boy, how was she going to explain to Farrah that instead of pushing him away, he might be tagging along for the ride?

"No, Antwan. I can't mix you up in any of this," she replied.

He narrowed his eyes. "Are ya trynna get rid of me?" he said and his tone felt somewhat sinister now. Menacing.

Feras simpered. "I don't want you to be caught in this mess. Let me tell you, it's been quite a hassle since I killed Trent, so…"

"How did ya kill him?"

"Excuse me?"

"Tell me how ya killed him."

She glimpsed into his eyes and saw… appetite.

You sadistic cunt. "It wasn't anything worth recounting. I pierced him with my sword," she explained rather dryly.

"Come on, Feras. After all these years o' wanting 'im dead, that's all ya did?" he said as though she had let him down.

She shrugged. She wasn't the sort of person to feign interest. In the past, there had always been a limit to how much she could bear pretending when she had seen him.

But she was also afraid of the repercussions. She knew enough about the captain of the *Red Skinner* that if she were ever to displease him, he would punish her for it. Since La Faux couldn't defeat her in single combat, he would use another to get back at her. This was something she was not willing to afford.

Hence, she had played on at these dangerous charades.

"Ya want to know what *I* would've done?"

Feras felt like raising her eyes to the overhead. "Do tell," she answered flatly.

He went on explaining in excruciating detail how he would have made Trent suffer for days on end as he ravaged him, inside and out. She shut her mind off at some point, repressing a sneer while she watched his deranged face, no longer listening to him.

"But ya know, I prefer 'em young."

She steered herself back to the conversation. "What young?"

Antwan repeated his words as though it was the most natural thing to say. "My toys," he explained, taking a sip from his almost-empty cup before helping himself to another drink on the bar cart.

She frowned and waited for him to sit down again. "You like your toys… young?"

He nodded. "Oh yes. Ya know, when they're that small, their little bums rip when…"

Feras yanked her chin down, shutting her ears to the rest of this sentence, though her brain was overflowing with images she wished she could forget but would haunt her for some time.

"They don't move much, easier to handle."

She leaned back inside her chair. "You know what, Antwan? You've convinced me."

"Of what?" he asked, tilting his head to the side.

Feras crossed her hands on her lap. "I would love for you to join us. I'm certain we'll make a great team."

Chapter 25

When Farrah spotted Feras on deck, she had to stop herself from running to her. Upon her waking, the first thing she had seen was the bulging, burgundy-clad hull of the *Red Skinner*.

She had assumed the corsair had failed in getting their guests to leave.

"What is *he* still doing here?" she asked Feras, trying hard not to sound accusatory.

Feras blinked at her. "Antwan will be accompanying us to Mondos."

Her lips parted in shock. "Are you punishing me for talking back to you last night?"

Feras rolled her eyes. "Would you stop being dramatic? Though I wish I didn't have to tell you this, *again*." She stared her down. "You need to trust me."

Farrah had no idea how a maniac joining them was a better thing than not. "Feras…" she began, but the pirate silenced her with a hand.

"Trust," she pointed her fingers towards herself, "me."

She hated not being in control and having to relinquish it. She especially hated it when she didn't know what was going on.

"I trust you," she replied, her tone more subdued. "If you would clue me in, I could understand your motives."

"Look, I'm taking care of the situation. Since I don't know if it'll work out, the less you know, the better."

"I can help."

Feras snorted. "Yes, but we'd just end up arguing and I'd rather conserve my energy."

Farrah ignored the teasing tone but knew the corsair would tell her no more. She hoped the pirate *did* have a plan in mind and wasn't veering this ship off course.

They were safe for now. Antwan had returned to his vessel late at night, his cronies alongside him. Any minute though, he was bound to wake up and pay them another visit.

Feras spotted the one person she had been looking for. "Alena," she greeted the woman.

"Captain?"

"I need your help for something if you are so willing," she explained. "I require your charms, your knowledge of Mondos and dreaded motivation for revenge. Are you interested?"

Alena grinned on command and put her arms up on her hips. "Aye, Captain, you can count me in."

Alena was the perfect person for this job. The woman knew how to get what she wanted and had a serious hate for Antwan.

Though she had escaped in time, he had tried to abuse her in the past.

She had come to Feras, her clothes in shambles, pleading for her help. They had been at the *Captain's Wench* tavern and were having one of their rare encounters with La Faux. Alena had, as per her usual self, unabashedly flirted with the handsome man. If anything, she had found him exciting.

Before they had made their way upstairs, Feras had told the woman to be careful, not to trust him. But Alena had not heeded her warnings. Antwan could truly be charming when he wanted to be.

Not long after, she had run back down and dove to Feras's feet, asking for her protection. Antwan had followed, buck naked and complacent.

This had been a pivotal moment for her; she was still in her early twenties at the time. With everyone's gaze on the scene, the man could not escape her wrath.

Offended, Antwan had professed how the girl had seduced him and been seeking the consequences. To Alena's dismay, most had witnessed their flirtatious exchanges earlier that night and considering his reputation and hers, not many had known what to do.

Feras had.

She had risen to full height, placed herself between the both of them and drawn her cutlass from her back.

Then, a strange thing had happened.

Antwan La Faux had dropped to his knees, begging for mercy. For anyone who knew of him, this behaviour had been most peculiar.

The cub had rolled back in a perfect example of the law of the jungle. Bullies, after all, only bow down to greater power.

Because of this, he'd already been vanquished, and she could no longer challenge him.

His gesture had been so respectful and so manipulative that Feras could only admonish him in front of the rest. She had ordered him never to put a hand again on any person of her crew and the man had agreed, though it had all been fun and games to him.

At least something had become clear between them on that day: Feras was the one in charge. Still, his loyalty was more than volatile. She knew he would turn his back on her in a jiff if it worked to his advantage.

Afterwards, and still in the nude, Antwan had grabbed a drink and acted as though nothing had happened. Alena had thanked her for what she had done, but Feras had felt that she had failed her. He deserved far greater punishment, but he had played his cards right and had gotten away with it.

Nevertheless, the man had kept his promise, and she had much preferred to have him on a leash rather than being at the end of *his*.

Well, things were about to change, but her plan required finesse and acting skills. Considering Farrah and the others had no talent in this regard, it would have to be hers and Alena's time to shine. "Antwan," she called out when he emerged onto her ship.

They began strolling together along the promenade deck, ignoring the quizzical stares of the crew members surrounding them. She clasped her hands behind her back and asked him, "You mentioned that Commandant Husar was looking for us?"

"Yes," answered the man, walking as though he had a horse between his legs, both thumbs clutching the inside of his trousers. "His command is down in Mondos, but his ships are searching the skies in its vicinity."

Feras hummed thoughtfully. "Here's my proposal."

"After we've landed the ship near Mondos, we'll make our way inside the city. Once there, we'll head for the research citadel and get our hands on those books you've been wanting. Mondos is crowded and flourishing; there are people galore coming from all over Iscar so that it shouldn't be too hard for us to masquerade as merchants amidst the throng."

"That seems a bit too easy, doesn't it?" Farrah replied, lips curving down. "The entire regime is after us. There are too many flaws in this plan, which could get us killed."

Feras intertwined her fingers before her. "Try me."

"For one thing, the ship…"

"Will be concealed far away enough that, yes, we'll have to stroll through the woods for half the day before we arrive in town. But we'll be well out of range of the city's radar. Next."

Farrah exhaled. "We'll have to get inside Mondos. There will be control posts at the entrance."

Feras nodded in agreement. "Indeed. Thousands of traders go through these gates. With the proper disguise, and bribe, we should slip inside unnoticed."

She glared at the corsair. "You think the placaters will simply let us march inside Mondos?"

"Oh yes, with the right motivation." Feras grinned. "In the end, it's just a man behind the red armour."

"Okay, suppose we do get in, we need to head over to the research citadel. Again, unnoticed."

The pirate waved it off. "I'll create a diversion. Their eyes will be elsewhere."

"Enlighten us."

"I'm taking care of it." And as she said it, Feras's smile became wider.

"Of course." Farrah crossed her legs under the table. "Still seems to me that a lot of things could go wrong."

The corsair sat on the edge of the table, body angled towards her. "Unless you have a better plan, it's the one we've got. One way or another, if you want to head over to the research citadel, we'll need luck on our side. Worst that can happen, we'll get into a fight. Though, I think it would be safe to assume that the odds are in our favour." She shrugged, looking standoffish. "Honestly, even a commandant is becoming no match for our abilities."

Aslor prodded his spectacles and cleared his voice. "Our abilities won't have a match as soon as we've figured how to conjure our gods on command.... But as things are at the moment, we're amateurs next to the extended theurgy training a commandant has had."

Feras did not appear troubled by his words. "Think about it this way, Mister Aslor..." She paused and grinned her sideways smile. "You've got me."

Farrah felt like rolling her eyes. "I'll agree with one thing," she admitted. "It's that we don't have another choice. If it comes down to a fight, let's hope that Commandant Husar is the only general in town." She drew her stare on the pirate, hovering above her. "Which leaves one problem. What about that friend of yours?"

"You know that distraction I was talking about?" Feras was looking very much like a rascal now. "It has to do with him."

"You're going to use La Faux to create a diversion?" replied Slay, eyes widening. "He's down with that?"

Feras's stare went elsewhere. "I'll make sure he is. In the meantime, you should know that he believes that our goal is to take out Husar and he yet has no clue on the whole god business."

This was at least something. Farrah didn't want word getting out on the nature of their quest for as long as they could keep it a secret, *especially* not to Antwan La Faux. Though she felt troubled that they were cooperating with this man, she liked the idea of using him for their means. A small consolation that was.

"How do you know he won't betray us?" asked Slay. "What if he's after the reward? I bet we're worth a pretty penny."

Feras's lips twitched. "Yes, the thing with crappy bastards is that they're unpredictable, I'll give you that. Though, I don't… think Antwan will betray us."

"How can you be so sure?" said Essan.

The corsair touched the edge of her blunderbuss. "Fame and money do not motivate him."

Farrah's expression hardened. It would be worth nothing to La Faux to get them arrested. What the man wanted was to inflict pain. Physical pain.

Essan rose and went face to face with the pirate. "Captain," she began, her round, innocent eyes looking up at her. "I don't like this man, can't we just… get away from him?"

Feras sat her palms on Essan's shoulder. "You have nothing to worry about. He's not going to hurt any of you; I'll make certain of it." She turned to the others. "And I promise we won't be having his company for long yet."

They entered Mondos's region a few hours later, after darkness had fallen. Feras had spent some time with Antwan, sifting through their plan, before waving him off. La Faux had returned to his ship, and they had begun preparations for their descent.

Feras had thought it safer for the vessels to go their separate ways in the meanwhile, and had arranged for a rendezvous point inside Mondos. While they would ground the *Dragon* somewhere in Mondos's vicinity, La Faux would change the colour of his sails, take down his flag and anchor his *Red Skinner* at the city's docks. He would then meet up with them in the early afternoon the next day.

After a while of scouring the fields adjourning Mondos, they found an opening inside the forest patch and Feras led the *Celestial Dragon* down its cavity. According to the pirate's calculations, a few hours of walking separated them from the city and they should be safe from prying eyes. Kerok would stand guard by the controls if they needed to make for a quick escape.

"Everyone should get to bed early. We're leaving at nine o'clock tomorrow morning," Feras told them.

"You do know that nine is not early, right?" replied Essan, giggling.

"Isn't it?" she answered, looking appalled.

Farrah and the captain had not spoken since their last conversation. There had been so many things to think about that she had preferred to keep her head level and avoid further confrontations with her.

While some of them had retreated to their cabins, she had gone instead towards Thorick's hulking form, sitting by himself on the sun deck. "You're recuperating well," she said and he answered with a contented expression. She took a seat by his side. "You know what I'm about to tell you, don't you?"

He glanced her way with a serious face but did not move.

"You can't come," she went on. "Your leg is not completely healed yet and considering there's a good chance we'll get into a fight, we'll probably have to run at some point." He contemplated the trees, dancing breezily in the cool night air. "Also," Farrah added, "if the enemy finds out our location, we'll need warriors to defend the ship."

Thorick returned his eyes to her and smiled. She knew he was aware that she was sheltering him and though he had agreed to her request with a gentle nod, his expression seemed worried.

They stood side by side for some time, enjoying the crisp breeze.

Being next to Thorick was like lying beside a cool, cascading river. Both had a way of soothing the nerves and giving focus to what really mattered.

Her eyes had carried over Feras, conversing nearby with the fair Alena. She suppressed a twitch inside of her belly when she did.

Though Feras hadn't demonstrated any romantic inclination towards Alena, there was an evident connection between them. It was hard to define in terms of feelings. Yet, she couldn't shake the thought that the both of them had a history together.

She also couldn't help wonder whether Feras found her attractive. If she was being honest with herself, she knew the answer was yes. This woman was an accurate description of the type of company the captain enjoyed. Had Alena been at all inclined towards women, Farrah knew that she would have jumped on the opportunity to share a bed with the corsair.

She let out a quiet sigh and realized that Thorick's gaze was on her. He had a soft expression and she had a suspicion that he somehow knew how she felt. Farrah didn't mind that. He was the type of man who understood and cared. She had nothing to hide from him.

She grinned and he gave her a gentle nod, his knowing eyes acknowledging whatever it was that she was feeling.

She looked away like a teenager caught having a crush.

Whatever Alena's and Feras's connection, she had to give it to the woman, she was not a bad person. Alena's business was her own, and so was Feras's.

While they had busied themselves for their departure, Feras had given a few last words of advice to Kerok if something were to happen to them, and the quartermaster had bade them good luck.

They began their trek amidst Mondos's fair weather and prepared for the upcoming challenges they were about to face when entering the city, talking sparingly and saving their energy for the day ahead.

Hours later, when they had neared the farming lands outside

the inner walls, they had taken a quick breather and rearranged their garments.

They put on loose layers of clothing they had found on the ship and concealed their weapons and gear under the fabric. As a finishing touch, they fitted masks retrieved from Keshui's merchant territories, which covered their faces from nose to jaw.

The crude Keshuian traders used these to shield their expressions when bartering, effectively offsetting any display of emotions in order to destabilise their customers. According to Feras, Mondos abounded with travellers from all over Iscar and though the guards at the gate would surely require they take parts of their costumes off, at least these would buy them some time.

They walked onwards along the main route leading to Mondos's entrance. Soon they had merged amongst the overflowing company of others also making their way towards the great research city of Iscar, their hovercars left abandoned in the huge parking lot outside the city.

Farrah's nerves kicked in as they neared the colossal gateway.

Feras was striding besides her, looking at ease. "You can relax," she said. "I've done this a dozen times before."

Farrah arched an eyebrow. "Dressing up as a merchant to illegally get into a city?"

She noticed lines folding the skin next to Feras's eyes and knew she was smiling underneath the mask. "Bribe the guards."

"Back then, you weren't so infamous."

"No. Simply famous."

"Feras…"

The corsair grabbed her by the shoulders with one arm. "Peace, woman. You can trust me." Farrah could almost see the mocking grin behind the visor.

She let out a breath but knew that she could trust her. Up until now, the pirate had never disappointed.

"In line, ye ruddy fools!" a voice clamoured when they added their numbers to the crowd that blocked the entrance. "One at a time!"

They were about to find out how right the corsair was.

The waiting felt agonizing as they edged ever closer to the placaters monitoring the gate, watching every newcomer making their way inside the city.

Feras had been peering at all three of the guards for a while now, scrutinizing their gait and tone of voice before she had gestured to one of them. "With me," she told the renegades.

They followed behind and positioned themselves in line so as to approach the soldier Feras had selected for their strip down.

She came up to him and discreetly, though rather dramatically, took out an impressive purse from underneath the layers of fabric she wore. Using a low voice, though just as theatrical as her gestures had been, Feras whispered in the man's ear and the purse vanished from her fingers.

The placater glimpsed at the other guards before glancing down at whatever had appeared inside his belt bag. He eyed them for a few seconds, then began asking her a set of questions.

The soldier then scanned his surroundings one last time and indicated with a hand that they could head on through.

Farrah started breathing again the moment they had passed the control post and entered the rich and dazzling city of Mondos, its gargantuan towers and alabaster facades rising mightily amidst this impressive demonstration of culture and wealth.

Gardens of lustrous fountains adorned the city's main parts while decadent citizens and merchants sold their bounty amassed from all over Iscar. This city had been, for more than a thousand years, the cradle of knowledge, arts and design. Its maze of streets, abundant in the lively scene of decorum, was a sight to behold. Mondos was, all in all, an aggregation of ornamental affluence.

"Come on," said a voice and she noticed Feras beckoning at the little group. "We have to make it to the rendezvous point on time."

They walked around the dizzying array of corridors and followed after the captain.

They eventually entered a quieter district where Feras led them to the entrance of an ancient-looking tower. She drew the front door ajar, not bothering to knock on it, and started up the spiralling stone stairs to the topmost room.

Expecting to find Antwan La Faux waiting for them inside, they couldn't help but gawk at the person they found instead.

"Fancy meeting you here," said Feras, taking her mask off and uncovering a cocky smile underneath.

"Oh, you know, I was in the vicinity," answered the tantalizing pink-haired woman.

"Everything went according to plan?" asked Feras while she removed the rest of her attire.

"Just as you said it would," replied Alena with a hint of amusement in her voice.

"Good girl," answered the pirate and headed over to the window at the far end of the room.

Farrah and the others were rooted on the spot. After a few confused seconds, they followed Feras's lead and took off the extra layers of fabric they wore over their clothes.

"Feras?" Farrah inquired as she came up to her, now sitting on the edge of the windowsill.

The captain nudged her chin down, pointing with her eyes to where she was looking. "See those hooded figures?"

Farrah squinted. In the distance, she found the people she was referring to, hanging around a fountain amidst a quaint city garden. "Yes?"

"We just need to wait a few minutes."

All the renegades stared at it, eyeing the patterns of the lustrous fountain. Before long, they overheard a sudden maelstrom of clanking noises, the unmistakable arrival of a fast-moving placater cohort heading their way. Or rather, passing by their place of hiding and continuing towards where the hooded figures were.

When the patrol entered the garden, they saw other battalions emerging in from all exit points around the fountain area. The men wearing black cloaks had jerked up in surprise and were spinning in place, caught within the collecting array of soldiers crowding them in the middle.

Breaking ranks from the mass of placaters came one man, sporting the formal commandant attire.

"By the gods," said Essan, becoming white. "It's Commandant Husar."

Farrah stared wide-eyed at one of the most hated of Daromas's generals, the sneering red-haired viper.

Husar was here, less than a hundred feet away, so near that if he were to glance up behind him, he just might spot them. "We have to go," she exclaimed.

Feras held up a finger. "That we do."

A fight had erupted below, the general engaging one of the hooded figures, his other acolytes fending off the endless horde of placaters rushing inside the garden.

Feras withdrew from the windowsill and headed towards Alena, also gazing at the scene with a look of absolute marvel. The captain bowed to her. "Alena, my dear, you've done excellent work. You may rejoin the ship at your earliest convenience."

The woman answered with a curtsy of her own and a beam on her lips. "It was my pleasure, Captain. I'll be on my way as soon as I collect the prize money."

Feras positioned her mask back in place, not bothering to retrieve the rest of her attire. "Shall we?" she told the others, voice muffled by the disguise.

They each pulled on their masks, Farrah frowning as she did.

"Care to enlighten us, Captain?" asked Slay.

Feras gestured up, bidding them to follow her down the stairs. "Must I explain who these hooded men were?"

"Antwan La Faux," Farrah muttered.

Feras nodded and went on, her tone hinting at bravado. "I did tell you I'd create a diversion, wouldn't I? What better than to set up one of the most despised sky pirates while, in the meantime, engaging the commanding officer and his troops, requiring both his time and diverting his attention from anything else happening in the vicinity?"

Farrah felt a disbelieving grin forming on her features. She was happy the mask she was wearing hid most of her face. She didn't want to show Feras how impressed she was.

"Yesterday, it became clear to me that you were right, Farrah," continued the corsair. "We cannot let Antwan La Faux be allowed to do as he pleases. Though I wanted to stop him, there was yet the problem of making certain he would not come after us if we were to make an attempt on his life."

They exited the tower and began walking towards their destination, the library of the research citadel.

"So I had an idea. How about killing two birds with one stone?" Feras went on. "We needed to create a diversion that would leave our way open, *and* incapacitate La Faux, all the while making sure we weren't the people doing the incapacitation. Since Commandant Husar was in town, I knew the man would jump at the opportunity to get his hands on what the government refers to as *the most villainous pirate there ever was*." She turned to look at them, her eyebrow arched. "Ironic coming from them, wouldn't you agree?"

She led them down another corner. "Naturally, I sent my best agent when it comes to seduction and convincing." Feras put her palm up matter-of-factly. "Alena, of course. She also happens to be from Mondos, which meant that she knew where to go and whom to talk to in order to get an audience with Husar.

"She left a few hours before we did and headed to a control post, claiming the bounty for information on the capture of the criminal La Faux. Did you know that his head is evaluated at quite a small fortune?" She pursed her lips and went on. "Anyway, I told Antwan to meet us at the *Garden of Knowledge*, and to await our arrival."

Farrah could feel the smug tone in the corsair's voice when she finished. "I almost wasn't expecting things to go this smoothly," added Feras. "Even Antwan doesn't stand a chance against a commandant. Right at this moment, La Faux is fighting his last battle. He *will* be arrested and sent to the Anemas where prompt execution lies ahead of him."

She looked sideways at Farrah, her tone becoming softer. "He won't ever hurt anyone again."

She had lost her voice. To say that Feras had caught her unaware wasn't coming even close to how she felt. Her actions had redefined her once more, shaping herself every day into someone she admired and cared for all the more. "Feras… I don't know what to say," she said, feeling touched.

The corsair grinned. "I've been putting up with this guy for too long. We may both be pirates, but this is a question of humanity. I agree with you; he doesn't deserve to live. I guess I just needed a little push." She gave Farrah a wink.

She drew her fingers up and touched Feras's arm. "Thank you."

When the corsair stared back at her, the wrinkles around her eyes had returned.

"That was fucking awesome, Captain," added Slay.

"And we don't have to worry about being intercepted, Husar's troops being occupied elsewhere," supplemented Aslor.

Essan hopped along a few steps and grabbed the pirate on the side, giving a quick but dynamic hug. "You did great, Captain," she said sweetly.

Feras's eyes smiled again and for a brief moment, Farrah envied the closeness they had shared, regardless of how friendly it had been.

She wished she had the confidence not to care so much about physical boundaries.

Feras beckoned them forward once more. "That's two problems out of our way, but we should yet hurry on the task ahead." She guided them onwards and they proceeded down the main road leading to the city centre.

"*I see you.*"

Farrah froze and her heartbeat accelerated. She turned around and called out, "Feras."

The pirate paused and wheeled back, arms crossing over her chest while she waited.

Essan and Slay had halted in front of a screen. A gigantic thing it was, standing on the side of the main street.

There it was. The magnified face of Daromas, the daemon, with those horrid mummified eyes looking right at them.

"*I see you at all times.*"

Shivers ran along her forearms. That voice had a way of doing that.

Ignoring the sensations, she drew back and grabbed Essan by the arm. "Don't listen to it."

"*I know where you are.*"

Aslor had turned his back on the monitor and was watching the pebbles at his feet as though they were the most interesting things he had ever seen.

"*I'm coming for you.*"

"Let's go." Feras's impatient voice came from behind.

Slay was slowly stepping back, eyes still darted up at the screen. "By the gods," he told Farrah giving his body a good shaking. "You never get used to them."

Farrah steered Essan around, and they started onwards again. She waved up at the long spire that rose over the stores' roofs a few streets away. "Come on, we're nearly there."

"*You are mine, my little moppets.*"

Chapter 26

Mondos's library was known for its impressive display of lore and learning. It counted fifteen levels, uniting most of Iscar's archives in a single place, each floor consisting of different overall topics where anyone could seek fuel for their knowledge.

Standing dully on the rusty-coloured quartzite entrance of the building, they gazed at the never-ending rows of books running all the way up to its distant cathedral rooftop, feeling dazed.

Slay let out a slow whistle. "How are we going to find what we need inside this endlessness?"

"We must access the system, it will lead us to the sections we require," answered Aslor, guiding them past the lobby and towards a panoramic circle of monitors that greeted visitors.

He took position in front of one of them and began typing, the others peering over his shoulder as he did. He had written the word *gods* on the screen.

His eyes sought Farrah's approval. "Good place to start?"

She inclined her head, unsure whether the search would be precise enough. As it turned out, thousands of titles appeared on the monitor. "Try adding *shrine* and *pillar*," she said.

He did and the list correspondingly became much shorter. However, an inventory of three hundred and fifty-four books was still too cumbersome for their needs.

"How much time do we have?" asked Slay, eyes scanning the crowd.

"Between days and minutes," Feras answered. "I'm hoping Antwan won't figure out we're the ones behind his arrest, which we can't be certain of. Regardless, we shouldn't waste a moment; the man might sell us out for a lesser punishment."

They all blinked at the corsair.

"I said I would buy us time, not complete anonymity," she argued.

For all they knew, even that guard that had accosted them at the gate could have reported something to the authorities.

"Let's narrow down that list," agreed Farrah, rounding on the monitor.

She added the words, *resting place* next to *gods*, and *location* on another row. The screen flashed to life once again, and a catalogue of seventy-six titles appeared before them.

"That's still too many," she muttered. "Let's go through the list and write the names of those we judge of particular relevance."

She took a piece of paper offered on a tray set next to the monitor and began scribbling down titles. Soon, they had an inventory of twenty books or so, which they divided between them, except for the captain.

"Feras," Farrah said. "Please remain on the lookout. I need you to come and warn us if anything happens. We'll leave you with the numbers of the floors we'll be on." She faced the others. "Everyone else, go and check on the volumes you have on your list. Get all that you can out of them and let's meet up in an hour. If we're discovered, or the placaters search this place, we'll reconvene here if we can. If not, we'll find our way back to the ship."

They nodded and headed towards the central elevator. They had divided the titles amongst each other by grouping them in similar sections of the library. As such, most of them would have only one level to conquer.

Farrah exited on the thirteenth floor and waved the others off.

She paced along the long circular walkway, filled with infinite rows of books and papers, gaze going up and down between the short list she held and the numbered shelves.

The books weren't too hard to track down, the citadel's refined system of categorizing being the best of its kind. After she had uncovered her five titles, Farrah had found a deserted place in a corner of the library.

She opened the first volume, *Our Mythical Saviours*, and started flipping through it. Though the book explained in great detail the rare occurrences in history when deities had made an apparition, it did not contain any information on their current whereabouts.

After a few minutes of going through its pages, she decided to try out another volume, *Iscar: Where Do We Come From?*

As time drifted by all too rapidly, Farrah began to feel the pressure of what little she had left.

This trip could not be all for nothing.

She set her book aside and picked up *Our Gods: All You Need to Know*. She went through the chapters on *Baltos*, *Birhn*, a deity already linked with Commandant Duras, and soon fell upon *Ekhon's* section. Farrah smiled when she saw the rather exaggerated, yet somewhat accurate, picture of him.

She scrolled through the vague and yet colourful account of the fiery deity and did a double take when she noticed the last line of the bottom paragraph: *The Baron of Fire is known to roam the mountains of Tharan.*

Pulse racing, she rushed through the following pages of *Endal*, then *Enamus*, the great Chevaleresse of Protection, a goddess of guardianship, she who had graced humans with her protection and wielded the shield against foreign invaders.

Her eyes focused in while she read through her description.

... known as the armour of defence...

... the strong barricade...

Farrah cursed internally; *nothing* on her whereabouts.

She looked up when she noticed people passing near her table. She touched the mask on her face, hoping the others had had the good judgment to keep theirs on as well.

She proceeded through the next pages, eyeing the paragraphs written on the gods, *Illmeth* and *Menthlos*, both also acquired by the enemy. Then she found *Mithland*, the Prince of Frost.

The god of ice, the bringer of snow. The deity who had given them the cold and the weather that came with it.

She glazed through the lengthy description of the spear-wielding master and her heart somewhat skipped a beat when she read: *This reclusive deity is presumed to occupy the harsh region of Threscar inside the caverns of Yor.*

This was it.

Of course, this lord of ice would reside in Iscar's coldest territory. The caverns of Yor were impossible to reach on foot. Threscar, which sat on the northern borders of Iscar, was an ancestral land where soldiers of defeated foreign invaders were left to die.

Those who entered this region were doomed to suffer a quick passing at the mercy of the unforgiving weather, an efficient way to kill off groups of men and women while washing your hands of their deaths. This harsh ritual had withered away with time, but the territories still held the skeletons of the fools who had defied Iscar.

Farrah wrote down every last piece of information she could gather from her text and shoved the paper inside the pocket of her cargo pants. She returned her attention to her book and went through the rest of its pages but was unable to locate other relevant clues.

She flitted her gaze up when she saw a person coming into her line of sight, half-trotting, half-walking towards her.

Aslor.

"Farrah," he whispered. "The captain said that we need to leave."

"What happened?"

"There's growing turbulence in the streets. We don't know

what's going on, but the soldiers are rushing all over the place and are erecting blockades."

Farrah got up at once. "We must warn the others," she said as they headed for the exit.

"The captain's already spoken to Essan, and Slay is on the floor below hers. They will meet us at the entrance."

They darted towards the elevator. When they arrived on the main floor, they found the library security guards yanking the bulky gates shut.

Farrah flew their way. "Wait, we need to get out!" she told them.

The man scowled at her. "Sorry miss, orders from Commandant Husar. They called for a shutdown of Mondos. We must barricade our doors and no one is allowed out."

"Shut down?" she repeated. "But they aren't even sounding the emergency alert!"

The emergency alert was a system implemented in every major city of Iscar. Whenever Daromas wanted his citizens to stay put, the shrieking noise would alarm all to remain in place and all buildings were to be placed on lockdown until the ban was lifted. Any person trespassing their area of confinement was to be immediately put to death.

The man glanced at his assistant. "No, but this is a different protocol. Not everyone has been notified yet."

"Why is that?" she insisted.

The soldier seemed unsure as he teetered on his feet. "Listen, miss, please step back, we've been asked to shut down the library," he repeated.

She bit the inside of her cheek and headed back towards the central elevator where Aslor had been waiting for her, fingers flicking together. A crowd had begun to amass in the entrance, also wondering what was going on.

"We're trapped," she told him in a low voice.

"They're looking for us, aren't they?"

"Seems like it," she replied, noticing the others coming towards them.

The rest of the group had to push their way through the congregating flock to get to them.

"We need to leave," said Feras.

"They've locked us in," explained Farrah. "From the look of things, they know we're in the city."

The pirate turned to stare at the doors. "Then we have no time to waste. Every second their troops are gathering and taking position is making our escape all the more difficult."

"What do you want us to do?" inquired Essan, expression fearful.

Farrah studied both security details, now explaining to other clients why they weren't allowed to leave. "They already know we're in the city."

"We bust out?" said Slay, looking pumped.

"We bust out."

She broke towards the entrance, glancing at Essan who had followed her. "Can you immobilize them?"

The girl grinned mischievously, eyes twinkling. "Don't hurt them," she added as Essan sped past her.

She sidestepped behind the first placater and moved her fingers up his neck before she did something that knocked him out.

The man dropped to the ground.

"What the…?" gasped the other soldier, wheeling round.

Just as quickly, Essan jerked his way and repeated the same actions. Screams escaped the crowd when the guard fell on his knees.

Without further ado, Slay splintered the chains that had been barring the doors with his hatchet and they bolted outside.

The streets had broken out in chaos. People were running for cover while platoons of placaters jogged in different directions. Amongst the turmoil, no one appeared to notice their exit as they made it down the main road.

"Should we separate?" asked Aslor, breathless with anxiety.

Farrah shook her head. "No, that'll make us easier targets considering the entire contingent is after us, not forgetting a commandant. We'll be safer as a group than alone."

They pushed their way onwards and past the people fleeing in disarray. "This way," said Essan when they noticed the blockade that had been erected midway through the street.

They turned left and followed her down the narrower walkway. In no time, they saw another patrol waiting ahead.

"Here," repeated Essan and they dashed down the next intersection they encountered. The girl had an uncanny feel for street running.

"What's the shortest path out?" asked Feras, weapons clanking against her back. "No one from around here, eh?" she added when no one was able to answer her.

Essan glanced over her shoulder. "It would have to be down the main road; it leads to the entrance gate."

"Right," said Feras. "Let's take the next turn and head back there."

Again, no one answered.

"The placaters will be blocking the way," Slay replied very obviously.

"Then we slap their arses out of it!"

The pirate rushed past them, took the lead of their charge and coerced their way back towards the main street.

When Aslor's fretful gaze inquired to Farrah, she said, "Follow her!"

Arms outstretched on both sides, Feras descended upon their first blockade, wiping out the mass of soldiers with a massive slash of her cutlasses. She had caught the placaters so unaware that they didn't even get an opportunity to retaliate as the renegades breached their ranks after her.

They rushed onwards. Shouts were bellowed and alarms resounded while the group charged through the next roadblock, firing a barrage of bullets when they neared it.

This time, the pirate grabbed her blunderbusses as she, Farrah and Aslor formed their own defensive barrier. Essan was spinning her shurikens down their throats and Slay was now the one opening the way, battering aside the remaining soldiers.

They continued their flight, revelling in the approaching sight of the entrance gate in the distance. The enormous metal-framed doors had been shut tight and a small army was standing in front of it, awaiting their arrival with swords in hand.

Feras abruptly stopped in her tracks and drew her palm to her face, removing in a swift gesture the mask that hid her features. The others stopped mid-course and turned to her when she did.

"Feras!" called out Farrah.

The placaters were catching up to them, swords and guns scintillating in the daring sun. Aslor and Slay flew past the corsair and covered her, taking out their followers while Feras remained immobilized, staring with unbreakable determination at the soldiers standing in front of the gateway.

Farrah ran back to her and took hold of her hand. "Feras, come on!" she pleaded, but the captain did not budge.

"He's asking if we want a lift."

"What? Please let's…"

"Don't worry, I've got this," answered the pirate before retrieving her fingers from hers and bringing her hand up towards the skies. It was beaming with a thousand specks of golden light.

Clouds began to gather and lightning illuminated their skeletons while thunder rumbled overhead. Out of the eye of the contained storm flashed an unbelievable sight.

It broke through the film of the nimbus. Hurtling down from the vault of the heavens came the mythological Dragon Emperor that went by the name of Baltos.

He spiralled downwards like a falling tornado, ending his graceful descent a few feet above them, wings opened to full length in a demonstration of power and sovereignty. His head angled down as he landed on the ground, destroying everything standing in the way of his huge form, dust swirling around him.

"*Come*," they heard him say in the solace of their minds, and he brought his claws down so they could climb on his back.

His face twisted towards the formation of placaters and the soldiers broke into a run, loosening their ranks as they fled from the dragon's sight.

The renegades heaved themselves onto his huge form and took hold of the sharp crest racing along his back. As soon as they had, Baltos lifted his wings off the ground and launched up. He rose above the city and outside of its walls while hundreds of gawking placaters and citizens alike looked up at the mighty dragon that was taking them away.

They clung to him as Baltos led them outside Mondos and into the landscape that surrounded it.

"I can't hold on much longer," yelled Feras after a while, voice muffled by the wind. "You need to take us down!"

Baltos obeyed at once and initiated his descent. As soon as his talons came in contact with the ground, the scales underneath the renegades began to glimmer, becoming aureate grains of light.

"Brace yourselves!" shouted the corsair.

The glow that ignited her palm had begun to fade as did the dragon that carried them.

They fell hard against the mossy grass of the forest, Baltos already gone from existence, the last specks of his light vanishing from sight.

They rose to their feet, hands dusting their clothes and taking off their masks.

"Captain, you sure have a sense of timing," said Slay, eyes bulging as though he could not believe he had just ridden a dragon.

"That was incredible!" added Essan, arms raised up as though she was still flying.

Feras graced them with one of her grins before lowering her palms to her thighs and bending forward, looking overexerted. "You can thank Baltos for that," she replied, somewhat panting. "He's the one who told me to summon him."

"*He* told you?" repeated Slay in wonder.

Feras huffed out a worn-out breath. "It's hard to put into words." She dropped her shoulder against the nearest tree and balanced herself against it. "Remember when I said that we should go down the main street? Well, I'm not certain it was my idea."

"It was Baltos's?" exclaimed Essan, eyes round with amazement.

Feras rocked her head from side to side before shrugging. "It felt like the right thing to do. I was too preoccupied with the chase to pay attention to what was happening in me. Thinking back on it now, I believe that Baltos was the one guiding my feet."

She squinted a little as though making sense of it all. "When we came in view of the entrance gate, I felt an overwhelming sensation bourgeoning inside of me, borne of emotions of disarray. That was when I heard his voice." She pulled herself up a bit as if recalling the dragon had given her back some of the energy he had taken from her. "He said not to be afraid, that he was here with me, that all of them were. That, even when we can't find them, they are never gone, because we are one.

"I remember thinking that it would be darn good if he could get us out of here. At this, he told me to trust in his power. I don't know *how* the rest came about, but my hand began throbbing and he appeared."

"I knew the gods were here for us...." murmured Essan, holding her fingers close to her heart. "In our times of need, they're listening."

"As long as we are so willing to listen to the god within," Farrah replied. She lifted grateful eyes to the pirate. "Baltos saved us back there. You did great, Feras," she said before turning her gaze on the rest of the group, her frown returning. "But we can't stay here. Husar is on our tail and we must go."

They nodded in unison and began their trek through the woods, Farrah keeping close to Feras, monitoring her pace. Though their journey on Baltos's back had been brief, it had brought them more than halfway down their path. They would have only a few hours left before being in sight of the *Celestial Dragon.*

Regardless, the renegades couldn't help casting their eyes behind them, wondering when a horde of placaters was bound to infringe on their route.

While they conversed on the subject of Feras's singular encounter with the dragon adding to the puzzle of the gods, Aslor suddenly threw his hands up, drawing their attention to him.

He tiptoed on the spot, gesticulating fast. "Which reminds me!" he began. "During my search at the citadel, I came upon a clue to the goddess Enamus's place of worship!"

"Aslor!" Farrah exclaimed. "Is this true?"

He readjusted his glasses. "It was written that her soul is bound to her spiritual shrine which inhabits the monastery built in her honour in the city of Egon."

Farrah could have hugged the man. "This is great news! And that's not all! I also found a god's resting place, which means that we just might have the last two deities that we need!"

"No shit! I guess, this book thing was worth it after all," replied Slay, head dancing back and forth.

Essan began walking backwards, facing everyone. "Two locations, the captain summoning Baltos, that creep Antwan arrested." She counted on her fingers. "Damn we're good!" she finished, pulling her hand down into a fist.

Moreover, Baltos's desire to appear in their time of need without his wielder's input further implicated the deities' support in their cause.

It felt to Farrah that as their numbers grew, the simpler it was becoming to convoke them. Perhaps the gods in their own plane were also banding together, reinforcing the links they shared with their wielders through the strength of their enhanced connections.

"Daromas will know of our plans," said Feras, taming their mirthfulness at once.

"The daemon will be furious," added Essan in a low voice.

"If we were already a threat to him, he will think of us as potential equals now," replied Aslor somberly. "Things are bound to change."

Yes, the line they were walking on was becoming considerably thinner. "We knew this would happen," Farrah said. "It was only a matter of time."

Silence had taken their tongues afterwards, their minds conflicted by thoughts of both elation and apprehension.

"When we board the ship," Feras said after a while, coming by Farrah's side, "where do you want it to fly?"

She retrieved the piece of paper she had folded inside her pant pocket and read it again. "Threscar. The god Mithland lives in the caverns of Yor. Do you think the *Dragon* could drop us somewhere down them?"

"If it can't, we'll go down the ladder and into the abyss," answered the pirate. "But mind you, ships don't fare well in these parts. The winds are treacherous and the cold is bitter for the engines."

She arched a brow. "Are you afraid?"

Feras pouted whilst rolling her eyes. "Oh, please. I'm just warning you, so we all know who to blame if the galleon shuts down and we crash to our painful deaths."

"Deal," she teased. "We'll be dead anyway."

The corsair seemed about to reply something but instead became silent. Essan, who was in front of the group, had halted in place.

Farrah said, "What's wrong?" But as she stared into the direction of the girl's eyes, the sight muted her as well.

"What the fuck?" Slay's voice called out from somewhere behind.

A short way off the path, the remains of a torn arm had been stuck inside the "V" shape of a branch.

Farrah's stomach twisted. Feras walked past them, a hand pulled behind her, ordering them to stay put. She removed a sword from her back and took a few steps along the pathway leading around the corner where the galleon was anchored.

She surveyed the limb, eyes rigid, before she trudged forth and disappeared down the path. Farrah beckoned to the others and they discreetly went along the same route the pirate had taken.

They walked down the improvised road and Farrah soon made out Feras's erect form.

She had fallen on her knees, cutlass limp in her fingers, head fixed in front of her.

There stood a mature weeping willow, its long, drooping branches harbouring a grotesque display of limbs and body parts. Interwoven amidst its thin diving offshoots were bits and pieces of something that used to constitute a whole.

A hand lifting to her mouth, Farrah came to stand beside Feras, eyes staring at the gruesome leftovers.

The woman's ears had been ripped apart, her fingers and hair had been left scattered amongst the different branches and now danced morbidly to the rhythm of the wind. A naked torso clung to the base of the tree, and what remained of her fragmented breasts dangled limply upon it.

When Farrah gazed down, she saw a head posing in a bed of flowers in front of the willow. The eyes had been pressed back inside their sockets and the woman's mouth stood open, drenched with the blood of its missing tongue.

That was when she realized whom it belonged to.

Farrah gaped at the monstrosity, now depicting the desecrated remains of Alena. Her veins ran cold. Her stomach churned.

She heard the gagging noises of a person being sick, and Aslor was now on his four limbs behind them. She then witnessed Essan's traumatized expression and Slay's pallid features, before her eyes drew her to the captain.

She stooped down and took Feras's estranged face inside her palms. "Look away."

But the corsair was frozen. Farrah forced her stare into her own. "Don't look," she said, holding Feras's shocked expression into hers. "We must go," she added and glanced up at the others. "Antwan is close by. He knows we came after him."

She grabbed Feras under her arms and heaved her up, trying to keep the pirate's sight from the carnage that lay before them as she did. "We need to go," she repeated more urgently and yanked on Feras's hand while gesturing with her head to the others.

They began a brisk walk, dreading the pathway they were trudging on, unwilling to suffer a similar vision as the one they'd just witnessed.

They heard a buzzing sound from somewhere behind them. The undeniable signal of an approaching ship.

The Imperial fleet was on their way and was descending upon the *Celestial Dragon*.

"Faster!" she yelled to the others and they broke into a run after her, jumped over fissured trunks and darted around trees.

They entered the clearing where the galleon awaited. The engines had fired up upon their arrival; the *Dragon* was already lifting at the sight of them.

The stepladder was thrown overboard while sounds of guns and cannonballs erupted, and a loud detonation echoed overhead. Blazes and debris began raining down on them when an explosion struck the hull.

"Hurry!" she shouted, shoving Essan first on the ladder.

As made their way up, Farrah felt a bullet graze by her ear. She gazed down below and witnessed hovercars flooding the area while freighters did the same above.

Worse, Commandant Husar's ship, the *Rise*, was also incoming, and was almost on them.

The *Celestial Dragon* was retaliating with its own arsenal. Some of the smaller vessels exploded on impact when hit by a few direct shots from their artillery, and some freighters even veered away from their cannons at the sight of them.

They hurried onwards, bodies rocketing in every direction, their grip slippery and footing deceitful. Another blow detonated above and they felt its bite reverberating down the ladder while the *Dragon* rumbled ominously. Fragments of wood and smoke fell on them as they continued their climb.

They made it aboard, the frantic crew urging them on by

pulling on their arms and limbs. Out of her daze, Feras ran up to the bridge, joining Kerok at the steering. "Hard over!" she yelled through the intercom.

The *Celestial Dragon* forced its way through the enemy's line of firing, Feras holding unto the wheel. "Start up the propellers!" she shouted, and a burst of energy shot from the back of the ship. They blasted into the sky, galloping away from their adversaries with increasing speed. But though the freighters began slipping out of range, the *Rise* was yet on their tail.

Feras's gritted expression had a ferocious look to it. The *Dragon* would win this race. Only the *Lethal Vulture* would have stood a chance against them and that ship was long gone.

They lifted away into the clouds, the land disappearing underneath, the commandant's vessel falling behind. As if Husar had known he would lose the race, the *Rise* drifted to the side, attempting a last manoeuvre.

It fired desperate cannonballs in their direction. They crashed against the galleon's stern and smoke erupted from the large gaps the blasts had created. The *Dragon* shivered but did not slow its ascent.

Husar's final assault had coerced his failure.

Feras kept her eyes ahead, forcing the engines on. She steered the *Celestial Dragon* away and fled the battlefield, leaving behind a plethora of vessels chasing after them.

Only when the *Rise* had fallen out of their radar's reach a few hours later did Feras finally step away from the bridge. "Keep on this course until nightfall, then change coordinates. We're going to Threscar," she told Kerok.

The pirate drew away from the wheelhouse and descended to the main deck.

She ignored the renegades' compelling gazes and continued on her way, expression constricted as she disappeared inside her sitting room, leaving her crew to their puzzled concern.

Farrah watched her until she was gone. Slay and Essan had

their backs against the bulwarks, hands on their knees, their stares empty. Aslor was by their sides, his back hunched and palms folded under his armpits.

"Hoy, mateys…" a voice called out from behind. "So… whar's Alena?"

Half a dozen other crew members surrounded Dahara, all raising questioning glares on them.

Farrah bit her lower lip and lifted a pained expression towards them.

CHAPTER 27

It was a mournful dinner that night. The pirates ate in silence, exchanging mute, sorrowful expressions. By that time, everyone had heard of Alena's tragic loss.

Farrah had spared them the details of her horrific death, keeping quiet what didn't need recounting. When she had been done with her wearing task, Dahara had thanked her for the explanation and the bereaved crew had left them alone.

"The Capt'n muss be devastated," the woman had said before retreating, shaking her head in grief.

Feras had not graced them with her presence and Farrah had wondered whether she ought to do something about it but had opted to leave her some space.

Alena was gone and it was because they had challenged Antwan La Faux. More than anything, she felt a deepening sorrow over this grim loss. If it hadn't been for how she had prompted Feras to betray Antwan, Alena would still be alive.

Essan had not eaten, admitting to feelings of sickness. Farrah had tried to console her, but the girl hadn't been able to silence the horrid vision from replaying constantly in her mind. Slay had been unusually quiet, and Aslor had been looking pale all dinner though he had nonetheless offered gentle words.

"Farrah," he had said, his tone warm. "You mustn't blame yourself for this." She had answered with a conflicted expression and he had smiled weakly. "This was a good day, we found the location of two gods." His eyes became aggrieved. "Even though we've lost someone, it was worth it. We knew La Faux could come after us, and it doesn't change the fact that he needs to be stopped. His actions today only reinforce that truth."

Farrah had agreed with him though that had taken none of the sadness away. It was indeed that, every time they took a step forward to make Iscar a better place, there was the possibility of one of them dying. What she found most unbearable was the notion that Alena had been an innocent victim who had not deserved to lose her life, especially not in the manner she had.

Not to mention that Antwan La Faux had escaped punishment.

He had enacted his revenge on them and just like Feras had warned, he had taken it out on someone close to her before vanishing and leaving them with desolation as their new companion. And many unanswered questions.

But Aslor was right. She couldn't wallow in guilt. It would never feed her as well as her anger. She *would* avenge Alena's death one day and La Faux would suffer for what he had done.

Though Farrah was trying hard not to let them drift, her thoughts had also brought her back to Feras. As the hours had trickled by since the pirate's confinement, the more uneasy she'd become.

After a few more failed attempts at convincing Essan to eat, she had left the others to their brooding and headed towards the entrance of the captain's sitting room.

She slid the door open, pulse beating faster than usual, and peeked inside the room.

There were no lights except for the moons shining through the back wall. She pushed the door further ajar and looked inside.

Near the end of the parlour was a long burgundy divan facing the large windows, offering a spectacular view of the boundless sky beyond. She paced into the darkness, eyeing the lone figure on the couch and sat on its other side, contemplating the corsair.

Farrah noticed the liquor bottle that lay flat on the ground, emptied to its last drop and stared back into Feras's moonlit illuminated features. Her eyes were bloodshot and the lines of her face were pulled taut.

"Feras…" she began.

The captain's eyes drew shut upon hearing her voice.

Farrah tightened her fists, her knees coming together, body angled towards Feras. "I can't imagine the pain you must be feeling…." she said. "I want you to know that if you need anything, we're here for you."

Feras's eyes remained closed, but her jaw had clenched, and so did Farrah's chest upon witnessing it.

She stared at her cramped hands for a few moments and slowly slid towards the pirate, pausing just within arm's reach. She then lifted her palm, hesitated for a second and placed it against Feras's metallic limb.

As though in a dream, she wondered once again if the corsair could feel it when someone touched her there. "I'm so sorry…."

Feras opened her eyes and craned her head to the side, looking at Farrah's palm. She batted her eyelashes a few times and raised a tear-filled expression on her. Her lips quivered when she took a profound breath. "I killed her," she whispered, voice thick, a single drop falling down the length of her cheek. "It's my fault," she added, her other hand rising to her eyes.

Farrah's fingers contracted around the pirate's arm, dejection clouding her mind at this sight. "No…" she replied. "It's not your fault."

She was reminded of a few days before, though it felt like a lifetime ago, when she had taken care of the corsair and how it had touched her so to witness her pain. This time though, she was sharing it.

Feras dropped her hand from her face, letting it rest limply on her thighs, her bloodshot eyes glowering at the carpet.

"It's Antwan's fault," Farrah continued. "He's the one who did this."

"She's gone," said Feras, chest heaving. "Butchered."

As she gazed into the pirate's honey-coloured eyes, Farrah saw the human aching for reassurance and felt torn that she couldn't give it to her. "What happened to Alena was a tragedy, but you need to blame the person who did this to her, and it's not you," she repeated.

She lifted her fingers and let them hover in midair as though an invisible barrier held them back. Expression almost frightful, heart beating, Farrah forced them to resume their path.

Hesitantly, carefully, she cupped the pirate's cheek with her palm and turned her face around.

"I beg of you, do not add on the weight you already bear and see the guilty party for whom he is: an evil man deserving our loathing." Feras's devastated features drew to her own. "We *will* avenge Alena and kill the person who did this to her."

Feras stiffened and nodded her assent. A renewed tear fell down the side of her cheek and Farrah courageously decided that if ever there was a time to take her into her arms, this was it.

Abandoning all pretences, she drew forward and brought the corsair near her breast. One hand embraced her shoulder blades while the other caught the back of her head. Their bodies closed in on one another, bridging every gap and caressing every curve, and a sort of warmth spread through her.

Feras smelled faintly of perfume and musk. Her sweat was feral and untamed, and Farrah wondered breathlessly if her lips tasted the same.

The pirate's arms had clasped around her back, trembling as she began sobbing softly.

Farrah could feel her own tremors—though for a very different reason. Ignoring her body's reaction, she whispered inside Feras's ear, "It's going to be alright," and at this, the pirate's head nudged against her neck as though seeking comfort in its fold.

They stayed like this for a few minutes, not saying anything, keeping each other close.

After too short of an eternity, Feras broke free, sat back, and wiped her eyes. Farrah had leaned away when she had, her skin growing cold the moment she had escaped the corsair's proximity.

In a murmur, Feras said, "I hope she didn't suffer too much."

Farrah had been worrying about the same thing but had been trying to spare herself the images that cautioned her against such thoughts. "I don't think so...." she replied. "He wouldn't have had a lot of time. I... think he would have been quick about it. His goal was to hurt *us*."

Feras nodded, accepting her explanation, but really looking as though she didn't have the strength to think on her own anymore. Farrah gazed into her striking features while the corsair held her temples with her palms.

"Do you need anything?" she asked.

The captain's eyes were drawn as she shook her head. "I don't feel well."

"Of course you don't...." she replied, daring to brush her fingertips against the pirate's thigh.

"And I'm drunk."

Farrah chuckled and said, "That's okay."

Feras creased her brows. "I don't want..." she began in a strange voice.

"Yes?" She leaned forward a bit.

"I don't want you to think that I'm..." She didn't seem to know how to finish her sentence.

"That you're... human?"

Feras laughed quietly. "That I'm a sensitive little wuss."

Farrah lowered her palm over the pirate's mechanical hand, feeling the cold fingers against her own. "At this moment, I think more of you than I ever have before.... Is this good enough?"

"My secret is out," she answered, grinning somewhat, some colour returning to her face.

"That you're a sensitive person?" Farrah replied, eyes rounding. "It might come to you as a surprise, but I already knew that. You care a lot more than you make it appear."

Feras searched her gaze and then smiled softly before her expression turned sober again. She sighed and looked outside the windows. Farrah waited, wondering what more she could say.

She decided that sometimes silence was the best word spoken.

Without warning, the corsair slid towards the ground and away from the sofa, dropping her whole body onto the floor, spread eagle.

Farrah bent over and asked, "Are you well?" with some concern.

Feras drew her arms high above her head, her breathing laboured. "My thoughts are spinning."

Farrah came beside her and sat back on her chins. "How about we take you to bed?" she said in a soft voice.

The pirate heaved a breath and nodded her assent. She crawled to her side and Farrah took hold of her elbow, helping her up. Her footing unsound, Feras raised her hand to her forehead and stroked it vigorously.

"Come on," she said. She wrapped her arm around Feras's waist and guided her to her chambers.

When they entered her room, Farrah led her towards the bed and Feras fell on top of it, her empty stare directed at the ceiling of her private stateroom.

Farrah stood for a minute or so beside the berth. "Feras," she said, inching closer. "Will you let me take your things off?"

The pirate grunted her consent, her lashes surrendering to exhaustion.

Farrah hesitated before edging forth and pulling on Feras's boots, just as she had done some days before. She set them on the side before attempting the difficult task of retrieving Feras's sash and layers of armour and weapons. She avoided making eye contact as she moved over her, and loosened the laces and buckles of her attire. The pirate only stirred when it came time to remove the leather straps caught under her back.

When she had left her with only her shirt and pants, Farrah put a knee on the bed and drew her arms up. "Let's get you under the blankets," she said, motioning with her hands.

Feras took her palms into hers and forced her washed-out form up. She then lay down again, and Farrah captured her legs under the covers. "I'll fetch you some water," she added before disappearing inside the bathroom that adjourned the corsair's bedroom.

She came back less than a minute later, Feras's tired eyes distinct in the faded lights. She pushed the glass of water into her hands. "You need to finish it," she said and when Feras did, she retrieved the cup and went to fill it once more, placing it this time on her bedside table. "If you want more, it's right here," she indicated.

Feras nodded, glancing off to the side. Farrah sat on the edge of the berth and pulled the blanket higher over her. Deciding there was nothing more she could do and that Feras needed sleep, she turned her head away.

"I'll… see you tomorrow." She remained in place for a second more before adding quietly, "Do you… blame me?"

Feras's worn-out expression became a frown. "You're not the one who asked Alena for help," she rasped. "I did."

She delved into the pirate's golden pupils. "I convinced you to stop Antwan. I'm…"

"I make my own decisions," cut in Feras, looking away. "Like Alena did… And so did Antwan," she finished, her lips tightening.

Farrah gave a forlorn smile. "If there's anything I can do," she said, rising to her feet, "don't hesitate."

Feras nodded as she left the room, closing the lights on her way out.

When Feras next awoke, her head was throbbing and her stomach was doing somersaults. She hadn't had a good night of sleep, and though the sun was shining through by now, she felt disgruntled.

She went to bathe herself and wash the alcohol away. She had drunk a lot, but she had had good reason to. Not that she'd forgotten any of the gross images that still haunted her, but she felt better.

Pirates couldn't afford to mourn the dead for longer than a day; too many lives lost, it was a part of the deal if you chose this existence. Maybe this was why they drank all the time—to forget some of the angst and grief. Not that they ever really did in the end. They simply hid it underneath, somewhere faraway on the inside.

She went outside, her features drawn as she blinked in the bold sunlight. Everyone was going about their usual business. It was as though Alena was already driven out of memory, or at least, they were pretending that she was.

She interrupted one of the crew members scrubbing the bulkheads and asked for some much-needed coffee. As she took the first few sips, she noticed Farrah sitting on a wooden crate, mindlessly gazing off at the clouds.

She stared at the content of her mug and twirled the liquid around, frowning. Only days before, the renegade leader had spent an entire night by her side. And last evening, of all people, she had been the one to soothe her sorrows.

The comfort of her well-established world had collapsed when she had seen the grotesque display of her lost friend. After they had escaped Husar's *Rise*, she had been unable to face the others, desiring none but the company of solitude.

When she had shut the sitting room's doors behind her, Feras had released her sorrow, all the while feeling estranged by her anguish. How cruel to be left with the memories of such horrifying images.

She had cried until she had been depleted of tears, certain of nothing anymore. After she had drunk some of the pain away, she had fallen to the arms of emptiness, drained of being. She felt sick at the notion of having abandoned Alena's body behind, denied a proper burial, and also with the world that had created a monster in Antwan.

When Farrah had approached her, her compassion had reawakened the sadness, and she had allowed it in.

What an unusual display of tenderness she had been offered. Farrah had given a bit of herself in the quality of her presence and unguarded self. More than anything, her gesture had touched her and deepened her worth.

Feras lifted an eyebrow and gazed for a second more at the woman, caught in this realization. She ended her daydream and headed towards her, taking a seat on the crate opposite hers, legs cradling the wood.

"So," she began, grimacing. Farrah opened her eyes somewhat at the sight of her and Feras glanced away, feeling coy. "I wanted to thank you for last night," she said, putting a hand to her hip.

The corners of Farrah's mouth had drawn up cryptically. Feras found her expressions puzzling at times. It was as though she was trying to keep her face to neutral but the innermost emotions underneath were bursting to reveal their existence.

Farrah was no doubt a passionate woman. Why hide it? Surely, this was her greatest strength.

"I'm glad I could be of help," she answered.

Feras drew her hand up and through her hair. "I'm starting to think that you're the person to keep around whenever I'm not well."

Farrah's smile widened though it appeared somewhat reserved. Feras felt unexplainably uneasy in her company. It was as though they had shared a moment of closeness that had deepened their relationship but felt too intimate now that things had returned to normal.

Since Farrah had elected to remain silent, she went on. "I'm sorry if I was overly emotional. I had drunk a lot and I guess it just got to me, considering what had happened."

Farrah's brow furrowed. "Don't apologize. I'm glad you didn't hide how you felt. Nor should you have."

She nodded a few times and peered around them, scrunching her eyes in retaliation to the morning sun. Minutes passed, and she felt awkward in the face of Farrah's mute appraisal.

"You liked her, didn't you?"

Feras blinked up at the other woman, her expression turning quizzical. "I'm not sure what you mean?"

"I mean… your relationship with Alena… was it of a deeper nature?"

Feras cocked her head to the side. "Alena was my friend and I cared for her as a person, nothing more if that's what you're implying." She made a face and squinted. "You know, she was a much better woman than you probably believed she was. She was searching for herself. All those poor chaps she went for, it was only a game to fill a void she couldn't satisfy."

Farrah looked thoughtful at this. "I'm sorry she didn't get the chance to find her peace in this life."

She lowered her gaze to her feet. "Maybe she'll find it in the next."

"I hope so too," answered the renegade leader, her tone of voice genuine. "I want to apologize again," she added. "You had warned me. I never—"

"Farrah," she cut in. "We did what we thought was for the best." Her brow became crumpled. "Though her death will haunt me forever, I have no regrets. And when all of this is done, we'll go together. We'll find him and when we do, we'll make him pay for what he's done."

Farrah's eyes filled with the depth of her willingness. "I'll be there," she answered. "I promise."

Feras smiled sadly and sighed. "Until then, we'll bide our time." She looked to the right and noticed Slay walking their way, staring at the renegade leader. She smirked and put her hands on her thighs before getting up, her head throbbing still. She winked. "Your boyfriend's coming." And then added, "I'll leave you to it."

Farrah's eyebrows dropped when she glanced at the approaching figure and Feras snickered.

She left off, feeling a bit better now. Not that she had the choice.

Farrah gazed at the disappearing form of the corsair, expression restrained.

"Farrah," Slay said. "The others are looking for you, they want to discuss the things to come." He stared back around, squinting in the sun like Feras had been. "Is the captain better? Coz she should join us."

She rose from her improvised seat. "I think it's best we give her some time," she answered and they both began forward.

Farrah felt thrown by Feras's comment, uncertain whether the pirate had meant it as a light joke, or she had been speaking her mind. She tried to ignore the barb, especially in the aftermath of what they had shared the night before.

She was upset by her growing attraction. Taking care of Feras had furthered the closeness she longed for: her desire to lose herself in these brief moments she sparingly had a chance to live.

She followed Slay inside the saloon hall, mindlessly stepping aside to let a pirate pass, thinking of Alena's fated demise. Her muffled jealousy vanquished, all that remained now was the sadness of the woman's loss. And her need to get revenge for her death.

She was wrenched out of her thoughts when they met with the rest of the group.

They spent the next hour discussing the clue she had found in Mondos, hoping that the author of the book, interred more a few hundred years ago, had been right about Mithland's location.

Earlier, Kerok had said that they would arrive in three days' time and would have to start preparing against the biting cold they were about to face. Even though the galleon was equipped with some of the best weather sensors for climate control, such harsh weather might prove too hard a battle for the *Dragon* to handle.

They had next discussed strategies in case their foes engaged them. Though Husar's ship had vanished from their radar, there was always a possibility the enemy would find them.

They had finished on the topic of the gods. They decided that they would practise their summoning every day from now on until all of them had the capacity to conjure their deity on command. Though the final battle was still some time away, they were nearing their goal and when that battle came, they would have to be prepared for it.

They had met on the forecastle deck and trained for the rest of the evening. Their stringent new regimen involved a mix of one-hour intervals of fighting and contemplation. Even Essan and Thorick had followed the same routine, readying their minds and bodies for the communion they would soon share with their future deity.

Chapter 28

The following days, Feras had joined in on their workout sessions. The captain had reclaimed her usual quirkiness and they had practised for hours, duelling each other until they had no longer been able to lift their weapons.

The theurgy training had become more feasible when everyone had done it together. It was as though their combined efforts had reinforced the bonds they shared with their deities.

Though none of them had summoned their god, all those who owned one had touched their spirits within. Farrah didn't know whether this was due to their collective strength, the myriad of time that they had spent on practice or their redoubled motivation in the face of what was coming. Whatever is was, they were on the right track.

Essan and Thorick were putting in as much effort as the others and the younger woman had even claimed that she had felt something calling out to her from afar. As for Thorick, he had worn this glint in his eye since he had risen from their last mediation, which Farrah had taken as a good sign.

There had been no more news of Husar or other pursuers for that matter, which was convenient but had left them feeling uneasy. Something was bound to happen at some point or another and they wondered all the time when that would be.

To Feras's delight, they were all turning into formidable combatants, and their practice was showing improvements on all fronts. For a while now, they had been training for hours on end every day and the results were paying off.

Those who had fought all their lives were becoming real threats for the commandants, and those who had known fewer battles were growing into forces to be reckoned with. Feras had even claimed that if they were confronted with a hundred placaters, their numbers would dwindle in the face of their abilities.

Thorick was recuperating well from his wounds, and though he had not pushed himself as hard on the field as he usually would have, he was coming back up to form. As for the corsair, she was free from the effects of the curse, and alcohol for that matter, and had sworn she would stay away from liquor for a while. Although, Kerok had leaned over Farrah's ear when she had, muttering, "'Tis the hundredth time she be saying that."

On that third day, Feras had met up with the group at breakfast in the saloon hall, and had told them that they were nearing their destination. She had then advised they rummage through the storage bins they kept in the hold below. This excursion would require far warmer clothes than the ones they wore.

As warned, the extreme change of weather had startled them when they had made their way outside. Throughout the night, they had entered the northern part of Iscar's territories and a blanket of white flurry had draped the arid lands below.

Though the wind sensors regulated the *Dragon's* temperature, they did not entirely keep the brisk air at bay, and the group feared the chilling storm that would greet their exit.

As the hours progressed throughout the day, the hefty breeze had become vicious and the weather had grown cutting. The moment they had flown into Threscar, the unforgiving lands of deserted cold, a veil of snow had begun draping their vision of the outside world.

Feras was standing at the stem, looking above the figurehead of the sandstone dragon, arms crossed over her thick leather and fur jacket. Though no flakes entered the periphery of the vessel, the blanket of white in front of their eyes was like a wall of rime just within reach.

"The ship's gonna be fine, eh Captain?" asked Slay.

Feras pointed at the hovering metal boxes flying all around the galleon. "The weather sensors are protecting the *Dragon* and its components from freezing over. Let's hope they make it through our trip. If they go down, that's when real trouble arises."

Aslor eyed the boxes. "You believe they could malfunction?"

"In these temperatures…" She gestured this time towards the tempest of icing snow blurring their vision. "It's possible."

"Let's be quick about it so we can soon be out of this place," decided Essan, hands wrapped around her midsection, attempting to warm herself up.

They murmured their assent, just as unwilling to overstay their welcome.

"We should be getting near the caverns of Yor. It won't be easy to make out their exact location in this unyielding weather," continued Feras. "I'll go and accompany Master Kerok at the controls. Be on standby for our arrival."

Less than an hour later, they had met up with the corsair on the bridge and had looked over her shoulder when she had motioned at the screen. Though their eyes could see nothing past a few feet around the ship, the monitor was displaying the caverns they had been searching for.

The *Celestial Dragon* was flying at its lowest speed. Feras was steering the helm with precision, her features tight while they pierced through the ever-falling curtain of snow, stare darting back and forth to the screen by her side.

"Wall!" shouted Kerok, and the galleon yanked to a standstill.

Mountains had appeared in front of their vision; the ship was so near their surface that had they gone any faster, the *Dragon* would have smashed on the rocks of its ramparts.

"Level the propellers, Master Kerok, and throw the anchor," ordered the corsair in a controlled voice, eyes glaring at the precipice.

"Is the galleon going to withstand the tempest?" asked Essan.

The harsh winds outside were relentlessly bombarding the *Celestial Dragon* while it shuddered over the abyss below.

Feras stabilized the wheel and checked on the monitors. "Let us hope so," she muttered, sounding a bit too unsure for their tastes. "Master Kerok will make certain the *Dragon* remains in flight while we are gone on our expedition. I would rather we be quick about our task. Though my ship is one of the best, I wouldn't dare defy nature's laws."

She found no argument there. Feras ordered the ladder be thrown and they gestured their goodbyes to the crew who had gathered on deck. "If we don't return, you know what to do," she told Kerok and lifted a leg over the edge of the railing, coming up last behind the rest of the group.

When they broached the invisible wall generated by the wind sensors, they were greeted with such a frigid barricade of ice that their breath caught inside their lungs.

More than once, they halted their descent, fingers clinging to the ladder while mighty flurries pushed them around, and hands grasping the rails so hard they were afraid it would break. Farrah also feared for Essan's small frame; it felt to her like a gust of wind could easily sweep her away at any moment.

Eyes stinging as razors of freezing snow cut through them, Farrah stared down at the gaping opening of the cavern's entrance below ground level, still far. Her fingers were becoming numb, and her face had been rendered senseless by the cold. She dared not look down again as they proceeded on their hazardous descent, apprehensive of losing her footing.

The winds suddenly grew so harsh that the ladder was propelled up, drawing them along with it. Farrah held on as her feet slipped and her legs dangled towards land.

She heard a yell.

Aslor had lost anchorage and she watched, powerless as he plummeted down the pit underneath them and disappeared inside its crater.

"Aslor!"

But soon, Essan had followed, and she could do nothing to prevent her fall when she tailed after Aslor down the abyss. Farrah prayed to the gods that they would be okay as she grasped on to her own life.

When the ladder reverted to a vertical position, they hastily continued their way down, pulse thumping in their chests and eyes narrowed to a slit.

As soon as they entered the depression, the winds stopped, and they were able to move faster though the freezing weather was as unforgiving as it had been before.

"Hey!" called out a voice.

Farrah was relieved to find Aslor and Essan's gesturing forms, stumbling out of a snow dent that had fallen inside the grotto, looking unscathed.

She jumped down the last few steps and fell feet first into the thick blanket of powder that adorned the ground. She trudged through the little hill, and staggered the last part of the way, hurrying towards the others. "Are you well?" she asked her friends breathlessly when she had caught up with them.

"If it hadn't been for the snow that cushioned our dive, I do believe we would have been goners," mumbled Aslor, fingers brushing the flakes that had covered his attire. "But as it is, we're fine."

"My heart stopped beating for a while, but I'm okay," added Essan, who appeared to have secretly enjoyed the whole experience.

Farrah glanced around the crater. An exit awaited on its other end, and it seemed to be leading towards some tunnels.

When they were done recuperating from their fall and the rest of the group had joined them, they went towards it.

As soon as they entered the cave, Feras passed around the torches that Thorick carried on his back and worked at igniting the tip of her own. Though they were yet freezing, the winds had all but stopped and they would be able to bathe in the radiating warmth of their fire sticks.

"No time to waste," said the pirate. She motioned with her head, and they began their way down the passageway.

The corridors were wide enough that they could walk as a group without touching their cerulean walls. The jagged trail took them up and down frosted pathways that had them climb around compact stalagmite formations growing on the ground and duck under stalactites hanging from the roof.

They paced on through the ice and delved deeper into the cavern, noticing its myriad hues of tarnished cyan and scintillating turquoise. It was as though thousands of diamonds of different shapes and colours were shining back at them.

Once in a while, they would enter larger chambers, rooms of natural art creations, blemished with heaps of sparkles and moulded uneven icicle figures. Any other would have gaped at the beauty of this underworld universe but the renegades went through it as though it carried nothing but gravel.

After an hour or so had passed, their bodies had grown so cold that Farrah had begun to fear for them. She had no idea how long they would have to walk or whether they would even find a god within this realm of frost.

"This place is eerie," muttered Slay at some point. "I don't like it."

"I mostly don't like the ice," said Essan, dense fog coming out of her pale lips as she spoke.

"Does anybody?" replied Feras, looking grumpy.

Eventually, they arrived at an intersection that branched into five different paths, each seemingly the same as the other. The group had stopped their advance and gathered outside their threshold.

"What now?" asked Slay, wiping cold sweat off of his forehead.

Perplexed, Farrah said, "We can't go down them all."

"We split up?"

"I wouldn't risk it," Aslor argued. "We don't know what's out there for one thing, and if anything happens to us, better be together than separate."

They didn't have the luxury of wasting even a minute, lest one of them died of hypothermia or the galleon broke under the added pressure of the violent gusts.

"If there's a god in here, perhaps we can ask for the guidance of the others to help us find him," Farrah said, thinking back on Leos's words, pronounced once upon a time while they'd been looking at some books.

"It doesn't seem to me that we can just talk to them on command," Slay replied as he blew on the frigid hand that wasn't holding his fire stick.

"We only need a direction, nothing more. With our combined powers, maybe we can kindle an answer out of them."

Sceptically, they circled around one another, keeping their body temperatures from dipping any lower, and brought the torches in the middle, creating an improvised pit out of them.

"I guess… we just ask," said Essan.

"Hmm, okay. Ekhon, are you there?" attempted Slay, gaze facing upwards as if expecting the deity's arrival.

Feras widened her eyes. "I think she meant *within*."

"Right…" muttered the islander while scratching the frost off his beard.

They sought out their gods. By now, Farrah could almost touch Endal on command. She knew where he was, could feel his nearness. The presence was bubbling, so close to the surface, and yet kept just out of reach.

They stood like this for some time, searching and praying for their deities to enlighten them about the way or give them some sort of clue. She could feel their combined energy buzzing, knew they were there. Not only Endal but also Baltos, Ekhon and even Thar—their figures like distant shadows floating in the space around them.

Talk to us, she thought.

Though they had surrounded her with their warmth, they kept quiet. It was like a balm to her soul amidst this cold place. *Please, show us the way!*

The vibrations became stronger as the shadows turned into lines, and the lines turned into shapes. They glided towards them and colours began painting their celestial bodies.

Farrah felt confused by their silence. It was as though they wanted to help but would not, their presence a source of comfort and nothing more.

Inside her mind, she witnessed Endal marching towards them, his benevolent features piercing through her. He lowered his forehead near hers and made contact, the rough and yet smooth surface of his fur burning like an ocean of suns.

Abruptly, she opened her eyes and the enchantment lifted, leaving the renegades alone inside the icy cavern. Her skin was still throbbing and she knew she had not imagined it.

They stared at each other, sharing mystified expressions. "Did anybody else feel them?" asked Slay, looking incredulous.

"Yes," answered Feras. "Though I can't anymore."

Farrah worried her lips. They had seem so gentle… why wouldn't they show them the way? "I guess we're on our own," she said before breaking the circle and facing once more the different pathways. She froze upon seeing the creature that greeted her.

Sitting in plain sight was a small, white fox.

Its tail, curled around its front paws, was almost the size of its entire body. Its ears were perked up on the top of its head and its dark eyes were elliptical-shaped.

Farrah lowered a palm in a reassuring gesture. "Hello," she said, her voice soft and forwarded a foot towards it.

The fox rose on its four legs and blinked up at her with its large eyes. It cocked its head to the side and took a short stroll down the tunnel before twisting its face back to her.

"I think he's showing us the way," murmured Essan, looking mystified.

Aslor grinned. "I believe we've received our answer after all."

They followed after the creature now trotting down the corridor, its movements so light against the frosted carpet floor that it was as if it was floating on it. They continued after the fox for almost half an hour, burrowing ever more underneath the ground, interred under endless piles of rocks and ice.

"Imagine there's an avalanche and we're buried alive," muttered Slay, glaring at the ceiling of the passageway.

Aslor made a face and wiped a hand over his runny nose. "How about we don't talk of this possibility?"

"Sorry," mumbled the other man, eyes still glowering at the frozen structure.

"You think the gods sent him?" Essan murmured.

Farrah glanced over, matching her tone. "It would be quite a coincidence if that weren't the case."

"What if he's guiding us down the wrong corridor, getting us stranded so we can't find our way back?"

"By the gods, girl," countered Feras, not bothering to keep her own voice down. "Aren't you the positive one?" She tipped her forehead towards the creature. "This little guy didn't appear by chance."

"I agree with her," replied Farrah. "I don't think he means us any harm."

"We're about to see for ourselves," added Slay.

Farrah looked ahead and witnessed an entrance at the end of the corridor. The lights on its other side illuminated the shadows of the passage they were walking in.

They were about to reach the deepest part of the cavern and would soon find out what that meant.

They followed the fox up to the threshold of the room and entered a large circular chamber.

Pillars lined its walls, holding the dome-shaped ceiling, and elongated candle sconces, emitting cerulean fires lit by an unknown source, decorated every column. Right in the centre of the chamber stood what they had been looking for: a shrine of summoning, glowing a fierce cyan colour.

Farrah eyed the fox as it coasted across the hall and headed to its other end where awaited the Prince of Frost.

Mithland.

His skin was as blue as the frost that covered his den, and his face was young and smooth. Unlike the previous gods, this one was of human size and resided on a superb carved chair of ice, wielding an upright spear in his hand. He wore a sash around his nude waist, made of elegant white material and gold definitions, and a mighty crown of similar colours sat royally atop his forehead.

He kept still, expression glowering as the fox went to him. It hopped on the deity's thighs and crouched down, front paws outstretched.

Farrah realized then that it had not been the other gods but rather Mithland himself who had sent the creature.

They made their way towards him, Farrah coming in first, Feras staying close behind; the pirate's presence reassuring amidst the energy of this dour-looking prince. She stopped at the foot of the stairs leading to the throne and kneeled down before it while the others followed her lead.

She lifted her stare and contemplated the deity's thin features. "Mithland, lord of ice, we humbly come seeking your aid."

The god did not budge, nor did his expression change. "*I was told of your arrival. I can hear my kin calling out to me at this instant, requesting that I lend you my help. But I do not know you and wonder why I would grant such petition?*" Like the others, his lips had remained unmoving though the sound of his voice was nonetheless deafening.

Farrah took a stabilizing breath. "We wouldn't presume to demand anything of a god, Prince of Frost. But you must know that the state of Iscar is on the brink of collapse and we come asking for the honour of your presence to put things back in their rightful place."

The deity's eyes narrowed at her words. "*Oh, I know why you stand before me, arch children of Iscar. I am aware of your past and dreams for the future. That is the affairs of the humans, not of the gods. You would have me partake in the business of men when that means little to me or to my kin?*" His tone was light and crisp, vibrant and haughty.

"Yes," she answered at once. "We may be small and insignificant to you, but this means everything to us. As you are aware, the gods have already joined the fray. Some have gone over to the side of the enemy, others are walking beside us at this moment. They have understood that Iscar needs them. Without your assistance, this world is doomed to suffer immense loss and the scars it has received will not fade before long. Perhaps you no longer associate with this plane but a part of you remains here and that is why I know you yet care for it.

"Join us, that you may help preserve the integrity of the gods who have created us and Iscar in their image! We are but mere reflections of your greatness. Lend us your hand and shape this realm into what it ought to be, a place that mirrors your magnificence."

At that, Mithland's smooth features twisted into an ironic smile. "*Your flattery is welcomed though your words are empty. You are but vain humans who cannot bear defeat and who would seek divine aid to work in their stead. We are not tools for the ego of the petty.*"

Farrah closed her fists but kept her voice controlled. "We wouldn't ask for your help if our enemies hadn't enlisted the help of others. How would we rival them if not with equal strength?"

"*You do not.*" The god tilted his head to the side. "*Bow to the divine powers already working in your lands and accept what is.*"

"I *cannot* accept that."

The Prince of Frost stared her down. "*You are just a human after all, what have I to teach a simpleton?*" he answered pompously, stifling a yawn with his hand.

Farrah rose to her feet and glared at the Prince of Frost. "I am not a simpleton for believing in what is right! Bring down your divine justice on me now if you think my words void of meaning, but

I know my fight is true." She opened her arms wide. "Look at me, lord of ice, and tell me that I am wrong!"

Mithland's mouth became lopsided. His features had taken a sharp turn, and his chin had lifted. "*Leave this place at once!*" he bellowed. "*Never return, lest my wrath avails itself upon you, you silly little thing!*"

"Lord, you must…"

"Farrah," came Essan's voice.

She had risen on her feet and was now right behind her, expression fearful.

Farrah stared at her companions.

Feras looked calculating, as though preparing herself for a fight. Slay and Aslor appeared uneasy, no, *scared*, and Thorick was gazing straight through her.

She saw his chest covered in blood.

Feras's limp figure on the ground.

Leos passing in her arms.

As these memories rushed back to mind, her resolve withered away like the dying leaves on a windy autumn day.

Farrah clenched her fists and lowered her head. She returned it towards the god. "If that is your answer…" she said quietly. "We respect it, Lord."

"*Mmphm,*" replied Mithland. "*You may leave now,*" he repeated haughtily.

Farrah peered into his regal face one last time and, chest heaving, turned around, the others following.

Her every step echoed with the sounds of failure.

"*You are the fool, Mithland.*"

She halted.

"*Listen to these humans and hear their truths, for it is also ours.*"

Heart accelerating, she wheeled around.

Mithland's eyebrows had lifted, mouth agape at the display of power radiating before him.

Farrah, Feras, Aslor and Slay's hands were all glowing, their own expressions bewildered as they looked down at their limbs.

"*Look into their souls and know what is real. We are needed!*"

The four gods appeared as shadows materializing before them: Baltos thundering over their heads; Ekhon, cleavers crossed in front of him; Thar, eyeing Mithland with her ghoulish gaze; and Endal, standing by Farrah's side.

The graceful Warden of the Forest approached the deity resting on his throne. "*Mithland, these lands are dying. It is our duty to breathe life back into them.*"

"*Endal, do not come into my home telling me of duty!*" the Prince of Frost answered loftily, looking annoyed by the arrival of his peers. "*Gods do not yield to petty humans!*"

"*Then you are an imbecile!*" replied Ekhon, voice booming throughout the cavern. "*It is not yielding to have the wisdom to know what is right! You hide yourself behind the closed eyelids of the ego!*"

"*My ego?*" spit Mithland back. "*It is these humans you cherish so who bathe in it! Their own hands are accountable for every wrongdoing in this world we gave them!*" He turned his cheek around, and pursed his lips. "*Let them deal with what they have created.*"

Baltos snarled and lowered his head down to meet with the lord of ice's gaze. "*You would punish innocents for the crimes of others and inflict responsibility on all humans for the evil of a few? Then Ekhon is right, my friend, you are indeed a fool.*" The dragon growled just as Mithland was about to talk back to him, efficiently silencing him. "*Look into their souls, and see them free of the ego you would speak of.*"

Endal came nearer, pausing midway along the set of stairs, his beatific head levelled with Mithland's. "*The problems of the humans are also ours. Do not blame them for the blasphemy of Israthel, Bearer of the Night. Their tribulations became the gods' responsibility the moment the deities of darkness have tipped the scales and undone the balance. It is only right we restore the proper order.*"

The Prince of Frost hunched his shoulders, scowling profoundly in his chair, looking like a sulking child. "*You are forcing my hand.*"

Ekhon uncrossed his cleavers. "*No, my brother, we are opening your mind. You must listen. There is no time!*"

Mithland pouted some more then glowered at Thar, who had yet to move or speak. "*And you, Mistress of the Underworld, what have you to say?*"

Thar drew her beak up and screeched. "*Balance must be restored. The land is screaming.*"

"*Even you must have heard her pleas,*" continued Ekhon, closing his fists. "*Or has your frozen castle sheltered you for so long that you have forgotten the warmth of the living?*"

"*I have no need for their pettiness!*" replied Mithland. "*They are but mortals, craving for more than their sort deserves!*"

Endal curled his lips, uncovering sharpened onyx teeth. It was an odd, frightening sight to behold on the otherwise tamed features of the Warden of the Forest. He glared into Mithland's face, the lord of ice recoiling under the fearsome expression. "*Do not refuse them, Mithland,*" he clamoured. "*Listen to their pleas, and know that Iscar needs you more than you believe! If you would not do it for them, do it for your pride and punish those of us who have transgressed our laws and meddled in the affairs of power-hungry men!*"

The Prince of Frost bowed his head, lips working on their purse. "*Do not misunderstand me,*" he replied more quietly now. "*I do not approve of the actions of the gods of darkness nor their association with the mortals they have become one with. I find it sacrilegious and condemn their behaviours.*"

"*Then help these humans, bring them justice!*" bellowed Ekhon.

"*Gaze into their souls,*" Baltos repeated. "*You only need but to look to know the truth. Or is this why you haven't yet?*"

Mithland scoffed, and Ekhon's stomp rumbled the ground underneath its foot. "*Is that it, Mithland? Do you believe that if you keep your head buried in the snow, you can pretend to ignore the purity of their bidding?*"

"*Will it gratify you if I indulge you so?*" Mithland exhaled through his teeth. "*Will you leave me alone?*"

"*You should have done so the moment they stepped foot in this place,*" answered the Dragon Emperor as though he had let him down.

"*You sent for them,*" added Endal softly. "*You care.*"

"*I was merely curious,*" argued Mithland, crossing his arms over his chest, the spear in his hand taking an awkward angle in midair.

"*No,*" Endal said. "*That is not the truth.*"

The lord of ice contemplated the other gods' disappointed expressions. No one talked anymore, nor moved. Everything had become still but for Mithland's eyes, which travelled to each of his peers, his mouth thinning as he did.

He then sighed and sneered at the group of renegades as though he had no choice but to comply. His scowl did not melt even as his cold gaze penetrated them and Farrah felt as though an invader had infringed on her spirit.

After a while, he yielded another exasperated sigh and muttered, "*These humans have worth, and their hearts are pure.*"

Endal gaze travelled to them. "*They are.*"

Mithland stared for a moment more at the room and opened his fingers, letting go of his spear. It fell on the floor with a ringing clash that reverberated throughout the chamber. "*Children of Iscar, you win,*" he declared half-grudgingly.

Farrah felt overwhelmed by this confounding turn of events. She bowed low. "We are eternally grateful," she answered him, meaning every word.

Mithland lifted the palm of his hand in mockery. "*Satisfied, Endal?*"

The Warden of the Forest's features softened, and he seemed to smile. "*Yes.*"

Mithland reclined in his seat. "*Well, then, whom of these mortals shall I bond with?*" he inquired, tone almost bored now.

Farrah grinned. "I know just the right person," she replied before looking over her shoulder and nodding at the youngest member of their group. "Essan will pair wonderfully with the Prince of Frost."

Essan quivered a smile but appeared nonetheless thrilled by Farrah's decision. She braved forward and paused at the bottom of the stairs, facing the intimidating deity. "If you'll have me…" she mumbled.

Mithland arched an eyebrow but raised no objections. He rose loftily from his royal seat, chin held high. "*Let Iscar know that the gods have not abandoned the humans. Let them remember who came to lend their help in combat when mortals were in need of them,*" he snarled.

"We won't," Farrah promised him.

He began to vanish inside a caged tempest of snow and ice, and the other deities did the same. Soon, a mist of gathering frozen droplets rushed towards Essan's palm like icicles aiming for her.

Essan dropped to her knees, right hand outstretched before her chest, gasping as Mithland became one with her. Farrah supported her through this phase of the communion, grasping both of her shoulders and muttering words of encouragement.

When it was over, Essan dropped her head forward and the hall returned to normal, the presence of the almighty gods all but gone.

Breathing fast, she removed her glove and admired the spear tattoo emblazoned on her skin. "Wow," she whispered.

Farrah caressed her on the back. "You did great, Essan."

The others surrounded them, praising the girl while she grinned in embarrassment. "Why me, Farrah?" she asked.

She chuckled. "Our friend Mithland seemed as though he needed a cheerful disposition to warm his heart a bit. Who better than you?"

Essan giggled. "Thanks…"

Feras bent over the both of them. "I don't like being the voice of reason…." She stopped and tilted her head to the side. "Actually, scratch that, I love it. But we ought to get a move on." She had gazed back, concern etching on her wrinkled features, and Farrah knew she was worried by her ship's bearing.

"Can you make it, Essan?"

"Yeah, I'm gonna be okay," answered the other woman, tottering up on wobbling legs.

They left, Essan walking with Farrah's help, and travelled back to the entrance of the hall of ice. They strode along the drawn-out tunnels, far too aware again of the ravaging cold. This time around though, their trek felt easier, the way it always was after they acquired the power of a god.

They reached the crevasse below the ship a few hours later, too frozen to speak anymore and drained of energy. Feras's features had relaxed when she had found the galleon still intact as though concerned it would have somehow crashed instead.

The pirate grabbed the rail first and pulled on it a few times, testing its solidity. "Let's hope the cold hasn't frosted it all over and we won't slip down sometimes midway."

Slay moped. "Thanks, Captain, I hadn't thought of that."

Feras snickered and started up the ladder, followed by Essan.

At this, a hefty hand had drawn her back and a paternal Thorick had glared at her, before gesturing over his shoulder with his thumb.

Giggling, Essan had placed both arms around his neck and had mounted on his back. He carried her up the rails, Farrah smiling after them.

Not a moment later, they felt the harsh flurry engulf them on their climb. Thankfully, the ladder brought them all the way back this time, the storm having calmed down somewhat since their return.

As soon as Feras had stepped aboard, she signalled Kerok for lift off and the ship creaked and whimpered as it twisted around.

It trudged through the mist without a problem and headed out of Threscar and its daunting snowfields towards the land of the living.

Feras had brought them inside her sitting room where a warm fire had already been lit. They had cozied up on the couches around it while she had kept near the mantle of the fireplace, elbow resting on it. "Where shall we go next, *leader*?" she asked, her stare on Farrah.

"Aslor," she said, "what about that information you found on the location of the goddess Enamus?"

The gentleman inclined his head and drew his frozen fingers towards the blazes. "Yes, yes. On the outskirts of the city of the gods, Egon, lies the Monastery of Prescue. Surely you've heard of it?"

Farrah nodded and so did Feras and Thorick. "It's an ancestral cloister devoted to the gods," Aslor explained to the others, who had looked questioning. "A historic shrine where pilgrims can ask for the blessing of the gods.

"Well," he went on, "this is Enamus's house of prayer. According to the author of the book I read, believers go there to catch a glimpse of the Chevaleresse of Protection." He grinned and said, "Known to appear every few years to grace the deserving faithful. Many have sworn to have seen her, and even more go on a pilgrimage to get a chance at meeting with her. It's apparently a most rare event, if real at all, but worth checking out."

"Most definitely," Farrah approved. "Can we get to Egon?" she asked Feras.

The corsair shrugged. "Of course, but I'll have to verify my charts. We're bound to be intercepted sooner or later and we'll have to leave the galleon far from the city if we want to keep it out of the enemy's line of sight."

"Do what you must," Farrah agreed.

Feras tipped her head and went searching for her quartermaster.

As the *Celestial Dragon* pulled away from Threscar, unknown to them, the entire fleet of Commandant Husar was making its way in the same direction.

Chapter 29

"I don't get it," said Essan.

"You're not supposed to get it, you're supposed to *feel* it," answered Slay with a tone that hinted at expertise.

They were sitting in a circle on the promenade deck out in the afternoon sun, feeling warm and comfortable, legs crossed and hands on their thighs.

"He's right. I know it doesn't make a lot of sense, but the harder you try, the less it'll work. You have to strive for it without forcing anything," agreed Farrah.

Essan slouched. "That still doesn't make much sense to me...."

They spent the following hour or so attempting to describe this process. Farrah could understand how difficult it was for Essan to get it. Though she had made immense progress, even now, she sometimes felt that she grasped nothing of the procedure.

Ever since all four gods had gathered to face Mithland, they had sensed a deepening connection with them. She now barely had to concentrate to visit Endal on the inside. Not that this had made the conjuring any easier, but they were getting there, and Farrah had actually summoned the Warden of the Forest... for a few seconds.

The deity had risen out of thin air before vanishing right away. She had been drained and weakened afterwards but content. This had been the first time one of them had convoked their god outside the midst of a battle or without them making an appearance of their own accord.

After she had accomplished her feat, she had left the others to their training, feeling the toll of her theurgy practice.

She had headed near the back of the ship and leaned against the handrail, her energy levels already returning. When she had first conjured Endal, she had been drained for much longer than this. She smiled privately to herself, thinking of how much they had grown.

"How is it that we summoned our gods back in Threscar?"

Farrah craned her neck around and witnessed Feras's arrival, coming to a rest by her side. She gazed at the pirate, appreciating her company as she pondered her query, one she had already asked herself before.

"I believe that the deeper our ties with our gods, the more they are free to become active participants in this realm and arise on their own when need be. In the face of Mithland's reluctance, they must have sensed and known where we were and whom we were talking to."

Feras rested her elbows against the bannister and intertwined her fingers, looking into the distance. "It's as though they have blessed our enterprise or something."

Farrah glimpsed sideways at the pirate. "Did you still have doubts?"

Feras's lips drew down. "Not really, but it's an odd feeling to know that there are deities rooting for us."

It was akin to a mystical dream every time Farrah thought of Endal and the others. Sometimes, she even wondered when the fantasy would end and they would awaken once more to the nightmare.

The corsair became silent and she felt pressured into saying something, afraid that if she didn't, Feras would go away.

She did not want that.

"You know, I had this arm made in Egon," Feras stated matter-of-factly, saving her from finding something else to say.

She admired once again the craftsmanship of the mechanical limb. "How did you come by it?"

Feras kept her stare away, eyes caught in the clouds. "Remember when Kerok and I escaped Prism Cove aboard that merchant vessel?" Farrah nodded. "They took us to Trasq. Kerok set out to track down the best engineer surgeon there was while I was rehabilitating myself. He returned with the name Hector Bristle written on a piece of paper, a man who lived in Egon. We bought our way on a cruiser and made it there." Feras grinned. "He had a waiting list of three years."

"What did you do?"

"I told him my name. He started working on my limb that same evening." The corsair held up the arm, scrutinizing it. "On the day he fastened it my spirit returned though the experience was rather unpleasant. You see, they have to attach the nerves and anchor the metal plate inside the skin so that the weight can't pull it right off. I was bedridden for a while afterwards."

"Kerok told me how you got your galleon back," she said, unsure whether Feras would approve or not.

The pirate raised a brow. "Did he now? I guess you know the whole story then." Farrah smiled and Feras kept her eyes on her, expression intrigued. "What about you? What's your story?"

At this, she unconsciously reared away from the captain. "What do you want to know?"

Feras drew her shoulders up and grinned. "What do you want to tell me?"

She looked away. She never talked of her past to anyone. How much was she comfortable telling Feras?

Everything, she thought as she glanced back into the pirate's handsome features. Yet, she knew that they weren't nearly as close as she wished they were for her to do so. "Daromas killed my parents when I was younger. I guess it made me into the person I am," she answered, knowing how vague she had been.

Feras narrowed her eyes, her expression soft. "Yes, I remember. What had they done to deserve the daemon's wrath?"

"They were threats to him. That meant they had to die," she explained. "But isn't that everyone's story?"

The pirate cocked her head to the side. "Thus, you decided to become a daylight vigilante?"

She mirrored Feras's posture and leaned her forearms on the bulwark. "I trained for years before that but yes, when I was mature enough, I returned to Letholdus with a few allies I'd made along the way and we began to take back what was ours." She glanced away. "Our lives."

Feras nodded a few times, looking entertained. "So, you became the leader of a rebel group, running the streets of the capital undercover, terrorizing our guardians of the peace. That it?"

She chuckled. "I guess that summarizes it...."

The corsair shook her head, grinning sideways. "You are something, Farrah."

She hid her face from the pirate's charming expression, boiling against her skin.

"Hey!" Slay was waving at them from afar, where the rest of them was still sitting on the floor. He was pointing to Essan. "She felt him, she felt him!" he called out at them.

"That's great, Essan!" Farrah shouted.

"That guy," Feras replied, shaking her head.

She drew her stare back on the corsair and bit her lip. "You know, he's not my boyfriend."

Feras's chin darted back. "I... it's really none of my business," she answered, but her expression said differently.

"I wanted to make that clear," she added, all the while avoiding the corsair's eyes.

Her face now one of puzzlement, Feras kept her gaze on her. Farrah peeked one last time at the pirate and smiled weakly before leaving her.

Feras tore her eyes away from Farrah, wondering what that last comment had been about. She knew they weren't together; Slay was great, but that probability was simply near impossible.

Farrah's tone, her expression, it was as though she had said these words for her ears and not for anyone else's.

She leaned her elbows backwards, ankles crossing in front of her and contemplated Farrah's crouched form beside Essan.

She shook her head, grinning. Better to keep herself in check; the last thing she wanted was to misinterpret intentions. That road was bound for disaster. She'd tried to steer Slay clear from it for good reason.

No wonder the pretty boy had fallen for the renegade leader. She was charismatic, caring and yet, self-assured, strong and independent, not to mention her immaculate looks which put most women to shame.

What Feras liked most about her was her presence, genuine and grounded, filled with a passionate calm. She was the work of a person apart, too good for the average lover. A woman who almost ought to remain celibate. An idea to admire from afar.

She rolled her eyes to herself. And it was best not to get anywhere near people like that, lest you wanted a charred ego. The islander was probably far down on that list of suitors and she had no desire to be another name written on it.

She left the renegades to their training and headed down the staircase towards the wheelhouse where her quartermaster spent most of his time, keeping watch on the ship's trajectory. "How are we doing, Master Kerok?" she asked him, eyes glaring at the screens.

"Freighters going in and out of our line of sight, Capt'n. Nothing abnormal."

Feras nudged the bridge of her nose closer to the monitor. It offered an overview of the surroundings that spanned a few miles around them. She saw the miniature vessel drawings that appeared in and out of her vision, moving steadily. Kerok was right, these freighters would never outrun the *Dragon*. Nevertheless, her growing disquiet had kept on expanding as recent days had passed by without any disturbances.

"You think it could be them?" he asked, leaning nearer.

"We can't know for sure. There's always going to be a ship on our radar no matter what we do. The sky is immense and the number of transports riding it, numerous." She patted Kerok's shoulder. "Keep on the lookout. If any one of them acts suspicious, I want to be told at once."

"Aye, Capt'n."

She left him to his duty and headed towards the main deck. She strolled around it for a while, checking up on her crew and making certain that everything was in order.

She met up with Danguer, the ship's boatswain, and inquired on the state of the *Celestial Dragon.*

"She's runnin' well, Capt'n," answered the rugged man. "O' course, that cold mother o' a weather got a few pipes actin' all hard-headed, but I got all thin's reviewed and she should be taken care o'."

"Good work," Feras said, hands clasping on her backs. "Make certain the galleon is ready for anything. We're not expecting an attack, but we can't be too sure."

The man tilted his head darkly. "'Twill be done, Capt'n."

That evening, the group gathered inside the captain's sitting room after dinner.

They were bound for Egon the following morning and if luck was on their side, they would acquire their last god.

It had started to dawn on them that they would soon have the means to challenge the daemon and that they were nearing the end of their search.

"I checked the maps and surveilled the territory," the corsair began. "The Monastery of Prescue is right outside the city, up on a mountain hill bordering the forestland. This should make our infiltration easier than previously thought, considering we won't be setting foot inside Egon. Cloisters being a place of spiritual mentoring for the pilgrims maintained by monks, few placaters should be in sight."

"That's convenient," said Slay. "Should be a piece of cake after Mondos."

Feras lifted her index finger. "There's a nice spot a day's walk away on the edge of the sea where we could dock the ship. I've calculated the distance and it should be well out of range of the city's radar."

"Better to keep away," agreed Farrah. She then stared at her hands and sat up straighter before she addressed them. "Tomorrow, if fate is on our side, we'll secure Enamus's aid. This signifies that our quest for the theurgy of the gods will have arrived at an end."

Essan fiddled with her fingers. "You believe that we're ready to take on the daemon?" she asked, expression seemingly doubting it.

Farrah shook her head. "No, but that doesn't mean we can't start preparing for the things to come. Our enemy is years ahead of us in terms of theurgy practice." She paused and then said, "I think we should retreat for a while."

The rest of the group shared brief looks between one another. "Retreat?" repeated Aslor.

"For as long as is required to get a solid grip on our theurgy," she explained. "We cannot rush in without proper mastery. Daromas and his commandants have trained for many years and there is but little time to achieve similar results, lest Iscar is left in a state of desolation for longer than it needs to be. Barging in without our full combat strength would only serve to lead us to our deaths and waste everything we've done up till now."

Feras lifted a leg on top of the other and put a hand around the top of her chair. "We can head back to Prism Cove. We'll be invisible to the rest of Iscar and have plenty of space to practise."

"I was thinking the same thing," Farrah agreed. "I'm not saying that we'll stay there forever, just until we're ready for the fights to come."

Slay hammered a hand against his thigh, holding his upper body's weight on it, eyes looking at the ground. "I'm with you, Farrah," he said, tone of voice grave. "But it feels kinda wrong to go on a retreat when, every day, more people are dying."

These thoughts had been haunting her since she had made up her mind. This particular road would surely lead to their demise if they followed it. "I know," she replied sombrely. "I wish we had another choice… but things being as they are, we're simply not ready to face Daromas."

All gazes lowered to the floor at this. Farrah noticed the relief in their expressions, as though the notion of battling Daromas could be forgotten as long as it was contained inside a distant future.

Fear wasn't nearly as palpable when it could be denied.

Essan dropped her cheeks into her palms, elbows resting on her knees. "The end is so close and yet so far. I wonder what life will be like when all of this is over."

Aslor put a reassuring hand around her shoulders. "Oh, I have a feeling that things are going to be quite different, dear Essan."

"I'm taking a vacation for sure," Slay answered and Essan gestured her immediate approval.

"My life's going to be exactly the same," Feras replied, arms stretching. "Only easier once I get rid of you people."

Essan pouted and threw a pillow in the corsair's direction. "Meanie! I know you like us."

Feras caught the cushion as it neared her face. "Perhaps, but I will forever deny it."

Though things would be different, Farrah had a feeling that her reality would not be any less complicated. She looked at the pirate, now flinging the pillow back and forth with Essan.

Feras had vowed that they would take revenge on Antwan. What Farrah wanted was to spend more time with her before they went their separate ways. She had known this would be inevitable at some point, but she didn't want it to be so anymore.

She wanted the corsair to be a part of her life, regardless of their future together.

Feras was a pirate. She would never be anything but that, and Farrah knew that her destiny was not to roam the skies for all eternity.

Truly, as she looked at all the renegades, she didn't want any of them to leave. Things would only really change for her the moment that they all took different paths.

"I'm off to bed," said Aslor, rising up. "We have a long day ahead of us tomorrow."

Feras got up after him and added, "I'll have the crew prepare provisions for our excursion. We ought to have docked by the morning. We should make for an early start on the journey ahead."

"It'll be the middle of the night for you, Captain," Essan jested.

She grimaced. "I know."

A door slammed against the wall.

Hectic footsteps were coming her way, heavy panting following their entrance.

Feras turned over on her berth, eyes blinking, arms lifting up on reflex.

"Capt'n!"

The desperation tainting the voice jolted her nerves awake.

Alarm bells rang in her foggy mind.

She drew herself up partway, trying to make sense of what was going on. She noticed the faint light of dawn piercing through the curtain of the night and pulled a palm up, eyes scrunching in the other pirate's direction.

Dahara was looking paler than a revenant that had crawled out of its grave.

"Capt'n!" she gasped again. "There be a host o' freighters comin' our way from Egon!"

Feras yanked herself out of her berth, grabbed her shirt and drew it over her head. "What's our position?" she asked as she put on her trousers.

"We juss entered the skies surroundin' Egon," answered Dahara while hurrying along to help her with her things. "There be more," she added, voice panicked as she brought her weapons to her.

"And?" she pressed her, growing agitated. She grabbed the sash from the woman's fingers and drew it around her abdomen.

"When we switched direction, ships on that side o' the map came in as well, and others be appearin' from everywhere. They be surrounderin' us!"

Feras cursed and lifted her dual cutlasses over her shoulders. She grabbed her tricorn and dashed out of her chambers, Dahara on her heels, going up the stairs two at a time. "Why wasn't I informed sooner?" she snapped.

"It all went real quick, Capt'n! We barely knew what was happenin' that already they had circled around us!"

Feras cursed once more. She drew outside and ran the length of the ship, looking out into the distance.

The sun was beginning its ascent, but she couldn't see anything with her eyes yet, which was a good sign. It meant that the enemy was still a way off.

She sped off again, encountering frenzied crew members hurrying to their posts, and climbed upstairs to meet with her quartermaster, who immediately gestured her towards the monitors.

"Capt'n!" he bellowed. "They're swamping us!"

Feras put her palms against the screen's rim where vessels by the dozens were flooding her vision.

On Egon's side, battle hovercars had stationed around the perimeter. By the looks of the *Dragon's* orientation, Kerok had attempted to move away from those as soon as he had spotted them.

All the same, overflowing the monitor on its other end was a warship accompanied by many freighters. "They're leaving us no opening," she said. "There forcing us into a fight."

She analyzed the *Celestial Dragon's* bearing. Though the vessels were still a few miles away, the enemy had erected a perimeter around them and was closing in on all directions.

"What's going on?" asked Farrah, looking out of breath as she and the renegades arrived on the scene.

"We've been followed." She indicated the largest galleon breaking through on the other side of the screen. "I'm willing to bet money that this is Husar's *Rise* at the head of Trent's naval fleet."

"I thought the *Dragon* was the fastest ship there is! How were they able to keep up with us?" said Essan.

"They've probably been staying out of reach of our radar, calling in freighters from around Iscar and reporting on our whereabouts, vaguely aware of our destination but remaining on our tail the entire time."

Feras cursed again, feeling like a fool, hand tossing her hair back. "It's normal to see vessels appearing in and out of our radar, so we don't pay them any heed. These ships were meant to keep us in check. Chances are that they've been trying to corner us for days now. When it became clear to them that we were travelling to Egon, they must have alerted the authorities and sent a blockade to stop us from entering."

"If this is Husar's armada, then he's been following us ever since we've left Mondos!" said Farrah.

She nodded gravely. "He lost the chase on purpose, staying never far behind, keeping track of us. This gave him more than enough time to set up his fleet, intentionally meeting us days later with the needed reinforcements while we were resting on our laurels." She exhaled through her teeth. "We've no other choice but to engage them."

Farrah peered overboard, gazing at the horizon. "What about the monastery?"

Feras did not answer. Her eyes scanned the tiny freighters she could now discern in the distance.

"Right," she decided. "We're taking on the hovercars." She pivoted to her quartermaster. "Turn back, Master Kerok, we're heading for Egon. We're keeping to our initial destination, the Monastery of Prescue, full speed ahead." She gave Farrah a look. "I guess there's no more use in hiding."

"What's your plan?" asked the renegade leader.

Feras took over the wheel. "I'm making this up as we go, but we need to steer clear of Husar's warship and his freighters; there's too many of them. We stand better chances against the authorities of Egon than the naval fleet."

The galleon turned when she maneuvered a hard starboard. "We'll disembark at the monastery while the *Dragon* continues along, drawing our foes away." She stared at her quartermaster. "Is that understood, Master Kerok?"

He agreed while he pressed on the controls. "Yes, Capt'n. We'll lead them astray."

"We'll try to escape Egon by other means. We can rendezvous back in Racketeer Bay in one week's time. I doubt it, but it's the only place we may yet be safe. Station the *Dragon* away from the main docks when you get there and drop the flag."

The land was now becoming visible and they could discern both battle cars and freighters coming their way as they readied themselves for an air raid.

Chapter 30

"Battle stations!" barked Feras.

The crew was rushing in every direction, posting themselves for the upcoming fight. Farrah left the bridge and ran all the way to the other side of the galleon, up the forecastle deck.

The ship was now entering the skyline above land, and she could see clearly the encroaching enemy. Dozens of hovercars were zooming in, aiming their heavy artillery towards them.

The *Celestial Dragon's* reinforced hull would never yield to such cannons. What worried her was the flock of freighters incoming on the horizon, the previously dot-sized vessels expanding into a building threat.

They were overwhelmed.

"Brace yourselves!" she heard someone yelling on the spar deck when the *Dragon* charged through their first wave of enemies.

"Farrah!" Aslor cried out, fingers grasping her elbow. "We're easy targets up here, we must clear away from their line of sight! Hurry!"

She followed him down where the cacophony of the pirates was head-splitting.

"Fo'c'sle cannon! Ready to blast off!" a man screamed near her.

Far above, the mouth of the white sandstone dragon opened to reveal the largest cannon she had ever seen.

"Fire at the enemy!" Feras shouted, her voice carrying through the intercom.

They heard a loud *bang* and the weapon drilled a hole inside the hull of a freighter that had been nearing their position.

Farrah sped back up the stairs of the wheelhouse. "There are dozens of them!"

"I know," answered Feras, eyes focused on her task.

"Entering enemy lines!" yelled Kerok.

"Fire!"

The cannons blasted off and a hundred merciless projectiles pierced through Husar's blockade. A ship ignited and its nose began pointing downwards towards the ground below.

"Again!" shouted Feras. "I want those cannons ready to discharge as long as there are foes flying the sky!"

The *Celestial Dragon* dove inside the belly of the beast. Enemy vessels were surrounding them on all sides while hovercars fired at them from underneath. Chunks of wood and metal parted ways with their construct whenever their assailants' cannonballs struck them, threatening their vision.

The galleon shook and creaked while its adversaries dropped around it like flies, their frailer structures yielding to its superior power.

"Capt'n!" shouted Kerok. "We've lost one of our rear propellers!"

Feras swerved and dodged a shattered hunk of wood that had tumbled down from the mass above her. "Maintain speed no matter what!"

Though the *Dragon* raced on, leaving the hovercars to trail in its wake, it soon became apparent that they were losing pace. "How far to the monastery?" she yelled over the commotion.

Kerok calculated the distance on his monitor. "A few minutes."

"We can make it," she muttered to herself.

The bombardments continued as the *Dragon* faced its enemies like a demon from another plane, destroying their insignificant frames and shattering their structures.

"Come on," she breathed through a clenched jaw.

They soared above the endless forestland that flourished below.

But when the city finally began taking form, so did an unwelcome sight on its other frontier

A colossal warship was emerging over Egon's skyline.

Even from such a distance, the vessel easily matched the *Dragon's* build. Pearly white and imposing, it rocketed above the city like a heavenly crusader calling down judgment on them. Numerous other battle galleons were rising alongside it, forming an offensive barrier sheltering their monstrous leader.

Her expression became still when she witnessed this foreboding spectacle.

"Another commandant?" gasped Aslor, growing paler.

Feras lowered her head, and her ardent gaze focused on the floor. "Not just any. This is Commandant Grieves's ship, the *Wall.*"

"What do we do?" Slay bellowed.

Husar's *Rise* was gaining on them, and the *Wall* had ended its sharp ascent. It was now stampeding overtop of the city, its flock following in its wake.

"There!" shouted Essan, gesturing with her finger.

The Monastery of Prescue.

It was sitting on the edge of town, atop a solitary hill near their vantage point.

Feras left the navigation to Kerok and ran to the trader's side, surveilling the picture that awaited below.

Before them stood Egon, Commandant Grieves's ship soaring above it. To their right rose the monastery on its mound, seemingly within reach and yet perilously far. All around, dozens of freighters were engaging the *Dragon's* cannons. And gaining on them from the rear was Commandant Husar's *Rise*.

She contemplated their options, knowing these were growing thin. "If we go towards the monastery, they'll be on us in seconds," she declared.

"Careful!"

A blaring explosion took the galleon by surprise. The vessel was propelled to the side, and they all collided hard against the bulwarks. They covered their ears as debris rocketed around them, blurring their surroundings with their particles.

A horrible yell resounded and a pirate went plummeting overboard, his flailing figure disappearing into the void below.

"Kerok!"

The man was on the floor. Cinders were falling around him, part of his body caught underneath a segment of the ship's structure that had toppled on top of him.

Feras rushed to his side and helped him out of the rubble.

"Capt'n… the monitors…" muttered the quartermaster. He hoisted himself up on shaking legs, holding his wounded arm with the other.

Feras witnessed the remnants of the main screen, fractured and forever gone. Her expression became inert while her mind assimilated the implication of losing this precious apparatus.

Farrah was looking at her, hands grasping onto her ringing ears. Grieves's *Wall* had finished turning to its side, and had opened fire on them, its immense cannons drilling holes into the *Dragon's* front hull.

"We need to take a new tack!" shouted Kerok over the noise.

Feras pulled fresh lines on her already tight frown. If they changed course now, they would no longer be able to outrun their opponents and would be forced into a fight with both the *Wall* and the *Rise*.

Dahara's voice arose from somewhere below, one hand up to her mouth, the other gesturing back. "Capt'n! We've lost our figurehead and the cannon. The sandstone dragon has fallen! We be stranded sheep!"

"Hard to starboard!" she barked and just as soon turned the wheel.

The ship creaked over to the right and the pirates went tumbling on the floor as the galleon pivoted abruptly. Feras held on to the helm while the *Dragon* tilted its massive form around, drawing itself up next to the *Wall*, discharging a wave of cannon blasts against it.

Commandant Grieves replied by sending a retaliation that rumbled her vessel to its core. Portions of the spar deck exploded; yells were bellowed as members of her crew were caught inside it. Some were surrendered to the mercy of the skies while others dove inside the open jaws of the collapsing floor.

Feras turned her head to the side when more debris came flurrying her way. Her hand flew to her face where blood was already pouring out of her ear. She gazed to her right.

Husar's *Rise* was nearing their position, battleships trailing behind it.

A detonation erupted nearby and collided wildly somewhere above her.

She stared up. The quarterdeck's mizzenmast creaked ominously and began collapsing under its weight. She was granted the opportunity to witness its dive as it tottered ponderously over her head. Shouts arose from out of the chaos, but her frozen expression remained immobilized on the crumbling structure.

"Feras!"

She stayed put as the towering mast came crashing down to her left, pulverizing everything that stood in its way.

She gripped the wheel, her whole body trembling as the ground ripped apart and cracked open. The mast plowed deep into the deck, slashing open a hellish mouth, plunging many a few pirates into its underworld. Smoke obscured her vision as numerous fires ignited both above and below.

Though she could hear the screams of the wounded, she couldn't discern them anymore. Everything had turned into a nightmarish blur.

Husar's galleon had finished rotating to its side and the *Celestial Dragon* was caught in a death trap between the *Wall* and the *Rise.*

In desperation, their own cannons blasted away, creating a splitting sound as they blew open large gashes on the enemy vessels.

A volley of bombardment came in retaliation, and knocked down parts of the quarterdeck. Glass shattered in a million rainfalls, heading for land in the form of shimmering rivers of ship tears.

The sitting room was no more, her stateroom and private parlour in all probability, also gone.

Baltos!

"Kerok!" she cried over the ruckus. The man was yet standing by her side, face covered in blood. "Fire up all that we've got! Full speed ahead! We need to fly out of here. We're being routed!"

The engines roared on and Kerok shared with her a look of alarm. "We've lost most of our propellers, Capt'n! Only the main one is still working, and we're operating on backups. Most of the monitors have stopped functioning, I hardly have any control at all left on the ship!"

"Fire up everything we've got!" she replied, feeling like a witness to an inconceivable bad dream.

"Feras!" yelled another voice, yanking her back into focus. Farrah was grasping her arm, her face a mask of desperation. "We're losing the battle!"

She gazed into the renegade leader's doom-laden expression. "I know," she answered calmly. "Take the wheel," she then told Kerok and left the both of them behind.

Dragon Emperor, you must *hear my plea!*

She went up the stairs by the bridge, wobbling along them as the ship shook underneath her feet and suddenly paused to glare at the nothingness that greeted her arrival on the quarterdeck.

The back of the galleon was missing.

When the rear windows had shattered, the rest of the floor had receded in their wake, the fragmented frame failing to support the structure. Everything was in ruins, the deck scarcely holding itself together, save for segments of the sidewalls that endured.

Feras let out a breath that quieted her surroundings for a brief moment.

Another blast discharged and smacked her off her feet and

down the stairs. She slammed onto her back, hands shielding her face from the smoke shrouding her vision.

Farrah's arms were already grabbing onto her, lifting her up by the shoulders as she lay dazed on the ground. "Are you okay?" asked the renegade leader, her far-removed voice brimming with worry.

With her help, Feras got back up on her feet. Mayhem reigned around them, a tumultuous symphony was blurring her senses.

"We've lost a good part of the ship's aft," she mumbled, barely registering Farrah's presence by her side.

She gazed away, her vision recovering, and flew off once again, Farrah calling out to her when she did.

Baltos, we need you!

She burrowed through the broken remains of the main deck, seeing wounded pirates everywhere she set her eyes, weeping and screaming as more explosions resounded around them.

She went up the forecastle deck. To her left, the *Wall* was catching up to them, drawing ever closer, attempting to board them. To her right, the *Rise* was reaching similar vicinity as both ships tightened their grip around them.

When she neared the top of the stairs, she chanced a glance to the side. The monastery was falling behind at a rapid rate. There would be no turning back to it now. They had missed their opportunity.

Oh, please, *thunder dragon. Please!*

Feras looked ahead at the stem and felt a pang in her heart.

The figurehead of the white dragon had disappeared, and only an empty space was left in its place.

The galleon trembled under her, and she forced her eyes away.

She gazed overboard at the damages the front hull had taken. There was no more denying it; the ship was tilting down. Not only was it losing speed, it was diving forward.

The *Celestial Dragon* would crash and there was nothing that could stop that from happening now.

Why? Why, Baltos?

A discharge exploded above her. She retreated a few steps and covered her face from the droplets of blazes that fell down from the heavens. The fore topsail was ablaze, its cotton canvas burning rancorously while the flames licked its membrane.

The galleon had turned into a demon ride from the netherworld, feasting on its content.

Feras sped back the way she came while the combusting deluge flowed from above. She jumped over the last few flights of stairs inside the hellmouth and landed on her hands, eyes level with the ground.

She tilted her head to the right and grew quiet. She was staring into the empty expression of the crushed pirate that lay by her side, her body angled awkwardly.

Dahara would never laugh again. Her features would instead forever be moulded into the misshapen horror of fear.

The woman seemed to have fallen from somewhere overhead. Perhaps she had gone up the mast, doing some damage control and had lost footing when a detonation had bombarded it and the sail had caught fire.

Whatever it was, Dahara was dead.

Feras stiffened and forced herself up, attempting the dangerous course back to the wheelhouse. She leaped over gaping holes, dove through lit fires and escaped near enemy blasts, all the while powerless to flee the terrifying sounds of her agonizing crew members.

She met up with the others, gathered inside the fragmented bridge and hardly made sense of their panicked expressions. "We need to abandon ship," she declared, tone of voice blank as she took control of the helm and angled the galleon to the left.

"Captain?" whispered Essan drawing close to her.

"Master Kerok, I have one last order for you."

The *Dragon* was losing altitude, its nose was dipping between the *Wall* and the *Rise*. Both vessels had stopped engaging them the moment they had dropped underneath their firing lines.

"Once the *Celestial Dragon* goes down, you will escape with the rest of the crew. Scatter through the forest to the north. We will be heading south. Assuredly the enemy will come after us and leave you be." She fixed her gaze on her quartermaster's. "May the gods accompany you, my friend."

The full comprehension of what she was asking had dawned on Kerok's features. "Aye, Capt'n."

"How will we escape?" Slay said, gesturing at the unsurmountable number of ships. "Husar will try to stop us!"

"If I am to crash my galleon, I will do it my way," Feras replied, tone implacable. She nodded to her quartermaster. "Prepare the crew for our collision. Abandon stations and hold on steadfast to anything you can! As soon as we've come aground, it's everyone for themselves. Leave the wounded behind, we can no longer help them."

Kerok stared for a second more at his captain, blinking a few times, before grasping Feras's arm in his. "It has been a privilege, my capt'n," he said, his gaze set.

He left her, not to turn back again.

Feras studied the landscape ahead, its myriad colours and shapes, and tightened her fingers against the darkened wood of the helm, feeling its smooth surface, its elegant design.

The sun shimmered into her face as its rays illuminated the *Celestial Dragon's* shattered carcass, forever glorious as it plunged into its ultimate descent.

A knot fastened inside her as she played witness to the final stages of its journey and the *Dragon* took its last voyage. At the conclusion of all things, she stood at the helm of her father's galleon.

Her legacy, her inheritance.

"Thank you," she muttered, her words surrendered to the wind.

A hand anchored around her forearm and she felt Farrah's gaze on her as she kept her own ahead. The horizon began to disappear, and the tree line took over her sight. They were nearing the end of their flight.

"You'd better hold on to something," Feras softly told her.

She locked the wheel in its current angle using the retainer that would keep it in place. Kerok had been right; most of the controls were no longer functional, but there was only one that she required.

She pulled on the power lever and the *Celestial Dragon* became eerily silent as the engines shut down and the galleon glided towards land. She pressed a few more buttons, headed towards the bulwarks and loomed over.

"Aren't we going towards a downhill?" Essan yelled, her voice distant though the girl was next to her.

"Yes," she answered calmly though no one heard her.

She went back and took possession of the wheel for the last time.

Her eyes became larger as she glared at the terrifying view of the impending collision, her galleon descending towards ground like a flaming meteorite.

The previous specks of forestland took the shape of trees and leaves, branches and boulders; and a canvas of shredded sails and burning wood encroached on the view.

Her sweaty palms tightened around the helm, heart thundering inside her chest.

Amidst the blur, she witnessed Farrah's eyes staring back into her own as they approached their fateful encounter.

Why did you abandon us?

The crash was scorching though her mind dissected every detail of it as though it had taken an eternity.

The bow splintered into itself. Foremast, forecastle deck and galleys disintegrated in an instant.

Most passengers were catapulted off their feet, many falling inside the ship's scalding holes. The demolition had crumpled those who had stood near the front section of the galleon.

Their cries echoed like daggers piercing through a hundred souls.

Feras had collapsed against the wheel, her head banging hard against the top segment.

Her vision dimmed. Blood entered her left eye, its hue drenching its sight with the colours of hell.

The main mast began tumbling downwards, catching screaming pirates in its path as the rudder proceeded towards the forest floor.

This second collision shattered the *Dragon's* foundations.

The vessel buckled on the land it had plowed up as the rudder caved in and the hull ruptured.

Muscles and tendons had ripped; skin had split; bones had fractured. The galleon creaked and wobbled like the fragmented skeleton of a crushed human body.

It began sliding along the steepest ground below, a wraithlike screech emerging from its cavities as some of its components were left in its trail.

Cries of panic echoed as the survivors held on for their lives, faces covered in blood, limbs broken.

After one last jolt, the ship tilted at a standstill, halted by the forest that now sustained it.

A sudden hush enveloped the surroundings.

Feras parted ways with the wheel, eyes falling on the leftovers of the greatest galleon there ever was.

She couldn't feel her fingers anymore, couldn't feel her breath. The sight her perception depicted felt alien.

Her ears buzzed with the silence. As it hummed with the throb of her numbness, it trailed a path ahead and opened up to the cries of the wounded. Their scourging whimpers clawed at her hearing like shards funneling through her eardrums.

She swept her eyes along the embers, watched the torn limbs and pools of bodily fluids. She saw the crippled, caught underneath the rubble, tugging desperately on their mangled parts as tears flowed down their cheeks.

Her vision became glassy. The wreckage of her entire life painted the portrait of desolation that lay before her, crumbled into ashes of a past wonder.

She found her breath again, mostly because she noticed it had grown scarce.

She searched for its source but couldn't pinpoint it. It was gone and she began panicking. Her breasts heaved with a loss of oxygen.

It felt like dying, and maybe she was.

Her palms flew to her chest, mouth gasping.

A figure appeared in front of her fogged vision. Arms had wrapped around hers, soft words muttered.

"Breathe."

I don't know how, she thought. The mangled wails clung to her ears, tearing her heart apart, abating her sight. *Make them stop!*

"Breathe."

The hands eased up to her face. Fingers embraced the skin of her cheeks. They drew her head nearer, driving her eyes into their own.

"Breathe."

And she did.

Feras heaved for air and emerged from the clutches of her suffocation.

Farrah's palm fell on her shoulder as she wiped the blood dripping into her eye with the other. They gazed at each other and Feras found herself again inside the woman's bottomless expression.

They heard a thrum over their heads, and it drew their stares above.

The freighters were advancing on them, hovercars echoing in the distance. They had crashed into a zone of no landing which meant that larger vessels would not be able to anchor nearby.

Hovercars, however, were a different story.

"We need to go."

It was her own voice that had spoken, its timbre unlike anything she had ever said.

She witnessed the rest of the renegades taking shape in front of her eyes.

Farrah's fingers wrapped into hers. Without another word, she turned around and braced ahead, drawing Feras along with her.

The able-bodied were throwing themselves off the ship, fleeing its carnage.

Others yet would be left behind, unable to fend for their lives.

And there was nothing she could do for them.

Her gaze froze on her surroundings. Farrah's hand pulled on hers again, and Feras allowed the renegade leader to guide her feet. They made their way through the fumes, the blood and the cadavers.

Farrah led them down a hole inside the gun deck and into an improvised path towards the hull. They pressed themselves between crumbling planks of wood and ripped titanium, contorted their bodies around the wreckage, and moved amongst the rubble.

They soon found an opening inside the stern section. Slay tested the jump and dropped onto the forest floor below before beckoning them over.

Was that Kerok running away in the distance?

Essan and Aslor leaped over and landed next to Farrah.

Isn't the captain supposed to be the last one to leave the ship?

She stared back at the flared remains of her *Celestial Dragon*, wondering how many pirates she was leaving behind—trapped.

"Feras!"

She gazed into Farrah's pleading face.

She hesitated a second more and jumped down.

Freighters overhead were circling over the wreckage like condors readying for a meal.

As they hastened away, she paused and looked back one last time at the *Celestial Dragon*.

The ship her father had owned. The vessel that had battled the daemon's commandants.

The galleon that had flown the heavens on the side of gods.

She lifted her palms up, back facing away. They trembled as Feras drew her gaze over them and at the lifeless form of her *Dragon*.

And she bowed.

They ran for hours, hiding inside thick bushes and taking cover beside trees every time they heard noises or a freighter flew above them. On a few occasions, hovercars drove by so suddenly that they had just enough time to duck out of sight, praying to the gods the vehicles would not spot them.

After a while, they took a short break, lest they alert the enemy with the blaring sounds of their breathing, and found a hollow by a river to replenish their sore throats.

Feras had leaned against the large boulder that hid them, head tilted back. Farrah joined her and slid along the surface of the rock where the pirate was. She cradled her elbows around her knees and gazed down at the ground.

They stood like this for some time, contemplating nothing.

"Dahara's dead," Feras said in a low voice. "So are countless others. I don't even know if any of them will make it through." The corsair's face was void of expression as she kept it ahead. "I'll kill them for this. I'll kill them all."

Farrah dropped her lips against her folded arms, unable to withstand the look Feras was wearing. She felt like shouting but kept herself from it.

Many lives had been claimed, their only means of transportation left destroyed. She pulled on her jaw as ache raced through her every fibre.

She flinched when fingers caught her elbow and began untangling her.

Farrah raised her head, her knees falling towards ground, chest lifting. When her eyes met Feras's, the pirate drew her hand away.

"But we're still alive."

Farrah kept her gaze on the corsair's gaunt expression.

"I don't think it's sunk in yet," Feras added, voice hoarse. "We'd better get a move on before reality comes crashing down on me."

"Tell me when it does," she said. "I'll be there."

They resumed their way through the woodland, avoiding hovercars and warships for what felt like aeons, their abated spirits somewhat lifting the moment they arrived in proximity of their destination.

"There," murmured Aslor, squatting on his haunches and peering through a bush.

The Monastery of Prescue.

When they neared the forest's exit, they noticed freighters by the dozens soaring above the city. Moreover, hovercars were cruising in and out of Egon, on the lookout for them.

"As soon as we leave the cover of the trees, we'll be easy to spot," whispered Essan, eyes glaring at the open land beyond.

Thorick tapped Farrah's shoulder twice and pointed somewhere to the side.

"Right on, Thorick," agreed Slay, catching his movement. "The forest continues all the way to the other side of that mound. I bet we could climb up there and sneak into the monastery from the back."

Farrah also peered where Thorick had gestured and nodded. "Let's go around."

They retreated inside the woods' safety and bordered around it, hoping the enemy wouldn't think of searching for them there. Though it stood on the brink of Egon's limits, it wasn't in its main periphery.

The trek around took another hour. The territory had slowly become steeper and soon they'd began to make out Prescue's outer walls, up on the mountain hill.

Close to the ridge, they were forced to climb over the last part. Thorick helped them up, lifting them with one arm when they neared the top.

Back on solid ground, they looked from left to right for signs of the enemy.

"Do we go around?" asked Essan.

They crouched somewhat and headed towards the building's rearmost stone facade. "We'll get caught," answered Farrah. "We have to search for another way in."

They hurried over to the side, bodies hugging the wall as they moved down its length, Farrah beckoning them forward until they found an entry beside a set of exterior gardens.

Slay opened the ancient doorway and peered around the empty passage. "There's no one," he whispered.

"The city is probably on high alert," murmured Aslor. "I'm guessing visitors have left and the priests have been confined."

They went down corridor after corridor of old reddish-brown cherry wood, passing through praying chambers and common rooms. Eventually, they had made it inside a large hall garnished with colossal statues of different gods glowering at them.

"Enamus's cloister must be at the end of the central gallery," Farrah said, indicating a pathway that originated between two particularly stern-looking deities.

They proceeded into the corridor, their footsteps reverberating against the creaking floor, and hurried down the pathway, which may well have been the length of the entire monastery. Gods' effigies welcomed their passage with their solemn glares. Though they recognized many of the faces that greeted them, the hardened expressions on them felt off.

They drew the gates at the end of the gallery ajar and entered the outer chamber.

Its walls were accessorized with paintings and busts depicting Enamus. Its cathedral roof rendered a picture of Iscar and antique double doors stood on its other side, garnished with elegant golden decorations. The rest of the room was otherwise empty, apart from the mosaic floor, whose thousands of hand-laid stones illustrated the portrait of a sun darting its rays, the symbol of the gods.

Before she could set foot on it, fingers reached for Farrah's shoulder. She peered into Thorick's gentle face, his palm holding her back as he came up beside her.

"What's wrong?"

He gazed at the doors, expression mysterious. He stepped forth, his hand leaving her side, and headed towards them, jostling the doors open as though they weighed nothing.

Farrah chased after him. But when she did, she hit a wall, as if an invisible barrier had risen between this room and the other.

Caught unaware, she raised a palm and drew it in front of her, feeling an unknown energy source pushing her back. Though she didn't understand it, she somehow knew that she ought not to fear it.

Inside the inner chamber, Thorick was staring back at her, smiling as the doors shut on their own and trapped him within.

"Thorick!"

Aslor came by her side and prevented her from forcing her way through the invisible wall. "I wouldn't worry, Farrah. I think the man knows what he's doing."

Though he was probably right, she could not forego her concern. "I'm not sure if it's okay to just leave him on his own."

"For all we know, Thorick might have been aware of things we were not," Aslor replied, gaze dissecting the carved doors. "The goddess that lies in these chambers is no enemy of ours. Enamus is, after all, the Chevaleresse of Protection. Our friend is safe, I have no doubt."

Wary, Farrah retreated from the barrier and slumped against the back wall, keeping watch over the inner cloister.

They waited in near total silence as time passed them by. Not a single sound arose from the other side as though the room had been empty.

Not unlike the rest of the monastery.

Farrah had glanced at Feras many a few times. The pirate had looked distant, caught inside the clutches of her mind. Though she had wanted to go to her, she had refrained from it. The alarming hush of the outer chamber somehow made any sort of conversation feel improper.

"What are we going to do?" Essan's small voice eventually said. It chimed across the room, breaking the reverent silence.

Thousands of soldiers were on the lookout for them. Countless ships were roaming the skies, and dozens of hovercars were doing the same on land. They had lost the *Celestial Dragon* and any means of leaving this place.

They were stuck and theirs were the most infamous faces in all of Iscar.

"We'll need to find food and shelter," she answered.

"I wouldn't mind taking a brief detour to the kitchens," replied Slay, and they could almost hear their stomachs rumbling when he did. "I don't think the priest guys will mind."

"We could ask for asylum," suggested Aslor. "Surely the keepers of the Chevaleresse of Protection won't refuse us."

Farrah shifted position. "To be honest, I'm surprised we haven't met any of them."

"This place *is* awfully quiet," added Essan, gaze flitting about.

They stopped talking for a while more, listening to any noises arising in the building.

"Feras," she then said, breaking the silence again. "Do you have friends in town who could get us out of here?"

The corsair shrugged, her voice sounding hoarse. "I know people all over Iscar, but they're not all trustworthy if you understand what I mean."

"Anyone trustworthy enough?"

Feras lifted her eyes to the ceiling and shifted her hand in midair. "People come and go, and I haven't had much communication with the outside lately. There's a tavern that I am familiar with near the docks. I trust the innkeeper, but I can't say much about the clientele."

"We'd still have to get inside the city," said Aslor thoughtfully.

Essan drew her knees up to her chin and began rocking her body from side to side. "Farrah," she whispered in a small voice. "I'm scared."

Farrah sat next to her, draping an arm around her shoulder.

In reality, Essan had spoken the words they all felt too well. Caught as they were, they were as rats, waiting to be drawn out. The enemy far outnumbered them and the control they had over their deities was, at the most, unreliable.

"Don't be scared," she answered softly but loud enough so the others would hear. "Gods are walking amongst us and Thorick will soon emerge from this room, Enamus by his side. I may not know what's going to happen next, and I won't pretend that we haven't lost a lot, but no matter what, we're here for each other."

Essan leaned against Farrah's shoulder and remained there for a while.

She sighed, feeling beaten but trying not to show it. Everything had unfolded so fast, now was the first time she'd had to reflect on the last events. Things had gone woefully wrong, and she wasn't sure how to rectify them.

She lifted her head when the door's hinges suddenly sprung open, revealing Thorick behind it, alone.

He stepped into the outer chamber, the doors closing shut behind him as he did.

His expression resembled the one a person has at the end of a hard day's work, satisfied with the labour finished and taking a moment to bathe in their accomplishment.

Farrah jumped on her feet and met up with him halfway. "What happened?"

Thorick drew a palm up, revealing a green tattoo that took the shape of a knight's shield. She grabbed his hand between both of her own. "You did it," she whispered.

He nodded. Though elated by this news, Farrah felt disappointed that she would never know what had come to pass in there, nor what made him look more in harmony with himself than he previously was.

It dawned on her that if any of them were to bond meaningfully with their deity, it was Thorick. How odd that he had been the last one of them to acquire such a connection. Perhaps it was supposed to be that way. She had no doubt that *he* would have the most ease finding the god within. He might have even found it already.

"Yay for Thorick!" exclaimed Essan, grappling him into a hug, which meant only grabbing a section of his arm.

Aslor folded his hands, grinning. "Will you look at that, we've actually done it.... We've acquired the theurgy of the gods."

They felt a peculiar warmth taking hold of them, reminding them of the unique task they had the duty to accomplish. It seemed to erase, if only for an instant, the angst of their failures and give them the courage to go on.

"As much as I'd like to keep this party going," said Slay, eyes looking at the entrance of the room. "Two commandants are chasing us." He then added, "And I'm starving."

Reality swept their reverie aside, and Farrah was forced to agree with him. "Let's head out."

They left the outer chamber and went down the corridor they had taken earlier.

"Ouch!" yelped Essan when they came at the end of it, bumping into Aslor. "Hey, don't…"

The rest of her sentence fell into non-being.

Dread washed over them.

At least half a hundred placaters had formed lines around the circling room of the main hall, pointing their guns at their group. Two of them stood in the middle, carrying themselves with the ease of men consumed by a power progressively turning them into human shells.

At once, Farrah recognized the one on the right.

Commandant Husar.

She also knew that the person at his side was Commandant Grieves, a lean and dark-skinned, frizzy grey-haired man wearing a sullen expression.

At once, they cowered behind the archway.

"Oh no, that will do no good," said the man to the left. "I believe the only exit is this way."

Chapter 31

They drew their weapons, the placaters lifting their own in retaliation, ready to shoot upon hearing the order.

"Put your arms down. We all know how futile this is."

Farrah glowered at Commandant Grieves, whose scowl sat upon his aging features. "You think we'll go quietly?" she answered, trying to buy some time.

Though the commandants all shared that same deadened look, something contemptuous had appeared on the expression of this particular one. "My dear, we are the least of your concerns." He cupped his hands before him. "You should see the welcoming committee waiting for you outside."

"We suggest you drop your weapons now," continued Commandant Husar, "lest you are in a hurry to die."

Something in his voice, and the sparkle in his darkened pupils, was daring them to try, and Farrah had no doubt that killing them would give the man immense satisfaction—if that was an emotion he still knew how to feel.

"Farrah?" whispered Aslor.

It was incredible how much one could get out of a single word. Though a simple name in its habitual state, profound distress now imbued this particular proper noun.

She was at a loss. They were facing two commandants and a

host of soldiers. Even if they engaged the generals, the placaters' bullets greatly outnumbered their own.

From the looks of things, even if they *did* get past the enemy lines, she trusted that both men had indeed come with backups.

"My dear," added Grieves in his drawling, caught-between-frequencies voice, "unless you are about to summon one of those gods of yours, I suggest you turn yourselves over."

Farrah's pulse took a leap. She cursed herself for her idiocy. Of course, they had known all along that they were heading for Prescue, seeking to acquire its goddess.

"I don't understand what you mean."

Husar laughed dismissively.

A commandant's laugh was an odd thing. It was akin to a person cackling on the other side of a long cylinder. Its echoes nonetheless felt chilling.

"Let us be adults about this and stop our little game of pretend." He glowered somewhat. "I admit that I was surprised when I saw that dragon in Mondos… I should give it to you, you're the first people in fifteen years to have figured it out.

"I should thank you for leaving the records of the books you'd retrieved at the research library; you made it that much easier for us to track you down. When we realized you were heading for Egon, we knew where your actual destination lay." He sneered. "Don't you think we've tried to get Enamus's powers before?"

He strolled towards them like a man who had nothing to fear from them, his body shuffling from left to right the way it always did. "We had hoped to take you down before you arrived here, but as I am gifted with these horrified expressions on your faces, I believe the wait was worth it."

He came to a stop, a few inches from Farrah's handguns, sunken eyes scrutinizing hers as they infringed on her space with their bottomless souls. "You keep those weapons in hand five more seconds and I swear I'll peel the flesh off of your bones, *layer by layer*."

The pupils, already bleak, had enlarged; the veins had bulged. Even his skin appeared to have taken an ashen colour.

"Five," he began counting, holding out his fingers in front of her.

Was it better to lose this battle in order to attempt to win the war? But if the enemy captured them, how would they escape? Everything would have been for naught.

"Four."

If they went for the commandants' throats, fifty guns or so would retaliate and put them down on the spot. They wouldn't even have the chance to summon their gods.

"Three."

She tilted her head to the side, trying to assess what her friends were thinking. They were all gaping back at her, expressions frightened.

"Two."

Husar's eyes shone and a carnivorous smile grew on his lips, revealing yellowed, rotting teeth.

"One."

Farrah's arms encountered resistance and her gaze flitted to the right. Feras had placed a hand upon them, applying pressure on her outstretched limbs.

"We give up," said the pirate.

Husar arched an eyebrow, seemingly in disappointment though his features had returned to neutral.

Farrah glanced into Feras's hardened stare. "We can't win this fight," the captain added in a voice that felt strained.

Her arms finally yielded and dropped fully.

Her weapons clanked on the ground as she let them go. The noise they made against the floor embodied the sound of cruel defeat.

The group was escorted outside where they were greeted by the aforementioned foreboding sight.

Hundreds of soldiers spattered the fields of Prescue's landscape, awaiting command. Battle hovercars were stationed on both sides of an improvised pathway, their artillery positioned for combat while dozens of ships glided above, pointing their cannons at them.

Feras had been right. They wouldn't have gotten out of this place alive if a fight had broken out. Farrah wondered whether saving themselves now meant suffering a more terrible death later.

The placaters had amassed their weapons to be brought and identified, and within seconds, had placed electric handcuffs around their backs. They were shoved along the endless rows of soldiers, and it was akin to walking through a river of blood. The red-clad soldiers were welcoming their defeat with their army of the dead.

Grieves was next to her. The expression he wore was the one of a man having done his duty and nothing more.

"Where are you taking us?" she asked, chin high and tone laced with spite.

He did not grace her with a look. Nor with an answer.

Feet pounding to the drums of their fates, Farrah wanted nothing more but to stare into the faces of her friends but was unable to do so. They were being held in a tight formation, forced to walk one after the other.

Before long, they had been separated, each member of their group boarding a different hovercar carrying a dozen placaters keeping a secure watch on them. Grieves had embarked on Farrah's transport and had sat beside her, arms lying by his side, expression still as though his batteries were charging. She noticed that Husar had boarded Feras's hovercar.

They took off towards the city, leaving the monastery behind. Six renegades escorted by an army of soldiers.

Farrah recognized the towers as soon as they were in sight.

Protian prison, one of the regime's four great prisons, residing in Egon.

After she had been dragged out of the hovercar, Farrah had been reunited with the rest of her group but not for long.

Commandant Husar had led Aslor, Slay and Thorick towards the rightmost tower, while Farrah, Feras and Essan were taken to the left one by Commandant Grieves. She had tried to lock eyes with her friends before they had gone their separate ways, but a soldier had pushed her shoulder and driven her forward.

Her stomach dropped to her ankles the moment she passed through the colossal archway entrance.

Bleak and empty, the vestibule seemed to vanish somewhere on the other side of the prison but only because she could not see much of anything beyond the first half of the room. To her right began the ponderous ascent, the notorious staircase that climbed around the different levels of the building.

Instead of taking them to it, Grieves guided their group towards a central elevator. Once inside, the glass doors of the car closed upon request and started up. Though the transparent walls of the lift allowed a brief insight into the content of the floors that flew by, each one of them turned out being the same. Darkened and grim.

Farrah was able to share a look with the others for the first time since they had left Prescue. Essan appeared frightened. Her face was pale, her eyes gaunt and searching for her direction, one Farrah was powerless to give. Feras was staring down, lips pulled tight and brow crumpled into a frown.

They went further up until the conveyor came to a halt on the topmost level. The cells were stacked next to the other around the circular structure of the room, ending where the slope of the winding staircase began.

The placaters began escorting them towards the middle of the floor. Farrah noticed that all of the cells on the floor were empty. They were the only prisoners on this level and she had a feeling that this had not been by chance.

Grieves clasped his hands behind his back. Face blank. Or rather, dead. "Ancient seals crafted during the wars of a thousand years ago riddle Protian prison. In case you still held farfetched hope of escaping, know that it is impossible to summon gods within these walls."

Farrah jerked her head around.

She knew he had waited until now to share this information with them, destroying any notions of freedom they had clung on to. Her fists clenched on her back while numbness clasped her with its cold claws.

The guard slipped a keycard inside the monitor at the right of the gate, and the barred door slid open. Essan's shackles were taken away before she was jostled inside the cramped compartment.

Farrah's heart sunk as she did, unable to bear the look of terror written on the girl's face.

She searched for Feras's eyes while the pirate's cuffs were being retrieved.

"Don't lose hope, Farrah," the corsair said as the placaters pushed her inside the following cell.

Farrah was brought to the next one. When she went by the commandant, she conjured the most hateful gaze she could muster, imbuing it with all of her loathing. Grieves answered with the slightest lopsided smile as she passed him by and entered the quasi-darkness of the room.

The door slid shut behind her and the vague muffled footsteps of the soldiers soon vanished from earshot.

An energy barrier protected the metal gate, most likely to keep the prisoners from escaping or prevent them from talking to each other through the bars. As such, even if they stood in adjacent cells, the renegades would not have the means to communicate between one another.

They were effectively silenced.

She moved past the tawdry single bed that took up most of the space in the room and sat instead on the floor, holding her back against the frigid wall. She dropped her head between the folded arms she had rested on her knees.

There was nothing else she could do.

They had lost.

Everything… was over.

As the renegade's mind descended into the madness of her desperation, somewhere in the corner of the room, the poster of a man wearing horrible receded eyes was staring at her.

End of Tome I

Acknowledgments

Behold, friends, the names of those brave warriors who partook in this epic quest.

To the beautiful and talented Elita Maalouf, I bestow my thanks and award thee with the title of Elita the Magnificent.

To my wonderful editorial team, Carrie Jones and Ashley Rayner, I bestow my thanks and the titles of Carrie the Generous and Ashley the Expert.

To my first drafts beta readers, my opinionated loyalists, Marie-Pierre Codsi and Laurence Bourcheix-Laporte, I bestow my thanks and award thee the titles of Marie-Pierre the Eloquent and Laurence the Champion.

And to everyone else who read this novel and escaped with me aboard an airship that once flew the heavens…

I bow to thee and bestow my heartfelt thanks.

www.ingramcontent.com/pod-product-compliance
Lightning Source LLC
Chambersburg PA
CBHW020242030826
48979CB00030B/2485/J
* 9 7 8 1 7 7 7 6 5 2 0 0 5 *